WALK THE EDGE

**Also available from
Katie McGarry
and Harlequin TEEN**

Thunder Road

Nowhere but Here
Walk the Edge

Pushing the Limits

Pushing the Limits
Crossing the Line (ebook novella)
Dare You To
Crash into You
Take Me On
Breaking the Rules (ebook exclusive)
Chasing Impossible

Other must-reads

Red at Night (A More Than Words ebook novella)

Look for the next novel in the Thunder Road series!

KATIE McGARRY

WALK THE EDGE

HARLEQUIN®TEEN

Recycling programs
for this product may
not exist in your area.

ISBN-13: 978-0-373-21162-3

Walk the Edge

Printed in U.S.A.

WALK THE EDGE

RAZOR

THERE ARE LIES in life we accept. Whether it's for the sake of ignorance, bliss or, in my case, survival, we all make our choices.

I choose to belong to the Reign of Terror Motorcycle Club. I choose to work for the security company associated with them. I also choose to do this while still in high school.

All of this boils down to one choice in particular—whether or not to believe my father's version of a lie or the town's. I chose my father's lie. I chose the brotherhood of the club.

What I haven't chosen? Being harassed by the man invading my front porch. He's decked out in a pair of pressed khakis and a button-down straight from a mall window. The real question—is he here by choice or did he draw the short stick?

"As I said, son," he continues, "I'm not here to talk to your dad. I'm here to see you."

A hot August wind blows in from the thick woods surrounding our house, and sweat forms on the guy's skin. He's too cocky to be nervous, so that dumps the blame of his shiny forehead on the 110-degree heat index.

"You and I," he adds, "we need to talk."

My eyes flash to the detective badge hanging on the guy's hip and then to his dark blue unmarked Chevy Caprice parked in front of my motorcycle in the gravel drive. Twenty bucks he thinks he blocked me in. Guess he underestimated I'll ride on the grass to escape.

This guy doesn't belong to our police force. His plates suggest he's from Jefferson County. That's in the northern part of Kentucky. I live in a small town where even the street hustlers and police know each other by name. This man—he's an outsider.

I flip through my memory for anything that would justify his presence. Yeah, I stumbled into some brawls over the summer. A few punches thrown at guys who didn't keep their mouths sealed or keep their inflated egos on a leash, but nothing that warrants this visit.

A bead of water drips from my wet hair onto the worn gray wood of the deck and his eyes track it. I'm fresh from a shower. Jeans on. Black boots on my feet. No shirt. Hair on my head barely pushed around by a towel.

The guy checks out the tats on my chest and arms. Most of it is club designs, and it's good for him to know who he's dealing with. As of last spring, I officially became a member of the Reign of Terror. If he messes with one of us, he messes with us all.

"Are you going to invite me in?" he asks.

I thought the banging on the door was one of my friends showing to ride along with me to senior orientation, not a damned suit with a badge.

"You're not in trouble," he says, and I'm impressed he doesn't shuffle his feet like most people do when they arrive on my doorstep. "As I said, I want to talk."

I maintain eye contact longer than most men can manage.

Silence doesn't bother me. There's a ton you can learn about a person from how they deal with the absence of sound. Most can't handle uncomfortable battles for dominance, but this guy stands strong.

Without saying a word, I walk into the house and permit the screen door to slam in his face. I cross the room, grab my cut off the table, then snatch a black Reign of Terror T-shirt off the couch. I shrug into the shirt as I step onto the porch and shut the storm door behind me.

The guy watches me intently as I slip on the black leather cut that contains the three-piece patch of the club I belong to. Because of the way I'm angled, he can get a good look at our emblem on the back: a white half skull with fire raging out of the eyes and drops of fire raining down around it. The words *Reign of Terror* are mounted across the top. The town's name, Snowflake, is spelled on the bottom rocker.

He focuses on the patch that informs him I'm packing a weapon. His hand edges to the gun holstered on his belt. He's weighing whether I'm carrying now or if I'm gun free.

I cock a hip against the railing and hitch my thumbs in the pockets of my jeans. If he's going to talk, it would be now. He glances at the closed door, then back at me. "This is where we're doing this?"

"I've got somewhere to be." And I'm running late. "Didn't see a warrant on you." So by law, he can't enter.

A grim lift of his mouth tells me he understands I won't make any of this easy. He's around Dad's age, mid to late forties. He gave his name when I opened the door, but I'll admit to not listening.

He scans the property and he has that expression like he's trying to understand why someone would live in a house so small. The place is a vinyl box. Two bedrooms. One bath.

A living room–kitchen combo. Possibly more windows than square footage.

Dad said this was Mom's dream. A house just big enough for us to live in. She never desired large, but she craved land. When I was younger, she used to hug me tight and explain it was more important to be free than to be rich. I sure as hell hope Mom feels free now.

An ache ripples through me, and I readjust my footing. I pray every damn day she found some peace.

"I drove a long way to see you," he says.

Don't care. "Could have called."

"I did. No one answered."

I hike one shoulder in a "you've got shit luck." Dad and I aren't the type to answer calls from strangers. Especially ones with numbers labeled Police. There are some law enforcement officers who are cool, but most of them are like everyone else— they judge a man with a cut on his back as a psychotic felon.

I don't have time for stupidity.

"I'm here about your mother." The asshole knows he has me when my eyes snap to his.

"She's dead." Like the other times I say the words, a part of me dies along with her.

This guy has green eyes and they soften like he's apologetic. "I know. I'm sorry. I've received some new evidence that may help us discover what caused her death."

Anger curls within my muscles and my jaw twitches. This overwhelming sense of insanity is what I fight daily. For years, I've heard the whispers from the gossips in town, felt the stares of the kids in class, and I've sensed the pity of the men in the Reign of Terror I claim as brothers. It's all accumulated to a black, hissing doubt in my soul.

Suicide.

It's what everyone in town says happened. It's in every hushed conversation people have the moment I turn my back. It's not just from the people I couldn't give two shits about, but the people who I consider family.

I shove away those thoughts and focus on what my father and the club have told me—what I have chosen to believe. "My mother's death was an accident."

He's shaking his head and I'm fresh out of patience. I'm not doing this. Not with him. Not with anyone. "I'm not interested."

I push off the railing and dig out the keys to my motorcycle as I bound down the steps. The detective's behind me. He has a slow, steady stride and it irritates me that he follows across the yard and doesn't stop coming as I swing my leg over my bike.

"What if I told you I don't think it was an accident," he says.

Odds are it wasn't. Odds are every whispered taunt in my direction is true. That my father and the club drove Mom crazy, and I wasn't enough of a reason for her to choose life.

To drown him out, I start the engine. This guy must be as suicidal as people say Mom was, because he eases in front of my bike, assuming I won't run him down.

"Thomas," he says.

I twist the handle to rev the engine in warning. He raises his chin like he's finally pissed and his eyes narrow on me. "Razor."

I let the bike idle. If he's going to respect me by using my road name, I'll respect him for a few seconds. "Leave me the fuck alone."

Damn if the man doesn't possess balls the size of Montana. He steps closer to me and drops a bomb. "I have reason to believe your mom was murdered."

Breanna

I HAD BUTTERFLIES.

It was a combination of the nervous type and the exciting type and then they died with the utterance of one question. It's difficult to maintain eye contact with Kyle Hewitt as he continues talking, explaining why he's asked what he has of me. He stands a safe distance away—a little over one purple locker's worth. "I need your help with this, Bre."

He uses my nickname, the name reserved for my two best friends and family. I hug my folder to my chest, uncomfortable he feels like we are familiar with one another.

People pass us on their way to the gym for orientation, but he acts as if we're alone as his just-above-a-whisper words cram together. "English is tough... Writing papers is tougher... Football practice this year has been harder than normal... My parents have expectations... In two weeks there will be college scouts... You're smart...everyone knows this... You can make life easier on me and I can make life easier for you."

Easy. Natural. Meant to be. The smartest girl in school assisting the athletic golden boy. Two of the town's finest helping each other succeed, but he hasn't really given a fine example of how this plan will benefit me.

"I'm not suggesting anything romantic." He waves his hand in a downward motion that suggests he'd rather slit his wrist than become involved with me. This guy seriously needs to reevaluate his selling methods. Nothing good can happen from insulting the potential buyer.

Kyle grins. It's all teeth, and until this moment, I used to adore his smile. He has black hair like me, but he's much taller than I am and, thanks to his lifelong dedication to the game of football, he resembles a brick wall.

He's handsome. Always has been, but he's never been the kind who notices me. For a few seconds, I had delusions of grandeur that the reason he called my name was because he appreciated my change in appearance and, in theory, my change in attitude.

I have never been so wrong in my life.

"What do you say? Will you do it?" Kyle shoves his hands into the front pockets of his Dockers as if he's the one who's nervous.

Like my younger brother wore for his junior orientation yesterday, Kyle sports a white shirt, nice pants and a tie. The football coach required his entire team to dress up on the day of their orientation. I think it makes them stick out, but my younger brother claims it shows solidarity.

School starts in a few days and tonight is senior orientation. My parents are currently in a meeting with my guidance counselor while I'm being propositioned.

Propositioned. My lips tilt up sarcastically.

My goal for this evening was to be noticed. Guess I succeeded. I was noticed, but not for my new choices in clothing, hairstyle, or because I dumped my glasses for contacts.

Nope, I was hunted for my brain. All exciting and swoon-worthy romance novels start off this way, right?

Kyle misreads my body language and his dark eyes brighten. "So you'll write my English papers for the year?"

Fifty dollars per paper—that's his offer. Standing in my sister's second-generation hand-me-downs of a sleeveless blue blouse, shorter-than-I've-ever-worn jean skirt and platform sandals causes me to consider his proposal if only for the course of a heartbeat. I'm the middle of nine children and, I'll admit, new and shiny gains my attention, but this…this is wrong.

"Do you know this is the first time you've spoken to me?" I say.

He laughs like I told a joke, but I'm not kidding. Snowflake, Kentucky, is a small town and everyone tends to know everyone else, but just because we breathe the same air doesn't mean we communicate, or act like everyone else exists.

"That's not true," he retorts. "We sat at the same table in fourth grade."

I incline my head to the side in a mock why-didn't-I-remember-that-bonding-moment? "My, how time flies."

He chuckles, then scratches the back of his head, causing his styled hair to curl out to the side. "You're funny. I didn't know that. Look, it's not my fault you're quiet."

Kyle's right. It isn't his fault I became socially withdrawn. That blame falls solely on me. It's a decision I made in seventh grade when I was publicly crucified.

Blending into paint for the past couple of years has kept me safe, but it creates the sensation of suffocation. Everyone says the same thing: Breanna's smart, she's quiet. On the inside, I'm not at all quiet. Most of the time, I'm screaming. "I'm not writing your papers."

Kyle's smile that had suggested he had a done deal morphs into a frown and acid sloshes in my stomach. Denying Kyle isn't what bothers me as much as it worries me what he'll mention to his friends. They're the reason why I went voluntarily mute in seventh grade.

Heat races up my neck as the repercussions of refusing sets in, but I don't even consider agreeing. Cheating is not my style.

Kyle surveys the hallway, and if it's privacy he's searching for, he'll be sorely disappointed. He slides closer and a strange edginess causes me to step back, but Kyle follows. "Fine. One hundred dollars per paper."

"No."

"You don't understand. My grades have to improve." Easygoing Kyle disappears and desperation is hardly attractive.

I steal a peek into the school's main office, hoping my guidance counselor will beckon me in. Half of me hopes she'll have life-altering news for me, the other half hopes to end this insane conversation. "What you're asking for is crazy."

"No, it's not."

In an answer to the one million prayers being chanted in my head, my guidance counselor opens her door. "Breanna."

Kyle leans into me. "This conversation isn't over."

"Yes, it is." But he ignores my reply as he jogs up the nearest stairwell. Great. So far my senior year is starting out as the antithesis of my wishes—back at this tiny, strangling school with a group of people who think I'm beneficial for only one thing: as a homework hotline.

My attention returns to the main office and my guidance counselor has already settled behind her desk. Mom and Dad sit in two worn particleboard chairs across from her and neither of them acknowledge me as I enter and take a seat.

Dad stares at his loafers and Mom has become fascinated with something beyond the windows as she fiddles with the office ID badge for the hospital where she works. Only my guidance counselor, Mrs. Reed, meets my gaze, and when she subtly shakes her head, my heart sinks.

I bite my lower lip to prevent it from trembling. This was a long shot. I knew it when I pleaded with my counselor to discuss this opportunity with my parents, but I was stupid enough to have a shred of hope.

No point in acting as if I'm not aware of the resolution of their conversation. "High Grove offered me a partial scholarship. It pays for seventy-five percent of the tuition and I called around. I can make money in their work-study program and then I found this coffee shop that said they would hire me and would be flexible with my schedule and I could even study while things were slow and—"

"And you'll be over two hours away from us," Mom cuts me off, then smooths her short black hair in a way that shows she's upset. "This is your senior year. Your last year home with us. I'm not okay sending you to a private school. It's not right."

"But did Mrs. Reed explain my schedule for this year?"

I've already mastered every class Snowflake, Kentucky's lone high school has to offer. Because of how my brain is wired differently, there won't be a challenge, and if I intend to preserve my sanity, I require a challenge.

I briefly shut my eyes and attempt to control the chaos in my mind. My brain…it never rests. It's always searching for a puzzle to solve, for a code to crack, for a test to grapple with, and not having one, it's like someone is chiseling at my bones from below my skin.

"Yes," Mom answers. "But Mrs. Reed also assured us

they'll give you extra work and you'll participate in some independent studies. Some of them for college credit."

My foot taps the floor as hot anger leaks into my veins. What Mom's suggesting, it's everything that makes me stick out, everything that makes me the school freak again. "I need this. I need something more. I need a challenge."

"And I need you home." Mom's voice cracks and she grimaces as if she's on the verge of tears. My eyes fill along with hers. We've had this argument, this discussion, this tearfest several times as I was applying.

"You're my baby," Mom whispers. "I already have four of you out of the house and next year you'll be gone."

I swallow the lump in my throat. Next year, I plan to be hundreds and hundreds of miles north of here. Hopefully at an Ivy League school.

"Don't cost me my last year with you." The hurt in her voice cuts me deep.

"I'll come home on the weekends." I risk glancing at her. "I'll call daily. I'll still be around, just not as much."

"But we need you here." Mom scoots to the edge of her seat as if being nearer to me will alter my view, but what she doesn't understand is I'm seconds away from dropping to my knees to beg her to change her mind.

"Joshua is more than capable of helping out around the house." My younger brother by just over a year. I'm cushioned in the middle between four older-than-me and four younger-than-me siblings. Each older sibling has served their sentence as being the one in charge. Heading to private school would be the equivalent to handing in my two weeks' notice.

"Joshua isn't you," Mom says. "He can't handle the responsibility."

"So you're saying I should screw up and then you'd let me

go to private school? Because that's the logic of your argument. I meet your expectations and I have to stay home."

"Mrs. Miller." Sensing a full-on argument, my guidance counselor interrupts. "This is a fantastic opportunity for Breanna. With her photographic memory—"

"Just a good memory," I correct softly. There's no such thing as a photographic memory. At least it has never been proved, though there are people like me who can remember random information very well, but, in other areas, can struggle.

"Of course." Mrs. Reed smiles at me, probably remembering the conversations we've shared where she insists on calling my memory photographic and I insist my memory isn't quite that impressive. Since my freshman year, she's performed an array of tests on me like I'm a cracked-out guinea pig.

"Regardless, Breanna has a fantastic memory and a high IQ. We can supplement her education, but High Grove Academy can offer her opportunities we are not prepared or equipped to give her."

Exactly. I sit taller with Mrs. Reed's well-thought-out, adult-validated argument, but Mom leans into her hand propped up by her elbow on the armrest and hides her eyes, while Dad...he remains quiet.

Gray streaks I've never noticed have marred his dark hair and he rubs at the black circles under his eyes. His typically fit frame seems smaller in his business suit. Dad's been under extreme stress at his job and guilt drips through me that I'm adding to his burdens.

I open my mouth, close it, then try again. "Dad, I will do everything in my power to pay for this myself."

"It's not the money, Bre." Dad raises his head and it's like he's aged ten years from when I saw him this morning. "It's the timing. The company lost a huge contract, and if I don't win over this next client, the whole town's in trouble."

Because over half the town works for the factory. They make paint. It's a lot of chemical reactions going on in a small, contained space, but it's a process that requires a ton of people.

"Your mom just received a promotion at the hospital and her hours are more than we thought they'd be. Give us a few months to get our feet underneath us and then, your mom and I, we'll do everything we can to help you with the college of your choice, but for right now, we need you at home. We need you here. This family would be impossible to run without you."

He offers a weak upward lift of his lips and Mom's beaming as if she thinks Dad's monologue will persuade me. As if his words will cause me to forget how each day that passes in this town makes me feel like I'm drowning under a million gallons of water.

This should be one of those proud moments—the ones I've seen on television—where I hug my father and tell him how I'm overjoyed by his faith in me, but on the inside I'm a rose wilting in fast-forward on the vine.

How do I refuse my parents? How do I explain that of our family of nine, I'm the one who's never fit in?

"I understand." I hate it, but there's nothing else to say. "I understand."

RAZOR

THE WORLD ZONES out as if I'm in a long tunnel encircled by darkness. The green of the trees and sunlight surrounding me becomes too far away to reach. In a mindless movement, I shut off the engine and the stillness becomes a weight.

"I have a file," the detective says. "In my car. I'd like you to take a look at it."

I slip off my bike and wait for him a few inches from the bumper of his car. There's a voice in the back of my head. One I'm familiar with. One I understand. It's tossing out warnings—tell him to talk to Dad, tell him to speak with the club's board, tell him to go through the hundreds of different protocols that have been shoved down my throat on how any of us should deal with someone who's not a member of the Terror.

But as he offers me the file, the sight of my mother's name muzzles the voice. There's silence in my head. A crazy, fucked-up silence. The type that can drive a guy insane.

"Open it," he says. Mom said the same thing to me once. It was Christmas. The box was bigger than the other ones and it moved. Doubt I'll find in this file, like I did with the box Mom gave me, a puppy inside.

I do open the file, and I trudge in slow motion for the porch as my eyes take in the typed words and the handwritten notes. With a flip of a page, I slump until my ass hits the top stair. It's a picture of my mom. A hand over my face, then I focus once again on the picture—of her, of my mother.

"Where'd you get this?" I ask. It's of Mom smiling. A real smile. The type where her eyes crinkled. I loved it when she smiled like that. It meant her mood wasn't fake.

"Your dad gave it to the local police force...when she went missing."

Went missing...

That night, Dad and the club had been out for hours searching, scouring for a trace. Dad left me with my surrogate grandmother, Olivia. My three best friends stayed with me at her place. I was ten and they watched me pet my puppy over and over again.

I crack my neck to the side to bring me back to the present— back to her picture. I resemble Mom. I'm more like Dad in build and height, but I have her blond hair and blue eyes. Problem is when I peer into the mirror, I don't see the deep warming blue of her eyes. I see ice.

"Does the club ever discuss what happened that night?" From where the detective stands, he blocks the sun, so I can look up without squinting. "About what they saw?"

An uneasiness tenses my shoulder blades. "Why would they?"

He doesn't answer. It's apparent pages and photos are missing from the file. There's a picture of Mom's smashed-up car, but not one photo of her inside. A report that is mostly blacked out and a slew of papers that appear like they should go together, but pages two, five and seven through nine are absent.

"What's this?" I show him a page full of gibberish. Numbers and letters in odd combinations spread like a crossword puzzle.

"I'm hoping that's where you can help me. Several of those have come into our possession, and we have reason to believe it's messages from within your club."

The edge in his voice slices through my skin. *Your club.* There's an insinuation there. One that causes a dark demon within me to stir. *Your club.*

"The Reign of Terror looked for your mother the night she went missing," he says. "They reported a problem with her way before normal people would have known there was an issue. She left work, and a half hour later they were on full alert. Sound normal to you?"

"Sounds like they were concerned."

A growling, disgruntled noise leaves his throat. "Sounds like they knew exactly what was going on. Especially since they were the ones who found her."

The second part of his statement trips me up and causes me to pause on the word *died* in the middle of the page. *They were the ones who found her.* The club had kept me in the dark on that piece of information.

"I've been investigating the Reign of Terror for the past year. Longer than you've been a member. The club claims to be legit, but they protest too much. There are secrets in this club. You know this, and so do I."

I've been a patched-in member for only a few months, but I'm a child of one of the club's leading men. Dad's the sergeant at arms. It's his job to protect the club, to protect the president.

You have to be a crazy MFer for that job. He's insane enough to love the position.

I was born and raised in the Terror clubhouse. This bastard thinks he knows the club because he's been "investigating" us. He knows nothing. He's one more asshole attempting to destroy what he doesn't understand.

"Aren't you curious how your mother died?" he asks.

"It was an accident," I snap.

"You believe it was an accident because you were told it was an accident."

It's better than the alternative—that Mom took her own life. I meet his stare, and we become statues as we carry on the eye showdown.

"I didn't come here to get into a pissing contest with you. I'm here to help you," he says like he's my priest ready to grant absolution. "Maybe give you some peace."

"Who says I'm torn up?"

"This involves your mother." He allows a moment for his words to sink in and for my stomach to twist. "A boy never gets over losing his mother. Some things are universal. Black, white, poor, rich, college-educated to thug."

I raise an eyebrow. I'm guessing I'm the thug.

"You've thought about your mother's death. Maybe you've even been tormented. I've been on this case for a while, so I don't come here lightly. I know what people say—that your mom killed herself—"

A storm of anger flares within me. "It was an accident."

"It was no accident. I believe there's one of two ways that night went down. There were no skid marks. Nothing to prove she tried to stop. Your mother either went off that bridge on purpose or she went off thinking going over was her better chance at survival."

My throat tightens. She died. My mother died.

"I've talked to people. They say your mother was unhappy. That she had been unhappy for months. They say she was preparing to leave your father and she was going to take you with her."

A strong wave of dread rushes through my blood, practically shaking my frame. "You're full of shit."

"Am I?" he asks. "People say your father worshipped you. That he wasn't going to allow her to leave with you. Don't you want to know how she died? Don't you want to know if the people you claim as family were involved? If you work with me, we'll find the answers you've been searching for."

My cell buzzes in my pocket and the distraction breaks the tension between me and the cop. I pull it out and find a text from Chevy. I'm late meeting him and evidently he was worried: Pigpen and Man O' War coming in strong.

"Do you hear that sound?" I say.

He's got that lost expression going on. "What sound?"

The phone in the house rings and the welcome rumble of angry engines echoes in the distance. He turns toward the road and I beeline it into the house. Two seconds in, the file is open and I snap as many pictures as I can.

"Razor!" the guy shouts from the other side of the screen door. My back's to him and he sure as shit won't walk in without a warrant or probable cause. "Bring that file back out here."

"Phone's ringing," I yell, knowing full well he can't see what I'm doing. I close the file, then wave it over my shoulder to prove he and I are good. The house phone goes silent, but then my cell's ringtone begins.

I answer and it's Oz on the other end. He and Chevy— they've been my best friends since birth. "You got trouble?"

"Could say that. How'd you know?"

"You're late to orientation, and Pigpen saw someone with Jefferson County plates headed down your drive. He gave you a few minutes to show on the main road, and when you didn't..."

Oz drops off. He doesn't have to explain. The club, as always, has my back. Especially Pigpen. The brother adopted me as his protégé.

The detective bangs on the door. "Come out here or tell me I can come in, but if you leave my sight with that file in hand, I will bust down this door."

"I gotta go." I hang up and stride out onto the porch. The cop snatches the folder from my fingers and his hand edges to his holstered gun as Pigpen and Man O' War burst off their bikes and stalk in our direction.

Pigpen earned his name as a joke because the girls fall over themselves to gain his attention. Blond hair, blue eyes...a late twentysomething version of what I hope to be. Man O' War acquired his road name because when he's in a fight, he's famous for causing pain.

"Got a warrant for something?" Pigpen asks in a low voice that's more threat than question. Less than a year and a half ago, the guy was crawling around in the muck in some foreign country as an Army Ranger. Even though he was recruited by the Army because of his mad computer skills, it was a bullet in the shoulder and chest he took saving someone in his squad that brought him home for good. The brother is damn lethal.

"Just having a conversation," the cop answers in a slow drawl, "and I was leaving."

Pigpen climbs the porch and Man O' War lags behind on the grass. I lean against the house and stay the hell out of the way. Most people say my wires are crossed, but even I know to grant a wide berth when these two are pushed into irritable.

Pigpen slides into the man's space and goes nose to nose. To the cop's credit, he doesn't flinch.

"He's still in high school."

"Razor's eighteen," the cop bites out. "Legal age."

"Leave and don't come back. You have questions, you bring them to the board. I hear you're slinking around him again, you're dealing with me."

"Is that a threat?" The cop cocks his head to the side like he doesn't give a damn Pigpen's in his face. What I find more interesting is that the two are talking like they've met before, or are at least familiar with each other.

Pigpen grins like a crazy man. "Yeah, it is."

The cop slips a white card out of the file and holds it out to me, but I keep my arms crossed over my chest. With his eyes locked with mine, he drops the card and it floats like a feather to the porch.

He walks down the stairs, across the yard, and within less than a minute his Chevy Caprice is crackling rocks under rolling tires.

Pigpen releases a long breath and glances over his shoulder at me. "Am I going to want to know what that was about?"

I shake my head.

"Will the board?"

The club's board—the group of men who oversee the members. They tackle the day-to-day operations of the club and they tackle any problems that arise. The detective suggested the club killed my mom, so, yeah, guess they will want to hear about this. I incline my head in affirmation.

"Shit."

Sums it up.

"Get to orientation. I'll set up a meeting with the board soon."

Pigpen swipes up the card, but I catch a peek as I head past him to my bike. The cop's name is Jake Barlow, and not only is he a detective, but he's part of a gang task force.

We're a legit club. We don't dabble in illegal nonsense. We aren't the clichéd MC that sells guns, drugs, or deals in prostitution. We're just a group of guys who love motorcycles and believe that family can mean more than the blood running through your veins. This guy, he was fucking with me. Just fucking with me.

"Razor," Pigpen calls as I straddle my bike.

When I meet his eyes, he continues, "Are you tight?"

I'm not a talker. Speak only when I have something worth saying. Everyone knows this, but this silence is beyond my normal. My mind replays the image of Mom's car. It was crushed almost beyond recognition. The cop said there were no skid marks, no signs she tried to stop. My lungs ache as if someone crushed *me* beyond recognition.

Am I tight? Hell, no. I look away and Pigpen says, "Whatever this is, we'll figure it out."

I nod, then start my bike. Not sure about the *we'll* part, but I plan on getting some answers and getting them soon.

Breanna

I KNOW THAT the capital of Bolivia is Sucre. I know that the average distance from the earth to the moon is 238,900 miles. I also know that blue whales can go six months without eating. Random, bizarre stuff. That's what my head is full of. Nothing that will boost my math scores on the ACT or secure me a date to prom. Nothing that will save me and my best friend from this being our last day on the planet.

While my brain is obviously wired differently, there are certain commonsense rules all girls in town comprehend. It's not knowledge that has to be taught, like when I was six and my oldest brother spent weeks teaching me to tie my shoes or how at four my older sister spared a few minutes from her overly important life to show me how to spell my name.

In fact, sitting here on the top step to the entrance of Snowflake High watching this potential disaster unfold, I search my memory for the first person who warned me to steer clear of the Reign of Terror Motorcycle Club.

There was no pamphlet handed out during health class. No sex conversation like the one my mom had with me in kindergarten because I referred to a certain male body part by the same name as a round toy. Stupid brothers teaching me their stupid slang.

But when it pertains to the threat that is the Reign of Terror MC, it's not learned, it's known. Like how an infant understands how to suck in a breath at the moment of birth or how a newborn foal wobbles to his legs. It's instinctual. It's ingrained. It's fact.

"Do you think his motorcycle will work this time?" Addison asks.

"Hope so," I breathe out, too terrified to speak at a normal level in fear of drawing the scrutiny of the men wearing black leather vests who circle the broke-down bike. *Reign of Terror* arches over the top of the black vest, in the middle is a half skull with fire blazing out of the eye sockets and drops of fire rain around it. It's ominous and I shiver.

Addison and I sit huddled close. Legs touching. Shoulders bumped into the other. We'd probably hold hands if we didn't have our welcome-back-to-school information folders gripped tightly to our chests. Because we can't spawn eyes in the back of our heads, we lean against the large pillar of the overhang so no one can sneak up on us from behind.

It's edging toward nine in the evening, but the August sun hasn't completely set. Darkness, though, has claimed most of the sky. Temperatures during the afternoon hit over a hundred and I swear the concrete stairs and pillar absorbed every ounce of today's sunshine and is now transferring the heat into my body.

Sweat rolls down my back and I shift to peel my thighs off the step. Why I thought it was a fantastic idea to wear the jean skirt, I have no idea.

I take that back. I do have a clue for my clothing choice.

Tonight was the first time my entire grade was together in one room since the end of last year. My goal for the year may seem simple to some, but to me, it sometimes feels impossible. I'd like to be seen, to be known as something more than freakishly smart Breanna Miller at least once before I leave this town. I'd like to somehow find the courage to be on the outside who I am on the inside.

An annoying sixth sense informs me that I'm about to make a huge impression—on the evening news: *two friends on the verge of starting their senior year vanish without a trace*. Because that's how motorcycle clubs would handle this—they'll kidnap us and then hide our bodies after they're finished with whatever ritual act they'll use us to perform.

My knee begins to bounce. Mom and Dad left after my failed attempt to convince them to let me attend High Grove Academy and they promised to return in time for pickup.

The senior welcome session ended at eight and the parking lot cleared out by eight twenty. The straggling parents arrived by eight thirty and that left Addison and me alone with blond-haired biker boy and his dilapidated machine.

He called his buddies around the same time I tried the various members of my family for the fiftieth time. His gang showed in a chrome procession in less than ten minutes. I'm still waiting to hear from anyone I'm related to.

"What's going on with your family?" Addison asks.

Besides I'm child number five of nine? "Who knows."

Maybe Elsie needed medicine for her ears again and the pharmacy was behind schedule. Maybe Clara and Joshua split with the cars, thinking everyone was home. Maybe someone's game went into triple overtime. Maybe my parents counted someone's head twice and assumed it was me. It's not the first time I've been forgotten in the car pool rotation. Won't be the last.

I don't feel nearly as awful about being forgotten by my parents as I do about Addison having to call her father to tell him she was going to miss curfew. My left knee joins the other in a constant rhythm as I imagine what's waiting for her at home.

"I can have my parents call your dad," I offer. "Make them take the blame." Because this horrible situation is their stinking fault.

Addison's mouth slants into a sad smile as she yanks on a lock of my black hair. "Stop it, brat. Don't make me regret telling you."

Addison and I have been friends since elementary school and we met the last of our trio, Reagan, in sixth grade. While Addison and Reagan are more alike, both natural blondes and have a take-no-prisoners attitude, it's me they entrust with the secrets. Like how Addison's bruises are hardly ever from catching the fliers on her cheerleading squad.

One of the gang members stands from his crouched position at the motorcycle and the guy we attend school with inserts a key, holds on to the handlebar of the bike, and when he twists it, I pray the motor purrs to life.

My heart leaps, then plummets past my toes and into the ground when the motorcycle cuts off with a sound similar to a gunshot. Addison's head falls forward, and I bite my lip to prevent the internal screaming from becoming external chaos.

Addison pulls her phone out of her purse and taps the screen. "I'm texting Reagan. If we go missing, I'm telling her to point the finger at Thomas Turner and his band of merry men."

Thomas Turner. He's the guy who swore loudly the moment his motorcycle's engine died again. Thomas is the name called on the first day of school by our teachers, but it's not the name he responds to. He goes by his "road name," Razor.

He glances over his shoulder straight at me and my mouth dries out. Holy hell, it's like he's aware I'm thinking of him.

"Oh my God," Addison reprimands. "Don't make eye contact. Do you want them to come over?"

I immediately focus on my sandals. As much as every girl is aware to keep a safe distance from Thomas and his crew, we've all sneaked a glimpse. Thomas makes it easy to cave to temptation with his golden-blond hair, muscles from head to toe and sexy brooding expression a few girls have written about in poems.

My cheeks burn and there's this heaviness as if Thomas is still looking. Through lowered lashes, I peek at him and my heart trips when our eyes meet. His eyes are blue. An ice blue. His stare simultaneously causes me to be curious and terrified. And I obviously have a death wish, because I can't tear my gaze away.

He raises his eyebrows and I lose the ability to breathe. What is happening?

Addison's phone vibrates. "Reagan said she heard you have to kill someone in order to be part of their club."

A guy in the circle clamps a hand on Thomas's shoulder and tilts his head to the bike as he says something. Thomas returns his attention to his motorcycle and I draw in air for the first time in what seems like hours.

"Killing someone sounds dramatic," I answer. "There's a ton of guys in the club, and with the low population of Snowflake the police would notice if that many people went missing."

"Phssh." Addison squishes her lips together as she texts Reagan. "They wouldn't do it in their hometown. They're smarter than that. They'd go into a city. Their top guy was shot by another motorcycle gang in Louisville last month. And sometimes they do horrible stuff here. Everyone knows the Terror had something to do with the disappearance of Mia Ziggler."

Every small town has this story. The one girls tell late at night during a sleepover. The one mothers use to convince their daughters to be home by nine at night. Five years ago, Mia Ziggler graduated from high school, hopped on the back of a Reign of Terror motorcycle, and she was never seen again. Ever.

"Anyhow," Addison continues. "Have you noticed the patches on their vests? I overheard Dad tell Mom that the diamond one on the lower left means they're carrying a gun."

My head inclines in disbelief. "Seriously?"

Because that patch is stitched onto Thomas's vest and he's still a teenager…in high school. Everyone was shocked when Thomas started wearing his leather vest with the skull on it to school last year. It turns out the only requirements for membership in the club are to be eighteen and own a motorcycle. Oh, and commit murder.

Addison looks up from her phone. "Seriously. I'm surprised you didn't know that already. That's not a random enough fact for you to remember?"

Truth? I never heard what any of the patches on the Reign of Terror's vest meant before, but because that was so random, I doubt I'll ever forget. Instead of confirming or denying my freak of nature ability to remember weird stuff, I send a massive text to everyone in my family: I AM STILL WAITING ON A RIDE!!!

I added an additional exclamation point in my head.

"Just because you don't acknowledge me on your memory,"

chides Addison, "doesn't mean I'll forget what I said. Someday you'll trust me enough to let me in your head."

"I trust you." The reply is immediate because her words stung—stung because they're honest. I love Addison, more than some members of my family, but I've never flat out discussed my ability to recall things. Being near me as much as she has—she knows.

I avoid talking to Addison about this gift, or curse, because she's one of the few people who make me feel normal, and there's a comfort in fitting in, even if it's just with one person. "I trust you more than anyone else."

At least that statement is a hundred percent true.

"Then why didn't you tell me how Kyle Hewitt cornered you in the hall and was trying to convince you to write his English papers for the year?"

My stomach rolls as if it had been kicked. "How did you know?"

She gives me the disappointed once-over. "I overheard you two when I was coming out of the bathroom. I stupidly thought that if I gave you enough time you'd tell me."

My mouth hangs open and my mind races as I try to formulate an explanation for why I didn't tell her, but the words *embarrassed* and *ashamed* and *terrified* freeze on the tip of my tongue.

Addison nudges my knee with hers. "I'm glad you said no. What did he offer in return for writing his papers?"

Then she must have not heard everything. "Money."

"Kyle is such an asshole. Reagan heard U of K may offer him a football scholarship if he can raise his grades. His daddy and granddaddy are all proud and I guess Kyle is trying to cover his bases with his offer to you."

"Do you think he'll talk crap about me now?" Because

that's what a lot of guys at our school do. They spread rumors. Some true. Some not true. Unfortunately, the truth doesn't matter once people start talking.

"Maybe," she says with a tease. "But being the shining star in gossip is better than being invisible, right? You know what will help make you shine this year?"

"Oh, God," I mumble. "Don't start this again."

"Cheerleading!" She lights up like a Christmas tree. "I'll work my magic and get you on the squad. I'm not talking backflips. You can be the girl who holds the signs during the cheer."

I grin because how can I not when she resembles a set of Fourth of July sparklers, but before I can respond a motorcycle engine growls to life.

Addison mutters, "Damn."

My head snaps up. I'm expecting to spot Thomas and his gang riding their bikes in our direction, but instead it's a sight that can rival whatever damage they could have done if they had abducted us.

Addison's father's impeccably white four-door eases to the curb. Dizziness disorients me as I imagine the expression he must be wearing beyond the blacked-out windows. I clear my throat. "I thought you told him you'd still ride home with me."

"He probably feels like being pissed," she answers.

The motorcycle engines cut off as Addison gathers her purse. I grab her wrist before she stands. "I am so sorry."

She yanks on my hair again. "You stress too much. See you tomorrow, brat."

Two steps down, laughter from the circle of men, and Addison pivots so fast her blond curls bounce into her face. "I can't leave you here by yourself."

She said the words loudly, too loudly. Loud enough that the men grouped near the motorcycle stare at us. Her father honks the horn. It's a shrill sound in the quiet evening.

"Go. I'll be fine." Though my palms grow cold and clammy.

The car's horn screams again into the darkening sky. Addison's eyes widen as her gaze flickers between the club and me. I can't go with Addison. Her father doesn't allow anyone into their house, car or lives. Each second that passes without her behaving exactly how he expects means his wrath will be worse when she returns home.

"Go." I hold up my phone. "They texted." A lie. "They're less than a minute out."

"Okay," she whispers, as if suddenly realizing she drew the attention of the people we've been attempting to avoid. "You text me the moment you get in the car."

I fake a smile a true friend will hopefully buy. "Promise."

Addison nods, then sprints to the passenger side of her father's car. She opens it, slips inside and sends me one last pleading glance before shutting the door. Her father pulls away. Not fast, not in a hurry. Slowly. Very slowly. Methodical even. Which makes sense because that's exactly how he is with Addison.

As soon as the red taillights of the car disappear from view, I spam my entire family. I am officially alone with the Reign of Terror. If I die, I'm holding each of you responsible.

A buzz and it's from my oldest sister, who is working a full-time job fresh out of college a few hours away. Dramatic much?

Me: No, I'm alone at school and there are at least six of the RTMC here.

Second oldest sister, Clara: Them driving by does not mean you are alone with them.

A pause, then she sends a second text. This is her lame attempt at attention. I win the pot. Told you she'd crack by her senior year.

Another buzz, from my oldest brother, Samuel. It's the middle child syndrome.

My oldest sister again: lol Like Bre would ever be in a situation that puts her alone with the Terror.

Clara, the forever instigator when it involves me: Bre's too good for that. God forbid she make a mistake. Miss Perfect would never be anywhere near them. She probably thinks she sees them from 2 miles away.

Liam, the oldest one closest in age to me: lololol True. Someone send her a text back and ask her to take a selfie with them in the background.

My fingers curl around the phone as if I could reach through and strangle each of them. I'm still here and each of you suck!

Silence as they realized they'd pushed Reply All. Even with my name at the top of the *To* section it's like I'm invisible. Everyone thinks they know me, but no one sees me.

"Everything okay?"

My entire body flinches with the sound of the deep male voice. As if sensing death peering over me, I slowly raise my head and a weight crushes my chest. Golden-blond hair. Ice-blue eyes. Black leather vest. It's Thomas and he's standing in front of me.

I jump to my feet, and my cell, my sole source of communication, my only method of calling for help, falls to the ground and cracks open.

RAZOR

HER FACE IS white against her raven hair. Ghost white. I'd bet my left ball she hasn't breathed since I spoke. Her hand is outstretched toward the busted cell on the ground, but her wide hazel eyes are cemented on me. I turn my head and I'm greeted by the amused faces of my brothers from the Reign of Terror who stand next to their bikes in the parking lot. They'll be harassing me on this for weeks. Fuck me for trying to be chivalrous.

"You okay?" It's a variation of the question I asked a few seconds ago, but this one she seems to understand as her body trembles to life.

"Um..." she stutters. We've been at the same schools since elementary age, otherwise I'd wonder if she was a foreign exchange student with limited English. "I only have twenty dollars."

The muscles in the back of my neck tense. "I'm not going to jack you for your money."

She quits breathing again.

"Nice to know your current bank account status," I bite out. "But I asked if you were okay."

Color returns to her cheeks as I pin her with my gaze. She accused me of trying to rob her. I know it, she knows it and she's now informed I'm not the asshole in this scenario.

"Yes," she finally answers. "I'm okay. I mean no... I mean... I broke my phone."

She did and that sucks for her.

Her eyes flicker between me and the phone like she wants to retrieve it, yet she's too paralyzed. Saving us from this torture, I swipe the pieces of the cell and lean against the wall.

The distance between us relaxes her and that gulp of air was audible as she tucks herself tight in the corner farthest from me. This reaction isn't new. I've seen it since I was a child whenever my father or anyone from the Terror entered a room full of civilians. To everyone outside of the club, we're the evil motorcycle gang bent on blowing the house down.

People and their hellish nightmare folklore involving us pisses me off. I don't know why I told the guys to give me a minute. I'm late for plans I made with Chevy and some girls, plus I'm on call in case the board chooses to meet sooner rather than later to discuss Detective Jake Barlow.

But something about how this chick appeared alone and frightened messed me up. It reminded me... The thought stalls and the emotional speed bump causes a flash of pain in my chest. Screw it, her expression reminded me of Mom the last time I saw her—the night she died.

My mom. I shake my head to expel her ghost. One visit from one bastard trying to use me and I'm being haunted by a past I can't change. That's what the detective was salivating over—to use me for info on the club. He's one of too many who believes our club is the devil's prodigy.

What he doesn't see is that we're a family—the type of family that comes when called. Obviously not like this girl's family.

"Is it yes or no?" It's damn difficult to shove the battery in now that the frame is bent.

"Yes or no what?" Her long black hair sweeps past her shoulders. She has the type of hair that would have to be pulled up if she rode on the back of my bike. Gotta admit, I like her hair, especially how it shines under the lights of the school's overhang.

"If you're okay." I survey the mostly empty area to prove a point. "If we leave, you'll be alone, and I don't care for that. There's some real psychos out there."

She swallows. I'd be number one on her list of psychos. With a snap, the battery lodges into place. The casing takes me longer, but I wrestle that back into alignment, too.

She wears sandals with a heel and has pink painted toes. The girl fidgets and it draws my attention to her body. Her jean skirt displays some seriously mouthwatering thighs and her sleeveless blue button-down has flimsy fabric that hints at the outline of her bra strap. She's this mix between conservative and sexy. Breanna Miller is bringing it our senior year.

Under my scrutiny, she bends one knee, then straightens the other. Bet she hasn't realized how half the male population drooled over her tonight as she walked down the hall.

What she does know? She's terrified of me. I stretch out my arm, inching her cell closer to her. If I were a great guy, I'd lay it in the middle between us and let her scurry to it from there, but I'm not a great guy. I'm just good enough to stay behind to protect her from being raped by some bastard with a meth addiction who could be wandering past the school.

Despite efforts from the Terror to help crack down on drug

dealing, there's a growing drug population in town. There's been some robberies, some break-ins, and I don't feel right leaving her alone.

"Not sure if it'll work," I say, nodding toward the phone, "but it's back together."

Breanna nibbles on her lower lip, then releases it as she shuffles toward me. She accepts the cell, and this time she rests her back against the middle column of the school entrance instead of rushing away. Still a nice distance in case she needs to bolt. "Thank you."

"You're welcome."

It's getting darker faster, and under her touch the cell springs to life and brightens her face. There's no way I'm abandoning her. On top of the meth heads in town, the Terror have had issues with a rival motorcycle club, the Riot.

There's a lot of history between the Terror and the Riot. Tip of the iceberg is that they're mad we won't give them money for riding in their "territory." We're mad that they believe they have the right to ask. Last I checked, America was still the land of the free.

Over the past two weeks, the Riot have taken to joyriding near our town. They're testing boundaries and the club's on edge wondering if our unsteady peace agreement is floundering.

All of us are waiting for them to cross lines they shouldn't and ride into town. If the Riot do drive by tonight and they hear we've been at the school, they might check it out. Leaving this girl alone with the likes of them is like offering fresh meat to a starved wolf.

"Need a ride?" I ask.

She waves her phone. "No, thank you. My family is on their way."

Breanna peeks at me between swipes of her phone and I don't miss how her eyes linger on my biceps. Good girls like Breanna like to look, but they don't like to touch. A few more glances and a clearing of her throat. She's dismissing me. Her life sucks because I'm not leaving.

"I'm Razor." Though I have no doubt she knows and, if not, I'm aware she can read the road name patch sewn to the front of my cut.

"I'm Breanna," she answers in this soft tone that dances across my skin. Damn, I could listen to that voice all night, especially if she sighs my name as I kiss the skin of her neck.

Yeah, I would like to see this girl on the back of my bike. As I said, I'm not a great guy, and earlier I was just going for good, but her luck ran out. My bad side took over. "I know."

The right side of my mouth tips up as her face falls. I'm about to play Breanna like she's never been manipulated before. I hitch my thumbs in my pockets and decide to enjoy the ride. "So, that twenty dollars? Why did you bring that up?"

"What?" She recoils.

"Do you have something you need me to protect?" I ask.

She's lost and that's my intention. "That's what I do—protect things. I work for the club protecting semi loads from being stolen. Can be dangerous. Sometimes I've had to pull a gun. I'm assuming that's why you brought up the money. You need me to protect something for you."

She blinks. A lot. I fight to prevent from smiling. I press her again, knowing she'll feel so bad for calling me a crook that the next time I ask, she'll accept that ride. "Is that why you brought up the twenty dollars? Were you trying to hire me?"

Breanna

IS THAT WHY you brought up the twenty dollars? And things were going so well. As in I no longer thought Thomas was going to kidnap me and kill me. I made a mistake. A huge mistake. I insinuated he planned on robbing me because… well…I thought he was three seconds from robbing me. I thought if I told him what I had, the experience would be less painful.

Literally.

My phone vibrates. It's my mother and I can hear her weary voice in the written words. Sorry, Bre. I could make excuses, but I thought your dad picked you up and he thought I got you and both of us were home and thought you were upstairs. Your dad left to pick up Zac and I let Joshua take my car. Liam's on his way to get you now.

Liam. My fate rests in the hands of my older brother who has the mental maturity of a grape. For the love of God, he got a Froot Loop stuck up his nose this morning—on purpose.

My shoulders roll forward as I groan. Loudly. So loud that

when I raise my head, Thomas is gawking at me like I've grown a unicorn horn.

That's it. I'm going to die a horrible death. I'm alone with a biker who has a patch that indicates he carries deadly weapons and he already admitted he uses a gun. He'll probably record my demise and upload a viral video as a warning to the rest of the world not to mess with him.

Twenty dollars. What reason can I think of for telling him about my twenty dollars that won't insult him? I doubt that saying "Hey, Mr. Biker Guy, I was totally offering it as payment so you won't kill me" would fly...or maybe it will. He protects things...semi loads...as a job... "Yes!"

His forehead furrows. "What's a yes?"

I bounce on my toes. I'm happy. I'm excited. I am not going to die! Muppet arms are in full force. "I was offering you twenty dollars because I was going to hire you."

He laughs. It's more of a chuckle, but it's a fantastic sound and it's a beautiful sight on an already gorgeous face. My heart flutters for a moment beyond the fear, but as his laugh wanes, he narrows his frozen blue eyes on me. My happy moment fades, and my arms fall to my sides.

"I'll bite. What are you hiring me for?"

I sweep my hair away from my face and steal a peek at the rest of his motorcycle friends, who are now talking among themselves and ignoring us. "To be my bodyguard."

"Your bodyguard?" he repeats while crossing his arms over his chest.

He's not buying it, but I'll try to sell it. "I knew you protected stuff."

"You did?"

I didn't. "Totally, and when Addison had to leave, I was going to walk over to you and ask if I could pay you to stick around until my ride showed, but you…" Scared me to death. "Startled me and I lost track of what I was going to say."

He works his jaw and my mind is ticking with what it might imply. Jaw flexing can mean a person's agitated, but in order to know I'd need a baseline of behavior to compare it to…

"Is that right?" He interrupts the weird flow of information in my brain.

Not at all. "Yes."

Thomas settles against the wall and he reminds me of an angel. An archangel. I was obsessed with them in elementary school. Easily consumed every archangel book in our town's library—both volumes. Archangels are the warriors of God. This guy, he's definitely beautiful enough to be a heavenly creature and he's also deadly enough to wield a sword, but I'm not convinced he dabbles on the side of righteousness.

"If I agree to be your bodyguard," he says, "you'll owe me?"

"Yes."

He nods like he's hearing something way more than what I said. "Then I accept."

Thomas holds out his hand to me and I stare at his offered open palm, then meet those cold eyes. I can do this and then all will be okay. I lift my arm and inch my hand closer to his.

"So we're clear." He stops me centimeters short of our hands touching. The heat from his skin radiates to mine. "The condition is that as long as I'm protecting you, you'll owe me."

There's a whisper nagging me to run. To do anything to escape this situation. It's more than the warning caressing the inside of my head, it's also the fine hairs on the back of my neck standing on end. He's gorgeous and dangerous. Like the fallen angel Lucifer must have been. This could be the equivalent of a handshake with the devil.

I'm minutes away from my brother rescuing me, so whatever

deal we're on the verge of forging will be temporary. Then this night will drift away like the nightmares I used to have as a child. A distant memory of something that will feel so unreal I'll wonder if it happened at all.

My hand slides into his and his fingers close around mine. It's a firm grip. One I couldn't slip from if I wanted. He doesn't shake our joined hands. Instead, he steps closer and lowers his head so that we're eye to eye. "When a brother of the Reign of Terror makes a promise, we don't break it, and we expect the same from those we do business with. Which means you can't walk from this deal without consequences."

The air rushes out of my body, but as I draw back to renege on my verbal agreement, our hands move up once, then down, then up again.

The deal made, the promise in stone, and a car horn honks. My entire body vibrates and I dash away from Thomas. My skin burns as if I had shaken hands with him in the flames of hell.

A rap song blares into the night and I look over to the curb to see Liam bolting out of the driver's side of his beat-up, extremely used car. The wrath of God blazes from his eyes. "Bre!"

Thomas eases back as if he's informing me to go. Almost dropping my phone again, I fumble with my purse. "I owe you money."

Granted he didn't actually "protect me" after the handshake, but I'll gladly pay him for not shoving me into whatever blacked-out van they have waiting.

Thomas waves me off. "You can pay me later."

Guess he does expect payment for the one second of services rendered.

"Bre!" Liam left the car door open and he's barreling in

like a freight train without brakes. Liam's taller than me, with black hair like mine, and he's toned from the years he played linebacker in high school. "Hey, asshole, get away from my sister!"

"He doesn't mean it." I stumble backward off the steps, toward the safety of my brother. I don't like how Thomas is watching Liam closing in, nor do I like how we have gained the complete attention of the guys near the motorcycles.

"Liam's a spaz sometimes, like a mental condition," I ramble, though truer words could never be spoken. "But I swear he's cool, I promise, and I'll pay you soon."

With his focus solely on my brother, Thomas edges his hand to the underside of his leather vest and my stomach lurches. "Get this guy out of here before he starts shit he can't finish."

Holy crap. Thomas does carry a gun, and if my stupid brother doesn't calm down, we'll both be witnessing it first-hand. I trip down the stairs and crash into my brother, shoving both of my hands into Liam's chest. I plant my feet into the ground as he throws his momentum forward.

Liam's dark eyes bore into me. "You weren't kidding, were you? The Terror have been here the whole time."

A flash of anger rages through me. "Obviously."

"Did you forget to pick her up?" Thomas's tone is too casual. So casual it sounds more threatening than any shouted words I've heard in my life. "If so, someone should school you on what family means."

"Did he hurt you?" Liam demands.

"I'm fine." But we're in danger if we stay much longer. "Can we go?"

Liam's eyes dart over my face, searching for the beating I

was originally terrified of receiving. "We need to go now," I urge.

He hooks an arm around my shoulders, but not without aiming a last death glare at Thomas. Am I happy to see my brother? Yes. Am I thrilled to flee from this situation? Hell, yes. But it takes everything I have to not ask Liam when he started to care.

Liam leads me to the car, his head swiveling from Thomas to the group of guys tracking us like vultures. With each step my brother takes, his fingers dig into my shoulder and he pulls me tighter to his body. Liam practically throws me into the passenger seat, rounds to his side, then accelerates so quickly that my head hits the headrest.

"Will you chill out?" I shout.

"Chill out?!" Liam checks the rearview mirror and the tires squeal as he takes a sharp right, driving way faster than anyone should in a twenty-five-mile-per-hour zone. "You were hanging out with the Reign of Terror!"

An internal snap. A loud internal snap. An extremely audible snap and my body jerks. "I was not hanging out with them. I was waiting for someone to pick me up. If you recall, I texted, but I believe the response was I was being dramatic!"

Liam hammers the steering wheel with his fist and I ram my fingers through my hair. My hands are trembling. I'm trembling. The adrenaline rush as I negotiated my life in a handshake with Thomas and my brother's unexplainable anger has me flailing near the edge of insanity.

My mind drifts in and out of foggy, rash thoughts, but one clear message slowly emerges from the mist. "You already knew Joshua and Dad had the cars when I texted for help, didn't you?"

His lips thin out as he remains silent.

I sit on my hands to keep from strangling his thick neck. "Did you know I wasn't home?"

Liam's fingers drum the steering wheel once and he dares to flash that oh-I'm-so-cute-that-girls-giggle-at-everything-I-say smile. "Listen, Bre, I was—"

"Don't you dare lie," I cut him off. "Did you know I wasn't picked up before you left and that Mom and Dad thought I was home?"

"Yes." A cloud rapidly descends over his face. "I knew."

My blood pressure tanks with his admission. "You suck."

"God, you really are too dramatic." My intestines twist at the sound of my sister's voice. Clara's lying flat on her back in the backseat. She taps a package of cigarettes against her hand, removes one, then puts it between her lips.

"Please don't smoke around me," I say before she has a chance to dig out her lighter. It's not a shock to find Clara with Liam. The pair is often attached at the hip.

"Please don't smoke around me," she mimics in a high-pitched voice, then resumes her normal tone. "Do you ever get tired of being perfect? For once, Bre, give the rest of the world a shot at not living up to your standards."

"I'm not perfect." Clara and I—we don't work as siblings. On TV, siblings get along, but Clara and I have been oil and water since my birth. She's four years older than me and I was supposed to be her baby to take care of. Turns out Clara didn't want a new baby. She wanted a pony. Guess who was disappointed when our parents brought me home from the hospital?

This summer has been hell with her and she's been more unbearable than normal since Mom and Dad announced she has to pay her own college tuition because it's her fifth year.

"Boohoo." A lighter clicks in the backseat followed by the

smell of smoke. "My family forgot me, so I'm going to make everyone drop what they were doing to rescue me."

"Quit it, Clara." Liam uses a gentle tone as he glances in the rearview mirror. He won't see her, only a stream of smoke rising into the air. "She wasn't lying. The Terror was there and they were messing with her. Why do you think I tore out of the car like I did?"

Silence from the backseat. Liam and Clara are inseparable. Like how I wish I was with any of my siblings. There's an exhale and I swallow the cough tickling my throat.

"How close?" she asks.

"Too close," he answers.

I crack the window for fresh air. Clara and Liam were together the entire time I was asking for help. Texting next to each other as I was alone. My family does suck.

"I'm sorry, Bre." Liam's apology sounds sincere, but there's a strong suggestion of anger seeping in his tone. "I already had to pick up Joshua and Elsie from practice and it was my sixth time this week. I'm in college now. I shouldn't be everyone's damn chauffeur and babysitter."

I wince at *babysitter.* Child number five is an odd position. The older four are a clique. Always have been, and for them, I'm the start of the baby siblings they've had to drag around.

My four younger siblings consider me a part of the annoying older crowd who "think they're boss" and "tell them what to do," which is somewhat true, as I've been their official sitter since my older siblings graduated from high school.

Clara sits up. "If you guys are doing this apologizing family bonding crap, I want out."

I roll my eyes. Typical Clara. She's the main reason why I'm on the outs with my older siblings. Clara forces them to choose between her and me. My sister wields a frightening amount of emotional power over me and there's not a day that goes by that I don't think of the damaged relationship between me and Clara.

"You and I are going to talk like I said we would," says Liam. "Let me take Bre home."

Clara places her hand on the handle. "Stop the car now or I'll open the door and jump. You know I'm not kidding."

Liam mumbles a curse as he eases over to the curb and then pleads with me using his eyes. Pleads. Like he wants me to offer to be the one to walk home. Yes, we are three blocks away. Yes, our neighborhood is safe, but I'm not the one pitching a fit like a four-year-old.

There's an awkward pause in the car as they wait for me to be the one to leave. I cross my arms over my chest. This may make me a horrible human being, but Liam's driving me home.

"Fine." Clara breathes out like she's choking on fire. "I'll be waiting here when you're done." She slams the door, then collapses to the curb in front of the car like a beaten stray dog.

I hate her. I hate Liam for not leaving. I hate myself more for considering getting out. Even though Clara does stuff like this to needle me, there's something about how she fixates on the ends of her brown hair that makes her appear broken.

"What's her problem?" I ask. Clara drops her hair like she's disgusted. Most of us in the family have black hair. She's tried dyeing hers black, but her hair never holds the color.

"She's going through some stuff. Big stuff. Clara needs a friend right now."

Don't we all.

"Clara's upset Mom and Dad asked her to pay tuition. She struggles with focusing."

Clara's brain is like mine. She also remembers things extremely well, but the craziness I experience when I'm not working on something—when I'm not solving a crossword puzzle or a brainteaser—Clara feels it constantly, and I hurt for her. I've felt like she does twice in my life and both times it was like someone blaring a never-ending foghorn. I've found ways to keep my brain active. Clara never discovered a solution to stay focused. At least a healthy solution.

"Handling how your brains work," Liam continues, "it doesn't come as easily to her as it does to you. It's like you're the same, but hardwired differently."

Clara has said that to me more than a hundred thousand different ways since we were young. My favorite being that I stole her ability to focus while we were still eggs in my mother's ovaries. Because that happens.

"She needs me," Liam says quietly.

So do I, but I don't say that. Instead, I lay my fingers on the door handle.

"Thanks, Bre." Liam smiles as if his approval should be enough of a reward. Unfortunately, I'm pathetic enough that a part of me gets sappy because I did earn it.

"I am sorry for yelling. The Reign of Terror are dangerous. They hurt people. If you knew the stories I've heard, seen some of the shit they pull, you'd understand why I was angry."

Liam's eighteen months older, but he consistently treats me like I'm eight instead of seventeen. I doubt there's a soul in this town who isn't aware of the Terror's reputation.

"And you were there with them. Alone. That's not good."

"I know," I say softly. "He approached me. It wasn't the other way around."

"Did any of them hurt you?"

"No."

"Scare you?"

Yeah, but somehow that feels wrong to say. "The guy that was near me fixed my phone."

Liam chuckles and it relieves some of the tension in the car. "It broke again?"

Against my wishes, the ends of my mouth edge up. "Yeah."

I need a new one, but with nine kids, three of them in college, money is tight. I bought that phone with money I earned selling soft-serve ice cream last summer at the Barrel of Fun.

"Jesus, Bre. Just, Jesus." The lightness fades as Liam rolls his neck. "Are you sure you're okay with this? It's only three blocks and Addison's house is on the way."

It's not okay, but what difference would it make if I said so. My response is to leave the car. I have the fleeting thought to ram my fist into Clara's stomach when she hops up from the curb and heads for the passenger seat with a smirk on her face. She played her hand and she won.

I hate her. I really, really do, and for the level of hate festering in me, when I die, I am probably heading to hell.

Liam U-turns and I watch as the headlights of the other passing cars blur into one another. I tilt my head back and stare at the first bright star in the sky. A long time ago, I used to wish on stars, but the act is useless. It's a fairy tale created to make us think we have some semblance of control over our lives. I used to believe in magic, but I'm seventeen now and I gave up on happy endings a long time ago.

RAZOR

THE WATER BEATS down from the showerhead and steam rises around me. I should scale back the temperature from boiling to near scalding, but the heat eases some of the anger tightening the muscles in my neck.

"Razor?" Dad calls, wondering if it's me. I come and go as I please and sometimes guys from the club crash here if they require a place to lie low.

A knock, then the door to the bathroom opens. Cooler air sweeps in and a thunderstorm of mist drifts overhead. My hands are braced against the wall and I dip my head so the drops roll along my face and not into my eyes. I've been in here longer than needed. Finished washing minutes ago, but I let the water fall over me.

It's five in the morning. Got in after midnight, and thirty seconds after striding in, I figured out Dad brought a girl home. Walked out and I spent the rest of the night nursing a beer on the steps to the porch.

"You okay?" he asks.

It's an awkward question, but because I'm biologically his,

he feels compelled to ask. We both know he doesn't want the honest answer. "Yeah."

"You've been in here for a while." Dad hacks and it's a reminder as to why I rarely smoke cigarettes. "And it's early. Sun's not up yet."

That's the point. If I wait in here long enough, Dad will have the opportunity to keep his promise. After Mom died, Dad and I were torn up—at least I thought we both were. I continually gasped for breath like a fish living on dry land and I had assumed Dad felt the same.

But then a few weeks after her death, I caught Dad kissing another woman at the clubhouse. I was ten and in tears. The blonde was barely old enough to drink and vomited after she saw my reaction. Dad was old enough to know better and dropped to his knees.

He promised he'd never disrespect me or my mother by bringing a woman home. His promise disintegrated two months after Mom's funeral, but he did offer me another oath. One that has stung less and less as the years have passed, but one I expect him to uphold—even tonight.

Dad swore to never let a woman sleep in the same bed as my mother. Never overnight. Not even for an hour. He would do his business and then she'd leave.

I remain in this shower because at two this morning the light sneaking out of Dad's bedroom door went out. The girl he brought home—she stayed.

The first rays of morning light will hit soon, and if I hang in here long enough, then Dad could possibly keep his promise—he won't further disrespect the memory of my mother.

"Razor?" he asks again, probably questioning whether he misunderstood my response and it's someone from the club in here. The door creaks as if he's opening it more and the last thing I want is to be naked in front of my father.

I turn off the water. "I'm fine. Give me a few."

There's a tension-filled silence. He knows what he's done. I know what he's done. Neither of us can fix it.

"I thought you would be out all night," he says. "Heard you and Chevy had dates."

Mom told me once Dad's a man worth forgiving. There are billions of other words she could have said before she walked out the door, but that was her chosen parting advice. One more confirmation that I am what the good people of Snowflake say I am: cursed.

I rub my face as beads of water track down my body. The girls and then crashing at Chevy's place—that was the plan. But thanks to Breanna Miller, I ran late, and when I met up with Chevy and the girls, my brain wasn't there, it was with Mom.

I had heard Dad was back in town early from his security run for the club, so I cut the night short. I was the moron to assume coming home might solve my problems.

"Told you I'd be home when you got back in town," I snap. "I *keep* my promises."

Silence. The word *promises* cutting through both of us like a blade.

The door shuts and I silently curse. A long time ago, in a world I barely remember, the two of us used to talk. About stupid shit. About anything. The sound a motorcycle makes before it drops into gear. The best spot to catch bluegill. Which MMA fighter deserved to win. Detective Jake Barlow said Dad worshipped me. Goes to show how jacked up his theories are.

I slide the curtain and the metal rings jingle. The cracked

mirror's fogged and it distorts my image—slashing my face in half so that one side is higher than the other. Creating an external image of what I am on the inside: unbalanced.

I take my time toweling off and slip on a fresh pair of jeans. When I open the door to the bathroom, the cooler air nips at my skin. Dad leans on his forearms against the chest-high narrow table in the kitchen area of the front room. His eyes switch from the television on the wall to me.

Dad has red hair with a brown tint and his recently grown-in thin beard is the same color. I matched his height last year and surpassed him in what he can bench-press the year before. When we're standing side by side, people can spot the minute ways we resemble the other, but I know what Dad sees when he looks at me: blond hair, blue eyes. He sees Mom.

According to the weatherman, it's supposed to be a hot day. Scorching. He also reminds those of us who don't live under a rock that tomorrow is our first day of school. In slow motion, I turn my head to Dad's bedroom. The bed's made and there's no one in sight.

The woman—she's gone. My wish was granted. As much as I thought her leaving before sunrise would heal the oozing wound inside me, it didn't. Sunrise wasn't my breaking point. I broke earlier this morning when the light flipped off. I was just living in denial.

"We need to talk," Dad says.

I agree. We do. About Mom, the detective, the file, but it feels wrong to discuss anything associated with Mom now. "I haven't slept yet. Later?"

"All right." Dad focuses on the coffee cup next to his hand. "Later."

I head for my room, and when I reach the door, Dad stops me. "Razor..."

I pause, but I don't respond. I'm not doing this and Dad knows better than to push me.

"I heard about the detective and we're going to hash this out—me and you."

He's aware of my stance on conversation this morning. Besides last night with Breanna Miller, I'm not in the habit of repeating myself.

"The club needs you to be reachable," he continues. "When all the board's back in town, you need to be there at a moment's notice. They're going to want to hear what the cop had to say. Plus the Riot's getting too close to town and Emily's coming for a visit soon."

Emily—the daughter and granddaughter of the two most powerful men in the club. Not to mention she's the girlfriend of one of my best friends. Over a month ago, blood was shed over Emily between our club and the Riot. All of us wonder if blood will be shed again.

"You see the Riot," Dad says, "you call the club. Only the board is allowed to engage."

I enter my room and Dad raises his voice so I can hear past my now-shut door. "I mean it, you don't engage."

I lie on my bed and pinch the bridge of my nose. I hope the Riot busts into town. There's an edginess inside me. Something stirring like a cold front on the verge of colliding with warm air. Too many demons are hovering near me and the one thing that can release the pressure is a good fight.

Bring it, Riot. Show me your worst.

Breanna

THERE'S A PICTURE on the fridge Mom and Dad had taken of the kitchen when they moved into the house. Back then this room was bright yellow, open, and there were vases of flowers scattered everywhere. Twenty-six years of wear and tear later and three meals' worth of dishes stacked up from nine people and you'd have today's version of the same kitchen.

Addison sits on the counter with her eyes glued to her cell while I prerinse dishes, then load them into the dishwasher. She lifts her legs as my two youngest siblings chase each other around the island.

It's after eight. One of them is in kindergarten, the other second grade. Because elementary and middle schools began a few days ago, you'd expect at some point my siblings would tire and pass out, but I'm convinced that when they're depleted of their own energy, they suck me dry of mine.

Elsie shrieks when Zac hits her and he howls when Elsie bites him in return. With a groan, I pick up the holy terror closer to me and sit Elsie on the island, then pull over a chair with my foot and deposit Zac into that. "Neither of you move for two minutes."

They scramble to the floor and run to the living room, calling me "mean." I should pursue them, but I'm exhausted, and in the end I don't care enough to discipline them again.

I am never having children. Ever.

Addison surveys the swinging door through which they disappeared like she's solving a math problem. "You know, they portray large families completely differently on TV."

I snort. "And how would that be? Sane?"

A laugh confirms that's exactly what she thought. "There's a hundred of those reality shows where they have five million children and they all seem happy 24/7. If they can be close and lovey-dovey, why can't you?"

"You should try sleeping instead of watching television late at night. It could help with your overactive and wild imagination."

The swinging door opens and Zac aims a water rifle at Addison and fires. She squeals and raises her arms to her face. Whooping, Zac falls back and Addison yells, "I'm going to kill you, you little freak!"

"Freak is Bre's nickname!" he shouts.

The door opens again and Addison stops from rushing the person entering when Paul walks in with a skateboard in his hand and heads to the fridge. "Bre's nickname isn't freak, it's Encyclopedia-freak. Ain't I right, Encyclopedia-freak?"

Paul flashes a what-are-you-going-to-do-to-me grin. I used to like Paul. Back when he was cute and had baby fat rolls. Middle school has morphed him into a demon that even Satan can't control.

Baby brother wants to test me, then I'll call his bluff. "Showers and baths need to start. You can take yours."

His grin fades. "Make the babies go first."

"Maybe next time you won't call me names." I shove a glass harder than I should into the top rack and it clanks against the others. If I were at private school, I'd be eating crappy cafeteria food that I didn't cook and didn't have to clean up and I wouldn't be arguing with the demon child. That is my version of heaven.

The pure hate radiating from his glare bothers me more than I wish it would. Back when he had the baby fat and dimples, I was his favorite.

"Do you know why we call her Encyclopedia-freak?" he taunts me by asking Addison.

Because that's what Clara calls me? I'm five foot six and right now I'm feeling two feet tall. I watch the water falling out the faucet and hold a plate in my hand. Addison's heard them call me the name. She knows bits and pieces of how my mind works and she's also aware of how it makes me feel so…different.

"What's the capital of Russia?" he says.

Moscow. Population of Russia: 143,025,000. Area: 6,592,850 square miles.

"Look at the freak go," Paul sings. "Her eyes dart when she's listing facts in her messed-up head, but she acts like she ain't weird."

A lump forms in my throat. Paul gives everyone a hard time, but with Clara home for the summer, it's middle school on repeat.

I slam the plate into the bottom rack. "Go take a shower or I'll tell Mom you didn't come straight home from school today."

He mumbles something not twelve-year-old appropriate, but he leaves. I hold on to the counter with both hands. This is the reason why I keep my little Jedi mind tricks to myself.

"Don't let him get to you," Addison offers. "He's an evil troll that will never get a date when he hits high school."

"He makes me feel like I'm reliving bad stuff."

"We aren't in middle school anymore," Addison says in a soft tone.

"I know."

"Sometimes I don't think you do." But she moves on before I can answer. "Jesse is following me again."

This is the reason we're friends—she doesn't dwell. Like when I told her Mom and Dad nixed my plans to leave. She shrugged an "I'm sorry" and then she painted my nails.

I continue with the dishes and run the spaghetti-sauce-stained bowl through the warm water. "I'm lost. Are we happy or sad or annoyed over this?"

It's Thursday and tomorrow is the first day of school. It's weird to start on a Friday, but the district thought that we, the high school students, would be better readjusted into the school year with this schedule. Because of this, Addison and I are completing our night-before-school-begins ritual of freaking out. This year, our worries about how the year will go are complicated by Addison's on-again, off-again boyfriend, Jesse, and their social media drama.

He unfollows her. She unfollows him back. He posts a picture of him and another girl and tags Addison. She cries. He follows her again, then tags her in some heartfelt message of how he's sorry. I was over it from the moment he unfollowed her.

Addison wrinkles her nose. "I don't know. I'm not sure I want to get back together."

"Then don't."

She sighs, and her pain is so palpable there's an ache within me. I'm not sure she liked being with Jesse as much as she liked that Jesse whisked her away from her house. Whenever, to wherever, with no questions asked.

There's a fresh bruise on her forearm that I'd bet is retaliation for my family forgetting us. I focus on how the water washes the crumbs from a plate. "Did your dad do that?"

"How is it possible that every time I visit there are a million dishes stacked up and you're forever doing them? It's like we're living in some strange sci-fi movie and your life is on an endless loop."

She switches subjects and I let her. Addison's mom won't leave her father or throw him out and Addison won't call the police because she's terrified they'll put her and her sister in foster care. Doesn't help that none of her relatives are willing to help. In other words, Addison's stuck.

"Look at me," Addison says.

I do and she snaps a photo from less than a foot away.

Her lips tilt up in a mischievous way. "Perfect."

"For what?"

"Your profile picture." She flips my cell to me and the blood drains out of my face when I spot my name, my age, my info and my picture.

Addison and I have had several intense conversations involving opening an account for me on Bragger. I agreed to it when she explained how people use social media to impress colleges and universities. She showed me articles on how colleges were dazzled when prospective students worked what the colleges shared on social media into their essays and when the students could make intelligent conversation online. And emotionally, I agreed that maybe this could help in my quest to break out of my shell. But now that it's here and I'm deciphering the hundreds of ways this could go wrong...

I lunge for the phone and she's off the counter and on the

other side of the breakfast island before I can reach her. We stand on either side and each time I inch one way, she edges in the opposite direction.

"You're the one that said you wanted to be noticed," she says. "Bragger's a community of people. You can post pictures or something short, something long, something funny, something insightful, and then people like and comment. Whatever your little heart desires. The main point being, you will be interacting with other humans. If you want out of the box you hide in, then you need to crack open the flaps and bask in some sunlight."

"Remember when we decided my wardrobe change was going to help?" I counter. "The result of that experiment was Kyle Hewitt trying to con me into writing his papers. Change is overrated and my box is comfy."

"You told me all summer that you feel cramped in the box." She's right. I did say that. "You're suffocating and I'm tired of watching you turn blue. This isn't middle school anymore. People have matured. If you be yourself around everyone else, they'll love you like I do."

My heart pounds hard, but I pause because what she's saying is what I want. For once in my life, I'd love to be myself around everyone else and be accepted for who I am instead of staying silent for fear of people mocking me.

Maintaining eye contact with me, Addison raises my phone and pushes Save.

The door to the living room swings open and my younger brother Joshua enters. He wanders over to us and his eyes flicker between us as Addison and I continue to stare at each other in recognition of how huge this moment is for me.

"What's going on?" he asks.

"Congratulate your sister," says Addison. "She's on Bragger."

RAZOR

IT'S A HUMID NIGHT. The day was so hot the air smells of melting blacktop. Bugs fly near the town's light posts and the promise of violence is so thick I can taste it. Chevy swings off his bike and straightens to his full six feet. His pissed-off glare could shatter the diner's window.

Since I arrived home last night to Dad's broken promise, I've been itching for a release. A scan of the diner and I catch up on why Chevy nine-one-one'd me and Oz. Never thought I'd be happy to see Chevy's ex-girl, Violet, locked in a kiss in the corner booth with the town's biggest asshole, but God does work in mysterious ways.

Oz's big black Harley rumbles up next to me. He kills the engine and his head is that of an owl as he swings his gaze between us and Violet's public display. A crowd of guys from school are hanging in the diner. They eat and shoot the breeze as the guy shoving his tongue down Violet's throat begins to move his hand near the hem of her shirt.

"Shit." Oz verbalizes how deep we are in this minefield. People are automatically scared of Oz, with that unruly black hair and don't-fuck-with-me attitude. Now that he officially has the three-piece patch of the Terror on his back, people fall over themselves to get out of his way.

He flips me the bird and I flip it back. Not ready for Dad's father-son talk, I went fishing at the Pond with Oz. Chevy texted a few minutes ago he needed backup, and Oz and I raced to town. I cut Oz off near the railroad tracks and he's pissed I beat him on my pieced-together bike.

"We doing this?" Oz asks Chevy as he sidles up to the two of us.

Chevy's dark eyes harden into an answer. He's one hundred percent a McKinley. Chestnut hair, brown eyes, tall as hell and a mean bastard when he chooses to be. Even at seventeen, his personality mirrors that of his grandfather and uncle— the two most powerful guys in the Terror. Each of them are laid-back, easy to talk to, but if you push their button wrong, they'll hurl you through a concrete wall.

"There's six of them," I state. And three of us. I thrive off those odds. "Two of those guys in there were some of the ones that stood back and watched when that asshole beat up Stone last year. I still believe a lesson should have been taught to them all." Not just to the bastard who we made cry when he picked on a kid four years younger.

Stone is the fourteen-year-old and awkward-as-hell kid brother of the girl currently giving us heartburn. Stone and Violet's dad belonged to the club and died in an accident a little over a year ago. Club takes care of their family now, but Violet's gone rogue, alienating anyone from the Terror, even us—the guys who have grown up with her since birth.

"Should I mention hanging with them is Violet's choice?" Oz asks. I level my glare on him. I want this action and logic could kill my one possibility of throwing a punch.

"Was that picture put on Bragger Violet's choice?" Chevy spits.

There's a damn account set up on that nonsense Bragger site called Snowflake Sluts. A couple weeks ago someone posted a compromising picture of Violet. Oz and Chevy confronted her on it and she laughed it off, claiming it didn't bother her. But then she showed at my house later that night trashed and crying to the point I couldn't understand her.

That's a lie. She did make it clear she would never speak to me again if I sought revenge on the asshole who posted the pic or ran the account.

Fucked-up part—none of us can prove who posted the pic, and because I'd prefer for Violet to come to me when she's in trouble, I haven't tried too hard to figure out who's responsible. But my gaze wanders into the diner again and it lands on the group inside.

I've heard rumors. Noticed the way girls targeted on the account look at those guys like they've stolen a part of their soul. As far as I'm concerned, that's judge, jury and verdict.

"That's our family in there being mauled by the biggest jackass we know," Chevy argues with Oz. "You think he respects her? You think he has her best interests in mind?"

"You think beating the hell out of them is going to make her like us again?"

"No." Even I notice the chill in the air associated with my voice. "But it will keep them from touching her. You graduated this spring, Oz, and the burden to protect anyone in school associated with the Terror falls hard on me and Chevy. She thinks she can blend in with this crowd at school, but we all know how this is going to end. We need to prove a point."

Violet eases back from her public display of torture and her face pales against her red hair when she spots us. Not really us.

Chevy. She used to be in love with Chevy. Still is in love from what I gather, but she blames the Terror for her dad's death. Though Chevy can't patch in until he's eighteen, he's Terror to his bones. He won't walk from the club. Not even for her.

Violet stands. The guys in the diner all look out the window, and one by one they cast down their eyes. Like most everyone else in the town, they'll talk shit about us, but they won't back up anything they have to say with action.

Chevy mutters a curse and pivots away like he's going to vomit. He lowers his head as he scrubs his face. "I can't keep doing this."

"Then don't," comes a familiar feminine voice. Violet sways by the door to the diner. I notice her lack of balance, and by the subtle way Oz readjusts his feet as if he's readying to spring toward her, so does he. She rubs her bloodshot eyes, then glances at her parked car.

Great, she's drunk and/or high. Night before school, too. This year's going to suck.

"We won't let you drive home." There's a sharpness in Oz's tone. Even when we were tight, Oz and Violet tore into each other. Violet claimed it boiled down to hair color—her fire-red hair and temper and Oz's black hair and attitude to match.

They've always fought because Violet pretends she's in control. Oz is the one in charge, Violet was our glue, Chevy's the follower, and me? I don't follow and I've never cared enough about leading to challenge Oz for the role. I exist.

Violet rolls her shoulders like she's preparing to attack. "Are you guys stalking me?"

"I wanted food." Chevy keeps his back to her. "Just some fucking food."

"We're going to get you home," Oz informs Violet.

Her hands wave in a huge, unbalanced way. "No. No way.

I'm staying. You don't have any say over me. The Terror doesn't—"

"Violet," I cut her off. I may not be vocal about every damn thing, but I understand Oz's anger and Chevy's pain. There's only so much of her mouthing off even I can stomach.

Her eyes meet mine. I've protected her secret like she's asked. I've broken Terror code by withholding the fact that she's shown at my house in trouble. But sometimes, we all have our secrets to keep. I've done this for her. She can shut up and let someone take her home for me.

"I'll do it," Chevy says. "I'll get her home."

Lines form between her eyebrows. The idea of being alone with Chevy clearly rams a stake through her heart. But as Chevy starts for her car, because there's no way she can hold on to him to ride his bike, Violet trails after him—swerving.

"I'll get Eli's truck," Oz says. Eli's the father of the girl Oz is dating. He's also a board member. "Then I'll pick Chevy up."

I nod. Not much else to say to that. We watch as the taillights of Violet's rusted Chevelle pull away. "We could still do it," I say. "Beat the shit out of those guys."

Because truth be told, there's this slow burn that's peeling away at my insides. The edginess is getting harder and harder to control. First the detective, Breanna's family leaving her for dead at school, Mom on the brain, Dad's woman at the house, and now this shit with Violet. Someone's got to pay for something. There can't be this much injustice in the world.

"I think one of them's behind that Bragger account." I'm dangling bait, praying Oz bites.

Oz gives me the once-over. "Do you have proof?"

I shove my hands into my jeans pockets and Oz shakes his head. "Then we can't make a move. Board told us we're frozen with the Bragger situation without proof and their approval."

"The board can kiss my ass."

Oz stiffens. He's a club boy. I am, too, but I color outside the lines. The rumble of motorcycles interrupts his sure-to-be-well-thought-out lecture on how I need to conform.

Two bikes tear past, and it's not the speed at which they are flying through our town that causes my blood pressure to rise. It's the patch on the back of their cut. It ain't a skull, it's a reaper. The Riot are a long way from Louisville, and they are currently in *our* town.

Breanna

"YOUR SISTER HAS officially joined civilization." Addison props an elbow on Joshua's shoulder, and because he's taller, her arm is angled up. Joshua stares at her like he died and went to heaven. He's sixteen and has been way too infatuated with my best friend for two months.

They look odd yet beautiful together. She's blond-haired and fair. Like me and Liam, Joshua also has black hair and is well tanned from summer.

Joshua clutches his heart. "I'm so proud. It seems like yesterday Bre was making up stories about being around the Reign of Terror. Oh, wait, it was yesterday."

Addison swats him on the back of the head, and when Joshua overly dramatizes his pain, she throws him a mock kiss as she walks over to me. She tosses my cell in the air. I catch it and sigh. Thomas just fixed it and, thanks to Addison, that cell was seconds away from breaking again. "How is it possible that I already have five followers?"

"I sent out an invite to everyone in your email contacts.

You now have to wait and see if the rest of your contacts will actually follow."

My stomach rolls. Great. A popularity contest and my senior year hasn't even started yet. "I can delete the account, you know."

"You could," Addison responds. "But you won't. I know you've wanted on Bragger but have been hesitant to do it. Consider this your push."

"Why are we friends?"

"Because I'm pretty," she says to me, then cocks an annoyed hip as she assesses Joshua. "That Reign of Terror stuff wasn't bull. We were terrified."

He eyes Addison in a way that suggests he's thinking things involving her that seriously gross me out. "You could have called me. I would have given you a ride."

I toss my arms out to my sides. "I asked for a ride! I texted, remember?"

"I said her, not you. Besides, Liam picked you up. FYI, I overheard Zac and Elsie conspiring to act like you don't exist again. That should make bedtime fun."

Pretending I don't exist. It's a fun game all my siblings have played on me. Liam started it when he was eight—mad we were forced to share a bike as a Christmas present. To this day, I'm not sure how he felt slighted. It was a boy bike.

"Then do me a favor," I say. "You give them baths and get them in bed. I've got dishes."

Joshua claims his keys from the hook by the door. "No can do. Mom called. She forgot her checkbook and told me to tell you to make sure they're in bed by the time she gets home."

"Ask Clara to get Mom."

He grimaces. "That would mean Clara would have to stop

living in a dark room feeling sorry for herself. I don't do angst. You want her help, you ask for it."

We both know the result of that conversation. I'm envious of Joshua, always have been. He's an island in our family. Calm. Tranquil. Maintains his distance from everyone he's blood-related to. Joshua learned quickly to befriend people outside of our family and he sticks closely with them—not us. And my family believes I'm the smart one.

"Have fun." Joshua waggles his eyebrows as he opens the door. I launch a wet dishrag in his direction and Joshua dodges it by racing out. The rag hits the door frame with a wet splat.

Glass crashes in the living room. I hold my breath and a split second later Elsie's screaming. It's not her fake cry for attention, it's the real one. I'm across the kitchen, slamming my hand so hard on the swinging door that it stings my palm, and breathe a sigh of relief when I don't spot blood pouring from her head.

Mom's last nonbroken vase is in pieces on the floor and Elsie is nursing her elbow. There's a small trickle of blood, but no bone sticking out of the skin. The small child who was bent on ignoring me for the rest of the night holds her hands up to me. I swing her up on my hip, then scan the room for Zac.

He's crouched on the other side of the sofa, waiting for someone to tear into him because his younger sister is hurt. Elsie sobs and sobs in my ear like someone ripped off her arm. A heaviness descends upon me and the urge is to go upstairs, crawl into bed and pull the covers over my head, but that isn't an option. At the moment, I'm the designated parent.

"Zac." Even I detect the exhaustion in my tone.

He stands and looks like a puppy someone hit with a rolled-up newspaper. I should ask what happened. I should tell him he has to play more carefully with our sister. I should tell him he knows better than to have that plastic sword in the living room, but I don't. I may be the closest thing they have to a parent, but I'm only seventeen and right now seventeen-year-old me wants to run away.

"Let's go upstairs and start baths," I say.

With his head hanging, Zac trudges up the stairs in silence. Middle-school-demon Paul watches me with wide eyes from his spot on the couch. I very much notice the controller in his hand and the paused game on the TV. He didn't listen to me. He didn't take a shower. He didn't even attempt to police our younger siblings or help Elsie when she fell.

A cell vibrates and I turn to see Addison offering me a face full of sympathy. "My dad wants me home."

She lives a block away. I nod and she slips into the kitchen. The outside door shuts and Elsie wipes her snotty nose on my shoulder, then sucks in a shuddering breath.

I have glass to clean up, a boo-boo to kiss and bedtime routines to keep. I have dishes in the kitchen, garbage to take out and a social media account currently tracking my popularity.

In my bare feet, I gingerly step over the broken vase and ask a hollow question. "Can you at least pick up the broken glass, Paul?"

He doesn't say yes. He doesn't say no. I'm going to pretend that he's going to do it anyway because he cares or feels guilty. I'll accept either as an excuse.

RAZOR

OZ AND I mount our motorcycles at the same time, but I block his path forward with my bike. "You're not on this."

"Last I checked, you don't call the shots." Oz revs his motor.

"You're not allowed near the Riot." This summer, Oz pointed a gun at the president of the Riot Motorcycle Club and it appears our unsteady peace treaty with them is cracking. He shouldn't be the Snowflake welcoming committee. Besides, our clubs are about to go Fat Man and Little Boy, and I'm ready for this fallout.

"Last I heard," Oz retorts, "neither are you. Only board members are allowed to approach."

I'm not wasting any more time. "Call this in and I'll tail them to make sure they leave town. We both know Eli won't allow Emily anywhere near Kentucky if the Riot's become a problem, and if the Terror don't make a stand now, the Riot might come back. Then Emily will stay in Florida."

Oz cuts his engine with a curse and pulls out his phone. Emily is his kryptonite. "You stay back from them, you got me? Do not engage."

I flash him a smile, and it's hard to keep the crazy welling up inside me from leaking out. "Sunday stroll, brother. All friendly."

"There's nothing friendly about you," Oz says in that way I hate. It's part joke, part sympathy. It's part truth, too. I twist the throttle, pick up my feet and tear off into the night.

The wind blows through my hair and my speedometer climbs as I chase after the Riot. Their taillights emerge like the red eyes of a demon, beckoning me to follow straight to hell. The needle reaches fifty, sixty, seventy. Each new speed makes the blood pump faster.

The front wheel of my bike catches air off an uneven hill over the intersection. I'm racing, but it's not with them. It's with the devil breathing down my neck.

"It's okay, baby." Mom was crouched in front of me, uncurling my fingers from her hands. "I'll always be with you."

I pass over another intersection, my motorcycle growling beneath me. I hit a patch of cold air and my skin prickles. Is she here with me? Because it doesn't feel like it. Instead, it feels lonely. So lonely it hurts.

A tight right turn, a twist of the throttle again, then I brake so quickly I have to slam my foot to the blacktop to prevent from spinning out. Five headlights blind me and tires squeal as two of the bikes come to a stop.

Three bikes fly by, and as I whip my head to see which way the Riot is headed, I spot the Terror patch.

"You, boy, are in a ton of trouble."

My head lowers at the sound of the gravel voice. It's Cyrus, the president of the Terror, and I got caught disobeying a direct order.

Breanna

"THIS IS GOING to be the best night of our lives," announces Reagan. Addison sits at the desk in front of me and Reagan's to the left of Addison.

I check the clock on the wall over our English teacher's desk. In exactly two minutes, the bell will ring and the first day of my senior year will begin. It's not only the first day of school, but also the first Friday of the school year.

Three years ago, Addison, Reagan and I promised we'd do something crazy on the first Friday of our senior year. After notifying High Grove that I declined their scholarship, crazy is exactly what I need. "Are you sure your parents aren't going to check on us?"

"Trust me, everything will be golden." Reagan uses the camera on her phone to fix stray pieces of her dirty-blond hair. She curled it this morning and much to her displeasure the curls are falling out. "Has Cass started following you yet? I told her you created a Bragger account."

I sigh and Addison scowls. She's less than thrilled with my lack of excitement. I currently have twenty-five followers.

It's better than none, but not nearly reaching Addison's and Reagan's totals. Not sure how this whole social media thing is supposed to be fun. It's like being back in elementary school and waiting to be picked for kickball.

"To gain followers you must post something." Addison has this teacher-to-pupil reprimand going on, and it's scary on her. "Don't make me start posting for you, brat. You're the one that wanted to join the world. Reagan and I are trying to catch you up on how to participate in the land of the living."

"Because everyone will love reading how I was up doing dishes until midnight," I say.

"Tell them you were doing it naked and half the boys in school will follow you." Reagan tosses me a sly smirk and I laugh. She's always saying things that push the envelope. "Tell them you'll post the picture if you reach five hundred followers. Watch your stats climb, girl."

"That would be interesting." A new voice joins the conversation.

I see jeans first. Actually, I see a rip in the jeans, and that rip is an inch above the knee, and I'm staring at a very muscular male thigh. I enter this weird zone, because there's this sinking feeling of where this is heading, and ominous sirens are sounding off.

It's like being stuck in slow motion as I glance up. My heart stops. Starts. And when it starts again, I find I can't breathe. Golden hair that's a little long on top. Light blue eyes drinking me in. All I see is a whole lot of gorgeous...and dangerous.

It's Thomas freaking Turner. He wears the same leather vest that he had on the other night, and underneath it is a black T-shirt with the name of an old-school metal band. My eyes automatically scan his patches and I wonder which one is the warning that he carries a gun.

His fingers skim my desk as he strides past. There are small cuts on his knuckles, and the skin on his hands looks rough—like him. For some reason, I find that attractive. It reminds me of him hunched in front of his bike as he was repairing his machine. The steady way he moved. The serious set of his face. The way the muscles in his arms flexed as he worked.

"Hello, Breanna." Thomas's voice is deep, smooth, and feels like a caress along my skin.

"Hey." It's hardly more than a whisper.

"How are you?" Thomas settles into the seat in the back corner behind me as if this is where he's determined to stay for the year. He kicks his long legs into the aisle and crosses one booted foot over the other.

"Good," I answer, able to attain a somewhat normal voice.

"Good," he repeats. "How's your phone?"

"Terrific." When did I become the queen of one-word answers?

"Terrific." His eyes are laughing. At me. With me. I'm not sure, so I return to facing the front. Holy freaking crap, Thomas Turner is attempting conversation with me.

I'm greeted by two wide-eyed and slack-mouthed friends. Addison's gaze flickers between me and Thomas so quickly that I'm afraid she's going to make herself cross-eyed. So… yeah. I left out telling Addison about my few minutes alone with the motorcycle boy, so that would mean that Reagan's also in the dark.

Please act normal, I mouth.

They tilt their heads as if I asked them to explain osmosis.

Addison blinks as she snaps out of her shock, then clears her throat. "So…it's settled. As soon as you break free from babysitting prison, we're going to Shamrock's tonight."

Thomas shifts in his seat and my neck twinges as I feel his

eyes on me. We live in a small town in a sparsely populated county. Everyone knows Shamrock's is a bar near the Army base. They allow anyone eighteen and older, but we're not supposed to drink. Rumor has it the Army guys have no problem buying alcohol for any girl underage.

I'm going to admit, I'm not eighteen. I've never drunk before, not counting a few sips of my mother's wine under her visual guidance, and a small glass of champagne at my grandparents' anniversary party last year. Other than that—nothing.

I'm also going to admit, I'm curious. About drinking and bars and Army boys. I'm excited about a dimly lit room and neon lights and a glittering disco ball creating a rainbow.

The sane portion of my brain reminds me of the parental talks and just-say-no lectures I've heard in my life. All that common sense is fighting against the notion of going, but like wearing the short skirt to orientation the other night, I'm ready for something new.

I'm searching for magic—not the Christmas-morning type, but the type of magic that can be found by being courageous, being the girl who takes chances, being the girl who will dance. I want to be the girl who is seen.

"Shamrock's can get rough," Thomas says loud enough we can hear, but low enough that the three of us can't figure out if he was intentionally joining our conversation.

The bell rings, the morning announcements start, and it's the *click, click, click* behind me that gains my attention. It's not fast, but persistent, and my instincts nudge me to turn to confirm it's his pencil, but that would mean looking at Thomas, and I'm not sure that's a good idea. I can already sense his warmth, and I recall how his fingers held mine when we shook hands.

Our teacher writes on the dry-erase board: *Zhofrph edfn, Vhqlruv!*

The sights and sounds fade as my mind rearranges and translates the letters. My notebook's open and my pencil scrawls along the white paper. *E* is the most common letter used in the English language. *T* would be next followed by *A, I, N, O, S.*

Our teacher's talking. Rambling how she'll give a hundred extra credit points to anyone who can solve the puzzle by the end of class. She's saying some other things, too. Like my name. After a push of Addison's elbow to my desk, I absently say, "Here." After another passage of time I'm pulled out of the zone when I hear, "I only respond to Razor."

Then our teacher says other things. Things I should possibly pay attention to, but can't.

The wheels are spinning. I write down each train of thought, watching the correct letters come up like dials of a combination lock. Each click audible in my head, and it sends me higher and higher, and when the last letter falls into place, my seat jerks beneath me.

Addison and Reagan turn at the sound, and so do others. I use my hand to cover my answer because I don't want anyone to know I cracked it. I will not relive middle school again.

Our teacher assesses me, then continues to summarize our syllabus. Everyone else eventually faces forward and I allow myself to revel in the solution glory.

Forty minutes eventually pass. We hear about rules and projects. Books we'll read and movies we'll watch. As always, there's a discussion of expectations. At the end, our teacher grants us ten minutes to tackle the problem and I spend that time doodling cloud-inspired sheep.

The bell rings. Addison and Reagan give me a quick 'bye

and bolt, since their next class is on the opposite side of the building. My class is down the hall, so I'm slow packing my stuff.

The booted feet that were beside me are now drawn back, and there's a squeak as the desk behind me tips forward. A quick scan confirms the classroom is empty. Our teacher stands in the doorway with her back toward us.

"Are you really heading to Shamrock's tonight?" Thomas is so near his breath tickles my neck and I like it way more than I should.

"What if I am?" I inhale to calm the blood racing in my veins. He's close, so close. Close enough I should be afraid. Close enough I wish he would edge nearer.

"I am your bodyguard." There's a tease in his voice and I laugh without thinking. Thomas chuckles along with me and a strange warmth curls below my belly.

I angle slightly. His head is next to mine and he's wearing that heart-stopping smile. The breath catches in my throat. How can someone so beautiful be so lethal?

I hear you have to kill people to be a member of your club. It's what I'm dying to say, but after my foot-in-mouth moment a few days ago, I choose safe. "I thought you weren't allowed to wear your vest at school."

Last year the school board freaked when Thomas showed to class with the vest on his back. They had a special emergency session and unanimously voted that his vest was the same as wearing gang colors and that anything gang-related was prohibited in school.

"I'm not." His smile widens and that's when I spot the lethal. While a part of me shivers, another part of me finds his mouth completely thrilling. Oh, God, I do have a death wish.

"Aren't you concerned you're going to get in trouble? I mean, if they write you up, it will be an automatic suspension, three weeks in detention, and it will go on your permanent record."

"Do I look like I care?"

I bite my bottom lip with the surge of adrenaline. I'm actually having a conversation with Thomas Turner. This is insane. This is suicidal. This is the most fantastic moment of my life. "I think you're looking for problems."

"Read the student handbook we received on Wednesday a few times?"

"Maybe." I read it once while eating a bowl of Frosted Flakes.

Thomas rises from his chair and I fully appreciate his massive height. "It's called a cut, not a vest."

Noted. Thomas hooks a thumb in his pocket and stands there as if he's waiting for me, and after the longest seconds of my life, I comprehend that he *is* waiting for me. I fumble with my purse and folder and eventually coordinate myself enough to make it to my feet and stumble down the aisle.

Thomas follows. When we breeze past our teacher into the hallway, Thomas's head swivels between me and our classroom. Then he gives it a slight shake like he's having an internal conversation about me, and I don't like that I'm not a part of it. "What?"

"Nothing."

"No, that wasn't nothing. That was something."

Thomas doesn't answer, and he leaves two feet between us as we walk down the hallway. There's a large enough gap that people easily stroll through, so it's then I discover we weren't really connecting.

My second period class comes into view and I decide to end this weird thing the two of us have going so we can return to our normal lives. "Hey, Thomas, wait a sec. Let me give you the twenty bucks I owe you."

He studies me as if he's trying to figure out if he likes the knee-length skirt and sleeveless purple shirt, and then his gaze drops just low enough he may be admiring a part of me no boy has explored before. The thought causes a rush of heat to crash onto my cheeks and it takes everything I have not to pull my hair off the nape of my neck in an attempt to cool down.

Thomas slips closer and I step back, colliding with the locker behind me. My heel throbs from the impact, but I'm so caught by the way his muscles rippled when he moved in my direction that I don't utter a sound.

"Call me Razor." This boy is immaculately pretty and he makes it terribly difficult to be coherent.

He told me to call him Razor. Razor sounds mean and menacing and he's sexy and brooding with his cut on, but I recall the tease in his voice earlier and the way he fixed my phone. "What if I'd rather call you Thomas?"

Those light blue eyes freeze over. "I'd tell you you're shit out of luck."

A chill paralyzes me as he flips to dangerous. "Razor it is."

Razor looks over my hair with intense interest and follows a strand to where it lies on my bare shoulder. "Do you know what I was going to do?"

I inch my head left, then right. My mouth has completely dried out and I couldn't speak if my life depended on it. Thomas freaking Turner—Razor of the Reign of Terror Motorcycle Club—is so close I can feel the heat of his body. He's close enough that with every inhale I can smell his delicious dark scent. He's close enough I'm not thinking of guns or abductions or of any warnings I've ever heard, but of how my body is begging to take one step forward and touch that gorgeous face.

"I was never going to take your twenty dollars. I was going to get you on the back of my bike and take you for a ride."

Dizziness sets in as I'm not sure if he means a ride home or a very consensual *ride*. And here's the thing: I'm not the girl guys consider offering *rides* to—either the way home type or the type that's making my toes pleasantly curl.

"And now?" I hate how my voice quakes with anticipation.

Razor picks up a lock of my hair and the skin he barely touched while lifting the strands tingles. He allows my hair to slide between his fingers and then he eases entirely too far from me, his warmth retreating with him. "And now I want something else for protecting you."

The bell rings and I'm thirty seconds from being late to class. Panic rips through me as being late is so not what I do. Razor pivots on the balls of his feet and leaves. It's like my world is being torn in two as I'm desperate to understand him while I fight this desire to remain the girl who obeys the rules. "Razor!"

He rotates and walks backward for his class. I'm guessing his "what?" expression is the most encouragement I'll get.

"I don't need you to protect me anymore."

He releases that soul-squeezing smile. The one that screams dark nights and perilous bike rides at breakneck speeds. The one that reminds me he's not a model, but a biker. "Yeah, you do. We'll discuss payment later."

I slip into the safety of my class and watch as Thomas Turner, Razor the motorcycle boy, strides into the classroom across from me. My hands tremble as I sit. My senior year just entered the realm of interesting.

RAZOR

WELCOME BACK, SENIORS.

It's the message our English teacher would have given us a hundred extra credit points for if we deciphered it. I didn't decode it, Breanna Miller did. Watching her do it in class was one of the most fascinating things I've seen and what kicks me in the nuts is that she didn't turn it in. Didn't take credit. Didn't receive her reward for a job well done. She sat there, slightly angled in her chair, with that sexy little smirk on her face as she admired her answer.

"Are you smiling?" Chevy sits on the top of the picnic table, the second beer of the night in his hands.

A longneck's also in my hands as I lean against the entrance of the clubhouse. One foot outside, the other one in. I'm waiting for my sentence for disobeying a direct order and Chevy's trying to forget Violet. I rub a hand over my face to wipe away any type of grin—especially the type I didn't know I was sporting.

The clubhouse is packed tonight. Row after row of motorcycles fill the yard and the crowd near the bar cheering on the

Reds' game is three men deep. The night's warm and, with the number of members around, the bay doors of the clubhouse are wide-open. A combination of the scent of burning embers from the bonfire and spilt beer enters my nose.

The Reign of Terror clubhouse is an old two-story four-car garage that's on property owned by Cyrus. I've spent a good majority of my life on this land. Some of it in the clubhouse, some of it in Cyrus's log cabin house, but most of it in the thick surrounding woods playing with Oz, Chevy and Violet as kids.

I swirl the beer in the bottle. Breanna keeps me from drinking too much. She said she's headed to Shamrock's tonight. I shouldn't care where she's going or with who, but the thought of her there irritates me. Dad says the worst indigestion to have is from a girl.

The other night, I was fucking with Breanna—messing around—but I did promise to protect her. She's not safe there. No girl is safe at Shamrock's tonight.

"What do you know about Breanna Miller?" I focus on the beer label, acting as if that question doesn't mean anything to me.

"She's sexy," Chevy answers. "Has legs that go on forever. Which I didn't notice until orientation. I don't remember her being like that last year."

Me neither. Those wide hazel eyes, nice curves, and that silky-to-touch long midnight hair. I like tunneling my fingers into hair like that when I kiss a girl. Yeah, Breanna Miller transformed over the summer. That's what I call blossoming.

Originally the plan was to convince her to hang with me for a night. A ride on my bike. Some kissing until she decided to stop, but after witnessing how her brain ticks, I need her for more. I plan on using her mind in exchange for my "protection."

"She's quiet. I'd only know her voice because it's the one

I haven't heard over and over again like everyone else's since middle school. I also know she's smart." Chevy puts down his beer and begins to flip a coin over his fingers. He's been doing sleight of hand since we were kids and, to me, it never gets old. "She's going to be one of those who leaves Snowflake and never looks back and then in thirty years she'll be ruling the world."

He preaches the truth. She's straight A, award-winning, and has never said much in class for the past four years. Breanna's one of those too-smart-for-her-environment types who's biding her time until she's eighteen and can get the hell out.

The coin disappears between his fingers, he claps his hands and when he shows me his palms the coin's gone.

"Are you going to pull a rabbit out of your ass next?" I ask.

"No, but I'll shove a rabbit up yours if you pull any of that shit again like you did with the Riot last night."

"I was playing."

He snorts. "Playing is dangling meat in front of hungry bears with anger issues. What you did last night was skipping through nuclear fallout. I'm not kicking you in the stones, man. I'm a friend trying to watch your back."

I nod because that's the best I got for him. The coin reappears as if from thin air and he's flipping it through his fingers again at a rapid rate.

"Remember middle school with Breanna?" he asks. "She did that science project that re-created the telegraph or some shit like that. I remember my head hurting because I couldn't understand half the crap she said."

I chuckle because I do remember. I also recall hating her because I was proud of my exploding volcano. The moment she opened her mouth, there was no way I was going to win.

"Remember how Marc Dasher treated her after that?" Chevy says with a hint of pity.

"Yeah." After her presentation, the bastard tortured Breanna. "We need to mess that guy up."

"Patience" is all he says.

My eyebrows lift. Neither Chevy nor Oz are the type to walk from a fight, but they never search for one like me. As I'm about to ask what I'm missing, my father's voice booms into the night. "Razor!"

The boisterous conversations cease and the droning baseball announcer is the lone sound.

"Find Oz," I say. "I need you two to ride with me to Shamrock's later."

"Shamrock's?" There's a question in his tone and I understand why. "There's going to be Army boys there causing problems tonight."

"I know." Breanna and her friends have no idea what they could be dancing into.

"Then I'm on it." He slips off the table as it's time for him to leave. Chevy's seventeen and can't enter his prospect period, the initiation time span when the club decides if someone should become a full-fledged member, until he's eighteen. No one underage is allowed at the clubhouse after eight oh one. "Good luck in there."

We smack hands, I take a fast swig from the longneck, then dump the nearly full beer into the trash. Everyone watches and half of me expects a muttered comment of "dead man walking," but they keep their mouths shut. The shit I'm in is too deep for a smart-ass comment.

Dad's already gone by the time I reach the door, so I head up the stairs. As the sergeant at arms, it's Dad's job to call people into the boardroom. It's also his job to kick people out. Wonder how this evening will end.

I walk in and the chairs at the long mahogany table are

filled. As president, Cyrus owns the head. He's got a long beard and ponytail to match. He's a bear of a man. I love him like a grandfather but have enough healthy fear to keep my distance when he's pissed.

Cyrus's son Eli sits on his right. The way Eli examines me gives the impression he's about to yank his gun out of his holster, unload a clip into me, and will happily spend a few more years in prison over it. He tugs at the plugs in his ears and his gaze falls over to my father.

Dad drops into his seat next to Oz's dad. There's no seat for me, which is fine. I prefer to stand while being fired at. "I didn't engage."

But I would have and they know it.

"You messed up," Eli states. "But the good news is you didn't actually come face-to-face with them, so we're going to call that one straight."

Interesting. Last time I disobeyed a decree from the club's bylaws, I was fined a hundred bucks and I had to clean bathrooms with the prospects for a month.

Eli stands and motions to his empty chair. "Take a seat."

My eyes find Dad's and he nods to confirm it's cool. I move slowly to the table, waiting for a trapdoor to fly open beneath my feet. As I sit, Eli draws a folding chair up to the other side of Cyrus and straddles it directly across from me.

Cyrus may have been voted in by the members as president, but everyone knows that Eli is the chief of this tribe. Not because that's how he wants it, it's because every man who wears a Terror cut respects the hell out of him. But because of Eli's stint in prison, he can't hold an official office. "What went down with you and the detective?"

I could do a play-by-play, but talking that much to anyone isn't my style. Instead, I pull out my phone, bring up the picture of Mom's car, then slide my cell to Eli. "He gave me a file to look at and said that Mom's death wasn't an accident."

There's silence. It's a silence so loud I can hear my pulse beneath my skin, the squeak of Cyrus's chair as he readjusts, the inhale and exhale of breaths. What I loathe in this silence is how it doesn't feel like shock or surprise. It's more like guilt.

Dad balls his hands on the table and turns red—the same pissed-off reaction whenever we discuss Mom.

Eli scratches at the stubble on his jaw. "Did you take any more pictures?"

I remain mute and I don't know why. The answer's there with a swipe of his finger, it's on the tip of my tongue, but then my sight lands on Dad again. He's not lifted his head yet. He hasn't said a word.

"What do you think of his claim?" asks Eli as he must take my lack of response as a no.

Honestly, didn't think much of it until I noticed this reaction. "The detective believes the Terror was involved in her death."

Eli's dark eyes snap to mine and there's a chorus of swears from around the room. It's hard to rip my eyes away from Eli's. His are as black as death, but with effort, I do, and I discover Dad's empty seat. He presses his hands against the wall with his shoulders rolled forward. Even from here I can spot the cords of muscles in his neck as they stretch.

"Do you believe him?" Eli's voice is pitched low. So low it's almost hard to hear.

I want to answer immediately. To prove I'm a man and that nothing affects me, but he's asking about my mother—the one person I loved more than my own life. "He said there weren't skid marks. That there were no signs she tried to stop."

"What are you saying?" It's a grumble from my father.

The detective was correct on some things. Mom and Dad did fight in those last months. The memories of listening to her weep between the thin walls as Dad tore off on his bike still haunt me. And he brought a parade of women home a few short weeks after Mom died and then one stayed the night this week. But the idea my father worshipped me? That's bullshit.

I suck in air and toss myself over the cliff. "Did she kill herself?"

"Razor," starts Cyrus, but my father turns toward us and raises his hand in the air.

"Do you think the Terror had anything to do with her death?" Dad asks.

I should keep my mouth shut. I've tried to discuss Mom's death with Dad. Each time, he shut me down, but I've never done it before in front of the board. Doing this could be a sign of disrespect, but it could also put pressure on him to grant me answers.

"I didn't ask about the Terror," I say. "I asked if she killed herself. I'm asking if she was so miserable with you and—" the words catch in my throat "—with me that she pressed on the gas and not on the brake and drove her car over the bridge."

"Are those the options?" Dad challenges. "That she either killed herself or that one of us, one of your brothers, one of your family, killed her?"

"Did she hate us so much that death was *her* only option?"

"It was an accident," says Eli, and I round on him too quick for it to be respectful.

"We all know that wasn't an accident!"

"So you're calling us liars?" Dad roars.

"Yes!" I jump to my feet because there's too much adrenaline coursing through my body. They stare at me like I've lost my mind. Maybe I have. Maybe I never had sanity to begin with. "I want the truth!"

"Say it, Razor!" Dad points at me. "Look me in the face and tell me you think one of us, one of your brothers, killed your mother."

There's pounding. The wooden gavel hitting the table. It shuts Dad up and that's when I notice it—Dad and I are angled toward each other, primed and ready to attack, chests pumping hard in hurried breaths. The solid table the barrier that's preventing us from going to blows.

"Sit down!" Cyrus demands.

Dad does, but I remain on my feet. "I want the truth!"

"We told you it was an accident!" Dad yells.

"And you're full of shit!"

Cyrus beats the gavel against the table again and one by one the men of the board give me the same damn look of sympathy everyone in town does and it's like someone has stoned me with sharp-edged rocks. Even now no one will tell me the full story.

"The cop said you and Mom fought," I continue, not giving a fuck I'm in violation of a direct order.

"Razor," warns Cyrus, but I ignore him.

"He said she was going to leave you. He said you notified the police of a problem with her way before you should have known there was one."

"Thomas," Cyrus tries again in a stronger voice, but even the use of my given name doesn't stop the flood.

"He said you were the first to find her. If what you've given me is the truth, then why the hell didn't I know any of that? All of it sounds like lies to me!"

"That's enough!" Cyrus shouts.

But it's not enough. It will never be enough until I get the truth. I'm dying and I'm begging. I'm mentally on my hands and knees willing anyone to tell me what I already know— that my mother committed suicide.

Because if someone tells the truth, maybe I can find a way to not be so screwed up.

But I don't get an answer. Dad edges back his chair, stalks across the room and then throws open the door with so much force that it bangs off the wall. My insides hollow out as I realize no matter what I do, no matter what I say, I'm doomed to live in this gray, haunted realm of the unknown for the rest of my life.

Before the door closes, Oz's dad is up and then the rest of the board abandon their seats and follow my father. It's a show of support, a show of solidarity, and it's not a show meant to praise me. I disrespected a brother, so therefore I disrespected them.

There's a chain of command in the club. A way of how things are done. A respect that must be given to the pecking order that's been created. I've had a hard time with it for the same reason I never cared to become the leader of my group of friends. I find it challenging to follow as much as I find it challenging to lead. That's why, as the board told me over and over again, I had the longest prospect period of anyone else in the club. I'm too unpredictable.

The door shuts and there's two of us left in the room— me and Eli.

Eli's eyes flicker from me to my seat. This time, I listen to his nonverbal request and sit. If only because the weight of what just happened is crashing down around me. "I want an answer."

I need an answer.

Eli threads his fingers together and rests them on the table as he leans forward. "Four months ago, you agreed to join this club. Yeah, we had to vote you in, but you had to accept. You chose to be a part of this brotherhood. You chose to believe in this family. Are you saying those vows you made to us mean nothing?"

He's questioning my loyalty, and maybe he should. "This is my family."

"I know, and, Razor, you're mine. This entire building is full of men who would die for you, but this back-and-forth—this rogue bullshit you pull when the wind blows east instead of west, it's got to stop. You're either with us or not. You either believe us or don't. If you can't trust us, we can't trust you. There is nothing more this board wants than to trust you, but to be honest, we don't. We voted you in because we know you love us, but we watch you with wary eyes. We don't know what shit you're going to pull next."

When I was ten years old, it was Eli who came to me at Cyrus and Olivia's before the sun had risen. Oz, Chevy and Violet had crammed themselves into the tiny twin bed I used whenever I stayed the night and each of them had curled up around me, providing a human shield from the emotional storm that had been brewing.

The three of them fell asleep, but I never slept a wink. When Eli walked into the room, he saw the four of us and lowered his head. Eli looked like the living dead himself, and when he met my eyes, he knelt and said the words that changed every thought, every emotion, every moment of my life. "I'm sorry."

So was I. He didn't have to tell me why Mom never arrived to take me home. I heard it in his tone. Noticed it in his eyes. My mother was dead.

"That detective," Eli continues now, "showed to fuck with

your mind. You're smarter than him. Better than him. Don't let him wedge a wall between us and you. Don't let him destroy you and your dad."

We all have choices to make; what lies we accept to believe. Since I was ten, I loved this family so much that I never questioned believing the lie that had been told to me—that Mom's death was an accident.

But in this moment, the biggest lie I've chosen to believe is the one I tell myself: that I trust the Terror. I've always believed there was more, and the detective was correct—if I'm going to find any peace, I have to learn the truth.

"Who are you going to believe?" Eli asks. "Us or him?"

"The brotherhood," I respond with so much ease it should scare the hell out of me, but it doesn't. The doubt's always been present. I've just now decided to no longer live in purgatory. I'm going to discover what happened. Not sure how, but I'll die trying.

I hold my hand out and, after a second of staring at the image of Mom's car, Eli returns my cell to me. With a flick of my finger, the photo disappears.

"It's my mom," I say as if that can explain away everything that went down. As if that can absolve me from any sin I'll commit here on out with the club. It's a low thing to say to Eli. His mother, Olivia, recently died.

A shadow passes over Eli's face and it's an expression that's all understanding. "I know, and I also heard what you came home to the other night. It's been a rough few days for you."

He allows me time to digest his statement and I wonder how many people are aware of the promise Dad made to me... or how many are aware he broke it.

"You and your dad—you two need to find some peace when it comes to your mom and you need to find some peace with each other, otherwise the entire club is going to suffer. That shit that went down with the detective—it wasn't right. He disrespected you and your father, which means he disrespected this club. Trust me when I say we'll take care of it."

I should feel justified the board is pursuing some course of action with the detective, but the truth is I might need the cop. He might be the lone person willing to inform me what happened, and in the end I'm not sure I do trust the club to follow through.

The picture of Violet on Bragger did come down, not of my doing, but by the club's. Regardless, it's on the web forever. Even with my computer skills, I still can't prevent copies from popping up. But what I'm really pissed at is that the club hasn't figured out who's responsible yet and nailed them to a cross.

Why should I trust them to watch out for me when they can't bring justice for Violet or look me in the eye when I mention my mother?

"Pigpen warned us the detective fucked you up," Eli says. "But we had no idea how bad. I'll talk to your dad, tell him that you need time and space, but you need to work through this. You need to find a way to trust the club and you need to work it out with your dad."

I nod, and when I stand, Eli stands with me. He walks around the table and pulls me into a strong hug. One arm high to keep from hitting my three-piece patch. It's a sign of utmost respect and I return the gesture with the same amount of emotion.

The club has been my family, my rock, my port in a raging storm, and what I'm about to do might cost me my family forever.

Breanna

WE BYPASSED MY curfew of ten hours ago. This is the first time I've been out this late with friends without parental guidance and I have to admit it's exhilarating.

Shamrock's is a hole-in-the-wall. Hole. Like a dig-through-thirty-feet-of-slime-then-let-it-fall-back-in-around-you hole, and I'm loving every single second. The music pumps from the speakers and vibrates against the walls. Every corner is dark and strobe lights create this crazy movement of people like we're pages flipped through a comic book. The stench of sweat from too many humans occupying one room mingles with the scent of something sweet.

I hated the smell when we arrived, but with a few more drinks and a few more songs, I don't mind it nearly as much. What I'm loving the most is that the rumors are true. Army boys do buy drinks and they are glorious dancers.

"You know what I love?" I say to Addison as she wraps her arms around my neck in the middle of the dance floor. We start to slow dance with each other during a song that has too many beats and too many chords.

"What?" Strands of her blond hair stick to her face and a sheen of sweat covers her exposed skin.

"I am not number five tonight!"

"No, brat, you are not! You, girl, are number one!"

We take each other's hands and spin like we did when we were six, except then it was in my backyard and the sun was shining. We slow, and when I search the room for Reagan, the world around me fades. I become concreted to the floor and my breathing hitches. He's here.

Blond hair. Blue eyes. A body so ripped that every girl near him is gaping. It's Razor. He's in the corner on the opposite side of the room. His elbows rest on a raised table, and he's staring at me.

As always, he's the perfect mix of heart-stopping gorgeous and dangerous. His hair is styled so the longer bangs almost cover his eyes, but not quite. He wears his black biker cut and in the darkness it blends into the black T-shirt that hugs the muscles of his biceps.

My mouth dries out. I bet he can dance. I bet he could rival any Army boy here. I bet he's every fantasy I've ever had and I bet he's a fantastic kisser.

I smile. He smiles. I melt.

Addison appears by my side and whispers in my ear, "What is up with you and Thomas Turner?"

I give her my best answer. "I don't know."

"He's hot," she says.

I agree, he is. I should stop looking at him, but I can't, and I love that he hasn't stopped watching me. He inclines his head as if he's assessing my outfit. To show off my dress, I cock a hip and even lift my skirt like I'm about to perform a curtsy. I'm here to be seen, to be someone other than the

Breanna everyone thinks they know, and I like being seen by Thomas Turner.

His response is a raised red plastic cup in my direction. The smile on my face grows and there's a tingle in my blood as the corners of his mouth tip higher.

There's a boldness I have in this moment I've never had before and I'm not done admiring all that Thomas Turner is. Not Thomas Turner—Razor of the Reign of Terror. "He's trouble."

"Sometimes a girl needs a little trouble." Addison howls as she twirls me, breaking my connection with Razor. "I told you this year was going to be different."

I've had three drinks tonight. My lips purse together. Maybe four. Is it normal to lose count? They were sweet and tasted like strawberries and I feel light on my feet and I also feel pretty.

I love my dress. It's formfitting, except for the skirt, which ends above my knees and flares out at the hem. The dress is royal blue and it reminds me of the pretend games Addison and I used to play when we were five. We dreamed we were princesses and this dress swishes in a way that makes me grin. What I really love is how a few guys have studied me like I was someone worth giving their attention to.

I keep spinning, but my feet don't and then my entire body jerks into something hard.

"Hi." The voice is gravelly, and when I glance up, I frown. Yes, this place is wall-to-wall testosterone from the Army base and, yes, we are not the sole girls from school who decided this was the first pit stop for senior year, but boys from school should not be invited.

Well, Razor can be invited, but that's because he's the type of guy who would show because he wasn't invited.

"Hi." I push away from Kyle Hewitt. It's not that Kyle's disgusting to look at. He's far from it. He has that grown-man baby face so many girls fall for, but after orientation I associate him with Satan.

"Do your parents know you're here?" he asks.

"Do yours?" I retort.

He smirks as he leans back against the bar. We're in the corner and beside him his friends regard me as they always do, as if they barely recognize me.

"I'm sorry I lost my temper the other night," Kyle says. "It doesn't make what I did right, but I've been under pressure. From my coach, from my teachers, from my parents…"

Kyle pauses on *parents* and there's a shifting in the hate I have for him. I never entertained much thought involving Kyle until he cornered me and asked me to write his papers in exchange for money. But when he brings up parental expectations—family expectations—I can understand.

How many times have I wanted to scream at my parents that I'm not a live-in nanny nor their prize-winning state fair intelligent pumpkin, but never do? "It's okay."

"Good," he responds.

I consider the conversation done and start to walk away, but evidently Kyle didn't receive the memo that I'm not in a talkative mood—at least with him. "Bre, I need this help. What can I do to get you to write these papers?"

There's the use of my nickname again—like he knows me, but he doesn't. "I'm not writing your papers."

"You're smart." He points to his temple as if trying to explain where my "smart" originates. "You're getting out of Snowflake easy. Me? I'm not smart, but I can play football. I'm good at it. I understand it. If I don't get my grades up,

I'm going to be stuck in this dump town working in that mindless factory like my dad and his dad. I'm desperate."

I can tell by the hurt in his eyes that he is, but writing his papers for him is wrong. Cheating is wrong. All of this is wrong. "I can help you. I can read over the papers you write. Give you some advice and pointers—"

"I'll tell your parents you were here," he cuts me off. "If you don't write the papers for me, I'll tell them you were drunk."

I laugh even though I shouldn't find his statement funny. "I am not drunk."

He smiles and it baffles me. Maybe he's not as bad as I think. "Yeah, you are. Come on. What do you want? A date to senior prom? Everyone knows Reagan talked one of her friends into taking you to junior prom. He told everyone she begged."

My stomach lurches and my hand lands on my midsection. I didn't know that and my forehead wrinkles as I try to figure out if it's true.

"If you don't want me to take you to prom, then tell me what guy you want as a date and I'll make it happen. Then I'll make sure no one but you, me and him knows. Hand to God, no one else will find out. Do you want to be on the homecoming court? I'll convince my friends to vote for you. I saw you joined Bragger. Do you want everyone at school to follow you? Consider yourself followed. Name your price."

I told Addison that for my senior year I wanted to be seen, but not like this. There's a dip inside me and it's like plunging into a ravine.

"Everyone's talking about you," he says. "That outfit you wore at orientation, how you were flirting with Thomas Turner today—"

"What?" I blurt. "I was not flirting."

Blood drains from my face. Oh, God, was I flirting with him? I was flirting with a biker. I'm breaking so many rules and they are not the ones to destroy.

"Being here tonight," he continues, "you're trying to be someone different. I can help make that happen and not in the way that will make people laugh."

Everyone's talking about you… Make people laugh… Trying to be someone different… People are laughing at me and I wasn't pretending to be anyone else, I was attempting to be on the outside who I feel like on the inside.

The colors and sights of the club merge. There's too many people. Too much noise. A few feet away a trio of girls from school are staring at me—watching me and Kyle. One gestures toward me. The other two laugh.

Nausea knots my intestines. I didn't mean to be the girl people laughed at. In fact, I craved the opposite. I wanted to be me for once, but to be me without the judgment and hate.

Wetness stings my eyes and I pivot away from Kyle. His fingers circle my wrist and he slides in front of me again. "Don't be upset. I can make this better. For one year, don't you want to be someone more than the weird smart girl?"

Sadness sinks past my defenses and creates an ache of pain, but then a flash of anger whips through me like a storm gale through trees. I tilt toward him as if he should be scared of me. "I am not that girl!"

"When did you stop? New clothes don't change who you are, but I can help."

He said it. Out loud. My fingers form into a fist. I should hit him. I should throw a punch into his face and hurt him exactly how he's torturing me.

"Let me get you another drink." His grip on my wrist

lightens and his thumb slowly moves across my pulse point. His touch sickens me. "And we'll talk."

"Leave me alone."

Kyle releases me, then sags like I crushed him and I find him confusing. He's the one causing me to suffer. He's the one causing the tears flooding the rim of my eyes.

"I'm not trying to make you cry." He crams his fingers into his hair. "I'm saying this wrong. Doing this wrong. I swear, I'm not trying to make you cry."

I'm terrified to peek across the room again—afraid the girls from school will be cackling like hyenas. I desperately try to cling to the anger, but it slips through my fingertips.

I turn and there's Addison. The elation that was on her face wanes as her eyes crazily take me in. "What happened?"

"Nothing." My lungs burn and I want so badly to curl into a ball and cry, but I can't. Not in public. Not with everyone gawking.

When she spots Kyle, she rolls her shoulders back. "What did he do?"

"Nothing," I say, and I'm moving. Through the crowd. Past guys who ask me to dance. Past Reagan, who's all smiles and tries to snatch my hand to join her and another friend. Past tables and chairs. I run past my name being called by multiple people.

I need air. I need to disappear. I need out of Snowflake and out of my home and out of this life and out of my skin and just out, and with a push of my hands on the door, I am out.

I suck in a breath when my heels click against the black-top, but then the door bangs shut and my heart jumps. No, I went out a side door. Not the front door. I spin and my fingers graze the smooth steel where a handle should be. It's a security door and I'm officially locked out.

"Crap!" I shout into the night, but no one is around to hear.

To the right is a Dumpster. To the left is another alley. Both are shadowed. I choose left and pray once I reach the corner there will be light. But as I go to walk, the world becomes disoriented. I throw my hand out to the wall when stumbling seems easier.

"Alone again?"

My head snaps back to the entrance and a surge of adrenaline shoots through my veins. Emerging out of the darkness is a large, looming figure. I stagger back. Away from the night of the alley, toward my hope for light, but there's a crunch of glass under my feet. I trip, my ankle twists and a spasm blasts from my foot up to my leg.

My already bad balance is completely thrown. My arms flail, there's a pain near my elbow as it connects with the brick and my body topples back.

I close my eyes, bracing for the impact of the ground, but as fast as I was falling, I hit something and then I'm ascending. My eyes fly open and I'm greeted by the most beautiful blue eyes. But then I shiver. Those eyes are as frozen as ice.

"You have the worst luck," he says.

It's Razor and he's cradling me in his arms. As my skin vibrates, there's a part of me that agrees with his assessment. But a small dissenting voice wonders if, in this moment, I'm lucky.

RAZOR

TEAR TRACKS MARK Breanna's face and mascara smudges near her eyes. The sight of her unhappy tugs at my soul. She's light in my arms and her hands clasp around my neck. She grabbed for me as I caught her. By the shock on her face, she has no idea how her fingers have started to play with the ends of my hair near the base of my neck.

It's a tickling sensation and it's causing me to want to hold Breanna much closer than she already is. "Are you okay?"

Breanna nods, but the answer is no. She's crying, she ran out of the club and she's in an alley alone with me. No part of that equation adds up to okay, but girls never make sense.

"I tripped," she admits. "You scared me and I tripped."

"Sorry," I say, and I mean it. "Let me get you over the glass."

She glances around, then trembles. Someone lost their mind in the alley and smashed entire cases of bottled beer along the walls and concrete.

"Wow." She cuddles into me.

"Yeah." The broken glass isn't by happenstance. It's the reason I tried to warn Breanna from coming here. New school year also means a new class of Army recruits. Drunk Army boys on a high after kicking another guy's ass doesn't spell a good night for a high school girl.

The glass crunches under my boots and her arms wind tighter around my neck as I guess she's noticing the blood trails along the wall and ground.

"What happened out here?" she asks.

"Army hazing."

"Please tell me you're kidding."

My silence is the answer. As we near the street, there's a lump on the ground and the whimpers confirm it's not a wounded animal. Thanks to the beams of light flooding from the parking lot, I spot the red of blood over skin.

"Don't look," I tell her, but by the way she sucks in her breath, she's already seen.

"We have to help him."

Footsteps at the opening of the alley and one of the Army boys Breanna danced with slides into view. This guy ain't bleeding, so that suggests he was one of the group doing the cutting.

"I know him," she confides.

"Don't look him in the eye." If he had given his name to her and believes she can identify him, he might have a problem letting us go.

G.I. Joe eyes me. His job is to keep the guy on the ground from standing. My job is to get Breanna the fuck out of here.

"Razor," she pleads as we reach the lump on the ground and the guy on duty.

"I mean it. Don't look."

"Please help him." Breanna buries her face in the crook of my neck and I get a whiff of her perfume. It smells sweet, like honeysuckle, and it reminds me how delicate this girl is and how we're both in danger.

"Please," she begs one more time, and her lips whisper against my neck. A shock wave registers through my body at a ten point oh. Helping this guy will bring hell. The Reign of Terror avoids Army drama and they stay out of our way. But the desperation in Breanna's voice... I want to kick my own ass.

The guy on duty angles his shoulder enough to show me he's letting me through, but... "Your buddy's had enough," I say.

"He's had enough when we say he's had enough."

True. "Friendly advice."

Pissed at my advice, he straightens. "Are you going to take me with her in your arms?"

Breanna starts to move, but I readjust her to encourage her to keep her head down. She doesn't need to see broken bones and she doesn't need to know that the Army boy who made her smile earlier was taking a break from a sadistic ritual act.

"Nope, but we will." Chevy sounds like he's asking the guy to drink with us, but that smile on his face as he steps out of the lamplight and takes his place next to me in the alley suggests he's ready for a fight. Possibly itching for it more than me.

Oz follows Chevy and his shoulder smacks Army boy's as he goes to hover over the lump. Oz's eyes flicker from Breanna to me, but he schools his expression. Saving girls, that's Oz's style, not mine, and her in my arms will make him jumpy. I'm the one he thinks is crazy.

"Reign of Terror have never given us problems before," Army boy says.

"No problems from us," announces Chevy. "Concerned civilians. Looks like a stray wandered into your woods and it appears we're helping her out."

Chevy winks at me and I'd punch him in the jaw if I weren't holding Breanna.

"How about you take care of things?" Oz jerks his chin to the parking lot.

How is it I'm the one who's been jonesing for a fight and I'm the one carrying out the girl? I ease past and Chevy calls out, "Your girl's bleeding."

I am never going to hear the end of this. Chevy and Oz know I don't get attached, yet in less than three days I've made Breanna my business twice.

I should carry Breanna inside, find her friends and dump her off, but instead I walk past the cars, past the bouncer and the line, and head to the back corner of the lot where we parked. She's shaking and I won't sleep tonight until I confirm she's okay.

Bleeding. Chevy said she was fucking bleeding. If she is, it's going to really piss me off.

"Is he okay?" Breanna inches her head away from my neck and onto my shoulder. The movement causes pieces of her hair to drift across my skin. My blood grows hot and suddenly my fingers become aware of her soft body.

Because of the way she's turned into me, my fingers press into the smooth skin of her arm and it's then I realize how warm my hand is on her leg. A peek down and I have to swallow the groan. Her skirt has ridden up and the sight of her thighs is enough to spur my brain to remember the fantasies I had of her in a dream last night.

She asked a question. I should focus on that and on the ground. She asked about the wounded guy in the alley. The guy who joined the Army and for some reason has ticked off his squad. Will he be okay? Fuck no. He'll receive worse later because we intervened now. "It's taken care of." For the moment.

"What are your friends going to do?"

Deniability will be her best companion. "Walk the guy on the ground out."

Breanna relaxes in my arms and a part of me hates that she's reading exactly what I wanted into my answer. She's too trusting. Like I've been too trusting of the club.

I drove my bike, but Chevy and Oz rode in Eli's truck. Chevy had plans to get hammered, but that field trip into the alley may be the release he was searching for. I lean Breanna into me so I can undo the latch to the tailgate, then gently place her on the bed of the truck.

Breanna slides from my arms, and because she's unsteady, I edge forward to offer her support with my upper body. Her hands slowly slip from my neck to my shoulders, then land on my chest. She looks up and those hazel eyes consume me like I'm some sort of savior.

She has rose-petal lips. They're perfect and begging to be kissed. I could do it. God knows she's not thinking straight. I watched her down two drinks in less than a half hour and everything from her body weight to her reputation at school screams lightweight.

Breanna tilts her head in invitation and suddenly I'm drawn to accept. This girl is gorgeous. There's an exotic beauty to her with that dark hair and tanned skin. How have I missed her all these years?

I hesitate. Tear marks and dark smudges around her eyes. Breanna was crying. That's why she bolted from the club, why we find ourselves on the back of Eli's truck.

Chevy's last words ring in my head. "Are you hurt?"

Her forehead furrows. "What?"

"Chevy said you were bleeding."

Breanna

RAZOR'S TALKING, BUT the words aren't registering. I'm guessing it's because his palms are pressed against the bed of the truck, near my legs. His thumbs move—a brush against the material of my skirt. Each slow circle sends a jolt of electricity from my thighs straight to my stomach, and it's a glorious feeling.

He's touching me. Thomas Turner, Razor of the Reign of Terror, is on purpose touching me. And if that wasn't enough, his body is wedged between my legs and he's leaning toward me, into my personal space. That angelic face is so close. Beautifully close. Close enough that seconds ago I was absolutely convinced he was going to kiss me.

My body hums with expectation, with this secret uncontrollable desire. I've been kissed before—at a party. It was freshman year and it was Reagan's birthday and there was a game. But that was awkward and this is a gravitational pull.

"Breanna," Razor says in this deep voice that rumbles to my toes. "Are you bleeding?"

My eyes snap to my elbow and Razor steps back, taking

my arm into his hands. Oh, God, my fingers had been lying against his chest. My face flushes hot with the idea of what has transpired between us and somehow that brief moment was important and I didn't fully appreciate any of it because my mind is swimming.

His rough fingers delicately sweep across the area near my elbow. "You peeled back the first thin layer, but it's not too bad. Bet it burns like a bitch."

It does, a little, but I'm more interested in the tiny electric shocks happening with his caress. "I'm fine. I ran into the wall when you popped out."

Razor keeps his hold on my arm, sliding his fingers gently along the scrape, and he doesn't talk. We look at each other and it feels oddly comfortable.

I could get used to this type of comfortable.

But then the entire world shifts and nausea twists my stomach. Strong hands grip my shoulders and I grab on to Razor's wrists as an anchor.

"The world's moving," I say. "And it's moving fast."

"The alcohol's taking over."

"I didn't drink that much," I whisper as the lights from a passing car blinds me. "At least I don't think I did."

"You drank enough."

I continue to use him as an anchor and he continues to keep me from drifting off into this dizzying storm. Eventually the spinning stops and I inhale twice before trying to salvage my pride. I am never drinking again. "I'm serious. I only drank a little."

"So you're a little drunk?"

My spine straightens. Kyle said everyone at school laughs at me. Why would Razor be an exception? I release him and I do it with enough of a shove that he retreats.

"Are you making fun of me, too?"

He's silent and I clearly hear the answer. Yes, he is. Yes, he thinks I'm a freak. Yes, I definitely made a fool out of myself.

"No," he says. "Is that why you bolted from the club? Was Hewitt talking shit?"

Yes. Yes, he was. I throw my head back and appraise the stars. I could tell Razor everything. Tell him how Kyle demanded I write his papers. Tell him how he offered me the ability to be seen in a way that won't be an encore of middle school, but where would that get me? Nowhere. Plus telling Razor would suggest we're friends, and besides the people who belong to the Reign of Terror, he has never done friends, not even in sixth grade.

The stars twinkle in the darkness and they remind me how small and insignificant I am. I came to the bar to kill off the old me and I ended up being reminded. It all feels rather hopeless. "Did you know we live in the outer edge of the Milky Way?"

His eyebrows rise like I'm crazy, but, hey, I probably am. "Astronomers think there are over a hundred million stars in the Milky Way and they also think there are anywhere between one hundred billion and two hundred billion galaxies, so that means there are…"

I pause because I should be able to add a hundred million stars to a hundred billion galaxies, but my train of thought floats away. Maybe I am drunk. "That there are…"

"A shit ton of stars."

"Yes." I point at him and my lips lift. "That. Do you want to know something else?"

"Sure."

What makes my smile grow is how his blue eyes that are always frozen slightly thaw with this brilliant light that somehow represents laughter. Not the mocking type of those girls inside the bar, but the type that lends itself to warm fuzzies.

"The closest star to our sun is Alpha Centauri, but it's not the brightest star."

"It's not?" Razor appears honest-to-God interested and I must be misreading him. No one is fascinated by my worthless knowledge. Not even Addison.

"Nope, that's Sirius."

"Gonna be an astronomer?"

"I don't know what I want to be yet, but whatever I do, it won't be in Snowflake."

Razor reclaims some of the space between us but leaves room. He has this sexy sway as he cocks a hip against the tailgate, then lazily hooks his thumbs in the pockets of his jeans.

Razor screams confidence. The way he talks. The way he walks. The way he stands. It's like he doesn't care about anyone or anything and I wish I could be him.

"Then why the astronomy lesson?"

There's a pain in my chest. The internal warning I've learned to live by. The one that's kept me from being tortured. It's the voice that has meant survival in the wild jungles of school hallways. Stay quiet. Stay unknown. Hide who you are. Keep yourself safe.

But tonight was for risks. I was supposed to break out of my mold and, for a few minutes tonight, I was a girl full of life. Maybe the clock hasn't struck midnight yet. Maybe there's some magic remaining in this night. "I came here hoping to be kissed."

Razor's face goes blank, and it's clear out of all the things he was expecting me to say, that wasn't it. He scratches his jaw and my lips twitch at his baffled expression. I confused a biker. There should be points to be won for this.

"Did that happen?" he asks in a low voice.

I shake my head. Sadly, no. I did dance, though. I danced and danced and danced to the point my feet hurt and it was tiring to smile, but when the guy eased close enough—his body practically on mine and the energy began to build—I lost the courage to raise my head and accept what I possibly could have been granted.

In the end, I wussed completely out.

"Why would you want to come here and do something like that?" he demands.

"People do it."

"What?"

"Kiss."

He nods like he understands what I'm neglecting to mention. That people at school and TV and books and movies show that people kiss just to do it and it's normal and obviously I'm not normal. My lips squish to the side. I bet Razor's beyond normal and has kissed plenty of girls.

Razor inches toward me and the thoughts of him kissing me reenter my brain. "I would've thought you'd be the type who only kissed someone she had feelings for."

"Because I'm a prude? Because I'm weird?"

"No, because you come off as a person who thinks things through."

"That's me," I say, heavy on the bitterness, "the logical one."

Razor appears unhappy with my response, but his happiness isn't my problem. But what he said, about kissing someone I cared for, that would be awesome—falling in love with somebody, but I don't have hopes of that happening anytime soon. If ever.

Sadness becomes a weight as I admire Reagan's borrowed

dress. The dress is gorgeous and I love it, but Kyle was right. I'm playing dress-up, just like I did at orientation. I'm not being myself. Tonight was fun, but like choosing silence at school, visiting the bar was a different type of escape. I thought I had the courage to be me, but I'm still hiding behind a facade.

"Most of us regret it," he says.

My eyebrows knit together. "What?"

"Kissing just for the sake of kissing. Most times, people regret it."

I roll my eyes. "That's not true. If it were, there would be more people like me and I'm obviously not the epitome of cool."

"Think what you want, but I'm telling you how it is."

Razor moves and it's slow and he regains my attention. My heart patters with each gained centimeter in my direction. Eventually, he's in front of me again and so near that my knees brush against his thighs. He reaches toward me and smooths my hair behind my ear. His fingers lightly graze the skin of my neck and I suck in a breath with the beautiful teasing tickle.

"Why here?" he asks.

I shrug. "Just wanted to be wild tonight. To act differently than I normally do."

"Wild?"

"Wild," I repeat, and I can't help the smile that accompanies the word. I must sound insanely silly to him.

"Kissing a strange guy at a bar isn't wild," he says. "It's cliché."

"Is that right?"

"It is."

He stares at my lips like he's having blush-worthy thoughts

that involve me. I should say something witty or intelligent, but I've been placed on mute.

"I'll tell you what," he continues. "If you want wild—if you want a kiss that breaks the rules, I'll give you one, but not here, not now."

I think my heart exploded. Razor of the Reign of Terror—the guy all the girls have dreamed about for years—has offered to kiss me. "When?"

"When I say." His lips edge up, sending a thrill through my bloodstream. "If you have the nerve."

"I'll have it," I exclaim.

"I'll remember you agreed to this."

"So will I. My mind is a steel trap."

He laughs and I frown. He said something earlier about me being drunk and maybe I am, but he doesn't understand. When I say I'll remember, I will. "My mind's messed up. Messed up like there's something wrong with me."

Razor's face falls. "What?"

I wave off his concern. "It's not brain damage. Well... maybe. I have this huge family, so maybe I was dropped on my head a couple times as a kid. It wouldn't shock me. You should have seen how many times Liam dropped Joshua, but anyhow, according to my parents I was born with my wires crossed. You see, whenever I learn something that's random, it stays."

Razor scratches his jaw again, and this time I notice how smooth it is. I would give anything to skim my fingers against his skin. Now, that would be bold.

"What do you mean, it stays?"

I flutter my fingers in the air, mocking a magician's assistant. "It stays in my head. All the random facts and knowledge, they never go away. Weird, right?"

RAZOR

WEIRD? THAT'S THE coolest thing I've heard. It also explains a ton about Breanna Miller. "You have a photographic memory."

She shakes her head too fast, and because she's drunk, she needs to stop or she'll get dizzy again. "Not even close. I suck at math. Like, suck. As in the moment a number is brought up, it's like I'm surrounded by darkness. And I don't remember everything, but I have this crazy ability to remember facts. Really weird, random facts. Like, by the time I was three, I knew the state capitals."

By the time I was three, I could recite the Reign of Terror creed. "All of them?"

"All of them." She curls her fingers in and out like a fighter pointing out someone in the ring. "Bring it. Ask me for the capital of any state. This freak show carny ride is officially open for business."

My finger taps against my leg. I'm curious, but I don't like how she's putting herself down. Breanna releases this sly smile. "Is the big, bad biker scared to play along?"

No one teases me, yet I'm captivated by her courage. "Fine. What's the capital of Indiana?"

"Psh, everyone knows that. Indianapolis. Another one. A harder one."

I search for a capital I know that I don't think anyone else does. "Rhode Island."

She claps her hands. "The boy knows how to play! Now, Rhode Island is the smallest US state in land area, but did you know it ranks number two in population density per square mile? That means there are a lot of people in each others' space. Oh, and the capital is Providence."

Damn. It's like watching reverse *Jeopardy*. "That's cool."

Breanna runs her fingers through her black hair, then fists her hand at the ends. "If only everybody thought that way."

The conversation I had with Chevy cues up. Middle School. Marc Dasher. The one time Breanna Miller attempted to show the world this trick. That year must have been hell for her.

"Random facts aren't the only thing you're good at, are they? You solved the brainteaser in English." Her cute, kissable mouth gapes and I forge ahead. "I was sitting behind you."

Breanna nibbles on the inside of her lip and studies me like she's questioning the past few minutes between us. "No one knows this part about me. Not even Addison and Reagan."

"I won't tell. Any promise I make is set in stone."

"You could be lying," she says.

"Could. But why?"

"Good point." She picks nonexistent lint off her dress. "Puzzles and brainteasers...that is like crack cocaine to me. It's another weird part of my screwed-up mind. The moment I see a puzzle or a riddle, I start dissecting it, then reconstruct everything so it makes sense. It can be annoying sometimes. My mind tries to find logic in the illogical. Sometimes life chooses to be random."

"Why didn't you turn in the brainteaser?" I ask.

She ducks her head to avoid my eyes. "It's easier to not be seen."

I like looking at Breanna and I sure as hell like listening to her, too. If the pricks inside that bar or at school can't appreciate what she has to offer, I do. "Hewitt made you feel bad."

Her silence is confirmation.

"I don't know you," I say, "and you don't know me, but I do have a good read on when people are full of shit and Hewitt and guys like him are a mobile home septic tank."

That gains her undivided attention. "Am I full of crap?"

"Shit," I repeat. She blushes like I told a dirty joke, and I can't help but grin with her. "Letting whatever Hewitt said get to you—that's full of shit. You standing out here letting their words make you feel bad—that's full of shit. Not turning in the answer for the bonus points—that was definitely full of shit."

Watching her dance with her friends and seeing her throw her head back and laugh—that wasn't full of shit. Listening to her explain how her mind works—that wasn't full of shit, either. "The Breanna Miller who danced and figured out the code wouldn't listen to some asshole guy."

"You don't get it," she says. "You don't care what anyone thinks. You walk around in your scary cut, and if you don't like what people say, you throw a punch or have a million bigger, badder biker guys who will throw a punch for you. I can't throw a punch, and besides Addison and Reagan, I don't have a million people behind me. I have less than one year left in this hellhole and then I can leave town and become anyone I want to be. In a year, I don't have to be Breanna Miller. Not number five in the line of nine and not the standby joke for boys at school."

"I do get it." More than she thinks. I'm the one who's

overheard the town gossip about how my mom died and why. Breanna goes to argue, but I cut her off. I'm not interested in discussing Mom, especially after what happened with the board. "I do get it. End of story."

She flinches, interpreting my words as a reprimand. Not my intention, but the conversation had to end. *I need you to help me figure out if my mom killed herself or if she was murdered, but I don't know how to ask.* "I'm your bodyguard, right?"

Breanna dramatically inclines her head and strands of her hair fall into her face. "Beyond words being used as knives, the only terrifying part of this town is the Reign of Terror. So are you saying you're going to protect me from you?"

She might need it. "I came here tonight to watch over you. You and I, we made a deal. We shook on it, and as I've said, once you make a deal with the Terror, you don't break it. But I'm going to give you a chance to back out with no repercussions." Because I like her and she shouldn't feel forced to hang out with me, no matter how much I need her help.

"You came here because of me?"

I already told her that and I don't repeat myself. I cross my arms over my chest and wait for my statement to sink in.

"You're taking this bodyguard thing seriously, aren't you?"

I keep to myself that she should be glad I upheld my end of our agreement. "I've protected you twice. Now I need something from you, but if you don't want to help me, I'll let you out of our deal with no hard feelings."

Breanna yawns and her eyes grow heavy. She's the type who gets tired when she drinks instead of annoying or weepy. It's one more thing I like about her. "What do you need?"

"Your brain."

Breanna

MY BRAIN. HE NEEDS my brain. Of course he does. Why else would he be talking to me? No guy would choose to be alone to kiss me. I practically threw myself at Razor, confessing I was hoping to be kissed, and he gives me a rain check, which I'm realizing is the equivalent of a gentle letdown. What was I expecting? Him to admit he lured me to the bed of his truck to ravish my body?

Yeah, I know. I'm supposed to be this twenty-first-century woman and obsessed with a man desiring me for my massive intellect. I am woman, hear me roar, and all that stuff, but for once, it would have been really freaking awesome to be the girl in the pretty dress left alone with the gorgeous bad boy who wants to kiss *me*.

I evidently expected too much out of the universe. "I'm not writing your papers."

Razor goes rock solid and I make myself smaller when those blue eyes ice over again. "Did I ask you to?"

"No," I croak.

"Do you believe what everyone says? You think I can't write my own papers?"

I know what he's referring to. People say he's stupid because he failed fifth grade, but until he brought it up, that fact had stayed stored away in the dark recesses of my mind. "No."

"Did I ask you to cheat?"

"No." Once again, I made a horrible presumption. "I'm sorry, I didn't think—"

"You didn't think. Remember that, now let it go." Razor pulls his phone out of his jeans pocket and flips through icons. A split second later he's showing me a picture.

I'll admit, my vision isn't the best. In fact, everything has a blurry haze on the edges. My eyes are drying out and my contacts are irritating the crap out of me. My goal in life is to find a pillow and my glasses. Give me that combo and I'll die a happy girl.

A blanket would be like sprinkles on ice cream.

I squint at the lit-up cell and the thoughts in my head disappear. I reach out, grab Razor's phone and use my thumb and forefinger to enlarge the picture. "What's this?"

"Some sort of a coded message. Can you decipher it?"

"I'm not a puzzle ATM where you insert the code and I spit out the answer."

"Do you speak to all bikers this way?"

I choke on a laugh or a hysterical sob. I'm too tired and light-headed to analyze which one. "I was raised to never speak to any of you."

"Guess that makes you a rebel."

"Guess so." But I'm too lost in the numbers and letters to enjoy this easy banter between us. "It's worked like a cross-word puzzle."

"Yeah."

"That'll help. It means some of these words share the same letters."

"There's another one." Razor switches the image. My eyes scan the code, attempting to force a pattern, but my mind is already stuck on the crossword.

"Does it matter which one I try to crack first? Because once I get going on something I have a hard time moving on until I figure out the current problem in front of me."

"You can pick one or do both. Order is up to you. Does this mean you'll help?"

There's a soft question in his tone that causes me to look up. In the brief time I've known Razor he's been as sharp and tough as his nickname, but that one plea made him sound vulnerable.

"What's this about?" I ask.

Razor shoves his hands into his front pockets and rolls his neck. He's uncomfortable and I like how we had so quickly moved past uncase.

"Whatever it is, you can tell me," I say. "If you can keep my secret, I can keep yours."

His expression darkens. "I think it's related to my mom's death."

I sway as if I've been punched in the stomach. Everyone gossips about how Razor's mom drove off a bridge. For some people, it's the go-to story when other conversation fails. *Hey, do you remember when that kid's mom drove herself off the bridge because she was so miserable...*

"I know what everyone thinks," he says. "But when it comes to my mom, my family and the Reign of Terror, this town doesn't know shit. Can you look me in the eye and say every rumor involving you is absolutely true?"

"No," I answer slowly. "I'm not sure anyone in this town really knows me."

"Then are you going to help?"

I incline my head as I assess Razor. All of him. Not just his body and beauty or the threatening cut and the patches sewn onto the leather, but his collapsed posture and the desperation in his eyes. "What do you think happened to your mom?"

"I don't know, but if you help me, maybe I can find out. I need this. I need some peace."

Agreeing will tie me to a boy I've been taught to avoid, but how can I say no? "I'll help you."

"Breanna!" Both Razor and I turn at the sound of Addison's voice. She's by the front of the club, her head swiveling as she cups her hands to her mouth. "Breanna, are you out here?"

"You should go." He holds his hand out to me.

I offer the phone back to Razor, and I'm shocked that after he deposits it into his pocket, he extends his hand to me again. I accept the invitation, and his strong fingers wrap around mine. As I hop off the tailgate, his other arm slides around my waist and my body presses into his as he settles my feet on the ground. My breathing hitches and I close my eyes. His body is warm and solid and he smells so deliciously divine.

The world swings violently and Razor rubs his hand up and down my spine. "You okay?"

Am I? Yes, maybe, no. Because of the way his hands caress me, I'm a melted puddle.

"You ask me that a lot," I whisper and then discover the courage to raise my head.

"Stop getting yourself into trouble and I'll stop asking." Razor's eyes are practically twinkling like the stars in the sky. Butterflies race around in my stomach and it's not the nervous type. It's the beautiful type of butterflies that I love to watch flutter about in the spring.

No one has ever used *trouble* to describe me, but in the

short time I've known Razor, I can't seem to avoid walking a tightrope. I should be ashamed I'm smiling, but I'm so not.

"Breanna!" Addison calls again.

"She's worried," I say.

Razor tucks a stray strand of hair behind my ear, then lets his finger gently trace the curve of my neck down to my bare shoulder. I shiver in the sensual moment. He lowers his head and his breath is hot on my ear. My heart beats faster. Is he going to kiss me? I want him to kiss me. I shouldn't want him to kiss me. I'll explode if he kisses me. My toes curl in silent expectation.

"She should be worried," he breathes into my ear.

"Why?"

"Because you're alone with me."

Yes, I very much am.

"Remember—someday soon, I'll help you with that wild kiss."

Razor steps back and it's only then I realize how much I had been leaning against his sturdy chest. *Dear God, please let this bizarre gift you've given me still work despite the alcohol. I need to remember Razor saying he'll kiss me. I need him to want to kiss me later.*

He keeps my hand so I can steady myself, but it's not going to happen in heels. I remove one shoe, then the other. When my feet contact the blacktop, I learn I'm much shorter than Razor than I had originally believed.

"I can walk you to her," he says, but I detect his hesitancy.

"I'll be fine." I withdraw my hand from his and head in Addison's direction.

A cool breeze blows across the parking lot and it carries Razor's low and seductive voice to my ears. "Hey, Breanna."

I glance over my shoulder. "Yes?"

"Be safe."

Those are two enticing and lovely words. "I will be. I have you protecting me, right?"

Maybe I'm misreading Razor, but his eyes travel my body like he might toss me onto the bed of the truck and kiss me in a way I've never been kissed before. "Don't worry. I completely have your back."

RAZOR

LAST PERSON I expected at my house was a middle-aged woman in a pair of tight jeans and a thick-strapped black tank cooking over the gas stove. I shut the door loudly with my foot and that wins her attention. By the way her face falls, she wasn't expecting me, either.

"Hello." She wipes her hands on her jeans. The scent of fried bacon hangs in the air. Dad could eat bacon every day, three times a day. "Your father didn't expect you home."

Home. My home, not hers. I scan the room and there's no sign of anyone else. My bedroom and Dad's bedroom are black and the door to the bathroom is open. Unless Dad's hiding from this chick in the closet, she and I are completely alone.

"I mean, it's your home," she says as if reading my mind, "so of course you would show, but your dad thought you'd be gone for a couple of days."

Eli said I needed to give Dad a break. I gave him two days. I spent Friday and Saturday night in one of the rooms upstairs at the club. Only showing at the clubhouse after I knew Dad would be gone. He texted this morning and asked if I'd be back tonight. I didn't respond, but I now know why he was interested. He's playing house.

"I'm Jillian, but your dad calls me Jill." She brushes her long dirty-blond bangs from her forehead as she stares at me, I guess waiting for me to speak.

Another swipe of her hair. "You're Razor, right?"

"Yeah."

"Would you like some dinner? It's breakfast, but it's dinner, you know." Her voice shakes and she twists, then retwists, her fingers. "It's your dad's favorite. He's on his way home. He'll be thrilled for you to join us."

Us. The word is like a hammer and I'm the nail. *Us.* As if she belongs here and I don't. *Us.* The world feels disjointed.

Two days away wasn't enough. Hell, thirty years may not do the job. For over thirteen years, my father was faithful— loving the same woman day in and day out. Since three weeks after her death, it's been this. An endless parade of women through a revolving door.

The detective's voice loops in my brain: *Your mother was unhappy… She was going to leave him.* My mother was on her knees in front of me when she told me he was a man worth forgiving.

My gut twists. What if this parade wasn't new? What if Mom was leaving and the stream of women was the reason why? Breaking at the seams, I burst and throw a fist into the wall.

A picture frame crashes to the floor and shatters. The woman jumps and there's an indentation in the drywall that's going to piss Dad off. The thought brings a grim sense of satisfaction.

"You're not the first. Cooking bacon isn't going to make you last any longer than the others." It's an asshole thing to say, but it's also the most humane. This woman's trying too hard and those are the ones who show here weeks later in tears trying to understand why it didn't work between them.

"It's not like that," she pleads. "Your dad and I—we aren't like that."

That's what he convinces the women he sweet-talks into sleeping with him. I should tell her, but this is Dad's mess to clean up. Not mine. I walk past her, flick the switch to the light in my bedroom and grab a bag off the floor. They want to play house, I'll let them. She can stay as many nights as she desires or until Dad decides to trade her in for a new model.

The door to the house squeaks and my drawer makes a whooshing sound as I pull it out. I toss in some boxers and socks. Slam that one shut and I dump as many shirts as I can out of the middle drawer.

Low voices. A feminine sob. My dad's deep tone.

"He didn't mean it," she says. "Please, don't. Not over me."

I don't need her fighting my battles. A hard yank and my bottom drawer drops to the ground. The corner cracks and little splinters of wood pepper the carpet. I jam every pair of jeans I own into the bag. The clothes are overflowing and I punch them down so I can zip it up.

"Razor!" Dad's in my doorway, red-hot as a five-alarm fire. "What the fuck are you doing making Jill cry?"

A menacing laugh rips from my throat. He's the one who broke the promise. He's the one who won't answer me regarding my mother and he's pissed I hurt the sweet-butt-of-the-week's feelings? I turn toward him and his eyes flicker to the bag in my hands.

He steps back. "Where are you going?"

Chevy's, Oz's. The clubhouse. Any of those are options. "Did you sleep around on Mom?"

Dad curls his fingers into the door frame. "Eli said he talked to you about trusting the club."

"This isn't about the club. This is about you, me and Mom. Did you sleep around on her?"

"That's where you're wrong. What happened between me and your mother was between me and her. You may be our son, but you have no right to ask that question."

"I remember the fights. I remember how the two of you went at it, but I could never hear what you were fighting over. She was miserable. I know this. You know this and then you get pissed when I ask the obvious questions. This is between you and me. Did you sleep around on her? Did she kill herself because you couldn't make her happy?"

"Dammit, Razor! You're playing into that cop's hands. He wants to isolate you. He's been doing this shit to all of us over the past year."

"What difference does it make if I'm being played?" I pound my open hand to my chest. "We're legit. Our club is just that—a group of guys who ride bikes. And the security business, that's legit, too. I ride along semitrucks full of bourbon. Babysitting it until it gets from point A to point B. If I call the cop and meet with him in thirty minutes, it doesn't matter. There is nothing for him to get from me. I'm not playing into his hands, I'm asking questions I deserve the answers to."

A muscle in Dad's jaw ticks and he takes several seconds before he responds. "Is that what you're going to do? Are you going to meet with the cop?"

I haven't ruled it out. If I do, I'm going against the club in a way that won't be forgiven.

"*This*—" he overemphasizes the word "—*this* is what the board's been talking about. Why you had the longest prospect period out of anyone. Why you aren't trusted with answers now. None of us know where your loyalties lie. Not even me."

"Mom had nothing to do with the club," I say.

"She was a Terror Gypsy." The women's support group. They are wives or serious girlfriends of members of the club and they work together to support the Terror.

"Not the same. I'm asking as your son that you answer me. I'm tired, Dad. I'm so fucking tired of not knowing. I'm exhausted thinking she killed herself. That she chose to leave me!"

There's a strange wetness in my eyes and a loss of strength in my hands. The bag plunges to the floor and a rush of air from the impact hits my legs.

"Thomas..." Dad says in defeat.

I rub both of my hands over my face in an attempt to drive the emotions away. My arms drop to my sides, and when I glance up, Dad's entered my room. He stands before me, hands in his pockets, looking at me with the same pity look everyone in town wears when they spot me. "Your mother's death... I can't talk about it."

"You can." I need him to. "I know it's hard. It hurts to remember her, but if we sit and—"

"You misunderstand," he cuts me off. "I've been ordered not to."

My vision tunnels. I must have misunderstood what he said. If he's been ordered not to discuss Mom's death, then... "Mom's death is club business?"

He holds up his hand. "I didn't say that."

Yeah, he did. "Then why else would the board silence you?"

"For the same reason you've been kept in the dark. We can't trust you."

"The club patched me in. The board voted—"

"Because if we didn't, by our bylaws, you would have never become a member. You'd reached the maximum time any-one's allowed to be a prospect. None of us were willing to let you go, but you weren't ready. You still aren't ready. That patch on your back—it's borrowed."

I stumble back as his words strike me like a wrecking ball.

"You have to learn to trust us," Dad continues. "This club *is* your family. Let us in, Thomas. Let me in."

"How?" My arms are stretched wide, begging for him to give me an answer, any answer that will end this torment. "Tell me how, because I thought I was trusting you. I thought I was trusting the club."

"Let your mother's death go."

The world tilts and nausea sets up in my stomach. He's asking for the impossible. He's asking me to bleed out on the street. "I can't."

"Then we can't trust you. Not until you trust us."

Fuck this. I swipe the bag off the floor, but Dad doesn't move. "This is your home."

"It was," I answer. "But then Mom died. This ain't a home. It's walls with a roof."

Pain flashes in Dad's eyes and he stiffens like he's paralyzed. I use the opportunity to stalk past. The new woman of the week hugs herself in the kitchen and opens her mouth like she's going to say something, but thinks better of it when I won't meet her gaze.

I'm out the door, down the steps, and I leave with no in-tention of coming back.

Breanna

KEEPING IN MIND the most frequently used letters in the alphabet, I'm toiling my way through the Caesar encryption method. It's a simple method. One I don't expect to work because that would be too easy, but it's what my English teacher used on Friday.

The library's busy; at least it is toward the front. Because of that, I selected a table in the back. Joshua had practice before school, so I've been here for the past hour jotting down possible solutions and crossing them out just as quickly. It's frustrating and exhilarating, and if this is what being employed with the CIA is like, I want in.

There's a low buzz of conversation. Occasionally some girl laughs too loudly for too long, but a shush from the librarian silences her. There are footsteps on the carpet and a pause behind me. A flutter in my stomach wishes it's Razor, but then the overpowering smell of too much aftershave squashes that hope.

The chair across from me is drawn back and Kyle drops into it. I've been going to school with Kyle since kindergarten. He ate worms. I strung clover together to craft necklaces.

We belonged to two different worlds then and nothing since then has changed, yet here he is talking to me again.

"I'm not writing your papers. I will help you, but I'm not writing them."

He scratches behind his ear and the action reminds me of a dog. Strands of his black hair now stick out. He rests his elbows on the table, then rests back in his seat, then forward again. A strange unsettling forms in my bloodstream. Whatever is about to happen will be bad.

Time to bolt. I turn off my phone, put it in my purse and scoot out of my chair as I sweep up my notes.

"You're going to write my papers," he says.

I stand and shove my wrong answers into my backpack. Mimicking my younger siblings, I ignore his existence.

"Did you know I have over six hundred Bragger followers? Thanks to football camp, I'm hitting close to seven hundred and I like to post stuff. Stuff some people may not want seen."

"So?" I empathize with those antelopes on the *National Geographic* specials that glance up from the watering hole and come face-to-face with a tiger. Like them, I'm terrified into immobilization.

Kyle rubs his eyes with his thumb and forefinger and I shift my weight from one foot to the other. If I run, maybe whatever it is he's planning will fizzle, but something warns me that no matter how fast I sprint, he'll be able to catch up.

"You're wanting to go to college, right? Knowing you, you're going to some Ivy League school, am I wrong?"

He's not. Not at all. I hunger to go far from here. To go where there will be other people like me. Someplace where I won't be the one who is odd, but the one who belongs.

"Coach had a meeting with us a few months back on how we have to watch what we do online. How guys who have great track records on the field lose chances at scholarships because of their behavior off the field and online."

The entire left side of my body goes numb, and I randomly wonder if I'm experiencing a stroke. Kyle's right. Universities do research people online. They do care about our personal lives when it pertains to coveted spots or scholarships—especially with the schools I'm interested in attending.

The wooden chair cracks under his weight and he yanks his cell out of his pocket. "Have you seen this site before?"

Snowflake Sluts. Every girl I know hates that site. The first few times it sprang up on Bragger, someone told the school's administration and it was taken down, but like a bad pimple, it pops back up. No one reports it anymore, since the next picture in line is of the girl who snitched.

"I know the guys who run it."

My eyes dart to his. Guys? There's more than one sick, twisted pig at this school?

Kyle moves his fingers across the screen, then slides his cell over the table to me.

Bile claws up my throat and a sweat breaks out along my hairline. I collapse into the seat. It's a horror show. One I crave desperately to flee, but can't.

It's a Bragger message on Kyle's account and I don't miss how it hasn't yet been sent into the universe. The picture is of me and Razor and beyond us is a sign for Shamrock's. I'm on the bed of the truck and Razor is leaning into me, settled between my legs. His head and lips extremely close to mine. My skirt is pulled dangerously up my thigh, exposing areas that no one should ever see, and Razor's hands appear to be touching my skin.

The picture is damning enough, but it's the words above it that causes my head to throb: #snowflakesluts #bikerwhore

"I won't send the picture from my account. It'll be sent from Snowflake Sluts'. I'm sure you noticed it has a nice following."

It does. Too many people. Way more than the population of our school, or town, or even county. This has a reach that could devastate futures. Specifically, my future.

"I've got more," Kyle says. "Of you drinking, but I figure this one would get more attention."

More...of me drinking. I'm sure the college scholarship and admission committees would love to see one of their prospective students participating in underage drinking at a bar and then appear to be about to have sex in a parking lot in a bed of a truck with a member of a notorious biker gang.

"I'm sorry," Kyle says. "But failing isn't an option. It doesn't have to be like this. I can still give you whatever you want. You can forget you saw this picture, and when the year is done, I'll delete it and the others I took. This can be a great year for the two of us. I pass and get a scholarship out of Snowflake. You can become the most popular girl at school."

I fight the compulsion to dry heave. "But nothing happened between me and Razor. We didn't even..." I choke on the word *kiss*.

"Doesn't matter what the truth is. Only matters what people think."

He's right. Kyle is so right I'm dizzy. "That's Razor from the Reign of Terror. If you hurt me by putting that picture up, you're hurting him."

"The guys put up a picture of Violet and the Terror didn't do a thing." It's the crazy in his eyes that scares me. "What makes you think he'll do anything for a one-night stand?"

"I didn't do anything with him." I grit my teeth. "He's my friend."

"Razor doesn't have friends. His own club is terrified of

him. Even his mother drove over a bridge to get away. If the Terror didn't save Violet, Razor sure as hell isn't going to help you."

"What if I still say no? What if I tell you to go to hell?"

He looks me point-blank in the eye as if he's a firing squad. "Then I walk away from here and tell the people who run the Snowflake Sluts account to push send."

RAZOR

Cyrus: I have something for you. Something Olivia
wanted you to have.

ACROSS THE YARD, the clubhouse is shut up and the yard
is empty. It's Monday around noon. Most of the guys from
the club who are employees for the security company are out
on runs. The other half of the club, the guys who work normal jobs, are out doing their thing. It's quiet—lonely—and
the only sound is the rustle of leaves moving with the breeze.

In front of Cyrus's log cabin house, my hand's poised on the
railing ready to go up. If it weren't for Cyrus's text, I wouldn't
be here. Dad said the patch on my back is borrowed—that no
one believes I've earned it. It's an open-palmed slap in the face
and being anywhere near the club wounds my pride enough
that my skin crawls.

But Cyrus brought up Olivia. I lower my head. She was the
one person in the world who didn't think I was fucked-up beyond belief.

"Are you coming in or not?" Cyrus appears on the other side of the screen door.

I climb two steps at a time and Cyrus holds the door open. The place looks the same as when Olivia was alive. She passed a month ago, but even if ten years had gone by, I can't imagine the house changing. We loved her too much for this to be anything less than a living tomb.

Eli bought the flat-screen television and sectional couch for Olivia, his mother, after his stint in prison. There's a throw rug on the wooden floor and picture frames are everywhere. Olivia insisted on having visual reminders of the people she loved.

There's a ton of pictures of people in the club: Olivia and Cyrus; Eli and his brother, James; Olivia's granddaughter, Emily; and then plenty of the brat pack: Oz, Chevy, Violet and me. We weren't born to her, but we were her children. She loved us when we were unlovable.

Cyrus enters the kitchen and I hesitate near a framed three-by-five of me and Olivia. Olivia's beside me and I have my arm lobbed around her shoulders. I'm smiling because she was laughing. Olivia had a contagious laugh and the world is too silent without it.

"Where did you stay last night?" Cyrus calls out.

Figures Dad would notify the club I left. Leaving: another thing I've done to add to the list of how unpredictable and untrustworthy I am. "I drove around."

"All night?" Cyrus pops his head around the door frame. He strokes his long gray beard as he watches me for the lie.

I did drive around, but then I went to the one place no one knows. A place that can soothe my soul. "I haven't slept yet."

It's an answer in a nonanswer and he accepts it. "Second day of school was today."

The combo of the fight with Dad and no sleep would have made me a lit fuse. Olivia said a smart man knew which battles to fight and which ones to abandon. I waved the white flag on the war otherwise known as school.

Cyrus reenters the living room with a cardboard box in hand. "Your dad reached out to the club to find you. You should call him. Let him know you're okay. Oz and Chevy went looking for you. You should reach out to them, too. They didn't like you being MIA."

Funny how Dad didn't call or text me, but Oz and Chevy did. I messaged them this morning that I was good, but they were pissed I wouldn't confess where I was holed up. They didn't tell anyone we had contact because the three of us are still tight.

"None of us liked you being AWOL." Eli strolls into the house and pats my shoulder as he walks past. "Why didn't you come to me or Cyrus last night? You know we're safe havens."

They wait for an answer. I've admired Cyrus my entire life and then worshipped Eli the moment he rolled into town when I was ten. Before today, before I was patched in, I relied on Eli and Cyrus like a second skin, but after Dad's admission that the club considers my membership the equivalent of a handout, I'm not sure what my relationship with them is anymore. In fact, I feel like a poser still wearing the cut, but I can't bring myself to remove it from my back.

Eli's gaze flickers from Cyrus to the box Cyrus holds in his hand. "*This* is the moment? Did Olivia choose this specific day or was it an event?"

"Event," Cyrus answers in a gruff tone. "Makes you scared, doesn't it?"

"Yeah, it does." Eli cracks his neck to the side. "Let's do this."

Eli motions for me to sit on the couch. I do and Cyrus

settles into his recliner as Eli pulls a wooden chair out of the kitchen and straddles it across from me. Eli rubs the stars tattooed on his forearm. The guy is hardcore, but ask him what his tattoos mean and most women will weep.

Cyrus gives Eli the box. This package is like a coiled and pissed-off cobra. If you're careful, you can escape unscathed, but if you move wrong, the result will mess up your day.

Eli strokes his thumb over the box. "Do you know what's in here?"

"Some of it." Odds are it's Olivia's ashes. Chevy, Oz and I have theorized this was Olivia's grand plan. According to her final wishes, Olivia's ashes were separated several ways, but how many ways and who the ashes were for was kept a secret.

"Do you know what's in it?" I return the question.

"Some of it." Eli steals my answer. "The unknown scares me. Cyrus, why now?"

Cyrus steeples his fingers as he leans forward. "Olivia's instructions were to give it to Razor when he walked out on his dad or when he no longer trusted the club."

Knife straight to the gut as those are both viable options.

"Fuck," mumbles Eli. He adjusts the box as if he's weighing it, then offers it to me. I accept and the room shrinks with the two of them studying me like I'm under a microscope.

I run a hand over my head. I can do this. I can open a box. I can deal with what's inside.

This summer, I said goodbye to Olivia and I made my peace with her death. This box contains a piece of her, not the part that's important—not her soul.

Peeling the tape off the box, I remove the same wooden box I've seen in Oz's possession. I flip the lid and inside is a plastic bag and I divert my eyes away from Olivia's ashes to the white envelope with my name written in Olivia's script.

My heart stalls. This is the last thing I'll receive from her. After this, it's all memories. I release a long breath, then slide my finger under the edge of the envelope.

There's a packet of stapled papers inside, and the front page is a simple handwritten note:

Thomas, I wrote Oz a long letter, but you and I know how you prefer brief.

I chuckle and an ache forms along with the slight smile on my face.

Won't lie, you're a ticking time bomb, but you're the type that implodes instead of explodes. As a child, you were a talker, and as each year passed your silence felt like a slow, silent death. If you're reading this, it's because either someone cleaned out the closet and found this box or you're physically pulling away like you have emotionally.

I love you too much to allow that to happen.

Read the attached. Read it often. Carry it with you. Memorize it. This is the life preserver you have been searching for. I apologize that it took my death to throw it out to you.

After you've found your peace, you'll know what to do with my remains.

I love you. I'm not letting you go and I ask that you please reconsider. Walking away from them is like walking away from me.

~Olivia

I turn the page and my eyebrows furrow together.

"What is it?" Eli asks.

I raise the packet of papers and Eli's dark eyes harden into death. Eli's reaction confirms I'm holding the answers to my questions, but I'm clueless as to what those answers are, especially when it's something I've seen my whole life. Something I had to memorize to patch in. It's the bylaws for the Reign of Terror.

A low rumble of a chuckle comes from Cyrus's direction.

"It's not funny," Eli snaps.

"No." Cyrus sobers up. "It's not, which is what makes it sadly hilarious."

"Someone want to fill me in?" I ask.

Eli abruptly stands. His chair rocks, then hits the floor. "It means Mom's mental stability was more fragile than we thought in those last few months."

His hand hammers the screen door as he leaves and the door comes back and slams into the wood. I glance at the bylaws. Olivia was a lot of things toward the end and one of them was lucid. Eli's hiding something, and when I peer over at Cyrus, the pensive stare in my direction confirms he's hiding something, too.

Breanna

THE WORLD HAS an unusual fuzziness to it. A haze I can't escape. The bell rings, I get up, go to class. My teachers talk. My friends talk. People around me talk. I stare at the desk. The bell rings again. It's an endless cycle until the day ends.

I'm grasping for some sense of normal. Anything that happened before eight this morning. Before Kyle sat in the seat across from me in the library. Before he slid his phone in my direction. Before I saw my entire life crumbling.

Whore.

Slut.

My privacy is being completely and utterly violated. That picture—it violates me. It's taking a private moment and exposing it to the world. It's painting pictures that people will gossip and laugh about forever.

A Reign of Terror biker between my legs and my skirt riding up. I was smiling. He was smiling. Nothing happened, but that photo suggests something entirely different.

It's my fault. I threw out into the universe that I wanted to be seen. That I wanted to be more than the quiet friend of Reagan and Addison. That I wanted to be known as more than the freakishly smart girl in seventh grade. I wanted to be seen and the entire world is going to see me in a way that causes me to slowly wither and die.

"You okay?" Liam comes to a rolling stop at the intersection near our house.

"Yeah." But I'm not. "Why did Mom send you to pick me up?"

"She said you needed a ride. I'm guessing what she really needs is for me to drive someone someplace." There's an edge to his voice. He's been angry since he saw me climbing into Reagan's car. The stink part of this is that he's mad at me and I'm not the one who dragged him out of bed after he worked third shift at the distribution warehouse.

Mom calls Liam when she requires extra help. One day, he's going to snap or leave.

"I should have never let them talk me into community college," he mumbles. Community college is still an hour's hike from here. Yep, he's definitely going to move away and never return. Like our oldest sister and brother have done.

"You're quiet," he says. "Not that you aren't normally quiet, but this time you're quiet and heavy. Plus with the way you're gripping it, you're going to poke a hole in that backpack."

I stretch my fingers. "I need to talk to Mom and Dad."

"Leave Dad alone," says Liam. "Work is killing him."

He's right. Either Dad wins over this new client or the company falls into bankruptcy. Half the town works for Dad's employer. There's no pressure there.

All day I've run through the countless possible ways I can make what has happened okay. *So, Mom, I lied and I'm sorry and I need you to be okay with what I've done because there's this boy and he's blackmailing me. He's going to show everyone a picture if I don't write his papers and I need help because I don't know how to fix this. I don't know how to fix any of this...and please don't tell anyone. Not Reagan's parents and definitely not Addison's.*

Addison. My breath catches in my throat and my hand settles at the hollow of my neck in an effort to halt the choking sensation. If I beg my parents for help, will they tell Addison's parents what we did? And if they do, what new bruises will appear because I'm weak?

My chest hurts as I try to inhale. This situation isn't fixable. None of it is. I'll miss any chance to attend college. To win a scholarship. Mom and Dad will be disappointed. They'll be angry. Addison and Reagan will pay for my sins.

But I don't know what to do. This problem...this picture...Kyle...this is bigger than me.

"Is it true that once something's on the internet, it remains on the internet?" I ask. Liam likes computers. He's the one who prevents our household from plummeting into the dark ages.

"Once it's out there, it never goes away," he says.

"But what if you delete it?"

Liam pulls into our drive. "The moment it's on the net, it's cached someplace. Doesn't take anyone with half a brain to find it."

"Even pictures?"

"It's worse if it's a picture. People copy stuff all the time. It's like ants at a picnic. You can kill one, but fifty of them are right behind."

He shifts the car into Park, then his face wrinkles as if he realized he was strolling in a thunderstorm without an umbrella. "Why?"

If I speak, I'll cry, and if I cry, I'll lose my courage. Mom. I need Mom.

I'm out of the car, leaving my backpack in the seat and the passenger door gaping. I burst into the kitchen and my heart stalls. The floor is littered with luggage and cardboard boxes of Clara's stuff. What bothers me is that Mom's suitcase is in the mix.

The swinging door from the living room opens and Mom rushes in like she's fleeing out-of-control flames. Her arms are filled with various items on the verge of spilling onto the floor.

"Oh, good." Mom's expression relaxes as if my arrival meant the end to world hunger. "I was scared Clara and I would be gone before you showed. Liam must have found you. I know sometimes you visit with Addison and Reagan after school. Help me unzip the middle suitcase. The purple one. I wonder if I forgot something. Bre, start listing things I could have forgotten."

Me? You've forgotten about me. "Where are you going?"

"Where are you going?" Liam ambles in and drops my backpack on my feet, permitting it to hit my toes. "Leave something?"

"Liam." Mom glances at the clock on the microwave. "Unzip that middle suitcase. The purple one, then go tell Clara goodbye. We should have left five minutes ago if we're going to make this work."

"Good. This is good." Liam's shoulders loosen and then he mock swats the back of my head. "You heard Mom, start listing things, Encyclopedia-freak."

"Don't hit your sister and don't call her that." Mom reprimands him with all the passion of an answering machine recording as she drops the contents in her hands into the already overstuffed suitcase.

Mom straightens, places three fingers over her lips as she

focuses on the mound of stuff, then mumbles a list of items—socks, pants, toothbrush…

I'm frozen to the ground, my entire body becoming solid. "What's going on?"

Her head jerks up like she forgot I was here, which means she did. "Oh, yes. Bre. *You* are very much needed to make this work."

She plucks an elastic band off her wrist and wrestles her short black hair into a ponytail. Mom rarely does this except when she's flustered. It's a vanity issue as the gray shows near the base of her neck. "I need you to take care of your younger siblings while I'm gone."

There's that word again—*gone*. Panic sets in as a trembling in my hands. "Will you please tell me what's going on?"

"It's Clara," she says. "You know how upset she was that she didn't graduate this spring and that your father and I are having her pay her tuition this year. Well, your father talked to the college. The administration worked with us and they agreed to let Clara into the fall courses she thought were closed. I'm driving her into Nashville tonight and we're going to be staying with Nora."

We're? As in Mom and Clara are staying overnight with my oldest sister? "When will you be back?"

Mom's face pinches like either I won't like the answer or she won't. The way my sugar level plummets, I'm thinking it'll be me.

"Two weeks," she says.

The world tilts. "Two weeks? I thought Dad was going to be working crazy hours and you were going to be taking time off from your job so you could handle his responsibilities and isn't he supposed to be traveling for part of it and why are you leaving with Clara?"

Mom waves her hand to ward off my verbal meltdown as if she's air patting me like a dog. "Calm down. Yes, your dad is busy. Yes, he will be out of town for part of it. Yes, I did take time off from work, but no, I won't be here. I'll be spending the two weeks with Clara. Your dad and I discussed it this morning. We have complete faith you can keep this house going. I'm sure Liam and Joshua will help, but, Bre, if anyone can run this house, it's you. We know you can do this. Out of all of my children, you are the responsible one. My thinker."

Mom grins at me like I should be happy. When my response is my wide-open mouth, she continues, "I need you to understand. Clara needs me."

She needs her? Is Clara being blackmailed? Will Clara's future be destroyed with a click of a button and one post on the internet? "Are you kidding me?"

"You'll be fine," she coos like I'm Elsie and she's trying to convince me to bathe. "You're the one that is always fine. You have practically raised yourself since birth. You run this household better than I do. Dad's okay with you ordering takeout and everyone will have to understand you can't get them to every practice."

My head is shaking or it's me shaking or it's the entire kitchen shaking. "But you don't understand. I need to talk to you."

Liam and Clara walk into the kitchen. They're both smiles until they see me. Actually, Liam still is, but Clara's lips fall into a sneer.

"Liam, Clara, carry this stuff to the car," Mom says. "The bursar's office is giving us until six tonight so we can get you into those classes."

My brother and sister hoist multiple boxes and luggage and Mom's giving me a verbal list of things I already know, like what time to start baths and who is on what round of antibiotics and lots and lots of stuff that means she's not listening to me.

Nausea roils in my stomach and her words become muffled and Clara and Liam laugh and my world is crashing around me. The pressure is mounting and my skin feels too tight.

"I need to talk to you," I say, but Mom's lecturing over me about how she's concerned Zac isn't coming straight home from school and that I need to stay vigilant with his time.

"There's this thing that happened at school." My voice is becoming higher in pitch and Mom's progressed to describing Elsie's problems now, and then Clara asks Mom where the keys are for the car, and when Mom pauses to answer my sister, I explode.

"They're there, Clara! By the door. On the hook. Where the keys always are. Where everyone in this freaking room can see, but that's not what it's about, is it? You have to be the center of everything and right now the entire world does not revolve around you!"

"Breanna!" Mom roars. "That is uncalled-for!"

"Selfish much?" murmurs Liam. Shame heats my face, but what causes the tears to burn my eyes is the sadistic lift of Clara's mouth. Mom never yells at me. The perfect, responsible daughter is plunging from the pedestal Clara created for me and Clara gloats in her victory.

"Go outside," Mom says to Liam and Clara, but it's me she pins with her ticked-off gaze. "Get the car ready. We're leaving in minutes."

The moment the door closes, I suck in a breath. "I'm sorry, but you don't understand—"

Mom cuts me off. "I know I'm asking a lot from you and

I know Clara has not been very good to you over the past two years."

Try since birth. In fact, for years she's done nothing but dump the burden of her unhappiness onto me.

"But your sister needs me."

I attempt to rush out the truth. To tell her about the weekend, to tell her about Kyle, to tell her I'm scared and terrified and that I crave nothing more than to be six and climb onto her lap and let her chase the monsters away, but my mother steps forward and places her hands on my cheeks, hampering any hope I had of confessing.

Mom's hazel eyes soften as they bore into mine. "Clara isn't like you. None of us are like the two of you, but Clara struggles with this gift. This past year almost broke her, and when she didn't graduate, I thought your sister was going to enter a depression I couldn't dig her out of.

"Your dad called in a favor and we transferred her to a school near Nora. We're hoping that staying with Nora will help ground Clara. Classes started last week, so she's already behind. If she focuses, then she can graduate this December. I'm staying for two weeks to help her get organized, to help her catch up on work she's missed, to help her with her confidence. Honey, these are things I don't expect you to understand because you're the one who has it together."

Her words are like small razor blade slices to my soul, and even though it's just a trickle of blood at a time from each wound, I'm slowly bleeding out. A bead of something warm escapes my eye and Mom catches it with her thumb.

"But there's this boy at school..." I start, but Mom talks over me.

"And I want you to tell me, but not now. I'm late and I need to focus on Clara."

My throat tightens. "But I need you."

Mom tilts my head so I have no choice but to spot her sincerity. "When I return, I am a hundred percent yours. I promise you. Right now, your sister needs me more. I'm depending on you, and your dad is depending on you. This project is a make-or-break moment for him. He needs to focus on that. I need you to focus on this family. I am begging you not to let me down."

But I already have. I've let her down in so many ways that she'll be sickened to look at me. I need my mother so desperately. I need help, but there's no hope to be had. Before I can respond with a yes or a no or before I could throw myself to my knees and beg for mercy, my mother collects her suitcase and leaves me utterly and completely alone.

RAZOR

"HOW'S LIVING WITH CYRUS?" Chevy asks. It's before school and the two of us are leaning against the lockers near my English class. Chevy's looking out for Violet's younger brother, Stone. I'm searching for Breanna.

She sent a text last night I didn't see until this morning: We need to talk. Can we meet before class?

I texted back yes, but nothing more from her.

Because of my absence yesterday, the last time I saw her she was climbing into a car with her friends at Shamrock's. She texted me Saturday to confirm she received the code, so I know she made it home safely, but there's this itch to see her I can't shake.

It's both annoying and addicting.

Breanna Miller—the girl with soft skin and gorgeous hazel eyes. Breanna Miller—the girl who can tell me about the Milky Way. Hell, she can probably tell me about anything.

"Are you smiling?" Chevy asks. "Shit, you're smiling again. That's the second time in days. Gotta admit, that scares the hell out of me."

I sober as I answer his first question. "Everything at Cyrus's is good." Since I left home, Dad and I have had no communication. Not sure where that leaves either of us.

"Does the shift in your normal fuck-off attitude have to do with what you've got going on with Breanna Miller?"

I don't respond. I already informed Oz and Chevy that Breanna's off-limits. She's a private person. So am I. The one thing Breanna has after we chatted on Friday is my respect.

Out of thin air, Chevy produces that coin of his and flips it over his fingers. "Remember when we were kids and we'd catch fireflies in the forest with Olivia?"

I nod and watch the coin appear and disappear up and over his knuckles. This kid could make a good living in the circus...or make a million dollars as a pickpocket.

"Do you remember how Olivia taught us how to catch them by cupping our hands after she explained how fragile they were?"

I nod again, wondering where Chevy's heading on this memory lane detour.

"Do you remember what happened next?"

I snort because I do. Chevy tosses the coin in the air and he catches it between his hands with a loud clap as a reenactment of what occurred that night. We squished the hell out of those first few little fuckers.

"None of you listen," Olivia chastised us. "Each of you are too excited to do what you want to pay attention—to learn."

"Not that you asked me." Chevy yanks me out of my brain. "But you need to be careful with Breanna. She's not from our world, and what's worse, she's not the type that's curious about the club. She's one of those quiet types and those girls can be fragile. Guys like us can hurt girls like her without meaning to."

There's a twisting in my gut. Years ago, I was the one who killed the most bugs. It was never my intention to cause harm. In fact, the desperation to capture one alive caused me to go faster, and in my haste, I crushed more. "You telling me to stay away?"

"I'm telling you that you keep pissing off people—people who love you. Starting shit with a girl outside of our world isn't going to help anyone. Your dad asked me to tell him if you get into trouble at school. Breanna could be trouble and I'm not looking to rat you out on anything. Guess I'm saying stop making life complicated."

"You're right," I say. "I didn't ask."

"You never do. Figured out what Olivia wants you to do with her ashes yet?"

I shake my head and appreciate the change in subject. I've read through the bylaws Olivia left me a dozen times over. Even compared them to the current copy I found in the club-house. Nothing is different. Everything the same. I can't help but feel like she's toying with me from beyond the grave.

"Makes me wonder what she has up her sleeve for me," he mumbles. It's what we all think—that she left her ashes to each one of the brat pack. That we will each receive the same wooden box and messed-up set of instructions. It happened to Oz and Emily after her death. Now to me. Maybe her mind was in neutral toward the end.

I should confess everything to Chevy—the visit from the detective, my thoughts and fears about Mom's death and the increasing paranoia that the club was involved, but I don't. As he clearly pointed out, I don't ask for advice and his anecdote reminds me why. In the end, even the people I care for the most believe I'm crazy.

Stone rounds the corner in that quirky way he walks with his shoulders rolled forward and his feet moving too fast. He's fourteen, a redhead like Violet, tall like a tree, thin like a sheet of paper, and the wires in his brain are crossed—not like mine, but more like Breanna's. Where she's supersmart, Stone is, too, but he's socially inept and he can't empty thoughts from his brain. Stuff circles and the loop won't end.

Asshole guys in this school try to harass anyone associated with the Terror, and Stone's connection with us combined with his personality has tattooed a target on his forehead. Good news—he's Terror family.

Rumor has it the two juniors down the hallway have been dared to bully Stone, and we won't permit that to happen. They block Stone's path and Chevy and I push off the lockers, but Chevy raises his hand. "I got this. If this goes bad and I get suspended, I need you here."

I withdraw and let Chevy run the show. Stone belongs to all of us, but because he's Violet's younger brother, Chevy takes it more personally. As soon as Chevy joins Stone, the two juniors retreat. Chevy glares at them as he passes and I wait for them to piss their pants.

"...okay, thank you."

My head whips toward the sound of Breanna's sweet voice. At the corner, she waves at our English teacher, then starts for our classroom. She holds her books to her side and a part of me lightens as if I heaved a hundred-pound chain off my shoulders.

Breanna has this fluid, effortless way about her that draws me in. Her light-colored skirt swishes as she walks and I appreciate the white button-down shirt that's tailored to her curves. One side of her midnight hair is pulled up and I love how it exposes her neck and the smooth skin I came close to tasting last Friday.

Breanna reminds me of slow-moving time and summer

nights. She's sexy, I'm attracted and we're on opposite ends of the social scale.

Breanna glances up before entering class and, screw me, a hint of a smile plays across her lips. "Hi."

"Hey," I respond, and in one of the rare times in my life, I search for something to say. Do that small talk that Chevy and Oz find easy.

Her expression falls as she scans my body like she's trying to discover a bleeding wound. "Where were you yesterday?"

"Out."

A reprimanding frown in my direction. "Obviously. We need to talk. Something's happened."

An adrenaline rush charges through me. "Is it the code? Did you crack it?"

"No. I haven't had a chance to dig into it yet. When I texted, I didn't think my problem through and we shouldn't discuss it here. Can we meet somewhere private later?"

The sights and the sounds of the hallway zone out as my mind tries to guess what has her spooked. "Tell me."

"Not here."

And I'm not waiting. "Spill. Now."

Breanna's fingers drum against her folder and she does a sweep of the hallway. This time when she speaks, she lowers her voice to the point I have to strain to listen. "Do you re-member when we were talking on Friday night and you had sat me on the tailgate and how you were...close?"

Whatever the hell is bothering her causes a scary stillness inside me. "Go on."

"We weren't alone."

Breanna's words are a straight kick to the torso and I ease toward her as something dangerous unfurls within me. "What do you mean, not alone?"

Her eyes dart to the left, and when her face pales out, I track her line of sight. A wave of anger rumbles through my bloodstream as I go eye to eye with Kyle Hewitt.

He slows as he walks past us, raising his eyebrows as his gaze flickers between me and Breanna. When the bastard settles his eyesight back on me again, he has the balls to smirk.

Something's wrong—off. Breanna shrinks and it takes less than a heartbeat for the deadly thoughts to click together. Breanna raced out of the club Friday night after this asshole confronted her. Breanna said we weren't alone, and my own thoughts about how some girls look at a certain group of guys haunt me.

Kyle Hewitt is a dead man.

Chevy joins me, no doubt sensing the storm that's preparing to make landfall. "You all right?"

"I need you to cover me." I barely catch his agreement as I start after Hewitt. Breanna's on my heels, talking, pleading. Begging me to stop so she can explain. She can explain, after I throw Hewitt into a wall and hear him beg for mercy for whatever he did to make her cry.

Hewitt has no clue I'm behind him as he struts down the middle of the hallway like a duck with an ego complex. People say shit as they see him. All fucking giggles until they spot me and they understand that I'm the reaper and Hewitt has seconds to live.

"Razor, please!" Breanna says loud enough that Hewitt turns. His eyes widen, and his mouth opens in a silent scream as I grab him and shove him into the bathroom.

Two guys are at the urinal and finish their business quickly as they watch me push Hewitt again. Hewitt's shoulder bangs into the wall of the stalls and I barrel after him. The other guys run out. I should be shocked as hell when Breanna appears in front of me, but I'm not. The girl can be a force of nature when she chooses.

"Stop it!" Both of her hands are out and her folders are gone. "You have to stop."

I don't acknowledge Breanna. In fact, I look over her at Hewitt, who's trying not to piss himself as he holes up in the corner of the bathroom. "You have thirty seconds to explain why Breanna's upset."

"Or you'll what?" He attempts a big and bad bravado, but his hands quake.

Or I'll throw him into the cement-block wall, smash his head into the mirror, and then I'll crack his skull on the sink. "I'm creative. Get talking."

"People will come in here!" Breanna says.

No, they won't. Chevy's guarding the door. "Twenty seconds, Hewitt."

"She didn't tell you?" he spits.

"Ten." I advance a foot.

He straightens for my attack yet yells at Breanna, "If he hits me, it'll go up and it'll never stop! That's not the only picture. They'll all go up."

All I see is red. Pictures. Breanna. The image of Violet crying uncontrollably at my house as she sobbed, *That picture has ruined my life.*

Breanna hijacks my arm as I launch myself at the bastard. "He's blackmailing me to write his papers! And he's doing it with a picture of me and you together."

Her desperation claws at me. "Nothing happened."

"But it looks like something happened." Her fingers dig into my skin.

"Yeah, it does." The pride in Hewitt's voice causes me to imagine killing him seven different ways until Sunday. He holds out his cell, and if it weren't for Breanna's grasp on my arm, reminding me that she's here, I'd tear off his balls and shove them down his throat.

Friday night seemed like a dream to me. Her so close, the feel of her soft skin. Her laughter, her trust, the two of us sharing intimate details of our lives, and in front of me is a picture that makes dirty for her a night I enjoyed. This damn snapshot could destroy her reputation.

"Are you suicidal, Hewitt?" I ask in a low tone. "Because it feels like you're begging someone to slit your throat."

He laughs like what I said is a joke. "You really are banging her, aren't you? I had no idea what we were going for was correct."

The crazy residing in me fractures and Breanna shouts my name as I bolt forward, curl my fingers into Hewitt's shirt and slam him into the wall. I'm eye to eye with the asshole and overpronounce my words in case he's a stupid son of a bitch. "You will not disrespect her."

His hands are on my wrists and he fails at freedom. Hewitt's face stains red and he breathes hard as I probably knocked the wind out of him. "I'm holding the cards, not you."

"Tell me who's mixed up in this." I give him another shove. "Tell me or I will start throwing my fist into your face until you cry."

"Razor!" Breanna's next to us. "I'll write the papers. Please let him go!"

No fucking way. He's torturing her and he's using me to do it.

Hewitt tries to kick me, but I'm stronger. "Leave, Breanna. Let me handle this."

He angles forward to gain my attention. "I will destroy her by the end of the day."

"Razor, please!" Breanna cries. "That picture can't go live. I'm begging you, let him go!"

The despair in her voice unbalances me, and for some screwed-up reason, I'm listening. She's asking the impossible. I don't back down from a fight. Everyone knows this and the fact I'm hesitating because she asked confuses the hell out of me.

"Please, Razor," she whispers, and it's then that I notice her touch on my arm. It's a gentle caress. One that causes the buzzing in my head to vanish. "Let him go."

I do, and Hewitt places space between us as he rights his shirt. "You're crazy, Turner."

Me? "I'm not the sick bastard blackmailing innocent girls. But if you want crazy, keep this up. I'll bring the wrath of the Terror down on you."

"Your club's not going to do a thing. They didn't do anything when we posted Violet's picture and, according to you guys, she's your family. But go ahead. Tell your club. Anything happens to me, there are others who will destroy Breanna for me."

I'm inhaling through my nose and pushing away the urge to kill him. Clearer heads prevail. How many times did Olivia tell me that? Too many. I crave to tear him apart limb by limb, but I won't, not now. He's playing smart, and so will I. "I hear you."

Hewitt scrubs his hands over his face like he's free from a death row sentence, but he's sadly mistaken. There are only a few hours left before he's chained to the table. "Look, I had no idea she meant something to you, so no disrespect intended. I saw what happened at the club and I know you didn't kiss. I thought you guys accidentally ran into each other and she blew you off. I had no idea she'd run to you and that you'd give a shit if we did post the picture."

He's waiting for me to offer my hand and say that he read me correctly—that I don't care if he took pictures of me with any girl, but instead I stay silent. Either Hewitt's mentally unstable or he lies way better to himself than I do.

When he gets no reaction, he switches to Breanna. "It doesn't have to be like this. We can forget about the picture. Name what you want, I'll give it to you, and you can write my papers."

I have to keep from flinching. I made a deal with Breanna, as well. Her brains for my protection. Does everyone use her?

Breanna lifts her head, holding herself proud, but I can spot the anguish on her face. "I want *nothing* from you."

"Your choice." He regards me again. "This doesn't involve you, so stay out of our way or she'll pay for your sins."

He breaks eye contact with me first, not even lasting longer than two seconds before bailing for the door. Breanna crumples with her head in her hands. The anger that had been pulsating within me disappears.

"Hey." I ease into her personal space and tuck her hair that had swept forward over her shoulder. "Look at me."

She doesn't. My fingers slip under her chin and I nudge until she lowers her hands and raises her face. I swear at the pain in her eyes. "I'll take care of this."

The warning bell rings and Breanna bolts. Damn. She doesn't believe me.

Chevy sticks his head in and looks me over for signs of a fight. "We good, bro?"

I meet his eyes and he nods as he understands that I'm not. He inclines his head to the hallway and the two of us head to class in silence.

Breanna

IT'S ONLY THE third day of my senior year and today already ranks as one of the worst three days of my life. The first being yesterday, the second one belonging to seventh grade, the third is award-winning today.

Reagan slides a tray of food in front of me. There's plenty on it—pizza, a hamburger, French fries—but there is not an ounce of me that is hungry. She volunteered to stand in line and buy lunch for the three of us while Addison and I claimed the outside picnic table as far from everyone else as possible.

"It's just rumors." Addison props her chin on my shoulder in an effort to draw my attention from my cell. "It'll die down by tomorrow."

It's a sunny day. Enormous blue sky. White fluffy clouds. It's hot, though, like sweat-through-my-shirt hot, and because of that, there are only a few people outside, which is why we chose to sit here for lunch. I need alone time to regroup.

I lower my head into my hands. "Todd posted *Razor from the Terror is trying to screw Breanna Miller*. Yes, I can see how this will die down by tomorrow."

"Could be worse," she says in a light voice. "They could be saying you are definitely screwing Razor. Everyone seems to have enough common sense to keep the rumors somewhat realistic."

My head slips down farther and my fingers creep into my hair. If Kyle posts that picture, that is exactly the story that will be flying around. Breanna Miller: Reign of Terror slut. There are girls who have earned that title from rumors and they have never lived it down. Boys harass them. Girls ignore them. The world has such a double standard and girls are on the bottom of this filth-ridden pond.

"I'm sorry for not finding you faster," Addison says. It's the millionth time she's apologized for the night at Shamrock's. She thought she saw me go into the bathroom after I ran from Kyle, and she'd been waiting outside the stall. My best friend was shocked when someone else walked out and then she went into panic mode.

"It's okay." And it is. Maybe life would be different if she had found me before Razor did, but I don't regret my time with him. I just hate Kyle.

Four more Bragger messages pop up. Because I'm a glutton for punishment, I click on the new messages, and sure enough, two of them involve me.

Lily @lilybear · 20 s
This morning was interesting. Is she sleeping with Razor from the Terror?

Because the use of pronouns and not my real name will mislead me to thinking the message isn't about me. Blah... just blah.

Deke @deke575 · 10 s
Y'all crazy. Twenty dollars @breanna212 is tutoring his stupid ass and he tried something and Kyle came to her rescue.

My heart hurts. I went to the bar to find magic and I did find magic—magic that combusted into a curse when Kyle invaded my privacy by snapping a photo. No one deserves to have their private moments put on display and to be called names. It's like we've regressed to age two and we all need to relearn basic kindergarten manners.

"Finally," says Reagan as she sits across from me and Addison, obviously reading my cell. She doesn't understand the term *personal boundaries*. "A reasonable explanation, plus points to Deke for at-mentioning you instead of talking about you like you aren't watching the feed. I should totally accept his invitation to next week's dance for that."

"What are people saying?" I peer over at Reagan and she purses her lips.

Reagan's small, but she's full of personality. One of those people you know is there the moment she jazz-hands her way into a room. She's shorter than me, shorter than most of the girls at school, but she's runway pretty.

She befriended Addison and me in sixth grade and, I won't lie, my relationship with her has had its share of ups and downs. Reagan is infatuated with drama. She's like watching a busy little bee bouncing from flower to flower and Addison and I are the home-base hive.

Addison clicks her tongue in disgust at Reagan. "You're a gossip. It's a compulsion for you. We're aware, so dish what you know."

At least Reagan has the decency to fidget with her rings in guilt. "I didn't really gossip about you, Bre, as much as I discussed your current situation so I could get an appropriate sampling of the thoughts of the student population."

She'd make an excellent politician.

"I've considered buying you a muzzle," Addison says.

Reagan flashes us her brilliant smile. "Put diamonds on that baby and I'm your girl. But I swear, I didn't trash you."

What she's excluding is how she didn't defend me, either, but that's a part of Reagan I've had to learn to accept...or not accept. We're friends, but we'll never be close.

"What are people saying?" I ask again.

Reagan rests her elbows on the table and there's a spark in her eyes as she misreads my question as forgiveness. "The story going around is that Razor tried to hit on you and Kyle came to your defense when you got scared. Razor was pissed Kyle interfered, so he threw him in the bathroom and they had a shouting match. I'm wondering if Kyle started that rumor because it makes him less assholey than normal."

She drenches a fry in ketchup. "Everyone thinks Kyle is all heroic for saving our poor, defenseless, quiet Breanna Miller from the clutches of the Terror."

Kyle is a psychopath. "No one thinks I'm sleeping around?"

"God, no." Reagan chokes on the fry and pounds her chest as if she can't breathe. I glance over at Addison and she rolls her eyes. As I said, Reagan's dramatic.

I release a relieved breath, but tension still cramps my muscles. I'm safe, but for how long? In theory, if I write Kyle's papers, then I won't be branded with a big scarlet letter for life, but it kills a part of my soul to think of helping him cheat.

"The bright side of the whole debacle is that your number of Bragger followers is going through the roof," says Reagan. "Everyone wants to see your response."

If it weren't for the fact that being on Bragger and following

Kyle's account is the only way I feel secure he hasn't posted the picture, I'd delete my account in a nanosecond. Bragger is proving to be a nightmare. "There won't be a response."

Addison and Reagan share a long look and I consider crawling under the table to die.

"A nonresponse is still a response," says Addison. "It means you're hiding."

"I *am* hiding," I mutter.

"Posting a cute picture of a kitten should do the job." Reagan dips another fry into the ketchup, then points it at me. "It'll say you're innocent, plus half the girls in school will share it. I'll find one and send it to you via email next period. If you don't post it immediately, I'll steal your cell on the way home and I'll post it for you."

Reagan would also make a great public relations savior.

"So…" Addison cuts the hamburger in half and takes a bite. "What really happened in the bathroom? And let's not forget you were in a boys' bathroom. I have to say, Bre, I had no idea so much drama would be coming from you."

Me, either.

The bell rings and I hop to my feet. "We'll talk later." No, we won't. I'm praying Addison's right and that the rumors will dissipate and everyone will forget. "See you."

I squeeze into the crowded hallway and, like a salmon, fight against the current of bodies to reach the stairs. There's three floors, and the higher up I go, the less populated it becomes.

Nausea crawls along my insides when I arrive at the desolate third floor. Kyle leans against the lockers like he was waiting for me. He jerks his head to a hallway off to the side that has a clearly marked no-trespassing sign.

I scan the hallway. No other students. No other teachers. Only two rooms are used on the third floor because the heating and cooling systems fail whenever they attempt to regulate the temperature in more than two classrooms.

I follow Kyle but stay near the corner in case I need to run. I could have turned and gone the opposite direction, but it doesn't matter if I run. He'll find me, and I can't deny he holds all the power.

Kyle acts like he's normal, but every hair standing on end informs me he's completely unstable.

There's an unnatural silence surrounding us compared to the echoes of noise from the corridors below. The air is stale, like no living soul has visited here for centuries. People have told ghost stories surrounding the third floor—a girl who killed herself a few years back, a boy who snapped the neck of another fifty years ago, the forever fables of homeless students who squat here because there's nowhere else to go.

I believed they were stories until now. What else would explain the cold chill slithering down my back?

"In case you're wondering," he says, "I have a plan in place if Razor touches me, or if I go missing or end up dead. That picture will still be posted on Bragger and then a letter from me will be sent to the police and you will be arrested for being an accomplice in my murder."

Talk about being dramatic. "Razor isn't going to kill you."

"You spend ten minutes alone with the most psychotic member of the Terror and you think you have them figured out? You heard about the Terror shooting in Louisville this summer, right? I'm sure you've also heard about how Razor was seen tearing through town a few days ago chasing after the rival gang involved in that shooting."

A sickening sensation causes a cold sweat to break out on my palms. No, I hadn't heard that. Being around Razor, talking with him, listening to him…it makes it easy to forget there are some rumors that are true—that the Reign of Terror are dangerous.

"I'm saving you by telling you to stay away. Remember Mia Ziggler? She trusted the Terror and no one's heard from her since. I'm doing you a favor."

"He's not the one blackmailing me."

"I'm not blackmailing you," he says in a clipped tone. "We made an agreement. You write my papers, I'll help you make this a great senior year, and I've already started on my part. Our problem is that I had no idea Razor would be pissed. The way the Terror runs through girls, I had bet he would've forgotten when that picture was taken and who he was with."

It's like he socked me in my stomach and I wince with the verbal impact.

Kyle eyes my reaction. "Did you think you were special with him on Friday night? I've seen this guy and his buddies work. Girls are like running faucets for them."

A stupid part of me did feel special with Razor. Special in how he listened, special in the way he touched and treated me. A lump forms in my throat. I threw myself at him, and the boy who goes through girls like toilet paper rejected me. Like Kyle, Razor's sole interest in me is for my brain. "The lies on Bragger, that's from you, isn't it?"

"I may have said a few things. Explained how Razor was bothering you and I was helping you out. The story took off from there. Consider it my gift to you for writing my papers."

"Everyone is focused on me and him. That doesn't feel like help. That feels like a threat."

"I'm reminding you to stay away from Razor and I will continue to remind you of that every time I see you together. I am not the asshole here. He's the threat, not me!"

"Keep telling yourself that."

"That's not true!" Kyle rams his fist into the cinder-block wall. I stagger back, a scream teetering on the tip of my tongue. He turns his back to me and paces like he's a caged tiger.

I should run. I should race down the stairs and out the building shouting "fire" the entire way, but it won't solve my problem with Kyle. I'm trapped in this inferno.

Kyle shakes out his arms and it's scary how fast he calms down. "Everyone thought of you as the freak, shy girl. Now you're the girl I stuck up for. I already had two guys on the football team asking if I bagged you this summer because I stood up for you, and I told them no—that you weren't that type of girl, that you were the type worth dating."

"Am I supposed to thank you?" I clutch my folders tighter to my chest.

He gives me a "duh" expression. "Yeah. I built you up to them. Those two guys are thinking differently of you and it's not as the school freak or the easy lay. They're looking at you as the girl to take home to Mom."

"Is that how it works?" Disgust swims through me. "Some closed-door boys' club in a locker room and a girl's reputation is forever set?"

Kyle shrugs. "I didn't make the rules, I just play along."

"You're a pig."

"I'm a pig that's going to help get you on homecoming court if that's what you want, or a date with one of my buddies. A real date. Flowers. Dinner. Respect. Stop being so negative and start looking at what we can do for each other. I have a paper due this semester on some book. *1980 something* by George somebody."

"Orwell. George Orwell and it's *1984*." I roll my neck to

stop the flood of information on him, like how he also wrote *Animal Farm* and he was born on June 25, 1903, and...

"Yeah, him." Kyle interrupts my crazy train of thought. "Five pages. Double spaced. One-inch margins and, I've been thinking, you should throw in a few grammatical errors. If it's too good, my teacher may not believe I wrote it."

"If you're that concerned, maybe you should write it yourself."

"Could, but I'm not. Look, the rules of this game are easy—write my papers, stay away from the Terror and tell me what you want from this arrangement. As I said, it'll be easier on both of us if we don't consider this blackmail, but an agreement."

The bells rings, and my head starts to throb. I don't answer him because there is absolutely nothing he has that I could ever want—besides that picture banned from the universe. I pivot and slowly walk to my classroom. It's hard to breathe as the walls close in.

RAZOR

THE BRAGGER MESSAGES are like taunts from a drunken frat boy begging to be punched:

Jenny @cutekitten · 30 s
Like she's a catch. If Razor feels like playing, I'll play with him. Bet he wasn't coming on to her. Bet she was coming on to him and she struck out.

Kyle @koaltime · 10 s
Everyone back off @breanna212. Not her fault the Terror are terrorizing her. @cutekitten

Lauren @laurenrose · 10 s
@koaltime @cutekitten I saw her crying after math. She looked scared. Thank you for standing up to the Terror Kyle. The Terror suck.

"How the hell do you play football with these assholes?" I whisper to Chevy. He's a great running back. Can read a defender like no one else. That is, when his coach will give him playing time. Being a kid of the Terror has stalked him onto the field.

"They're not all like that," he replies. They aren't. Just like how all bikers aren't criminals on parole.

Another round of messages involving Breanna, and the pencil in my hand snaps with a crack. Using those fast hands, Chevy swipes his cell off my desk and tucks it into the pocket of his jeans before the teacher can spot what's set me off. The bell starting sixth period rings and it takes everything I have not to lose my shit.

People stare at me like I'm about to go nuclear bomb fall-out. The guy in front of me scoots his desk forward. Yeah, asshole, I'm going to knock the hell out of you because someone else is putting lies on the internet.

He glances over his shoulder and I glare. On second thought, maybe I should beat him and every guy in this room senseless as a warning to mind their own business instead of expressing an opinion on someone else's life. Piping in to join the masses because they're grateful they aren't the one being picked on. The kid in front of me with the overgelled hair turns red and mutters to his buddy next to him that I'm crazy.

"Fucking right I am," I say.

"Is there a problem, Mr. Turner?" my science teacher asks.

I shake a no. The incredulous expression on her face says she doesn't believe me.

This town has talked shit about me since Mom died, and most of the time I can tune it out, but this bull involving Breanna pisses me off. They can talk trash regarding me all they want, but they need to leave her alone. The only sin she's committed has been being in the wrong place at the wrong time—with me.

Chevy's writing in his notebook, then sliding the paper toward me. On it is the one word that makes me feel like a dick: *firefly*.

As an answer, I cross my arms over my chest, slouch in my seat and kick out my legs, letting my combat boots hit the chair in front of me. The kid flinches like he's terrified. My lips edge up but then fall back down as Chevy's message circles my mind: firefly. I spend a few minutes alone with Breanna and I'm killing her.

Our teacher has begun to bore us with her theatrics when Mr. Duncan leans in from the hallway. He's a tall man, grayhaired, old enough that he taught my dad and Eli, and is built like a linebacker. His best attribute? He's one of the few people in town who's a friend of the Terror.

"Sorry to interrupt," he says. "But I need Thomas Turner."

Chevy peers over at me and someone does that annoying "Ohhhh" in a singsong voice, like getting called into the principal's office is the equivalent of being sent to death row.

I grab my notebook and haul it to the hallway before my teacher asks questions. Duncan starts toward the stairwell and I follow him down.

When I catch up with him on the landing, he speaks. "Talked to Cyrus, Eli and your dad today. They're on board with what I'm about to tell you."

When he knows I'm solidly listening, he continues down the stairs. "Remember those tests you took at the end of the year? Not the state ones, but the ones to figure out placement?"

We take a shit ton of tests. Sometimes it feels we test more than we do actual learning.

Duncan pauses outside his classroom. "Turns out you did well."

My forehead furrows. "What?"

"Enough seniors tested high enough that we were able to create college credit classes for the other subjects, but only four of you passed the science AP exam. We received permission from the state to set up an independent study for AP physics. You'll sit in the back of my earth science class and watch videos, take tests online, and there will be projects you'll turn in to me on occasion. You'll need to buddy up with one of the students for projects. I'll leave it up to the four of you to decide who is paired with who."

I nod to confirm I'm absorbing. Gotta admit, it's a high to hear I've done well.

"Either you can do this on your own or you can't. If you act like a fool, then you'll go back to biology. Some of the administration are balking at you being in this program, but I stuck my neck out for you. If my head gets chopped off because you act like an idiot, then I'm tearing your balls off, son."

Besides the fact that his son is our brother, his attitude is why he's a friend of the Terror. "Yes, sir."

A grin cracks onto that weathered face and he pats my back. "I also told the administration you'd start leaving your cut at home."

"Tomorrow." I strode into school with it, and if I don't leave school with it on, it'll be the same as shuffling away with my tail between my legs.

"Tomorrow. There are four computers set up in a study room in the back. If you have questions, find me before or after school and I'll answer."

Duncan walks into his classroom, which sounds on the verge of going *Lord of the Flies*. He shouts at them to "Quiet down," and because he can be an intimidating son of a bitch, they do. Then every eye lands on me.

Someone mutters, "Great," and my eyes hit Kyle Hewitt

in the back left corner. There's no way this moron made it into an advanced class.

"Is there a problem, Hewitt?" Duncan asks.

"Not as long as you sit him far from me." Kyle assumes he has the upper hand. Poor boy will cry when I nail his coffin shut with him in it still alive.

A knock on the door and two more guys appear.

"Is this the room for AP physics?" one of them asks while cowardly sizing me up.

"You're late," Duncan says, ignoring the guy who's trying to explain why they're late. "This is Razor, he'll be taking the class with you. I want partner matchups turned in to me this afternoon. What are you, morons?"

Duncan's across the room and yelling at some kid who has his hand caught in the blinds.

"Should we wait for the fourth person before we partner out?" one of the guys suggests, but I'm no longer listening as my gaze meets wide hazel eyes.

Breanna blinks when she enters the classroom and I want to kick myself for not thinking ahead that she'd test into this course. She scans the room full of students, spots Kyle fuming, and I decide it's time to start fucking with the boy.

He demanded that I leave the situation with Breanna alone—threatening to destroy her if I interfere with his plan—but according to his rules, he can't do shit if I'm hanging with her because of school. Time to inform him he's not the only one holding some strings.

"Duncan," I call, and that stops the low murmur of conversation that had started when Duncan went to untangle the idiot in the back.

"Yeah?"

"Miller's my partner."

Breanna's head slowly tilts to the side as if I spoke in another language and she's trying to translate what I said.

"Works for me." He gestures to a room in the back. "Get in there and get working."

The two guys head for the room, and when Breanna stays cemented in her spot, I wave my hand like a gentleman for her to go before me. I follow her as she trudges down the aisle. This time when Kyle looks at us, he doesn't smirk. This time he's pissed and I lift my lips in grim satisfaction. Game on.

Breanna

"ARE YOU INSANE?" I whisper-shout. "Have you absolutely lost your mind?"

Razor drops into the corner seat in the long, narrow room built to inventory textbooks. The walls are floor-to-ceiling metal shelves and have become a holding cell for me and the other AP physics students.

He angles his head so he can peer past me, and when I glance over my shoulder, I notice how the other pair reside as far from us as possible an entire classroom length away.

"Most people do think I'm crazy." Razor kicks out his legs and folds his hands over his stomach. He wraps his booted foot around the leg of a chair and angles it toward me like he's encouraging me to sit.

I collapse into it, then push back in an effort to create space between us. I prop my elbow on the table that houses our computer and lean my head into my hand as my stomach plummets. This situation is absolutely hopeless.

"Kyle's mad," Razor states.

"No kidding," I mumble. "And he's going to post that

picture because of it. Do you care to explain how this helps me or were you lying to me about the whole protecting me garbage?"

"We do have an agreement." An unfamiliar tremor runs through me with Razor's deep voice. "Hewitt thinks he holds the power. I'm letting him know the power works both ways."

"He's going to post that picture!"

Razor reclines forward and his blue eyes pierce me. His body is so massive that he fills the windowless, cramped room that has more dust bunnies than square footage.

"Hewitt needs you. Never forget you also have power. I get you don't want the picture posted, but that bastard is using fear to control you. You hired me and I'm covering your six by showing him we aren't scared of him."

My throat tightens. "But I am scared."

"Don't be. I'm telling you, that picture won't go up."

My temples throb and I slip the spiral-bound, printed-out wannabe textbook off the table in an attempt to pretend these past two days never happened. My eyes scan the page as if I'm interested in the words, but I'm not. I'm mad at Razor. At least I should be, but with each second that passes, the anger recedes.

"I heard what's going down on Bragger," Razor finally says. "You deserve better."

I bite my lip, then summon the courage to look at him. "I'm sorry, too. People have said terrible things about you and that's not fair, especially when what they're saying isn't true."

"People talk shit. It happens. Don't worry about me. You okay?"

Not at all. "I'll be happy when people move on to talking about someone else. Did you also watch Bragger today with agonizing despair?"

"I avoid shit like Bragger, but Chevy showed me some of the feed. I'm not interested in what most people have to say to my face, much less what they have to say when they have the safety of a computer to hide behind."

"I wish I was more like you."

"Sorry to break it to you, but only men can join the Terror. But if you're completely heartbroken, you can try to join the Terror Gypsies. That's the women's support group."

"I wasn't talking about joining your gang," I say.

"Club," he corrects. "Not gang."

What's the difference? "Fine—club, but even if I were, I don't know how to ride a motorcycle." Like that's the sole thing stopping me from dancing over the line into crazy.

Razor rests his arms on his thighs, causing his golden-blond hair to fall forward. Through the strands, those beautiful eyes capture me, holding me completely and utterly under a spell. "I'll teach you if you want."

My mouth dries out and Razor's eyes focus on my lips as I lick them.

"Teach me what?" I whisper.

"To ride," he says in this slow seductive slide as he inches forward in his seat. His knee brushes against mine and a zap of electricity shoots up my leg to very private places.

My temperature spikes and I have to remind myself that inhaling is essential. Razor eases back in his seat but extends his leg so that our calves are touching. A ball of energy zings to life from the small amount of friction between our bodies and it races through my blood. I take a deep breath, gather my hair and pull it off the back of my neck.

"Hot?" There's a definite tease in his voice.

Sizzling. This entire room is sizzling. From his voice to his eyes to that dimpled half smirk to those ripped muscles in his arms. Razor is so hot the fire alarms should be blaring. I wave my hand toward the ceiling. "There's no vents in this room—no flowing air. It's stuffy."

"Mmm." That's his response to my attempt at logically explaining away my attraction to him. I have never felt like this with a guy before—like a moth drawn to the raging inferno. My entire body hums breathing the same air as him.

"Do you want out of our deal?" he asks, and the humming stops.

A mental pause. The real question he's asking is do I believe he can keep the picture from going up…if I can trust him to help me. "I've heard your club kills people and I don't want that. I'm mad at Kyle, but I don't want him dead. I want out of the deal if he's going to get hurt."

Razor steals a few seconds of silence as he methodically rubs his hands together. There's a hard glint in his eyes that causes a spark of fear within me.

"Our club isn't what you think," he says as if he honestly believes he means it. "Are you saying you don't want to work on my code?"

"No, I'm saying I'm not okay with hurting people even if they've hurt me." It's an honest answer. "I've seen the code. Even if I wanted to stop working on it, I can't. My mind won't stop turning over the possible solutions."

I raise my fingers to my head and they flutter about like the movement can help him understand the organized chaos. "I don't know how to describe it, but when my mind doesn't have something to work on, I feel like someone's peeling off my skin. My mom says I never relax, but how do I explain that crossword puzzles and those mind games on my phone are what help me unwind?"

I wish I would learn to shut up around him. I've spent too

many years trying to keep this part of myself locked tight so no one can use it as ammunition against me and here I am handing it out freely.

"You're the coolest damn person I've met," he says.

On the inside, I'm smiling like an idiot. I may also be smiling like an idiot on the outside.

"If you're working on my code," he says, "then I'm still your bodyguard. Deal's still in place, and if it makes you feel better, then I won't involve the club."

My happy moment withers. "You know the whole bodyguard thing was a sham."

Razor's mouth edges up and my breath catches. Good God, he's gorgeous with a frown, but he's perfection with a smile. "I thought you were trying to hire me last week."

"Would you hate me if I told you that you scared the hell out of me last week and I said some stupid things I'm sorry for?"

"I'd like you more than I already do for being truthful. There's not too many people who can do honesty."

The way he stares at me, as if he likes who I am, causes me to become shy. I run my fingers through my hair and pretend I'm crazy interested in the ends, because I have no idea what to do with myself now.

Razor doesn't propel the conversation along, so I do what any other self-respecting seventeen-year-old would do: change the subject. "Mr. Duncan told me about this class yesterday and he let me take the book home, so I read the syllabus and—"

"You memorized it," Razor cuts me off with a grin.

I bob my head back and forth. "Maybe." Yes. "Anyhow, there are projects and Mr. Duncan said we can do them together, but I'm not sure you'll want to work with me, because—"

"I do."

I blow out a frustrated sigh. "Razor—"

"We're working together. You're smart, I'm not."

"You're one of four people who tested into AP physics. I'm not buying what you're selling. But anyhow, you need to remember how I explained I'm not good at math, and there is math in physics, so—"

He slices his hand across his throat, ending the discussion, and I snap my mouth shut. While me and big, bad hot biker guy may be forming some sort of strange friendship, I'm not pushing him into conversations he doesn't want to have.

"Back to the deal." There's a glint to Razor's eyes that's a hundred percent mischief and I'm tempted to play along. "You crack my code and I'll continue to watch your back, and I'll even sweeten the pot. If you and your friends want to go out dancing, I'll be DD, mop the floor with any boys that try to cop a second-base feel, then I'll make sure you get safely home."

I swallow at the thought of Razor being the guy stealing a second-base feel. I haven't been that far before. Bet he has. I bet he's full of all sorts of fun, fascinating moves. "Thank you for the offer, but my clubbing days are officially over."

"That's a shame." His eyes wander the length of my body like he sees beyond my clothes. "I loved the blue dress."

Um… I've lost the ability to speak or to think or to do anything, so I flip through our textbook. Words. Words would be good. Any word. Preferably words that make sense.

"If we're working together, then you'll need to read the syllabus today. The first video is tomorrow. Did you know that everything falls at the same rate? Like if someone was to chuck you and me off a building at the same time, we'd both fall at the same rate of motion because of gravity? It's called acceleration of gravity. If you exclude wind resistance, everything, and I mean everything, falls at the same rate of 9.81 meters per second. You, me, cats, dogs, hedgehogs. We'll be doing a project on that."

Yep, words.

"We're going to toss hedgehogs off a building?" he asks.

I try not to giggle at his bad joke and fail. "An egg."

"Good on the hedgehog. That could get messy. Speaking of throwing people off buildings, we have two options of how to handle Hewitt."

And the conversation was going so well... "What do you mean?"

"I can try scaring the hell out of him," he says, like we're discussing the weather.

"You already tried that and he said if you get involved in any way someone else will post the picture. I was in the bathroom, remember? Scaring him didn't work."

His mouth twists up in a deadly way. "That was me being friendly."

I shiver despite the heat of the cramped room. "What's the second option?"

"We get rid of the picture."

"How?"

"By being smarter than them."

It's like he's set out a puzzle and my mind is desperately trying to sort the pieces. "Only way to get that photo is to know who is in the group associated with the site and then hack into their computers and phones to delete it or destroy the hardware."

He doesn't even blink at my words.

"I'm not a computer hacker," I say. "And I have no clue who he's working with."

"You're not, but I know a few things about computers and you're smart. Together we can figure this out."

I fiddle with the corner of the syllabus. "I don't want to write the papers. If I do it for him, it's a lie he could hold over me forever—just like the picture."

I could lose my chance at a scholarship or admission into my colleges of choice for cheating. My skull starts to feel as if it's collapsing in and I rub my temples as if that could help. I wish this problem would go away. I wish none of this had ever happened.

"Breanna," he says, then goes quiet. I glance up and he continues, "You won't write the papers and that picture will be deleted, okay?"

I nod and Razor seems to accept my answer. His eyes dart around my face as if he's waging an internal war. "It's going to be hell on you to be seen with me."

It's not a question. It's a statement. A very, very true statement.

"If we're sharing," he says, "I'm going to catch hell being around you."

My eyebrows rise at this. "Because I'm the epitome of trouble?"

He laughs and it's a glorious sound. One that warms my insides. But then the laugh turns a bit bitter and dies out. "I've been warned I could hurt you without meaning to."

My stomach sinks and my posture deflates along with it. Addison said the Terror have to follow orders or there are consequences. "Have you been told to stay away from me?"

Razor's expression gives nothing away and in the silence I can hear the whispers of the boys on the other side of the room. I clear my throat and try a different question. "Are you going to get in trouble for hanging out with me?"

"I'm running out of allies. Hanging with you might piss off one of the few I have left."

It's not really an answer. A million questions spring to mind about his club and who his allies are and who is warning him away from me and why, but the one single thought that wins out is… "I don't want you to get in trouble over me."

Razor offers a crooked smile that I guess is meant to comfort me, but all I see is sadness. "I'll worry about me so you don't need to. I hate to ask, but beyond us working together in class, do you have a problem with keeping whatever this is between us a secret?"

He nudges my leg with his own, rekindling the fire that had begun to burn minutes before. "The fewer questions I get from the club about you, the better it will be, and it'll be easier on you at school the less we're seen together. Besides, being a secret makes the flirting more fun."

I should be annoyed at what Razor is saying, at the idea that he doesn't want to be seen with me in public. Instead, a thrill runs through me, so fast, so strong, that goose bumps form along my arms. A secret. Me and Razor from the Reign of Terror—a secret. There's something magical in the idea of there being a secret between us. Something exciting about being allowed to explore this newfound friendship without the prying eyes of the rest of the world.

Life just went from awful to incredibly fantastic. "I can absolutely live with that."

RAZOR

Breanna: Apples. Your turn.

I DON'T KNOW why her answer causes my lips to curve up, but it does. It's eleven at night. She texted to let me know she wasn't making much progress on the code. I texted back that she should take a break. Now neither of us seems eager to end the conversation. Our texts took a turn toward random and we've been sharing favorite foods. Breanna's moved us on to fruit.

Me: I don't eat fruit.

Breanna: Liar.

I laugh. Maybe I am.

It's been a few weeks since Breanna and I made our deal. She's been working on my code and, with a few glares from me, Kyle Hewitt has gone mute about me and Breanna, which is what I wanted. He's scared of me, yet with time passing, he's relaxing. Tonight I step up my game to nail the bastard.

Breanna: Kyle's paper is due soon.

The rare happy moment dies. Me: First step to getting K out of your life starts tonight.

Breanna: When are we going to shoot the rockets?

Classic Breanna. She switches the subject to school when she stresses out. Her brain operates so fast I'm not sure she's aware of the defense mechanism. Me: Tomorrow? I know a place where we can shoot them off.

Breanna: Sounds good. I get off work at six. I don't have a ride so can you pick me up?

My smile grows. Twenty dollars she has no idea what she asked for. Me: Yeah. Wear jeans and boots. It's going to be a fast ride. I gotta go.

I pocket my cell and chuckle as it vibrates with her frantic responses. I suck down half my beer and consider grabbing another. People surround me. Over a hundred of them, but for a while I lived in a world where there wasn't chaos, only me and Breanna.

Music pounds from speakers, there is beer on tap and two chicks are on top of the bar I'm leaning against—stripping for anyone who cares. I haven't looked up once, even when a bra was tossed in my direction. My mind has been focused on Breanna and the meeting that's about to take place tonight. Plus it doesn't help that across the room is a picture of my mother.

The clubhouse is packed and it's not just the mother chapter filling the place. Chapters from as far as California have made the pilgrimage.

It's the annual remembrance party thrown for the members of the Terror and Terror Gypsies who have died. Some of the people we're honoring are Eli's blood brother and Chevy's father, James, Violet's father and, because life is cruel, Olivia and my mother.

A new beer with sweat running down the sides slides into view and Pigpen sidles up beside me grinning like a crazy man. "Everyone's dying to know who you're texting with. It's like you're a twelve-year-old girl chained to that damn cell. Have you started your period yet?"

"Fuck you."

He punches me in the shoulder. "Seriously, who's on the other end?"

I drink the beer while maintaining eye contact. He should know better than to ask questions he won't get answers to. He motions to my cell. "I could hack it and find out."

Proved he could this afternoon after the two of us hacked into emails of someone who's been targeting a client. "You won't."

He tilts his head in annoyed agreement. A brother wouldn't disrespect another brother like that. "Is it a girl? If so, tell me you're being smart and covering up. This club has had enough teenage baby bullshit to last us a lifetime and the last one was born seventeen years ago."

"I need something," I say, ignoring his jab at Eli.

"Finally! Name it and it's yours. That's what we've been waiting for, brother. You to come to us."

I shift to look at his reflection in the mirror on the wall

beyond the bar. He appears too damn happy and that causes a wave of uneasiness.

Pigpen curses. "You're asking me for something you don't want the club to know about, aren't you?"

I promised Breanna I wouldn't drag the club into this, but if Pigpen agrees, I can solve her problems and keep my promise. I'm hoping he'll help me as a friend.

He rests both of his elbows on the bar and has that expression that tells me he's contemplating putting a bullet in my head. "You trust family and we are your family."

"I'm trusting you," I say.

"That's not enough. Two voices can't do shit, but together, this group, we're fucking loud." To prove his point, he shouts, "Reign of Terror."

The answering roar causes my ears to ring. Pigpen stares at me, unblinking as the mantra is repeated three more times followed by over a hundred men howling into the night.

I sip my beer again. Point taken. When the room returns to normal chaos noise level, I say, "I gave my word I'd do this on the down low, but I need your help."

I don't give my word often, Pigpen knows this, and the confusion causes him to scratch his jaw as he surveys me. "What do you need?"

"A virus that will give me a back door. Something that can travel from a cell to a home computer if it's hooked up. Nothing I've found will do the job and I need it to be undetectable."

Anyone else my age making that type of request would have their parents grounding them for a month. Pigpen goes deep in thought, then nods his head that he has what I need. "I'll send you the code tomorrow, but next time you have a favor or a problem, it's time for you to man up and come to the club. I don't care how many promises you made to other people. You got me?"

"Got it." Pigpen hugs me and I hug him back. I'd be lost without him.

With a sly smile he flickers his gaze over my shoulder. "Enjoy the rest of your evening."

A warm body pushes up to my back and then her scent surrounds me. I take another drink. I made a mistake with this girl and, tonight, I hate the reminder.

"It's packed," she says into my ear, and I turn to discourage her from touching me again. Amy combs her light brown hair away from her forehead. She's showing off her tight body in a pair of painted-on jeans and a red corset. "Wasn't sure I was going to find you."

Yet she did. I like Amy. She doesn't laugh too loud to gain a guy's attention, doesn't act like a fool when she's drunk. Amy's older than me, in college, majoring in business, and she loves to play at the clubhouse on the weekends as a middle finger to her iron-fisted daddy.

Trying to find the attraction I had for her, I scan her from head to toe. It's gone, and that causes me to be unbalanced. I haven't thought of being with another girl for weeks. Can't bring myself to do it. None of them compare to Breanna Miller.

I gesture from the prospect tending bar to Amy. He hands her the usual—Fireball. She downs it, then takes a burning gasp. "Thank you. You're a classy guy to buy a girl a shot."

I snort and peel the label off my beer. Funny how I found plenty to say to Breanna, but I've got nothing for the girl I lost my virginity to. It was the night I patched in. We did it twice and then I hooked up with a friend she brought along for the evening. The friend was Amy's idea, and at the time I thought she was brilliant.

"Are we going to play tonight?" she asks. We've played since I patched in...multiple times, but we haven't fucked. I regret that part of the night. In the morning light, I felt like I had morphed into my dad.

I kiss her cheek and walk away. She follows, smacking my ass, and smiles as she shoulders by me. "You're too young to be in love, Razor, but whoever it is, she's a lucky girl."

I snatch her wrist before she disappears into the crowd in her search for her rebound good time. "I'm not in love."

Amy sadly laughs and it's the type that hits her eyes in that sympathetic way I hate. "I lied about just now finding you. I've watched you text for the past half hour. Me and you—we had fun together, but I never made you smile."

She touches the edge of my lips. "You should smile more often, but if whoever it is makes you sad, you know where to find me."

Here on any Friday or Saturday night. "Have fun tonight."

She waggles her eyebrows. "Will do."

My back pocket vibrates and I leave the clubhouse, striding past the bonfire and groups of guys cutting up. The night is dark, no moon, and it's even darker when I enter the tree line and head for the towering oak Chevy, Oz, Violet and I used as home base. I can almost hear Violet singing, "Not it."

There's a shadow of a form leaning against the tree and I'm impressed she showed. It's taken me two weeks of groveling to get her to agree to this, but I did grovel because this will be my first solid lead. "You missed your dad's memorial."

Violet powers on her cell so the two of us have light during this clandestine reunion. "It's the club's fault he died. Why would I participate in something that will ease their guilt?"

I cross my arms over my chest, not caring to get into a pissing match with her. "The picture of you that was put up on Bragger, were you being blackmailed?"

She goes pale against her red hair. I smacked the nail on the head.

"How did you know?" she whispers.

"It's happening to someone else."

"Who?" she asks, then answers her own question with an annoyed huff. "Breanna Miller."

I don't verbally confirm it, but I do meet her eyes.

"That sucks," she says. "Not that it should happen to anyone, but she's too nice for someone to be messing with her."

"This stays between us."

Violet nods and I can't decide if I'm comforted or mad that the two of us fall so easily into our friendship even though she has shit on everyone else I love.

"What's going on with you and Breanna?" she asks.

I shrug. "She's helping me with something personal, so I'm going to try to help her with this, but I need to know what I'm dealing with."

"No way. My life may suck because of that picture, but I will not have club blood on my hands. Does Breanna know she's making a deal with the devil?"

"This is on me, not the club. I promised her they wouldn't be involved."

Violet's head jerks back. "You're lying to the club?"

Why is she shocked? "I kept what you've told me quiet."

"Yeah, but I didn't think you would, which is why I didn't tell you everything. Razor—if the club finds out you're hiding something big like this from them, they'll kick you out."

She's not wrong. The club would want to know about anything involving Violet. She was the daughter of a brother who died. They feel it's our job to protect her now. As for the stuff going down with Breanna, they probably would be pissed if they knew that I'm seeking retribution without their knowledge or consent. Then again, Violet doesn't understand how close I am to being thrown out to begin with. "That's my problem. Is it Hewitt that blackmailed you?"

She's silent as she weighs whether or not she should tell me. What's seriously jacked is that I have a cut on my back that says I have an entire clubhouse of men who should trust me, but the only ones putting that trust into action are two seventeen-year-old girls.

"No," she says. "I had no idea Kyle was involved. Not until you just told me that Breanna's being blackmailed, and, by the way, how is that possible? The girl is a saint. What on earth can he have on her?"

Tension forms in my neck and I pop it to the right. "He has a picture of me and her together, and before you go there, don't. We didn't do anything."

She smirks. "You must have been doing something, and go you for 'not doing anything' with the smart girl. I bet her family must be thrilled she's not only into a Terror boy, but she's dating *the* notorious Terror boy."

"We're friends."

A "psh" leaves her. "You don't have friends, but for shits and giggles, let's say you are just friends—keep it that way. Don't mess up that girl's life by dragging her into the club."

My patience level is depleting fast. "Who blackmailed you?"

"Promise no club involvement."

"I already gave my word to Breanna."

"Great, but you gave it to her for her situation. I want your word on my situation."

Keeping a secret from the club regarding Breanna—I could

justify that. She has no club involvement. But keeping a secret of who has caused Violet pain and misery, the secret I swore to tell the board the moment I found out—I'm entering near damnation. Good thing I've been teetering on this ledge for a while. "You have my word."

Trusting I'll stay true, she immediately answers, "Rob McEntire."

A muscle in my jaw twitches and Violet shrinks. That's the asshole she was making out with the night the Riot flew into town. "What was he blackmailing you for?"

Violet raises her chin and creates a fist with her fingers. "Something that I took the risk of not doing, and you saw how that blew up in my face."

I'm a damn pot on the stove getting ready to boil. Violet's smart. If she said *sexual favors* out loud, I would already be on my bike and would be seconds away from ripping his heart from his chest with my bare hands. "He's still blackmailing you."

She looks away now, at the tree, and her foot begins to tap. "I lost my chance at a scholarship out of this dump town over that picture. I was a finalist and they called and I was happy and Mom was happy and a few days after the picture went up the college called back and told me what they found on the internet and that I was no longer—" she uses her fingers to create quotation marks "—*material that lived up to their standards.* So, yeah, I said yes to Rob and in return he took the picture down."

But it's still out there. And other places now. She knows this. I know this, but like Kyle had warned Breanna, they probably had more.

"You should have come to me," I say.

"I did!" Tears form in her eyes. "You demanded that we

go to the club when I needed my friend. The moment I said a name, Chevy, Eli or Cyrus would have taken a gun to his head."

"What makes you believe I won't?" I ask. "I'm the crazy one, remember?"

"You're emotional," she says. "But you think before you leap. They don't just leap—they go psychotic. Eli went to jail over a temper tantrum gone wrong and I'm sick of it. I'm sick of living in this damned town!"

My fingers curl in and out because the need is to shout. To throttle her because she knows this club is legit, that they never would have killed anyone, but then there's a question in the back of my head. A lingering doubt. *My mom.* I have to swallow the hurt tightening my throat.

Something caused Violet to walk away from her family, and whatever that something is, I wonder if it's on the same level of agony as my mother.

Violet hugs herself and she looks so damn pathetic that my chest aches. I swear under my breath, then wrap my arms around her. Her shoulders shake and each deep breath she takes to keep from crying causes the anger inside me to build. My heart breaks for her, for the friendship that's been floundering this past year, and for how Breanna must also be emotionally crumbling.

"I'm going to fix this," I say as I hold my best friend. "I promise I'm going to fix this for both you and Breanna."

Breanna

I AM NEVER using public Wi-Fi again. I researched what Razor told me last night after we hung up and it's frightening how unsafe technology is. Razor divulged his scheme and I've been worrying since over this insane plan. He has the simple part. He sits back and types. I, on the other hand, have to speak with the devil.

Nervous adrenaline leaks into my system as the bell to the diner rings. I walk in and, as he promised, Razor's in the corner working intently at his laptop and, like clockwork, Kyle is on the opposite side of the diner eating lunch with his friends.

This is what Razor has been doing for the past couple of weeks—following Kyle. Understanding his routines and rhythms. Kyle doesn't seem to know that Razor has his life dissected and documented to the minute.

My cell vibrates. It's Razor. Don't look so terrified. He touches you and I'll stick this dull steak knife through his skull.

Me: It's not him touching me I'm afraid of.

Razor: Is it me you're afraid of touching you? If so, I promise you'll like it.

My temperature jumps to triple digits. Razor touching me. It hasn't happened yet beyond a few careless brushes of his body against mine while in physics. Regardless, my imagination goes to places beyond him caressing my face or holding my hand and beyond PG-13. I suck in a breath to regain a logical train of thought. Me: I'm afraid he'll find out what we are about to do.

Razor: All the same. You say the word, I'll use the knife. Or say the word, we leave now and I'll give you that ride we keep talking about.

I never know if he's joking. Me: Let's stick to the plan.

Razor: You're no fun. All work and no play...

I smile, and when I peek at him, his eyes are still glued to the screen, but he's grinning, too. Digging deep for courage, I choose the side of the diner Kyle and his friends are at, select a booth by myself and study the menu. There's no way I could eat anything without regurgitating.

"Hey." Kyle slithers into my booth. Per part of the plan, I texted Kyle last night and asked if we could meet to discuss his paper, and like Razor thought he would, Kyle suggested the diner. It's scary how everything Razor said would happen is coming to fruition.

"Hi." I make a point of looking over my shoulder at Razor. "I didn't know Thomas would be here."

Razor's real name feels weird on my tongue.

"He's been coming here for a few weeks. Waitress says he comes for the Wi-Fi, which makes sense. I heard he lives in a box of a place in the middle of nowhere."

Reception is sketchy for everyone in town, which is why Kyle doesn't question a thing—whenever any of us comes into the diner, we switch to the Wi-Fi because it's reliable.

I fiddle with the napkin. Razor said to act as if I'm terrified of him and I thought it would be hard to do. But it turns out it's easy to act afraid, because I am—of Kyle.

"Are you sure we should be in the same place as him?" Razor's suggestion for me to say. Reverse psychology.

"It's good for him to know he's not in control. Besides, I thought you two were best friends." Kyle extends his arm along the back of the seat.

"He's too intense, plus he's mad at me." I glance over my shoulder again like I'm worried.

"Are you okay?" His question is part concern, part confusion. Like he actually cares about my well-being.

Please buy my lie. "If I tell you, you're going to tell everyone at school, then it'll be on Bragger, and then he'll really be mad."

Kyle's eyes dart over my face. *Get him to trust you,* Razor had said. I read an article that said people bond quickly over two things: gossip and joint misery. If it's true, then gossiping about how Razor's bothering me ought to be a friendship gold mine.

Kyle plops his arms on the table, encompassing too much space. "I won't tell anyone."

I roll my eyes and I don't have to pretend for that. "Sure."

"No. I mean it." He scratches behind his ear. "Look, between me and you, Razor's been scaring the hell out of me. There's something not right about that guy and I don't like the idea of you being wrapped up in him. You're too nice of a girl for a psychopath."

I attempt to squash the anger flaring within me. Razor's not the crazy one, it's him, but Kyle needs to believe we're bonding. I clear my throat and use the hurt from Kyle to convince him my emotions are about Razor. "What happened at Shamrock's was a mistake."

A mistake that Kyle created by snapping a photo of me in a private moment.

"You're too good for him, Bre. I hope you can see that. I don't want to put that picture up any more than you want it live, but if you think that picture would shatter your life, it would be nothing compared to if you did get involved with him. The guy is a nut job."

I hate that he uses my nickname. I hate how he thinks he knows Razor because he's listened to rumors. "You're right about Razor." He's wrong. "Working with him in AP physics has scared me and he's mad I'm trying to switch partners."

Kyle swears like he cares and has the nerve to reach over like he intends to touch my hand. I withdraw it as if I didn't notice his kind gesture and twist my fingers in my hair.

"It's okay," Kyle says. "You're in public around him. Nothing will happen."

"So this is what I was thinking." I'm so ready for this charade to be over. "I want to work with you, not against you. If you say the picture won't go up, then I believe you."

"Now you're talking." If he had given me that smile last year, I would have been happy. "Tell me what you want for writing my papers and I'll make sure it's yours."

For you to be castrated. "There is one thing you can do."

He stretches out his arms like he's willing to give me a hug. "Anything."

"Send me a copy of the pictures. All of them."

His forehead furrows. "Why?"

"I want them as a reminder," I say. "Of how stupid I can be and how I made a wrong choice." Like believing the rumors involving Razor.

"You shouldn't be hard on yourself," he says. "He's conned a lot of girls, not just you."

The empty aching at the thought of how many girls Razor has possibly been with overwhelms me. I could try to convince myself that his female companionship issues are a lie, but even I've seen him in action. Each time, he was getting biblical with them, but not in the godly fashion.

"Will you send them to me?" I prod.

I sag with relief when Kyle produces his phone and swipes here and there in order to send me the photos. My heart picks up speed as my cell pings with his message and then as I ask if he still has the email from his English teacher that describes what he needs to do with the paper. With each second he's on the Wi-Fi, I experience a high and a panic.

Can Kyle tell what's happening? Will his phone beep like NORAD and he'll realize we've deceived him? But none of that happens. Kyle interacts with me as if we're friends and I let him talk, encouraging him to keep hunting for things on his phone.

If Razor's true to his word, this nightmare is on its way to being over.

There's ice cream in my hair. Why wouldn't there be? In the tiny employee bathroom of the Barrel of Fun Ice Cream shop, I lower my head, run water over the sticky strands, then yank so many paper towels I can hear trees in the rainforest screaming in protest.

I squish the towels to my hair in an effort to dry it and the rumble of a motorcycle causes my stomach to fill with a million anxiety-ridden butterflies. Oh my God, I'm getting on a motorcycle with a member of the Reign of Terror. Scratch that. I'm getting on a motorcycle with Razor, voted by my school as the most feared member of the Reign of Terror.

I peer at my reflection in the mirror to see if I've gone insane.

My eyes are brighter than normal. My cheeks are flushed. In front of me is a girl I barely recognize. Texting with Razor, the occasional chat on the phone, the way we flirt when we're together in independent study—all of that is crossing dangerous lines, but this...leaving with Razor? Being alone with him? I've lost my mind, and I'm loving the girl staring back at me.

A buzz of my cell and I fumble with it in my haste. It's not Razor announcing his arrival, but Addison: What are you doing tonight?

My parents think I'm working until nine and my fingers hesitate over the letters. I trust Razor—but seventeen years of Reign of Terror doctrine is hard to combat. Me: I'm doing homework with Thomas Turner.

I wince at how quickly she responds: WHAT?!!!!!

Me: I'll explain later, but keep this between us.

I pocket my phone and step outside. My phone pings every few seconds. My best friend will strangle me and then demand Razor details.

On the other side of the lot is a familiar angelic face, golden hair and a black leather cut that spells trouble. Razor leans against his motorcycle. His biceps are gorgeously flexed as he crosses his arms over his chest.

Adrenaline pumps into my veins as I walk toward him. Razor spots me and this devilish smirk forms on his face. A thrill runs through me and so do a million questions about what exactly will happen when we are completely and utterly alone.

Razor straightens when I reach him and then glides into my personal space so that we're close. Super close. Almost as close as the night at Shamrock's. I inhale to calm my beating heart and I detect his dark, spicy scent.

"You ready?" he asks.

"Yeah." I swallow, as I sounded crazy raspy. "Do you have our rockets?"

We built them this week during our independent study.

He gestures to a black leather bag attached to his bike, then raises his fingers. Wrapped around three of them is a rubber band. "Figured you wouldn't think of this."

Riding a motorcycle. My hair. Lots of wind that would create tangles. Nope, didn't contemplate it at all. I go to accept the rubber band, but Razor pulls back his hand. I frown, then freeze. Razor gathers my hair at the nape of my neck and pleasing goose bumps tickle along my skin. I suck in a breath of air to keep my heart from exploding with his touch.

There's a gentle pull as he twists the band around my hair. Tingles. Beautiful tingles. When he's done, he lets one finger trace the length of my chin. I can't breathe.

"A few things before we go," he says.

I nod, because speaking is officially impossible. He slips his cut off, then shrugs out of his leather jacket. "Put this on."

I raise an eyebrow. Don't get me wrong, the idea of wearing something of Razor's makes me want to squee with joy, but... "It's warm today. Like high of eighty-one warm."

"Better you sweat than scratch the hell out of yourself if we take a spill."

My stomach twists. "Spill?"

"Not planning on it, but I'm not taking any chances."

I accept the jacket and draw my arms into it. It's heavy and huge and smells like him and I'd die a happy girl if I never had to give this back. Razor produces a helmet. "When we get on my bike—"

"Wait up, Kyle." The voice is unexpected and unwelcome. Near the Barrel of Fun, Kyle and two of his friends stand by the outside back bathroom entrance. Cold fear rushes into my veins.

Razor blocks me from their view. "I'm not ready for him to see us out like this yet. So short lesson. Climb on and hold on to me. If you're scared, pinch my thigh and I'll stop. Got it?"

I'm blinded when Razor places a helmet on my head. He adjusts it so I can see, then snaps the strap under my chin. It's not one of those full helmets, just the type that covers my head.

He straddles his bike, eases his cut back on and glances at me. After wiping my palms against my jeans, I hop on behind him. Razor reaches back, gathers my arms, and I close my eyes when my fingers touch a very hard stomach. I slowly breathe out. Oh my God, this is happening.

He squeezes my fingers, lets me go, and within seconds the motorcycle roars and vibrates between my thighs. A fleeting moment of panic becomes a hiccup in my brain. I could pinch his thigh. I could jump off the bike. I could run.

But I do none of those things. Instead, I rest my chin on his shoulder, readjust my hold on his waist and press closer to him. When Razor turns his head to look at me, I swear he's smiling.

RAZOR

BREANNA COVERS HER face with her hands. "This is impossible!"

It's not, but knowing any response I have will annoy her, I avoid commenting. Instead, I grab the paper she had been murdering with an eraser. She slams her hand on her notebook in an effort to capture it, but I'm too fast.

"I can do this," she says. "If I get a new brain maybe, but I can do this."

"Let me try." I also steal the notebook and pencil.

"Fine," Breanna huffs, then collapses back onto the tall grass. Beside us are the remains of our three rockets. Our job now is to mathematically prove why one went higher than the other.

"It really is pretty here," she says, and I glance over at her. The early autumn day is warm and the brittle grass surrounding her is green and yellow. Above us are trees colored with orange and red leaves. I agree it's a sight under the clear sky, but not for the reasons she believes. Breanna's the one who's pretty.

"I can't believe I've never been here before," she says.

"No one comes here." It's why I like it. This meadow is a quarter mile from my home. I stumbled across it the summer after Mom died. I couldn't stomach being home, especially on those days Dad brought a girl to the house. Since that summer, this place has been my refuge.

It's encircled by trees, and during the spring and summer, flowers of multiple types bloom. But what I found interesting as a kid was the abandoned railway trestle. I've walked over that bridge more times than I can count. I've even climbed to the top.

Breanna's a vision with her black hair sprawled around her. There's not a soul around for miles, which means this place is perfect for the two of us.

A distant rumble and the ground vibrates. Breanna rolls over to her stomach and I have to tear my gaze away from her tight ass to watch as a train flies around the bend and crosses the current railroad trestle farther down from where we're settled. It's because of the newer trestle that I was able to bring Breanna here. There's an access path off the main highway. It's dirt and it was bumpy, but Breanna rode the back of my bike like a pro—like she belonged there.

Like she belonged with me.

"It seems impossible, doesn't it?" she asks.

My heart stops. Is she also thinking about us?

Breanna points at the paper in front of me. "The math. It's impossible."

The math. *Get your shit together.* "If acceleration is equal to gravity, then the number would be…"

"Negative 9.81 meters per second squared," she rattles off. I'd give up my bike for a week to be inside her head for a minute.

She's quiet while I focus on the problem, which I appreciate. When I solve the equation, her face brightens. "Wow."

I prop my arms on my raised knees and pretend to admire the field. Yeah. Wow. If only everything in my life came as easily as it does with numbers. I wasn't just admitted into AP in science, but in math, too. School told Dad my science score teetered on admission to the program, but it was my knowledge of numbers that pushed me over.

"You're the anti-me, aren't you?" she says.

I chuckle and it comes out bitter. I am. She's beautiful and smart and all that's good with the world. "Yeah."

Her forehead furrows as she reads my expression. "I mean with math and the hacking stuff. Your brain is built for math whereas mine isn't. Like how you knew how to apply the kinematic equation. I know the equation, but I have a hard time applying the knowledge. I'm saying you're smart."

"It's a small town, Breanna. You've heard the rumors about me. Some of which are true."

Breanna sits up, then regards the old abandoned trestle. It's not the first time today she's studied it with curiosity. "Do you ever go on the trestle?"

I nod.

"Is it safe?"

Evidently not for trains. I stand and extend my open palm to Breanna. She's eager to explore and I like seeing her smile. Breanna slides her fingers into mine and our eyes meet. We stay that way, staring, our hands twined together. I've never held a girl's hand before. Not in a way that means something.

Her skin is soft. Very soft, and I begin thinking thoughts that would cause Breanna to demand a restraining order—like how the skin of her stomach might also be this soft.

The pressure of her delicate fingers is heavier than most

weights I've lifted. It's like holding on to a promise and it causes me to be nervous. Me nervous. About what? About kissing her? About touching her? I've done things with girls a million times over, but not with Breanna.

I gently pull and she hops to her feet. Breanna didn't need my help, and as I attempt to release her, she squeezes my hand and offers a shy smile. Something within me shifts.

No, I don't get nervous, but Breanna transports me to all sorts of new places. It's not her physical proximity getting to me, it's the fact that she makes me feel.

We let go of one another, but we walk close through the tall grass. The sound of the rushing water grows as we approach the bridge. Her hand bumps into mine, and I consider reclaiming her fingers, but I have no clue if she sees me in the ways I'm beginning to see her.

Breanna inhales, then pushes out a question. "I heard you failed fifth grade. Is that true?"

"I was held back." We reach the foot of the bridge and I shove my hands into my pockets.

She toes the wood of the track and assesses the rusting iron. "You're smart. A hell of a lot smarter than most. Definitely smarter than what—"

She cuts herself off and I finish for her. "Than what everyone at school thinks."

Her frown is an admission and an apology.

"I know the rumors. Stupid Razor. Only kid who repeated fifth grade."

"As I said, you're smart," she responds. "So why did you repeat?"

Because of the steep incline, the river is a class-three rapid. We've had a steady amount of rain and the water roars and splashes against the sharp rocks about thirty feet below.

I remember the first time I stood near the edge. The sun was setting and the sky was bleeding pinks and reds. I gauged the distance, the spiked rocks and the racing current. Back then, I had considered jumping.

"I missed too many days of school." Admitting this feels strange. There are too many rumors, too many lies surrounding me and my mother, so it's been pointless to speak the truth. Somehow, Breanna's the person to say these words to.

A breeze cuts through the trees and Breanna's hair soars. She raises her face to the sky and it's like the wind dies off at her command. Breanna seems powerful enough to control nature. She gets me to talk. That in itself is amazing.

Multiple wheels spin in that brilliant brain and her hazel eyes flash with understanding.

"Go ahead and ask," I say. She's the one person on this earth besides my father I'd allow this question, and I can guarantee that, at least with her, there won't be shouting.

"Was that the year your mother died?"

I flinch and Breanna notices. "Yeah. I was too messed up to go to school at first and then Dad had a hard time getting me there. By the time the club stepped in to help, the damage had been done. Too much time missed. Too far behind in class."

"I'm sorry. About your mom and about how people talk about you."

Me, too. "I'm sorry they talk about you, too."

A cloud sweeps over Breanna's face, but she forces her lips up like that will remove the sting from my words. "The gossip from the first week has blown over."

"I wasn't referring to earlier this year."

Breanna sighs so heavily that she seems to shrink. "It's going to get better, right?"

There's a dip inside me because it's the same prayer I say at night.

"Like when we graduate, all this stupidity will go away, because I am so tired of pretending to be something I'm not. If I act like who I really am, I'm crucified. If I hide, I feel like I've chained myself inside of a one-foot box and I'm dying to break free."

Breanna strokes her hands over her arms as if she could wrench her metaphorical chains off her body. "Everyone says it doesn't matter what anyone thinks, but you know what? It does. Yeah, I walk into school with the attitude of screw them. I'm going to answer every question. I'm going to show the world who I am, and I'm not going to apologize for it, and then..."

She fades off. "And then people stare at you as they cover their mouth with their hand, lean over and whisper. Then people whisper back, all while staring, and they laugh. Then that rare burst of confidence—shatters."

A strong gust rips through the trees and I don't like how near to the edge she is. She's a small thing and another surge of wind could cause her to tumble to the swirling water below.

"I can handle the whispering," she says. "But it's the people who like a show that make it unbearable. The people who get a kick out of making me into a spectacle. The jerks that stand in front of everyone, call me names, and then when I do say something back, I'm the one that doesn't know how to take a joke. When my face turns red and my neck gets hot and tears form in my eyes, I'm the one that's too sensitive. I'm the freak."

Her cheeks do turn red and then she pulls her hair off her neck as if heat does curl along her skin. A pulse of anger runs through me when I see tears forming in her eyes. I'm going to kill the next person who gives Breanna any type of crap.

She drops her hair and wipes her eyes. "Maybe I am too sensitive. Maybe I'll never belong anywhere. Maybe this is how life is supposed to be forever."

I'm desperate to find a way to soothe her pain. "At least you have a big family. Your brother came at me hard the night of orientation."

"I'm even the oddball in that group. My older siblings never talk to me. My younger siblings act like I'm their mother. Because I'm not their actual mom, I just get the hate part. Joshua's married to the football team. Liam worships Clara, so that means he and I will never be close, and Clara...there is not a word strong enough to describe the hate Clara has for me."

She's told me about her older sister. "Clara's a raging bitch."

"Clara can't find a way to calm the chaos in her brain. It's hard turning it off. Finding peace is even harder. She's like me, but honestly better. She remembers things and she's a whiz with math, but she struggles with the constant noise. It's like neither of us can win for losing. Clara was picked on for not being able to focus. People assumed it meant she was stupid and then I came along. I could process everything I remembered. I could find a way to keep my mind in check. Because of that, my parents used to show me off as a parlor trick with the moronic capitals, and if I was Clara—" Breanna chokes on her words "—I'd hate me, too."

She rubs both her hands over her face as if she can scrub away the hurt. Those nights I've spent in scalding showers prove neither of us can wash away the misery.

"Want to cross?" I ask. We both need the distraction. "The bridge. We can cross it."

She surveys the wooden planks across the metal rails. Huge fat gaps exist between the planks and there's a narrow strip of metal off to one side of the bridge that's barely wide enough to balance on. There's no railing on either side.

Breanna leans over the edge, no doubt making a mental note of the rushing, raging water and mammoth rocks. "Will you go with me?"

I shouldn't do it. I should tell her we've completed our project and we're done for the day, but instead I offer her my hand again and tempt her to hang with the devil.

She closes the space between us, and the moment she lays her palm in mine, I grasp her hand and lead her onto the bridge.

Breanna chooses the narrow strip of metal and I tempt fate on the aging wooden planks. The wood cracks under my weight and Breanna holds on to me like she could keep me from falling through into the river. "Walk on the metal."

A sadistic tilt of my lips. "It's the danger that makes it fun."

She shakes her head, but I spot a smile. Guess she doesn't want to admit it's why she's on the bridge—why she's with me. This is the girl who was on the dance floor at Shamrock's, the girl who cracked the code in English. This is a girl full of life and searching for a challenge.

When we're halfway across, she hesitates and scans the length of the river. She squints. In the distance beside a canopy of trees is the bridge of Highway 109. I step onto the metal next to her and support my back against the metal girder.

Breanna's eyes widen, and I see the puzzle pieces fall into place. She's quick, and while I normally admire how her brain ticks, this time, I wish she would have ignored the clues.

"My mom died in this river," I say, to answer her silent

question. My mouth curves down and the horrible pain from that day covers me like a shroud.

"Why do you come here? Why put yourself through this?"

How many times have I asked myself the same question? I could say I experience a connection to Mom here, but I don't. I come because… "I need answers."

"What type of answers?"

"How she died." My statement hangs and for the millionth time I wonder if it had been calm before Mom reached this area. Were her thoughts peaceful or chaotic? Was there a screeching of tires or did Mom spot the opening off the road as a way to fly into freedom?

"The club told me it was an accident and I said I believed them, but I don't." I've never told anyone that and I speak slowly, like the words might set me on fire. "Everyone in town says the same damn thing. My mom and dad were fighting. She wasn't happy. Things were bad."

Day after day, hour after hour, heartbeat after heartbeat my mind swims with the questions and doubt. She left me. She died. She did it on purpose. I was never enough.

My mind dissolves into chaos and it's cluttered and I can't cling to a single thought that doesn't cause me blinding pain. "Fuck it!"

I stalk away. Off the bridge, onto the grass, and pause by the river. I expect Breanna to walk past, to flee, to leave. It's what people do. It's what my mom did. It's what my father did by sleeping with a harem of women after Mom's death. He may have been in the same household, but he ran. He just escaped by staying still and damning me to hell.

Her footsteps are light against the metal of the bridge, and when she's close enough, I say, "I'll get you home. Give me a second to—"

Air rushes out of my lungs with the unexpected impact and my feet rock. Breanna is tight against me, her arms wrapped around my body. She's hugging me. Breanna Miller is hugging me. She lays her head against me and her voice vibrates against my chest. "I'm sorry about your mom."

I can't remember the last person who hugged me. Not a fast pat hug from the club. A hug that shows affection. Just hugged. I hugged Violet last night, but she didn't hug me back. Was Olivia the last person who hugged me? My mother? Besides them, most people avoid me, easily leaving two feet between us, and here is this little warrior trudging into battle without armor.

Terrified I'll break her, I weave my arms around her and hug her back. My eyes shut when she settles further into me. I rest my cheek on her head and simply breathe.

"I'm sorry about your mom," she repeats. "I'm sorry about what everyone has said about you, and I'm sorry everyone's words have made it worse."

Me, too. I inhale her sweet fragrance and enjoy the rare moment of peace. "It's okay."

She lifts her head and genuine emotion fills her eyes. "It's not. None of this is okay. Your mom, the people at school, the people in this town, none of it is okay."

Breanna swallows and her delicate throat moves. "It's like this town is diseased. Gossip and rumors and people playing with everyone's lives. Sometimes I feel like I'm going to drown."

I run my fingers through her flowing hair, tucking it behind her shoulder. I'm touching her because she's describing my emotions. Because if I do, then maybe she will no longer feel like she's drowning, and maybe I'll continue to stay afloat long enough for a mouthful of air.

"I've hated Snowflake for so long," she says. "But then I met you. And you're the person this entire town has trashed, a person belonging to the group I've been raised to believe is evil, and you're the only person who is able to make me feel as if every part of me is beautiful."

She is beautiful. Inside and out. My fingers tunnel into her hair again, but this time, I gently knot them in. My heart beats hard, and I open my mouth, hoping that doing so will force the right words. That I can explain how being near her makes everything that's impossible about me seem possible.

But the words become lodged in my throat and silence paralyzes my tongue. Breanna blinks and the hope that had been on her face disappears as she misreads my hesitation.

Her hold on me loosens and she ducks her head. "Don't listen to me. I say too much around you. I was being stupid. I..."

More words meant to wipe away her admission spill from her mouth, but I'm not listening. My grip on her hair tightens, I lower my lips to hers and I kiss Breanna Miller.

Breanna

I'VE FORGOTTEN HOW to breathe.

Razor's kissing me and I desperately try to remember how to kiss back. His mouth is warm and strong and a shock wave of awe ripples through my body as my cells tremble with anticipation. I lean into his body, thawing from the way his fingers gently caress my neck.

He lowers one arm, locks me to him and tilts his head. His tongue slips along the seam of my mouth. It's a tickling sensation that heats parts of me I never knew existed.

Razor's lips continue to move, and I hesitantly follow along, enjoying the way his kisses entice and coax. I'm a struck match on the verge of becoming a full-blown fire. Bolder than I've been in my life, I explore. My hands in his hair, along the hot skin of his neck, and when my fingernails skim down his spine, Razor groans against my mouth.

My lips edge up. The most dangerous guy at my school—the lone person who makes me feel safe—is reveling in the way I am touching him.

Razor pulls away, leaving a centimeter between us. That

devilish smile I adore graces his beautiful face. "Enjoying yourself?"

There's a definite tease to his tone and those blue eyes sparkle as they drink me in.

I bite my lip, loving this moment. "Maybe."

His smile widens. "Know how I promised you a wild kiss that breaks the rules?"

I nod furiously as my excitement grows.

Razor bends, and before I can register what he's doing, he swings me up into his arms. I squeal, then laugh when Razor eases down to his knees and rolls us to the ground. He's lying on top of me. His thigh is over mine and his knee rests on the ground between my legs. Razor props himself up on an elbow, and he raises his other hand to trace the grin on my lips.

My blood tingles and I ache in very good ways.

"Tell me to walk away," he says. "Tell me to take you home."

It's what I've been trained to do. It's what's expected of me. To be responsible. To follow the rules. To make logical decisions and use this precious brain, but Razor's teaching me there's more to me than logic—there's also a ton of passion.

Butterflies and fireworks and a craving that curls my toes and melts my heart. All of these foreign emotions belong to him. "No way. You're the one that keeps telling me a member of the Reign of Terror never breaks a promise."

"I do, don't I?'

"You do."

I want magic… No, I demand it, and I'm done being patient. I want to be the girl who's kissed, but there's no reason why I can't be the one doing the kissing.

I lift my head and draw his lower lip into mine. Within a heartbeat, Razor deepens the kiss, taking possession of my mouth. I lie back and begin to function on pure instinct. My hands seek the strong muscles of his back and shoulders and Razor's hands also deliciously roam.

His fingers discover the curve of my waist and they meticulously inch up my shirt. I'm in the middle of an inferno and I'm clinging to the flames. He shifts and parts of his body fit perfectly into me. I turn my head and gasp with the jolt of sweet electricity.

Razor continues the kisses. Along my cheek, down my neck, and I'm completely lost in the sensation. All of the sensations. The way his lips press on my skin. The way our bodies have started a slow rhythm. The way his fingers tickle and tease the now-exposed skin below the material of my bra.

I hold my breath, half hoping he continues his expedition, and then my heart drums so hard at the idea of him caressing areas no one has touched before that I might die of excitement.

The two million thoughts in my head disappear and the only language spoken is by my body. Of how my arms tighten in consent, of how my foot wraps around his ankle to tempt him closer, of how my hips arch, of how my butt...vibrates?

I jerk and Razor's forehead furrows as he stares down at me. My butt continues to vibrate and I blink as I return to reality. My phone. "Someone's calling me."

Understanding causes the wrinkles to disappear and he sits up, pulling me with him. I yank out my cell and release a relieved breath when I see Addison's face. I reject her call but send her a text: I'm still alive.

Addison: I can't decide if I should call the cops or celebrate.

Me: Celebrate.

Addison: If you leave one detail out I will never speak to you again.

Me: We'll talk. Later.

I pocket my phone and find Razor crouched across from me. The awkward part? I have to guide down my shirt and rearrange my bra acting as if it wasn't entirely dislodged.

Razor kissed me and I kissed him back and I have absolutely no idea if that means he cares for me like I care for him or if he's driven to touch and kiss me like I've been fantasizing of cuddling with him since the night we met.

"That was definitely wild." I try to smile past the strange ache. With a tug of the material to the left, most of me falls back into place and I'm dying of embarrassment. I thought I could do it, just kiss a guy and not be attached, but…

"It was." Razor offers me his hand "But it was more than that. Least it was for me."

Thank God. I lay my hand in his and he leads me to a towering oak tree. He sits against it, then encourages me to settle between his legs. I do, enjoying the warmth of his body.

Razor's arms circle my stomach and his fingers graze along my sides. My head rests against his shoulder and he switches between scenting my hair with his nose and resting his cheek against mine. Both create a pleasing thrill in my bloodstream.

"I don't know if this is a good idea," he murmurs against my neck.

His lips on my skin? It's a terrible idea. So terrible that I'm close to begging him to do it again. "What do you mean?"

He inhales deeply in the way my mother does when she has bad news. A twinge of fear strikes my heart. Razor lifts his head but keeps me tucked to him. "Us."

My happiness evaporates and the cool breeze that rushes through the colored leaves causes a chill.

"We're from two different worlds," he admits. "I have no plans to leave the club and I'm not sure you could digest certain parts of my life."

Nausea claws along the walls of my stomach. It's here, the opening I've been searching for. The moment to ask all of the questions, but if I'm deep-down honest, I no longer crave the answers. "Do you hurt people?"

He chuckles and it's such a sad sound. "Yeah, I hurt people. I mess up everyone I meet."

"That's not true." Not with me. "I meant for your club. I've heard things about how your club does things. About how they treat people."

He goes silent and it's not his typical moments of quiet. There's a heaviness that weighs the air around us.

"That's one of the things I'm not sure you can swallow about me—I can't talk about club business. Not with you. Not ever. I'm a brother of the club first and that's something any girl who's with me has to accept. But I can tell you we're a legit club and the business I work for is also legit. We do our best to abide by the law, but we do play by our own rules. There are things you wouldn't agree with, and being with me, you'd have to find a way to be okay with it."

I'm dizzy with the whiplash. I've been number five of nine for so long that taking another step back in any relationship makes me physically ill.

Razor slowly brushes the top of my hand with his thumb and the gesture is so heartbreakingly sweet it causes a flash of pain.

"There are good things about the club," he continues. "We're a family. Take care of each other like we're blood-related. There isn't a need that isn't met. Not a guy that wouldn't have my back when I'm against the ropes. If you're with me, those guys would also take care of you."

I snort and Razor stiffens behind me. I angle forward and rest my hands on my knees. He doesn't move, choosing to stay supported by the tree.

"You don't believe me?" he asks as if my actions stung him.

"I'm from a big family, so that Hallmark card you're trying to sell me isn't going to fly."

The leaves beneath him crackle as he readjusts so that he's sitting next to me. In typical Razor style, he's silent as he studies my expression. He then picks up a lock of my hair and plays with the strands. "We have our problems. That code you're working on is my problem with them. I love the Terror. More than I've loved anything, and the thought of not being a part of them rips me in half, but..."

He drops my hair, then mimics my position—his arms on his bent knees. Razor surveys the field, but from the hollow look in his eyes, he's not seeing the grass or the flowers or the red-and-orange leaves drifting to the ground. He's seeing something in his mind that's causing him to suffer.

"But what?" I urge him to continue.

"But if I don't find out what happened to my mother...if that code you're working on doesn't pan out...it may mean the end of the road for me and the club."

A pit forms in my chest. "Why?"

"They'll either throw me out for what I'll do next or I'll walk because I won't be able to stomach looking at them after the betrayal."

"Betrayal?" My mind is running in a million directions. "What are you going to do?" Then I recall what he said. "Or can you not tell me?"

Razor rubs his arm, and when his sleeve lifts, I spot a tattoo. It's a rain of fire. A lot like the picture on the back of his cut. He worships this club enough that he's forever marked himself for them. Leaving them would literally be like peeling the skin off his body.

"There're parts I can't tell you, but there are parts I can." And he does. He tells me about how a Jefferson County detective visited him the night of our orientation. He tells me about the file and how he found the code. He explains how he's now full of questions and desperate for answers.

More important, Razor is talking. Openly. Candidly. With heart and emotion. This moment is even bigger than the kiss we shared. I love that he's trusting me, love the sound of his voice, but hate the agony in his tone.

"If you don't crack the code, then I'm left with no choice but to talk to the detective."

"So what if you talk to him?"

Razor's jaw works as if I've stumbled across a crime in progress. There's a sinking inside me. He means what he says. There're things he won't discuss.

I flex my toes and, with my arms hugging my knees, I rock. "Does it change? When people get married? Your friend Oz, the one who graduated this past year—his mom works with my mom at the hospital. Would her husband talk to her with what you can't talk to me about?"

He shakes his head no and my feet collapse to the ground. It all feels hopeless. How can you be with someone who won't talk to you about the most important part of their lives?

"Are you saying I know everything about you?" he asks. "That even if we were married with ten kids, that you wouldn't keep a secret your best friend swore you to protect?"

"That's different." I think of how I promised Addison I would never divulge to anyone that her father hurts her and her mother.

He hikes a skeptical brow. "Integrity's integrity. Not too many ways you can split hairs on that subject."

Though I don't like it, I understand, then decide to let it go. "The club—it's your family?"

"We're fucked-up enough to be blood-related."

I giggle, and he pushes me with his shoulder. "At the end of the day, the shit you take is worth being part of your family, right?"

My mind wanders to Clara and Liam and Zac and Paul. I reminisce about dishes and years of diapers and how I'm the outsider. "I love them, but I'm not sure I belong." Or if they even believe I belong with them. "I'm not sure I belong anywhere."

His eyes soften. "Maybe you belong with the Terror. Most people who join, they say the same thing—that they never felt like they belonged anywhere else, and when they found us, they found a home."

His words hit a place too raw and I try to smile my way out of the ache. "I'm a girl, remember? You said only boys were allowed."

His gaze travels my body and my cheeks burn hot. "Never forgotten for a second you're a woman, but if you're with me, you become a part of us."

It's like someone stabbed me with an EpiPen. Pure adrenaline shocks my system as I replay his words. "Are you asking me to be your girlfriend?"

"Yes."

My heart leaps.

"And no."

A verbal slap across the face.

"I talked to you in public one time and you saw a fraction of the backlash this town will unleash if you're with me. I like you, Breanna. More than like. We can do this and try to keep it on the down low, but someone is going to figure it out. I need to decide if I can live with being the person who puts you in the line of fire, and I want you to think long and hard about being the girl associated with the Terror."

It makes logical sense, but it honestly hurts my heart. Because of how people gossip, my lone sin with Razor could be to hold his hand and kiss him good-night on the front porch steps, but the moment everyone sees me with him, I'll be labeled biker trash for life.

"Plus you'll need to come to the clubhouse. At least once. To see if you can handle some of what I'll be around if you choose me."

"What kind of stuff are you talking about?"

Razor picks up a stone and rolls it in his hand. "Drinking. Partying. Girls." He shuts his mouth into a firm line, then opens it again. "I had sex for the first time last spring—the night I was patched in. Didn't just have it once and I didn't do it with the same girl. I was drunk and I was curious and I did it. Before that, I messed around with girls but never took it too far, and I haven't taken it that far since. But…

"That night wasn't right. Point is, if you're around enough, you're going to run into some of those girls. If you end up with me, someone will tell you the stories. They'll tell you because we're talking shit or because someone's out to make you feel bad."

My hand presses against my abdomen, as if someone had kicked me in the gut. "I don't know."

"I'll never cheat," he says in a tone that suggests I don't question him. "I swear to God, if you're with me, I'll be faithful. I'm capable of a lot of things, but cheating's not one of them."

His eyes bore into mine and my head is swimming with so many thoughts and emotions. Even with the turbulence, there's no doubt I can depend upon that promise like a life preserver.

"Do you kill people?" Because I can't be with him if the answer is yes.

"No, and you watch too much TV. We're a legit club. I won't lie, I carry a weapon for my job. If some bastard shoots at me, by law, I'm allowed to shoot back. It's called self-defense. But I only carry my gun when I'm working for the security company. When I'm off, it's locked up tight in a safe at the club. I'm not interested in carrying any other time. A gun's a heavy burden. I never forget that when I carry. Life means something to me and I don't plan on stealing it from anyone else."

My face practically twitches as I attempt to process that tidbit of information.

"Do you trust me?" Razor asks.

I survey the field and listen. The lack of people's voices or the sound of traffic on the road confirms my answer. I'm already alone with him, so… "Yes. What do we do now? Take it one step at a time? Go from one day to the next until we get caught or decide to do something different?"

Razor cracks a grin. "Works for me. Especially if I get to kiss you."

I laugh and my mind is hunting wildly for the logic, for the pattern. There's a slow throb when I wind up chasing my tail. We're a couple, but we're not. We're together, yet we're supposed to be figuring out if we want to or should be together. We care for each other, yet we're keeping it a secret.

The boy everyone sees but nobody knows is with the girl who everybody knows but nobody sees.

There's no plan, no pattern, and while every part of me that relies on rational thought to make my decisions screams in protest, the part I hardly ever lead with, the part that has never led the way before…my heart…it takes a stand. "That works for me, too."

RAZOR

IT'S MONDAY AND I'm playing a mixed-up version of hide-and-seek. Breanna said she hangs in the library before school, but she was nowhere to be seen near the tables at the front where everyone else is. But as Breanna's proved time and again, she's not like the rest of the sheep in this herd.

We kissed this weekend and made a lot of nondecisions. Since the moment I dropped her off a block from where she lived, I've been dying to see her again…to touch her again.

I cut down the first row of stacks, take a right and spot Breanna sitting on the floor with her legs stretched out and an open book in her lap. Her long midnight hair has fallen forward, shielding her mood from me. Once again, she's in a skirt, but today she has a white button-down sweater over her blue top.

We're alone and it's what I want. This plan will work only if Kyle thinks Breanna's abandoned me for him. I'm not surprised by the lack of people. She's loitering in the 500's. Doubt anyone is eager for early-morning reading on quantum physics. "Hey."

"Hey." Breanna brightens. She closes her book and I readjust my footing when I catch the title. She was reading about quantum physics. Should have guessed Breanna would be the exception to the rule. She often causes me to feel...unworthy.

I fail at masking my thoughts and Breanna places both of her hands over the title of the book before glancing away. I'm such a fucking ass. "You're still cool."

"You looked at me like I'm suffering from leprosy and my nose is dangling from my face. I've been well versed in that expression since seventh grade, so don't bother lying to me."

I edge near her. "What you saw was me feeling bad about myself." Wondering what's wrong with me that I can't be more like her. "People take their insecurities out on the thing or person that makes them feel threatened."

She rolls her eyes. "Whatever."

"Like everyone else in this damn town, I wish I had a quarter of what's in your head. You have a gift that makes people scared there's something wrong with them because they're nothing like you." Being a child of the Terror, I'm also well versed in taking the brunt of people's fear.

She rolls her eyes again and I ignore her attitude. "Tell me something you've learned."

I stare at her. She stares at me. When it's clear I could do this all day, she caves. "Well...did you know if you removed the empty space from atoms, you could fit all of humanity into a sugar cube and that there are things that can travel faster than the speed of light and that light sometimes travels slower than...well...the speed of light?"

I had no clue. "Nope."

"Now you do, and so do I, so if we run out of things to talk about, then we have that."

I crouch next to her and realize how weird the smile on my

face feels. The first couple weeks of smiling, I didn't know I was doing it, but now that I've been continuing, I notice. Maybe because I'm exerting muscles that have been frozen for too long. "Humans suck and light has traffic issues—I'm keeping up. Any reason for your choice of reading material?"

She squishes her lips to the side as she fiddles with the zipper of her pack. "I was curious if time travel was possible. Stupid, I know, but it was either that or redoing a crossword puzzle I had already done, which doesn't help much with the itch in my brain."

"Why time travel?"

She tilts her head as if I should already know and my gut twists.

"Do you wish you never met me?" I ask.

"No," she rushes out. "Not at all. It's Kyle I'd like to dissect from my life."

The peace she always brings unbalances me. I settle my hand over hers, which is fidgeting with the bag. "I'm glad we met, too."

I look into her eyes for one second. Another. Breanna's searching my face longer than anyone I have known and it's not for a battle of dominance. It's as if she honestly likes what she sees. I hope she finds something redeemable in me, because I like what I see in her.

A thump. Breanna jumps and withdraws her hand from mine. I stand and survey the area. Someone must have dropped a book a few rows over. I'm stupid for letting down my guard in public. There's a reason why I sought her out so early. "Kyle's been busy on his phone."

Breanna beams. "And?"

"I found your picture on his cell, his home computer, and

I've figured out four of the five people in his group." It helped that I knew two names instead of one.

She blows out a breath and her shoulders relax. "All of this from one computer virus."

I nod. Pigpen taught me how to upload code from the internet and how to get it on people's computers and phones so I have a back door to their network. So far, the code he sent me is complete magic.

Words to live by: never use public Wi-Fi. Protecting our clients means discovering who is after them and almost everyone leaves a digital trail for someone savvy enough to follow.

"You keep surprising me," she says.

It's nice to prove to Breanna that I also have a few smart tricks up my sleeve.

"What about the fifth person?" she asks as she stands. "And are you sure you have the correct three other people and can you delete the pictures without them knowing and how will you know you get them all and what if they find out and..."

The bell rings and I risk touching her as I lay one finger over her soft lips. She goes absolutely still and it takes massive amounts of self-control not to tunnel my fingers in her hair and press my mouth to hers.

"Breanna?" I say, and it comes out much lower than I had intended.

She licks her lips. My eyes briefly shut as her warm tongue grazes my finger. She turns red and I'm haunted by images of her doing that again, but on purpose and slower. I clear my throat and continue, "Trust me."

I lower my hand and she breathes out, "I can do that."

Breanna: What if this first one isn't a code? What if it's the cipher?

I lean against the seat of my motorcycle parked on the side of the road. Next to me is a stranded semitruck full of fine Kentucky bourbon. It's a cold autumn night, which means this winter is going to be a bitch. My cut is on over my zipped-up leather jacket. My fingers are numb as I discarded my gloves so I could text with Breanna.

In the past month, on this same road in the mountains of the Tennessee/North Carolina border, three other rigs not under Terror Security have met the same fate of two blown tires. Those trucks were jacked of their cargo at gunpoint while the driver had been fixing the problem.

With the black night surrounding us and the occasional flash of headlights from passing cars, there's an eerie sensation to this scenario. My neck itches, like there's a scope of a high-powered rifle trained on me.

Me: Cipher?

Breanna: The key to the lock. I'm going to take a look at the second code and see what I can do with that and let my mind play on the idea of the other code being a cipher.

This is the first night in two weeks Breanna and I haven't talked on the phone. I even called last weekend when I was on break, but there's tension in the air tonight. The foreboding feeling of everything going to hell in a matter of seconds.

Me: Sounds like a plan. Gotta go. Break's up.

Breanna: Be safe.

Be safe... I can hear her gentle voice saying the words and it wraps around my bones like a caress. Damn, this girl has me tied in knots.

Off in the trees crickets chirp, and to my right Eli and Pigpen scan the area with their backs toward the driver who's repairing the tire. Pigpen has his fingers on the piece strapped to his side. Eli's hand rests on the gun holstered to his back. Man O' War is up near the front of the rig. We're rotating watch every ten minutes to stay alert.

Am I safe? No. None of us believe we're safe. We're on borrowed time until someone strikes. When I explained to Breanna what I do part-time for the security company, her forehead wrinkled and she fell silent. I never miss how her eyes linger on the patch on my cut that informs law enforcement that I carry a weapon.

The patch is there as a warning to anyone who wants to fuck with me and it's a calling card to police that I'm legal and papered up on my weapon and that I won't draw unless someone tries to shoot me first.

It's hard to witness Breanna's struggles not to ask the million questions forming in her head or accept when I won't answer. Some days, I think we'll make it. Other days, I'm not sure.

The door to the cab of the truck shuts. Man O' War and Pigpen hang near the front of the rig and Eli strides over to me. "Driver's almost ready to go."

I crack my head to the side in an attempt to push away the growing unease. In the red taillights glowing from the back of the truck, Eli appears more like the devil than a friend. It's too damn dark outside. Too damn quiet. Even the crickets have gone mute.

"Someone's out there," I say.

"Faster we get moving, the better. You've been a good man to have on this. We knew this trip could be trouble, and I picked you for this run because I knew you could handle it."

It's high praise coming from him and I savor the moment.

"Your dad misses you at home," Eli says simply.

Dad's texted a few times. Each message a reminder of business with the security company. Stuff he's aware Eli already told me. Then there are times at the clubhouse when I've caught him staring at me from across the room with an expression that suggests he might walk over and talk to me—but he never does.

"Have you thought about moving back?" Eli asks.

"Yeah." It's an honest answer, but I leave out the rest—that I can't return. Not until I know how Mom died.

"You're letting what the detective said get to you, which means you aren't trusting your father, the club or me. Each day you spend at Cyrus's is a confirmation of that."

"Would you prefer I go home and pretend?" I pretended before the detective and I'm not lying to myself anymore. Unlike Dad, I own some integrity.

"No." He pauses. "Have you visited with the detective again?"

I straighten and my fists tighten at my sides. Barlow hasn't contacted me. Either he's listening to Pigpen's warning and staying away or he's trying me at home, not realizing I bailed weeks ago. And I promised to keep my distance from him. "Are you calling me out on my word?"

A stick snaps in the trees and adrenaline pumps into my system. Eli and I turn toward the sound. Instincts flare and my hand goes for my gun. A shadow of movement to my left and I'm throwing Eli to the ground. Bullets whistle past. I cover him as we smack the blacktop.

Two pings into the metal of the rig meant no bullets into skin. Those were so damn close that the air near my ear moved.

I'm rolling and so is Eli. We jump to our feet, crouched low with guns aimed and triggers pulled into the darkness. The vibration of each round fired jerks through my body, but years of practice keeps me strong and true. My shots are a deterrent, to warn them to stay away.

The rig roars to life and the vibration of the working engine rumbles through me.

"Get the truck out of here!" Eli yells. A motorcycle parked near the front growls. There should be two bikes and the idea of a brother down scares the shit out of me.

Leaves shake on the bushes in front of me. "They're coming in!"

The truck lurches forward, the gears shifting with a whine. More shots ring out. Blinding pain rips through my arm and my entire body whiplashes with the impact. "Son of a bitch!"

"He's hit! He's hit!" Pigpen flies into view, gun drawn and on the prowl to kill.

Eli's firing. Round after round into the darkness. The sound is deafening and white lights appear in front of my eyes as my damn arm screams in agony. Urge is to go down. To surrender to the burning torment, but the need to survive forces me to ignore the wetness running along my skin.

Two shadows in front of me and I aim my gun. Last-second recognition halts my finger from pulling the trigger. Eli and Pigpen walk backward as a human shield as they fire, edging me toward my bike.

"How bad?" Eli shouts.

I'm fucking fantastic. Blood's pouring down my arm and it feels like I've been branded by a hot iron. "I can ride."

They protect me as I straddle my bike. I ignore the pain as I lift my arms to provide cover as Pigpen, then Eli, slip on their bikes. No one's shot back. Odds are they're long gone, but I'm not in a gambling mood.

Eli revs his engine and I grimace as I rotate the throttle. Eli's on my left and Pigpen on my right as we take off. Both have their guns still drawn and their expressions are deadly.

The world around me zones in, then out. The blood streaming down my arm is more than a trickle. Coldness numbs my fingers and my grip on the bike weakens. Eli drives ahead of me. Gravity beckons to me and the last thing I see is headlights.

Breanna

MY MIND WHIRLS and my hand can barely keep up with my racing thoughts. The pencil scratches against the paper, my handwriting unintelligible to anyone other than me. This code was much easier than the first. Each letter clicks into place and each word that is created causes blood-tingling euphoria.

There were too many letters in one continuous sentence. Too many Q's. Too many Z's. As if they were a placeholder for spaces. I purposely blurred my vision and letters started rearranging in my head and that's when I saw it—these letters need to be reorganized into columns. My entire body trembled and I dug in, entering the most intense word search of my life.

Consider this your... My cell pings and my muscles convulse as I snap out of the trance and back into my bedroom. Another ping.

My breath catches in my throat. Razor. It has to be him. I scramble for the cell, which is lost under a heap of wadded paper balls. I slide my finger across the screen and my happy feelings die.

Message 1, Kyle: We should get together to figure out what my paper will be about. Maybe I can help you with the research.

Message 2, Kyle: You still need to let me know what you want in return for writing my papers.

Disappointment tastes like stomach bile. His paper is due soon, and if Razor doesn't find out the identity of the fifth person, I'll become something I never wanted to be: a cheater.

I roll my neck in an attempt to ward off the sore muscles caused by hunching over the code for too long. A quick check of the time and it's no wonder I'm stiff. I retreated to my room after I put my younger siblings to bed at nine and I'm still sitting cross-legged in the middle of the single twin bed at midnight.

I scroll through my messages, hoping I missed one from Razor. Friday night, Razor and I texted while he was on break and then…nothing. I texted him again, but he never responded. It's Sunday and my chest aches. I understood why we couldn't talk Friday, because of his job, and I'm sure that's why I haven't heard from him, but I miss him.

My cell buzzes and my stupid heart leaps. One glance down and the bitter nausea returns. Kyle: You look sad at school sometimes. I didn't do this to make you sad.

How exactly did he think blackmailing people would make them feel? Ecstatic? Included? He's freaking psychotic, but Razor has told me to play nice. Me: Things have been tough at home lately. I'm fine. We'll talk about your paper soon.

I power off my cell and toss it onto my nightstand. If it's off, then I can pretend Razor's contacting me instead of knowing he isn't.

A knock on my door and my eyes widen when Mom walks into my room. Exhausted is the best way to describe her. Her black hair is knotted in a clip at the base of her neck, but several strands have broken loose. Dark circles are under her eyes and it's like a few new worry lines have formed near the corners since dinner.

She's in a Bellarmine University T-shirt, a gift I'm sure from Clara, and a pair of sweatpants. Mom's in her early fifties and tonight is one of the rare nights it shows.

She smiles as she closes the door behind her. "Hi."

"Hey," I say. "I thought you were in bed."

"Elsie had a nightmare and then Liam stopped by to talk."

I had heard his car rattle into the drive about two hours ago. He works third shift and sometimes stops by here for leftovers before he clocks in.

Mom scans the room and I know what she sees: empty.

The bunk beds pressed into the corner are waiting for daughters who will probably never return for longer than a one-night visit. With Nora and Clara gone, the walls are barren except for the thousands of pushpin holes put there by my sisters in the blue paint. I could add my personality to the room, but it seems useless. As soon as I graduate, I'll join the ranks of gone.

Mom sits on the edge of my bed and her forehead wrinkles as she notices the clutter. "What's this?"

I gather up the papers and stuff them into my backpack. "Schoolwork. How's Elsie?"

I should ask how Clara is, but I won't. Liam told me Clara is having a rough time transitioning into her new environment, but he thinks she will graduate. Maybe she will. Maybe she won't. I have to be honest, after being abandoned on the side of the road, I don't have it in me to care.

"She'll be fine. I'm sorry we haven't had a chance to talk—just the two of us—since I've been home. Your father said you did a fantastic job taking care of everyone while I was gone. Thank you."

Not like Dad would know how things went. He was on the road more than he was home, but no one perished, nor was anyone physically scarred for life. It's too early to judge the mental repercussions of me being in charge for two weeks.

Mom reaches over and curls over the ends of my hair as if that will give the straight locks some life. "I'm proud of you. Not just for stepping up when I was gone, but in everything you do. Your dad's proud, too. He told me you're living proof we did something right."

I flinch as if she's shoving a pickax into my chest.

"So…" Mom grins. It's forced and it's more tired than cheerful and it causes fear to tiptoe through my stomach. She's not here because she was passing by my room. She's here because she's smelled blood. "I'm late, but as promised, I'm all yours."

It's impossible to meet my mother's gaze. If only she'd said those words over a month ago maybe everything would be different.

Mom returned two weeks after Kyle began blackmailing me, and the moment she strolled in the door, Zac vomited. Paul and Elsie weren't too far behind. Mom seemed to have forgotten her promise of being "all mine," but I was okay with that. Kids puking trumps kid not puking.

Guess I could tell her, but instead of Mom just being disappointed in me for going to Shamrock's and my time spent with Razor of the Reign of Terror, I'd also have to explain how I'm days away from writing a paper for Kyle. This is a grave I can't seem to stop digging.

"What did you want to talk to me about?" she asks.

That I'm a failure. "Nothing."

"It was something, and I know I didn't handle things well when you came to me." The way she speaks, it's like she's coaxing a spooked kitten from behind a couch. Too kind. Too understanding. She can't even imagine the damage I've sustained. "I can't change the past, but I'm here now. Talk to me, Bre."

I wish I could. I wish I hadn't been swept up in this storm, but I have and there's no turning back. "There was some stuff, but it worked out and I'm okay now."

Mom's silent and the lack of response from her creates a heaviness in my chest that causes breathing to be a labor.

"Liam visited me this evening to talk about you. He told me about Thomas Turner."

My bones practically jump out of my skin. "What?"

I expect wrath to be pouring out of my mother's eyes, but instead I discover sympathy. She places her hand over mine. "Liam hung out with some old friends on Friday night."

Meaning Liam hung out with people I go to school with. He was on the football team in high school and he still attends the games to cheer on his home team. My head falls back. Translation: Liam chatted with Kyle.

"Liam heard from a friend that Thomas Turner is in some of your classes this year. He also heard there were some rumors going around about you and Thomas at the beginning of the year. Liam put two and two together and realized that was what you were upset about the day I left. He feels bad for how we treated you and I feel worse."

Blood drains from my face and I'm sorting through the possibilities of what she heard, but I keep landing on the same spot: Mom heard about the rumor floating around school.

The one that says that Razor tried to ask me out. Because if she heard Razor and I were body to body at Shamrock's or that we're dating/not dating, she's handling the idea of me lying to her way too well. It also means Kyle is throwing out a reminder to me to stay in line.

"What did Liam say?" I ask.

"Nothing I believe. Nothing Liam believes." Mom squeezes my hand and she inhales a quivering breath. "Liam told me what happened the night he picked you up from orientation. About how you were alone with Thomas, and then he told me about the rumors going on at school..."

"What rumors?" It's odd how distant I sound. Like I'm stuck in a tunnel. Even odder is how I've become detached— from my body, from my mind.

"That Thomas Turner was bothering you at school and that people were jumping to wrong conclusions. He also said Kyle Hewitt got into a fight with Thomas in order to protect you."

I'm not sure if I'm in shock or if I'm relieved.

"Please talk to me," she begs. "The Terror have their own way of living and it can be frightening. I want to make sure you're okay. I want to be here for you. Liam's scared something more happened the night of orientation. He's feeling a lot of regret and...so am I."

Did he also spill how he forced me out of his car? That he dumped me on the side of the road? Mom swallows and she grows overly interested in the bedspread. Maybe he did confess. Maybe the two of them commiserated over their guilt.

"Did Thomas Turner hurt you?" Mom asks.

"Thomas Turner stayed behind at orientation because I was alone. He stayed behind to protect me." If Razor and I do end up together, I should lay some positive groundwork, but what if Mom uses her spidey senses and figures out how deep I'm into him? "He and I...we're working together in our AP physics class. He's not that bad. Actually, he's nice."

"Nice?" Mom eyes me as if she's weighing what to say next. "That's not how the Terror operates. Odds are he's being nice to you for a reason. I'm grateful your brother showed when he did at orientation, and I think you need to keep your distance from Thomas outside of class."

"Isn't it possible everyone is a little overdramatic about the Terror?"

"I worked with Thomas Turner's mother."

My heart stops beating. "What?"

"And I'm sure you've heard the rumors about how his mother died."

Slightly ashamed, I nod. I've spent my life hating rumors, but I've had no problem listening to them. I guess I was thankful they weren't slandering me.

"Layla wasn't from Snowflake. She met her husband at a party in Louisville when she was in her last year of college. She wasn't who you would have thought of as a Reign of Terror wife. Supersmart, lots of honors when she graduated. When she arrived in Snowflake, she was so full of life. I purposely would switch my shifts around to work with her."

Mom's eyes glisten with sad tears. "She was a lot like you. She could have done anything. Ended up anywhere. And she wound up married to a man that made her unhappy."

My throat constricts. These may be the answers Razor is so desperate for. "Did she tell you that? Did she tell you she was unhappy?"

Mom shakes her head. "Layla was private when it came to her husband. It's the way the Terror operates—they expect complete secrecy, but she arrived in Snowflake one person, and over that last year of her life, I saw the light in her eyes wither."

"Some people say she didn't commit suicide," I say. "That it was an accident."

"Maybe. Only God knows the truth, but I do think the rumors regarding the Terror have weight. If you want me to be perfectly honest, most rumors are based on truth."

Her words strike me in the stomach. "So you believe the rumors about me sleeping with Razor?"

Mom's head ticks back. "No. I told you, neither your brother nor I believe that, but we are convinced you gained Thomas Turner's attention and that scares me. What upsets me even more is that you tried to come to me and I shut you down."

Confirming this would be a betrayal of what I wish she would have done that day.

"You have been so withdrawn. You're home and you do what you need to do, but you aren't here. Something happened and I want you to talk to me."

Kyle is blackmailing me and I'm not sure you'll believe me when I say that Razor is a good person. It's there on the tip of my tongue, but then I realize what has happened since. How I have kissed Razor and I'm forming feelings for him.

She would never permit me out of the house if she knew how much I long to touch and kiss Razor more. I've tumbled down a rabbit hole, and no matter how I fight for a way out, I slide deeper. There's no saving me from this situation.

"It's over now—the rumors. Everything. I'm fine." I'll remain that way if Razor succeeds...or if I write Kyle's papers.

"I'm so sorry I wasn't there for you."

So am I. There's this ache. It's in an area so deep that the pain can live there forever—as if it's a cancer along my soul.

Mom has no idea how badly I wish she had been there for me. But she wasn't and now it's too late.

I long to confess my sins and find unyielding grace, but I've done too many things wrong. Chosen too many paths she'll never be able to forgive.

"I'm okay," I say. "I promise."

RAZOR

I'D GIVE MY left ball if I could flip onto my side, but the fire shooting down my arm whenever I try stops me. It also keeps drawing me out of sleep. Doesn't help that half my face burns and my side feels like it's been shoved through a shredder.

My muscles are sluggish and my thoughts are slow, like I'm dreaming while being aware.

"...could have been the Riot." It's Eli. I'd know that serious-as-a-freshly-dug-grave voice anywhere.

"I've thought of that," says Cyrus. "I flipped through the police reports on the other truck robberies. This hit was different. In the other incidents, they attacked as soon as the driver got out. In this hit, they waited too long and they waited for Pigpen and Man O' War to be out of range—for you and Razor to be alone."

"Think the Riot knows the detective talked to Razor?" Eli asks.

"I sure as hell hope not," Cyrus answers. "If so, our boy has a huge target on his back I'm not sure we can erase."

Erase...

Erase...

Erase... The word seems important. It referred to another word, another idea that also felt critical, but it fades with a hand that grips the back of my neck and lifts my head.

"Drink, son." It's a voice that's familiar. Low. Rough. "You need to drink."

Sounds like my dad, but Dad hasn't given a shit about me in weeks. Gotta be one more jacked-up dream in the line of dozens.

Something grazes my lips and cold liquid sinks down my throat. When my head rests against the pillow again, the pain slips away and I finally can sleep...

There's a caress across my forehead and my hair moves with it. I should open my eyes. It's what the soft voice is insisting I do, but instead I attempt to shift again. I want to sleep on my side. Maybe then, I can sleep deep without the dreams.

"Has he responded to you at all?" the soft voice says, and I angle my head to the sound. It's Oz's mom—Rebecca. She's nursed me back to health several times in my life. Damn—when the hell did I get sick?

"What he's doing now?" Dad says. "He turns his head toward whoever's speaking."

"What did you give him?" Rebecca asks.

There's an answer I can't discern and Rebecca curses. "I told you Tylenol. You fucking men drive me crazy. Give him any more of that and I'll castrate all three of you. He's always been sensitive to drugs, or do none of you remember his appendix surgery? I should shoot you. Lord knows there's enough guns in this place that I can find a spare."

"We gave him something different," Cyrus says. "We gave him—"

Rebecca cuts him off with a "Fuck each of you," then descends into another rant.

I almost died after the appendix surgery. I was six and Dad said Mom rocked me in an ICU room for hours begging me to wake up. I'm allergic to some shit. Something I should remember but can't as the need to sleep threatens to drag me under a black veil.

There's another brush of fingertips across my face and Breanna appears in my mind. The bed dips with her weight and she touches my hand. "Thomas, I need you to open your eyes."

Thomas. I told her to call me Razor, but I like the idea of her saying my real name. My hand twitches as I capture hers. She's here and I want her to stay. Everyone else can leave and I need her to lie beside me. Maybe then I can sleep. Deeply.

"That's right," Breanna says again, but she sounds off— more like Rebecca, but it's her hazel eyes that bore into mine. "Come back to us. You did great with taking my hand, but I need you to open your eyes."

Damn, I'm trying, but they're glued shut.

"We need to take him in." There's an edge in Breanna's tone and also a hint of fear. I don't like her scared. Not with me. I rub my thumb over her skin. *Don't be scared with me.*

"There's no way to hide the gunshot wound," Eli says. "The hospital will call the police. Razor understood what he was taking on when he agreed to let us patch him here."

"You're putting him through this to save an account with your company?" she spits.

"I'm doing this because we don't want the police to know he's been hit. It'll be public information then. Fuck the company. This could be the Riot, and I will not have them thinking he's weak. If they think that, I might as well sign his death certificate now."

"He's our family, Eli! Basically my son! I can't let him die because of an allergic reaction!"

"He's my son, too, my fucking brother, and I'm trying to keep him alive!" Eli snaps, and I grasp firmly on to Breanna's hand. Damn, I need to open my eyes. Going toe-to-toe with Eli is like playing with a loaded semiautomatic weapon with the safety off.

"You don't think it's killing me to see him like this?" Eli yells. "You said the shit we put in the IV would help!"

"I said it might help!" she shouts back. "But he's not responding!"

I swallow and it's like the middle of Arizona in my mouth. "Don't, Breanna."

Silence.

"What the hell did he say?" asks Eli.

Another squeeze of my hand. "Open your eyes, Thomas."

Too many muscles involved in hoisting my lids. I crack them open and blink to force the blobs of color to merge into something recognizable.

Breanna's missing, and in her place is Rebecca. Her dark hair is pulled back in a bun, and she wears her blue nursing scrubs. Dad stands behind her, and he rolls his neck like he's relieved.

"Welcome back," says Rebecca. "How do you feel?"

I swallow again, and my throat's as bad as my mouth. "Like I've been shot, then I used my skin to scrape off some blacktop."

Chuckles in the room and Eli mumbles something about telling everyone I'm coming around. Rebecca's asking me questions. My full name. How old I am. Her name. Everyone in the room's name, then road name. She's checking an IV bag that's attached to a pole. Inspecting my wounds. Looking at my eyes.

"How bad?" I ask.

"Flesh wound with the bullet," she answers. "Good thing you were wearing jeans and your leather jacket when you took the spill. It could have been worse."

I nod as a fuzzy memory of already having this conversation squeezes out. Blood loss from the flesh wound and sinking blood pressure made me dizzy and I wiped out on my bike. Club got me back here banged up, bleeding and bruised.

We were hired by the company because they wanted their loads delivered safely and they preferred no bad press if there were problems, which means we keep everything quiet. Eli's right, I agreed to be treated by friends of the club away from the hospital, but Rebecca is also right—dying from an allergic reaction wasn't on my bucket list.

"I'd feel better if you stayed awake for a while," she says.

Cyrus, Eli and my father congregate in the doorway. When they notice me staring, they all give me a chin lift of approval.

There's a round of cheers from below and that's when I realize I'm in one of the private rooms in the clubhouse.

"The club's been sitting vigil. Oz and Chevy are ready to start throwing fists if they don't let them up soon," Rebecca whispers as she peels back the bandage on my arm.

I scrub my face with my other hand and I'm smacked with an IV line. No way I heard her correctly. "Thought I was the black sheep of this club."

"Sweetheart, you're all black sheep." Rebecca winks. "And, by the way, when you've had a few minutes to get your bearings, you're filling me in on who Breanna is."

"Fuck," I mutter, then close my eyes again.

Breanna

ME: I'VE FIGURED out the second code. I don't understand the meaning, but maybe you will. It's the third time I've texted this to Razor and it makes me dizzy with nerves that he has yet to reply.

I twine my fingers around a lock of my hair and pull as I scan the hallway again. The internet articles I read on the Reign of Terror circle my brain: Reign of Terror member shot by a rival club in Louisville this summer, Reign of Terror member killed in a hit-and-run accident last year, and an article from a few years back that detailed carnage between the Reign of Terror and another club not mentioned by name before my birth.

It's been three days since I've heard from Razor and I'm losing my mind.

"Bre!" Addison blocks my view of the hall and I blink at her harsh tone. "You aren't even listening to me."

No, I wasn't. "Sorry."

"I'm serious about this. If you're going to date him, you need to tell somebody."

Addison was jump-up-and-down-with-joy when I told her that Razor and I were in an undefined relationship, but with each day that passes, my forever-positive best friend has developed into a worrywart.

"You count as somebody," I say.

"Not what I mean." She slips in front of me again when I turn my head, searching for Razor in the hallway thick with students waiting for the morning bell to ring. "You need to tell someone else…like your parents."

The loud voices and laughter vanish as Addison gains my undivided attention. "They would freak if they found out I was dating him."

Addison innocently bobs her head. "Yes, they will, which is the point. I liked you flirting with him and then you guys kissed and I was cool with that—you know, like you were busting out of your shell. But falling for him? That's too far. He's part of the Terror. Being with him is not safe."

"You're buying the rumors. You know over half the stuff everyone says is lies."

Addison grabs my hand. "Which means half of the stuff they say is true. People around the Terror get shot. People who hang with them end up in bad situations. Mia Ziggler was a real person. She did get on the back of a Terror bike and she did disappear. I don't want that for you."

My body sways with her words. "So if I go public with Razor and the entire school calls me a Reign of Terror slut, does that have truth to it? Does that make me a whore?"

My best friend backs away like I smacked her. "No. How could you say that to me?"

Tears burn my eyes. Because that's what I've been facing regardless of my relationship with Razor. Maybe Razor is right. Maybe I can't cut it as his girlfriend, but the thought of breaking it off hurts my heart. "I like him and he likes me."

Addison's eyes soften and she halfheartedly yanks a strand of my hair. "You aren't making being your friend easy this year, brat."

She drops her arm and I catch sight of a huge bruise. I snatch her wrist and draw up her sleeve. Disgust swims through me. "Things with your dad are getting worse, aren't they?"

Addison jerks back and pushes down her sleeve. "It's fine."

"No, it's not fine. This has to stop!"

Fire rages out of her eyes, reminding me of the Terror patch, as she raises a pointed finger in my direction. "You get to preach to me about my dangerous life if you do something about yours. Until then, I'll back off you and you'll back off me."

It's like she's reached in and fractured my soul. "Addison—"

But she's already gone, disappeared into the crowd of people, and has left me alone. My foot edges in the direction she retreated when fingers wrap around my wrist. A grip, then a yank.

Adrenaline shoots into my veins. It's Kyle. He's been doing this more and more. Dragging me into stairwells and hallways. Begging me to tell him what he can give me in return for the papers. Explaining that he feels bad, that he's having nightmares, that he's consumed with guilt. That he's going insane.

In a flash, I'm in the stairwell and I'm greeted by red hair and blue eyes. It's Violet, a girl I've never talked to before, and now we're close to very alone.

"I need you to meet me after school," Violet whispers as she leans into me.

Talk about being on an upside-down roller coaster. "What?"

"It's Razor. He's been shot and he's asking for you."

★ ★ ★

It's after school and I'm in free fall. Two million thoughts in my mind and I can't hold on to a single one. Violet's charging through the green forest and I'm on her heels. We parked a quarter mile away and she's spitting out a laundry list of warnings like...

"You're supposed to be smart. Everyone says you're smart. Why would Razor be asking for you? Everyone knows to stay away from him. Everyone! And he goes and says the name of the one girl who should have the brains to stay away."

Razor was shot. With a gun. Metal entered his body at speeds of hundreds of miles per hour. Razor said he valued life. He said he took owning a gun seriously, but obviously other people don't share his point of view.

He could be dying and I might not ever see him again and Violet won't answer questions, at least not directly, and her nonanswers cause bile to continually inch up my throat. "Why isn't he in a hospital?"

I'm in my sandals and have a hard time keeping pace with Violet's blistering speed. Because I'm wearing a skirt, the long grass swats at my legs and stings my skin.

"Because they're fucked-up, that's why." Twigs crack under Violet's feet as she glances over her shoulder at me. "Razor used to be a normal kid. Well, as normal as you get being raised by thugs, but then they messed with him."

"Who's they?" I stumble over a root and catch myself on the bark of a towering tree. Leaves of three on a vine. I flick my hand away.

"Who do you think? The club." She pauses. "He's screwed up in the head, Razor, I mean—you know that, right?"

A crow caws overhead and there's a rush of beating wings as an entire flock of birds take flight. We're surrounded by a green canopy, but the growth is so thick that the forest floor lacks full afternoon light. Despite the heat of the October day, goose bumps form on my arms.

"He's been good to me," I say.

The tough expression she wears at school dissolves, and in front of me is a girl I'm not sure many people have met. "You're probably the only person in the world who would ever admit that."

"If I'm not allowed at the clubhouse..." Violet explained that females aren't allowed in there without a member sponsoring them. She also said no one under eighteen is permitted. If I could pass either of those qualifications, it wouldn't matter because the clubhouse is on lockdown—whatever that means. "And if you hate Razor so much, then why are you doing this?"

She flinches. "I never said I hated Razor."

"It seemed implied." In our short time together, she's blasphemed the Reign of Terror MC to the point I've been ready for her to sacrifice an animal to complete the curse.

"You don't understand me or the Terror. Nobody understands. All this town is good for is gossip and lies."

I agree. I don't understand how a guy everyone is terrified of makes me feel safe. I don't understand how a guy who stayed behind to protect me when he didn't know me has been shot. I don't understand how a guy who carried me out of an alley full of shattered glass is the enemy everyone is warning me about.

Violet's mouth trembles as if whatever she's holding in is causing her pain. "My father is dead because of the Terror. My reputation has been ruined since kindergarten. My mother is a mess, my brother has issues...my life has been damaged by the club, so excuse the shit out of me if I'm not their biggest fan."

"Then why are you taking me here?" I ask.

"Because..." She struggles to breathe. "It's Razor and he asked for you."

When she exhales, it's like she's flipped an emotional switch from on to off. Not sure which one I prefer—the girl who felt everything or the girl who appears stone cold. "I don't know why he asked for you, and I sure as hell don't understand why you agreed to come with me, but some advice?"

I nod.

"Break this off with Razor, because there's nowhere for it to go. I know who you are. Everyone at school has your number. You're the supersmart girl who's going to leave Snowflake for good, and I can also tell you aren't clubhouse girl material."

My knee bends as I shift my weight and I feel oddly overdressed in my sweater and skirt. Something about the way Violet said *clubhouse girl* brought up the image of less clothes and more confidence.

"Maybe Razor doesn't want a clubhouse girl." Whatever that means.

She laughs. Throws her head back and laughs. "As I said, you don't understand. He won't walk away from the club for you."

"I'd never ask him to."

Her eyes narrow on me as if she could choke me with her glare. "I sneaked into a party once, know what I saw? My dad doing body shots with a woman who wasn't my mother—his wife. Women swinging their bare tits as they danced on the bar. You aren't the kind of girl who's going to let a strange guy do body shots off you and you sure as hell aren't the girl who's going to strip for shits and giggles in front of a crowd. Are you telling me you're going to be fine being with a guy that calls that a typical Friday night?"

A lump hardens in my throat and I stagger back. No, I wouldn't. In fact, the idea repulses me. Razor's words haunt me... *I had sex for the first time the night I patched in...*

"And let's say you can get over all that," she continues. "I seriously doubt you'll be okay being harassed by everyone in town and by the police. You're going to resent every whispered rumor and judgment, which means you are going to resent everyone in the world. And then there are those dark, silent and lonely nights you wait by the phone to hear if the people you love have been shot or killed. The MC path for a woman isn't a life—it's a death sentence."

I look behind me, over my shoulder, back to the way we came. This is what I've heard my entire life...what I've been told over and over again. And this girl—Violet—she was raised with them, she knows what no one else knows, has seen what no one else has seen, and she's telling me to run.

There's a crackling of leaves and my head snaps back in Violet's direction. A woman with dark hair appears. She's older than me but younger than my mother and she eyes me and Violet warily. "What's going on, Violet?"

"This is Rebecca," Violet says to me as she studies the new woman. "I texted her for help. This is Breanna."

Rebecca inclines her head as if she understands why my name should mean something. "How did you know?"

It's a question to Violet and Violet's response is a shrug. "I'll wait here for her. Breanna mentioned she has to be home by four thirty, so the two of you might want to get moving."

"Club's on lockdown. Neither of you would be permitted near the property."

"Then I suggest you don't get caught." Violet crosses her arms over her chest. "I'll take her home now if you want, and that will prove what I've always known—that the women involved in this club are puppets."

Rebecca straightens and lifts her chin. "Your father raised you better than to disrespect your family."

Violet and Rebecca enter a staring contest that feels more like a duel with pistols. Violet severs eye contact first. "Either take her or don't. I did this for him, not for any of you."

Rebecca cups a hand to the back of her neck and surveys me. "You aren't what I thought he would have picked, and in case you're wondering, that's a good thing...for him maybe, but not for you. Let's go. You need to be quiet and do exactly what I say as I say it, do you understand?"

I take another step back as a cold sensation floods my limbs. "Maybe I should go home."

"I agree," says Rebecca, "you should, but you won't. Your name was the first off his lips when I was convinced he was going to die. Women don't walk away from that type of commitment easily. I'll guarantee your safety if that's what you're worried about. I'm married to a board member, so I wield some influence. We need to get moving as we're both wasting time."

My hand drops to my stomach. "Did you say you thought he was going to die?"

Rebecca stretches her arm toward me and wiggles her fingers, encouraging me to lay my palm over hers. "Let's go see him."

RAZOR

"YOU MOVE LIKE an old man." Chevy sits on the dresser and shuffles cards. He cuts the deck, then fans them in his hand as if that shit is easy to do. "You act like you were shot or something. Then you let your bike slide out from underneath you—that's sad."

"Fuck you." The entire right side of my body is bruised from the fall on the bike. I'm sore, but I'm living. The doctor the club brought in told them I'd get tired fast, but I'm on my feet and haven't collapsed yet.

"How was school?" I dig, and Chevy raises an eyebrow. In eighteen years, I've never asked that question. In fact, I rarely ask anything. My cell busted in the fall and I haven't been able to contact Breanna. I'm not curious about school as much as I need to hear Breanna's okay.

"Good," he answers. "Boring."

I glare at him and the end of his lips tilt up. "I'm assuming you're referring to a girl with black hair, real smart, and has a habit of glancing in your direction from across the room. Same girl you can't take your eyes off whenever she's around."

Yeah. That would be the one.

The humor flees from his face. "It was one thing when you were infatuated with her, but she's been watching you as much as you've been watching her. I know you don't want to hear this, but I don't see options for how this game you're playing ends well."

"Why?"

"Because she's not from our world. Breanna's not the girl looking for a quick ride. She's the girl who wants flowers before the sit-down dinner. She belongs to the family that has probably printed up just-say-no-to-the-Terror pamphlets."

She's a good girl, I'm all that's bad and Chevy's convinced I'm capable of destroying anything good. "Oz and Emily are working."

"They're different," he states. They are. Oz is badass, but he's never been feared like me, and Emily is a good girl, but she's Reign of Terror blood.

"And if you want to know, I've seen Kyle Hewitt talking to Breanna in hallways and stairwells. She might be looking at you, but it's him she's being seen with in public."

A dangerous anger curls within me. "She was what?" Breanna's kept that tidbit private.

"Go do your thing." Chevy's eyes flicker to the bathroom, halting the conversation. I'm taking my first shower since the accident and Rebecca's bent on someone being near in case I pass out.

I crack my neck to the side. Breanna and I, we need to talk. "Where's my new phone?"

"Shower, then food, then phone."

Showering had been the priority, but calling Breanna stole first place. Knowing that I'm seven degrees of angry, Chevy wouldn't give me the phone even if I whipped out my knife, and to be honest, a shower might make me feel human again. "I don't need a babysitter."

Chevy wields the cards so they fall like rain from one hand to the other. "Cyrus says you do. He's going to be real pissed if you pull that I've-fallen-and-I-can't-get-up bull in the shower and I wasn't here to play hero and catch you."

This treating me like an invalid crap got old the moment I woke. "If you go anywhere near that shower while I'm in it, I'll slice you open."

"Taking your blade in with you to shower? That's creepy, man."

"I will if you don't leave."

"You're a cranky son of a bitch." But Chevy smiles. "I'm glad you're alive."

Me, too. I nod at his words. When he nods back, I have to look away before emotion gets the best of me. "Get out of here so I can shower."

He hops down. "Hungry?"

Stomach felt like a garbage dump last night, so I didn't eat. Rebecca said it was the result of the painkiller the guys gave me. I rub my eyes. Guess I'm allergic to anything that brings me peace. "I should eat."

"What do you want?" He's dead serious on feeding me.

He'll think me weak if I ask for soup. I'm standing and I'm walking, but Rebecca said it could take days for me to reach one hundred percent. "Whatever, as long as it's hot."

"I'll be back, and I'm serious, no passing out—if you fall in that shower and bleed all over the damn place, I'll kick your ass."

I flip him off. He flips it back. I love the bastard.

"Hey." I stop Chevy before he leaves. "Did you hear anyone talk about the Riot?"

"No, why?"

I shrug, but the conversation between Eli and Cyrus repeats in my mind. Problem is, I don't know if it was real or if my head was off its rocker. Chevy points at the shower, and when I don't say anything, he leaves. I pull off my shirt, kick off my jeans and enter the tiny bathroom.

Breanna

I'M COLD. I'M HOT. I'm on the verge of fainting.

What I really am is flush against a wall in an industrial kitchen. Beyond the fact that I can't begin to comprehend why a motorcycle club needs an industrial kitchen, I'm questioning my decision-making skills and sanity.

Even if I wanted to bolt out the exit, Rebecca has pinned me to the wall with an arm she threw out like a mom slamming the brakes. She's peeking out a serving window, and men's laughter roars from the adjoining room. It sounds happy, but there's a sharpness to the chuckles and I tremble.

As if she felt the vibration, Rebecca offers what I'm assuming is a reassuring smile. "When I say go, we're heading up the stairs. Me first, and when I make sure the area is clear, I'll get you to Razor."

Razor. He was shot. He's the reason I'm risking my life, because if I had chickened out, there's no question I would have regretted it. What if he's critical? What if he's dying? What if he dies? There's a sinking inside me that causes me to be dizzy.

Rebecca scans the other room again, grabs my hand, then drags me up the stairs. She doesn't want me to get caught and what will happen to me if I do? This must be a sacred place to them. It has to be if they use terms like *lockdown*.

We reach the second floor and Rebecca slows and I don't like the change in pace. She holds tighter to my hand and nausea disorients me as we creep along the narrow corridor. There are multiple doors and each of them is closed.

"What happens if they discover me?" I whisper.

"Let's not find out."

A door behind us opens. Men's voices carry out. Rebecca whips her head to the sound, jumps in front of me as if her outstretched arms could protect me, then demands, "Go in the door on the right—now! Don't leave until I come for you."

My hands shake as I turn the knob, then stumble in. I shut the door behind me, my back collapsing against it in an effort to stay upright, and then gasp.

It's Razor.

He's standing with his back to me, and he's absolutely breathtaking. Shirt off, jeans riding low on his hips, just enough that I can see where his spine curves to meet his gorgeous rear. A tattoo of the half skull with the fire blazing out of the eyes marks his back, but that's not what has gained my attention. It's the beads of water rolling over the pronounced muscles that have me absolutely captivated.

Razor drops the towel from his face and glances over his shoulder at me. Dear God, he really is an angel. Those deep blue eyes immobilize me and a single globe of water drips from the wet blond hair that's partially covering his sight.

He's sculpted and ripped and he's alive. My heart beats hard twice and my eyes burn with a sense of relief. Razor is alive.

My best friend has warned me to stay away. Violet, a girl

raised by the Terror, has warned me to stay away, but even after digesting her advice, knowing the rumors and experiencing what I have, I can't leave. The bandage on Razor's arm and the cuts and bruises along his side testify to how dangerous his life is, but with one long look into those beautiful eyes, I know that I'm a lost cause to logic. I've already fallen in love.

RAZOR

I NEVER WOKE UP. The painkillers sent me into a coma and I'm hallucinating. No, I'm dreaming. Hallucinating suggests something bad and everything about Breanna Miller is all good. From the long raven hair that frames her face to that body with the right hint of curves.

As always, she's the epitome of summer nights. A vision in her pleated skirt made with flowing material that ends above her knees. This skirt shows more thigh than the ones I've seen on her before and a shock wave of lust hits me in places she'd blush to ponder.

"I heard you were hurt," she whispers like she's in a church.

"Just a bullet graze. A couple cuts and bruises."

Her head falls back, hitting the door. "Just a bullet graze. There's nothing 'just' about that statement."

According to her world, this entire situation is fucked-up. "What are you doing here?"

"Violet brought me, then Rebecca sneaked me up."

My head rises—Rebecca sneaked her up. The club doesn't know she's here. Breanna is bolder than any person I have met.

Before Breanna, I never kissed a girl I cared about. I kissed girls I was attracted to, kissed girls because they were there and I was lonely, kissed girls because kissing girls is what it seemed like I should do…it's what I saw Dad do and I thought maybe I was messed up for not craving to replicate his behavior.

But never did I gaze into eyes that were so deep with emotion as I have with Breanna's. I've never been with anyone who would risk sneaking into the clubhouse of the most feared group in town just to see me.

A surge of feelings rush through me and I don't understand any of them. They're foreign, but I do know that if Breanna doesn't leave now, then I'm not sure how I'll be able to let her go.

Breanna wears an off-the-shoulder white sweater with a tank underneath. The urge is to stalk over, pick her up so that her face is level with mine, encourage her to wrap those thighs around my body, crush her back into the door and kiss her until we both forget boundaries.

But that would scare her. It would do more than scare her. It'd shock her into never speaking to me again, but then she's still here—in this room. She's entered Terror territory, meaning she's on my home ground. Her eyes are dark with lust and her tongue slips out as she licks her lips.

"I need you to make a choice, Breanna. If you want things to stay as they are between us, then I need you to walk out that door. Otherwise, it's going to change."

She tilts her head as if she's as lost in emotion as I am. "It's already changed."

A part of me mourns for her. She's the firefly I'm not sure I'll be able to keep alive, but I shove those thoughts away. Breanna is here and she isn't leaving, which means she's mine.

Breanna

WHEN RAZOR MEETS my eyes again, there's a hunger in them I've never seen before. Something feral. Something dangerous. He begins to walk. His body one constant ripple of hard muscle. Instinct screams at me to run, but my body begs to stay. With each step he takes toward me, my temperature runs hotter and hotter.

Within the last three inches of meeting me, Razor quickens his pace, slides his body into mine and winds his arms around me. He wastes no time as he lowers his head and kisses me. No, devours me.

His mouth is moving against mine and it's a dance that's easy to follow, easy to get lost in. Tongues exploring, nibbles on top lips, the sucking in of lower. Razor's hands roam—in my hair, skimming along my spine, winding me tighter and tighter and tighter.

I'm hesitant touching him, terrified of his wounds, frightened of losing complete control and burning in this building inferno. Razor leans his body into mine and I collapse against the door. His lips leave mine for a brief second as we gasp for air and I incline my head to expose my neck. Razor accepts the silent invitation.

Deep kisses along my skin. Ones that may leave marks, but I don't care. I allow one hand to grasp his healthy side and the other to travel into his hair. Razor's lips tickle and tease and send this zap of energy straight to the underside of my belly. There's a curling warmth there. This pulse that is growing in intensity.

I grip his hair at the foreign and fantastic sensations and Razor moans. The sound vibrates along my skin and I press closer to him. The heat from his bare skin radiates through my clothes and I pray this moment never ends.

A knock on the door and I jump. Razor grabs my wrist, pulls me behind him, then shoots me a frozen plea that keeps any question I might have had stuck in my throat. "Stay behind the door and stay quiet."

I nod as he rubs his thumb over my hand, a reminder that we did just share that mind-blowing moment. He places a hand on the knob and whoever it is knocks again. Razor looks over at me, leans in and kisses me lightly on the lips.

"I promise I'll take care of you," he whispers. "You're safe with me."

Even with an army of motorcycle guys outside that door, I firmly believe him.

RAZOR

BREANNA SITS CROSS-LEGGED at the end of the bed looking completely sexy and adorable. Her hair is ruffled from when I ran my fingers through it and her lips are still swollen from kissing. The best part is the light in her eyes and that contagious smile on her face.

When I grin back at her, she squeezes my ankle, completely unashamed that less than two minutes ago we were going at it. Damn, she's fantastic. I sit near the head of the bed and finish the cup of soup Rebecca brought in after I opened the door.

"What time do you have to be home?" I ask.

"Four thirty. Joshua doesn't have practice, so I asked him if he could pick Elsie and Zac up from school, but he gets overwhelmed with them, so I promised to be home to help. So, that whole near-death thing wasn't from the gunshot wound, but because you're allergic to painkillers?"

I nod and she squishes her lips to the side. "And if I asked what happened or why they wouldn't take you to a hospital, you would say?"

"That you need to trust me when I say I'm fine and that

nothing illegal happened." It's true. By law, I'm allowed to carry the gun and to protect myself if fired upon. Not reporting the attempted hijacking of the truck and the shooting crosses into the fuzzy area, but I work comfortably in the undefined.

Her lips squish to the side and I change subjects before she overthinks. "I've heard Hewitt's been chatting it up with you."

Breanna pales out and that's not the reaction I was expecting. I swallow the last bite of soup and set the bowl on the nightstand. "I know I told you to make him think you were on his side, but is he overstepping into your personal space?"

"He's acting weird. Texting. Saying he's sorry. Obviously not sorry enough to tell me he's deleted the picture. He's… anxious."

Anxious is good in that he realizes he doesn't possess all the power, but bad if he's attaching himself to Breanna. He could flip out and I don't want her anywhere near him in case he creates collateral damage.

"You should have told me."

"Like how you told me how you got shot?" she snaps. "A bit hypocritical, don't you think?"

I scratch my jaw. I'm the emotional one of the two of us, which means that outburst is a strong sign something's brewing underneath. Could be Kyle. Could be me. Could be a combination. Most people would have already cracked under the pressure she's battling. The urge is to press her for answers, but even I know when I'm on the verge of detonating a land mine. "Come here."

She inclines her head in a cute pissed-off way and I mock like my arm is in pain. "Are you going to deny a man who almost died comfort?"

Breanna rolls her eyes, but she crawls up the bed. I stretch out and encourage her to settle into my left side. She gingerly places her hand on my stomach, careful to avoid the scratches and bruises. Her cool fingers burn against my bare skin. I should have put on a shirt for her modesty, but I've enjoyed how Breanna's been appreciating my body.

Exhaustion consumes me the moment my head hits the pillow. I nuzzle my nose into Breanna's hair and her sweet scent relaxes me.

"You terrified me." Her lips move against the skin of my chest as she speaks, and if I wasn't so damn tired, I'd seduce her until she was underneath me and then I'd kiss her until she was breathless.

"I'm good." Now that she's here.

"Is this what it's going to be like with you? Will I constantly be scared of losing you?"

I turn her words over in my mind while tracing a path up and down her arm. Goose bumps form under my caress and I love how she reacts to my touch. "No more than I would be scared of you figuring out that my world is too much for you and leaving."

"I've never done this before." Her soft tone dances along my skin.

"What? Visit a guy with a bullet wound? I sure as hell hope this is a first."

She huffs. "Not what I meant. I've never lain with a guy in a bed before."

The innocence of her statement is like a hug and an ache at the same time. A reminder that she's as fragile as those fireflies from all those years ago.

Since the day in the field, we've kissed and I've had blue balls from purposely keeping our private time tame. Doesn't help that I fantasize about sliding my hand along her soft skin, lowering her bra straps off her arms and hearing her whisper my name when I cause her to experience the rush of being physical with me.

"Are you uncomfortable?" I ask.

Her head rocks with a no.

Because she's aware of my dirty laundry... "How far have you been?"

I don't remember her dating anyone, but I could be wrong. Staying current on town gossip has never been my priority.

"I've been kissed before."

Maybe she did have a boyfriend. "Someone I know?" And damn me to hell for the jealousy leaking out of my voice.

She giggles. "Nosy much?"

Fucking jealous, and I rap the back of my head against the pillow at how much this girl is starting to own me. "Yeah, I am."

The giggles fade. "It was freshman year and it was at Reagan's birthday party. There was an empty two-liter and it was spun and I was either really lucky or unlucky."

This gains my attention. "Who?"

She props her chin on my chest and looks up at me. "I'm not telling because it doesn't matter, but I will tell you that he slobbered—like a dog. It was seriously disgusting."

The laughter rumbling out of my chest surprises me and I love it when Breanna's eyes sparkle. I brush my finger along her cheek. "The night I had sex, it wasn't right. When I do it again..."

I can't describe the confusion. Did I physically enjoy that night? Fuck yeah, but then I didn't enjoy the heated shame. The feeling I had let myself down. The fact I did to two girls what Dad's been doing for years. It was physical, no emotion. They stumbled out of bed, searching for their next thrill, and I was left wondering where the hell I fit into any of it. In the end, I hated that I had been used and that I had used them in return.

"You don't have to worry about me pressuring you. You say stop, we stop." That sums it up without my having to overexplain. "But I'll never complain if you cop a feel above or below."

I wink and Breanna laughs so loudly that she slaps a hand over her mouth.

Parts south on me support any action she'd take. As if on cue, Breanna glides a finger along my stomach, and it's like she's poured liquid electricity into my veins.

One breath in. Another out. A steady buildup of sexual tension. So thick that the air between us grows warmer. Her fingers wander lower, near the waistband of my jeans, and I bite back a groan. My hand eases to her hip and I begin this slow circle. The material of her skirt lifts with it and her breathing hitches. I wonder if she can feel my heart beating.

"When we kissed..." My voice is deeper than normal. "When my hands wandered here." I draw my hand up and it gently grazes the underside of her breast. She edges closer to me as if she enjoys the touch.

Her tongue darts out and wets her bottom lip. "Yes?"

We're playing a dangerous game I want to continue. "Was it your first time for that?"

She nods, then meets my gaze. My lips tilt up with the excited wildness in her eyes.

"There's been no other touching for you, then?" I'm referring to south of her and I return my fingers to the skin of her thigh, but this time, it's closer to her inner than outer thigh.

"No." A mixture of curiosity, nerves and lust merge together to create that sexy hooded expression. She'd like to experience the answer to my question. If there weren't stitches in my arm, I'd be willing to satisfy her desire for this new knowledge.

"Someday," I tell her. "Someday, I'll be better and we'll be alone."

"My heart is going to explode," she whispers.

"Mine, too."

We lie together. Her next to me. Me holding her. The chemistry brewing between us is an undercurrent not willing to be ignored.

"I almost turned away," she says. "Violet was telling me things that frightened me—things about your club—and I almost told her to take me home."

My heart stops beating and I freeze. "What changed your mind?"

Breanna's silent and I count between her inhales and exhales. Each second that passes becomes excruciatingly longer. When I'm about to bust out of my own skin, she says, "I couldn't stay away."

"Why?"

"What if I said I don't know what love is?" she asks like she's testing out the words. "That I've read about it—in textbooks and psychology books and in novels, but it's not something I can pin down the meaning of. Like, I know I love my parents and my brothers and sisters and Addison, but that's what is expected and all I've known. It's always been a part of me, and then there's meeting you..."

She drifts off. I loved my mother. Loved my father. Loved Olivia, Oz, Chevy, Violet and this club. Then there was meeting Breanna and the emotion of being around her is nothing like that definition of love. This is heartbreaking and consuming and addictive. It's terrifying and peaceful, crazy and serene. It's a million things in one brief moment and it's something I don't understand and never want to live without.

"I'd say I don't know what it is, either. But if I had to guess, it would be like when I'm with you."

Breanna does what hardly any other person can do—she stares straight into my eyes without hesitation. "Yeah, it would be that for me, too."

She loves me. That damn smile that I never knew was a part of me spreads across my face and I love the answering one she has for me. I burrow my fingers into her hair. "Kiss me."

Worry shadows her expression. "But you're hurt. Your arm and your side and there are cuts and brui—"

"If you don't lean your body this way and kiss me, Breanna, I'm going to roll you underneath me and threaten to tear open my wounds so *I* can kiss *you*. Your choice."

She purses her lips as if she's annoyed, but she slips closer. Her hand claims my stomach, her knee brushes against mine and that tempting mouth is only a few centimeters away. "Your logic completely sucks."

"Nothing logical about it. This is all instinct." I grab her hips and drag her across until she's straddling me. I fight the urge to laugh at the shock washing over her face. Eyes wide. Mouth rounded into an O. Her skirt gathers around her thighs and she's settled exactly where I've pictured her being.

"You really are bad." She adjusts to her new position and I'm about to lose my mind with the sensations that that movement brings.

"Just now figuring that out?"

"Maybe."

Doubt it. She's smart. The girl has had my number since we met, but damn if she hasn't fallen for me anyhow. "Are you going to make me repeat my request?"

"Unfortunately, yes. I'm not sure if you know, but I have this nasty habit of forgetting things..."

I tangle our fingers, pull her to me and take her lips with mine. Our mouths open and our tongues dance. Asking and giving, possessing and relenting.

My hand is along her back, drawing up her sweater and tank, and when Breanna shifts, granting me permission, I have the material up and over her head. We're close to skin against skin and my mind becomes a whirlwind. She's heat, softness, curves and sighs. Hair that's like silk, kisses that cause earthquakes and she has a sweet scent that drives me insane.

A flick of my fingers, a clasp undone and the gentle pressure of all of Breanna is too much to bear. Our bodies move, my lips are on her neck, my hands are memorizing, and Breanna whispers in my ear, "I don't want to hurt you."

There's no pain. Only a building heat and an impending rush. I shake my head to calm her fears and reclaim her mouth. The momentum grows and she presses closer to me as I press closer to her. It's fast and out of control and there's a light pain in my right arm, but I shove all that away as I grip her hips, encouraging this rhythm to pick up speed.

She's kissing me and I'm kissing her, then she turns her head as she gasps and shifts so that we're no longer in sync. Both of us are struggling for air and my body pulses with the need to continue. Breanna sits up, still straddling me, and looks down with wild and apologetic eyes. "I'm sorry...it's just a little..."

"Fast," I finish for her. "It's okay. Don't apologize. Never apologize."

I rub my eyes and scrub a hand over my face to try to ease the blood now pounding in my head, then encourage Breanna to lie next to me.

Her body becomes pliant and she settles against my side

again. This time her arm and leg drape over me. My fingers knot in her hair and I kiss her lips several times. Each of the kisses soft. Each of them a promise that this moment is forever burned in my brain.

She's my girl now and I'll do anything for her at any time. I'm in love with her.

Breanna snatches her bra, tank and sweater and I do my best to school my expression so she can't tell how I'm admiring the view or of how I find her innocence cute when she slips the tank and sweater over her head and then clumsily puts on her bra underneath them.

Before me, she'd only kissed a boy and she's in my territory now. We visited new areas and I want her to trust me enough to return to those places with me.

"Are you tired?" she asks. "Do you want me to leave?"

I'm fucking beat. "Stay." It's a request in the tone of an order.

"I have to leave in enough time to sneak out and make it home by four thirty."

If she's staying… "I'll get you home in time."

When she's done rearranging, I tug on her hand to indicate for her to lie down next to me, and she does. Her head's on my chest and my arm keeps her tucked close. My world, for the first time in years, is full of peace. "You're my girl, Breanna. You're my girl."

If she says something back, I don't hear it as dreams have already started to invade my mind. It's no longer nightmares, but dreams of Breanna and an open field and her wrapped tight around me.

Breanna

I'M HIS GIRL. His statement brought on a wave of excitement mixed with an intense dose of fear. Razor's chest rises and falls and his heartbeat against my ear is steady and strong. He flinches in his sleep and what I love is how he angles closer to me each time he readjusts.

I outline one of his bruises on his stomach with my fingertip and appreciate his chiseled chest. Walking away in the forest would have been the smart, logical Bre thing to do, but I like who I am when I'm with him. I like how, for once, I belong.

Razor has an angelic face, but he doesn't look like a man old enough to be carrying a gun, protecting semi loads of goods, and whatever other responsibilities he has in being part of a motorcycle club. He shaved, so he has this smooth baby face I itch to caress, and the tips of his hair barely kiss his eyelids.

A light knock on the door and Razor rouses from his slumber. He opens his eyes as Rebecca pops her head in. "Are you decent?"

"Yeah," Razor answers. "Come on in."

Oh my freaking God, did she really ask that and would she be okay if we weren't? Razor gives me a swift kiss before sitting up. "Rules are different here."

"So you keep saying," I mutter as I slip off the bed.

Razor pulls a shirt over his head, shrugs into his cut and then shoves his feet into his black boots. He grimaces once in the process and I wonder how it's possible to hide the pain.

"You're giving me too much credit, Rebecca," Razor teases. "I'm still on the mend."

Rebecca snorts. "You're an eighteen-year-old boy. When it comes to girls, it's amazing how fast you can recover."

He chuckles, she laughs and I'm mortified because we did make out.

Rebecca genuinely grins at me. "You'll get used to us. What's taboo in the real world is fair game around us." Then she speaks to Razor. "When are you introducing her to the club?"

Razor rises to his feet. "Now."

"What?" I'm not the only one shouting the question. Rebecca appears equally horrified.

Razor leans down and kisses Rebecca's cheek. "I'll tell them I met her in the woods. None of this will blow over on you. I can't have her sneaking out of here like I'm ashamed of her. She's walking out of this clubhouse with her head held high."

"I'm fine with sneaking out," I offer, but neither of them are listening to me.

Rebecca smiles like my parents do at me when I win an academic award. She hugs him and avoids touching the patch on his back. "You're such a good boy."

It's weird watching this moment. One that's too intimate. One that I would have never thought of as possible for the Reign of Terror. It's so...normal.

"With that said, no. One, Breanna looks like she's about to pass out."

He immediately glances over at me and I weakly wave.

"Two, we're throwing a club dinner in your honor on Friday. That would be a better time to bring her. The Terror Gypsies will be here, so will all the kids. The board will also be more welcoming of her if you give them advance notice that you're bringing a guest."

"She's special to me," Razor says, and I can't help the warm fuzzies he creates.

"They've been asking you to play by the rules and I understand how hard that is for you. Waiting until Friday will speak volumes. Waltzing her down now will upset them because we sneaked someone in without their permission. If you won't do it for yourself or for me, do it for her."

Razor keeps his gaze on Rebecca as he tilts his head to the door. As if she's fluent in nonverbal communication, Rebecca leaves without a word.

He heads over to me and cups my face with his hands, and I could stay in his warmth forever. "You're my girl, and I can't let you leave like you don't mean something. If sneaking you out makes you feel like shit, I'll take you down now. If it makes you feel better to follow the rules, then I'll bring you on Friday."

"I like not making waves," I admit. "I like the path that keeps me from being the center of attention."

His forehead furrows as if I've confused him. "The girl I've fallen for is fearless, so where is this coming from?"

I release a long breath. "I'm not as fearless as you think."

"You need new eyes."

I roll my old eyes in a "whatever."

Razor has that predatory expression again and excitement

curls within my belly. His hand goes to the small of my back and in a sudden motion presses me to him. I suck in a pleasing breath and he lowers his head so that his lips are a whisper from mine. "One day soon, I'll be healed and we're going to be very, very alone."

Fantastic shivers run through me. And I thought what happened earlier was magical.

A knock on the door and I jump. The code. I haven't told him about the code. "I figured it out."

He blinks. "What?"

"The code. I took a look at the second code, and I solved it." I break away from him and fumble with my book bag until I find the folder. "It means nothing to me, but something tells me this references the one I can't figure out."

I hand Razor the paper and watch as his eyes dart over and over again from left to right, repeatedly reading the few words: *Consider this your warning shot ~RMC*

He rips his stare to me. "That's it? Nothing else?"

"No, but I swear to you I'm working as hard as I can on the other code."

Another knock and Razor roars, "In a minute."

He rams his fingers through his hair with so much force that I study the bandage on his arm to confirm spots of red don't bleed through. "Don't do the other code."

Shock strikes me with such force, I'm dizzy. "What?"

Razor grabs both of my arms. "Don't do the other fucking code. Leave that folder here and delete everything off your phone. And don't ever mention to anyone what I asked you to do and you never tell anyone what you learned from that code, do you hear me?"

My mouth gapes, but no words come out. This code has been my life for the past two months. I've researched it. I've thought nonstop about it. He doesn't understand, it's impossible for my brain to let it go.

"Breanna!" He shakes me slightly. "Tell me you understand."

When I remain speechless, he releases me and tears off across the room, and my folder is in his hand. My heart gallops. Two months of my life is in his grasp. "What are you doing?"

"I'm saving your life. Get the code off your phone when you get home."

"What do you mean, saving my life?"

Razor breathes hard as if he had run a marathon, and the way his eyes freeze into ice, I know that I could beg and plead and he'd never tell me.

Another knock, the door opens and Rebecca walks in. "We have to go."

Razor picks up my backpack, hands it to me, but keeps my folder. My mind is a train wreck, but I accept my backpack and the swift kiss from Razor, but it's like I've entered another dimension as I follow Rebecca out of the room.

The folder isn't a complete loss. I read and wrote everything in there, so I remember it. I could have it back on paper in a half hour if I wanted, but what frightens me is Razor's warning. He implied that if I continue I could be in harm's way.

But Razor doesn't understand how my brain is twisted. I have to work on the code because I'll never be able to function without noise until it's solved. Days like today, I realize that my mind is most definitely a curse.

RAZOR

I'M IN A CAGE and it pisses me off. I crave the wind on my face and the power of my bike pushing me forward. Because everyone is still treating me with kid gloves, Pigpen's driving me in his pickup truck, blasting music that's more screaming than music. I prefer electric guitar over voices, but it's not my fucking truck.

Two guys ride on bikes in front of us. Two behind. It's like our own messed-up version of an honor parade.

Pigpen takes the wide curve on my dad's property and my bike's sitting pretty under the carport of the garage. It shines in the evening sun, sparkles even. I was told it's been buffed up, gassed up, and it's ready to go. Everyone knows I've been staying with Cyrus, so the fact that they dropped my bike off here feels staged.

Pigpen pulls off the gravel road near the house and severs the engine. I go to open the door and he stops me. "Talk to me for a second, and I don't mean me talking and you nodding your head like that's acceptable conversation."

I release the handle of the door and look in his direction.

It's the best I got at the moment, especially with the cracked code weighing on me: RMC equals the calling card of the Riot Motorcycle Club.

A million questions form in my mind. How current are those codes? Do they have anything to do with my mother? The detective said he found them recently, so it may not be related to her, but could be shit going down with the club now: the Riot shooting Eli this summer, the detective coming to town, the RMC running through the streets of Snowflake when they've never done that before...

"What's going down in your brain?" Pigpen asks.

"Who shot me?"

"We don't know." The way he makes direct eye contact, he's not lying.

"Do you have ideas?"

"We got shit we're looking into, but nothing definite. You gotta trust us that we won't let you down." Which means they aren't letting me in. It also means I could dump what I learned about the Riot onto Pigpen and he'd once again shut me out.

I stare out the front windshield and watch as Dad greets the guys who drove over with us. That woman, the one with the blond hair, she walks out of the house in a black tank and a pair of jeans and smiles when she wraps herself around Dad. "What's she still doing here?"

Pigpen taps his steering wheel. "He's in love with her, but he won't fully commit until you're on board with her or at least talk to him again."

The muscles in my neck tighten. "Commit? Commit how?"

Pigpen inclines his head for the obvious answer and I swear. "He doesn't know how to commit. Do you have any idea the amount of women that've been through this house?"

"He married your mom and was with her for over thirteen years before she passed."

I could ram my fist into Pigpen's face for bringing up my mother, but because of club code, I'm not allowed to strike a brother. "Yeah, Dad did commit, but that was before she drove herself off a bridge. Where's the keys to my bike?"

"That's not how it went down. You gotta learn to let this go, because if you don't—"

"Save the bullshit."

"It's not bullshit. You need to trust—"

"You want me to talk?" I cut him off. "How about this? You weren't part of the Terror when my mom was alive and you sure as hell weren't there when she cried herself to sleep and you sure as hell weren't there when Dad brought home his first drunk chick to sleep with. So you can shut the fuck up about what I should or shouldn't do."

Proving he's a crazy son of a bitch, Pigpen flashes me that guilty-by-definition-of-insanity grin. "See, was talking so bad? A few weeks with me and you'll be ready for full-on family therapy."

"Fuck you."

Pigpen goes silent and that causes my bones to quiver. The two of us get along because I'm the silent one and he's the one who can't shut up.

"Your dad would do anything for you. He's been arguing with the board. Disagreeing with them. I shouldn't be telling you this, but this fight you got inside you, it's not with him."

I'm terrified to believe him because if he's wrong and I let myself have hope that my dad and I could work through this…that false hope could kill what's left of an already weary soul. "Keys to my bike would be nice."

"Your dad has them and you can't drive until tomorrow. Guess you're stuck here."

With another curse, I'm out of the truck, slamming the door to piss Pigpen off. He follows as I go up the stairs, then brushes past me when I pause.

He grins at me from over his shoulder before opening the screen door. There's a loud round of laughter and, in a house as small as ours, it doesn't take long for the noise to be unruly. The scent of meat loaf teases my stomach and I turn away. That's my favorite and I'd bet this new girl is trying with me...again.

My heart clenches and I bend over to rest my arms against the railing. Attached to it are the flower boxes that have remained empty since Mom's death. Every fall she'd plant mums. Different colors and sizes. Every year I'd help. I never got enough of being beside her.

The screen door creaks and Dad steps out. I focus on our property and the surrounding woods darkened with the fading evening light. He leans on the railing beside me and the creak makes me wonder if the failing wood can handle both of our weight.

"Proud of what you did out there, son. Eli said you had his back and shot true, even when you were injured."

I join my hands together and continue to scan the woods. I'm not quiet because I'm proving a point. I'm quiet because I have no idea what to say to the emotions tearing me up.

"You scared me." His voice is so low I can barely hear it. "There were a few minutes this weekend I was scared I was going to lose you...like I lost your mom."

There's hurt in his tone. The same agony mirrored within me.

"I don't want that." He talks like the words are a struggle. "I don't want to lose you. Not to death... Not in life. I miss you here... I miss you at home."

"Do you remember when Mom would laugh?" Because I'm not sure I can continue to listen to him. He's saying what I want to hear, but it's stuff I'm not sure how to process.

"What?" He's confused and I understand why.

We don't talk about Mom… I don't talk about Mom. "Do you remember when something would hit her as funny and she would laugh?"

Because sometimes when I dream, I remember, but as each year passes, the memories become foggier and her laughter seems too far away.

"She'd get the hiccups, then she'd laugh harder."

I smile at the memory that's a mixture of a balm and acid on my heart.

"Your mom liked to laugh," he says.

She did, and I hate I can barely recall the sound. "She cried that last month she was alive."

Dad drops his head and doesn't deny it.

"I tried to make her better before she left for work that day." I clear my throat as I tell Dad something I never told anyone. "I gave her flowers I had picked outside."

I half expected her to be mad. Three of them were from her flower box, but they were red and that was her favorite color.

Mom hugged me. Longer and tighter than she had before. She hugged me like she'd never hold me again and I held on to her believing that a ten-year-old's love was enough to fix any wound. There's a burning in my eyes and I fucking hate the loss of control.

Mom peeled me off her, grasped my shoulders and said those last words. Words that have haunted me since. *Your father is a man worth forgiving.*

I lower my head and scrub my hands over my face. *I don't know how to forgive him, Mom. Not if he hurt you. I don't know how to forgive him for disrespecting the memory and love I had for you by bringing a parade of trash through our house. He kicked and spit on every good memory I had, and if you left me on purpose, then you destroyed anything that was good in me to begin with and I'm not sure I can forgive you for that.*

"I miss her," Dad says. "Every damn day."

"Then why did you do it?" I demand. "If you loved her, why did you bring those women to her house? To my house? To our home?"

Dad grimaces and the fading rays of the sun hit the red in his hair. Mom loved his hair, saying they should have another child—a girl—so they could have one with hair like his.

"I wanted to forget the pain," he says like he's broken. "I wanted someone to erase the hurt, but the sad part was, they never did. Not one of them did."

"Until now?" The pain leaks out of my voice before I can stop it.

There's hurt in his eyes and I'm not sure why. Because he's still in love with my mother, because he's fallen in love with someone else, or a combination of both, I don't know and after what's taken place between us it's hard to find a reason to care. But fuck me, I do. I do care about my father. He's all the blood family I have left.

"Can we put away the shit that's between us?" Dad asks. "For tonight. I promise our problems will be there in the morning, just like they have been since your mom died."

I nod, and when I straighten, Dad hugs me high. Hands off my patch and he's careful of my arm. It's fast and strong and I hug him just as quick and with the same amount of emotion.

Dad keeps a hand on my neck as we walk in, and if I didn't know better, I'd say he had wiped his eyes. The door shuts behind us and Dad calls out, "Let's eat!"

Breanna

THE DEFINITION OF AWKWARD: riding home with a girl who knows my boyfriend better than I do and yet we have absolutely nothing to talk about on the twenty-minute drive.

Violet is pretty. Fire-red hair, a bit taller than me. She has this bohemian look I've envied since middle school. Why it works with her—the ton of bracelets on her wrist, the whimsical way she can wear a pair of ripped jeans and a tank top with gemstones in a way I can't pull off—is because she has the I-don't-care-if-I'm-not-going-the-same-way-as-the-world outlook.

Pathetic thing? I just now realize it's not the clothes she's wearing that make me envious, but the attitude. I wish I could be in every aspect of my life what Razor says I am—I wish I could be fearless about telling Kyle that his pictures have no power over me, but in this area, I'm drowning in defeat.

"Can I ask you something?" I probe.

Her car is old, possibly older than me and her combined. The windows of this overly large bucket of metal are rolled down because either the car was built without air-conditioning or the system is broken. Because of the age, either is feasible.

"Sure. It'll beat the hell out of ignoring each other."

"It's personal."

"You saw my mother's bra on a wall. It doesn't get much more personal than that."

I choke and she smirks. It's true. When Rebecca and I raced past the main room, I spotted bras hanging on the walls of the clubhouse. "Is your bra on the wall?"

Violet breaks out into a full grin. "No. I've never decided to donate one, and even if I did, I'm not sure they'd accept it. As much as I try to push them away, they still consider me a child of the Terror, which means each man in that club tries to act like my father. It would creep them out if their 'daughter's' bra was on display."

"So those bras..." I drop off.

"Are a contribution to the cause—whatever that means. There're different stories of how and when the first bra went up, but since then when women come to party, they see the rainbow of colors and want to add theirs to the mix. It's become a thing. A thing I don't get, but a thing."

Violet glances over at me and her hair blows wildly in the wind. "I would love to have been in your head for thirty seconds when you saw it. What horrible story did you invent for how the bras got there?"

Honestly, none. When I first darted by, I was too sick at the thought of getting caught, and the second time, I was still numb from Razor declaring me done with the code.

"Half the stories about the Terror aren't true," she says. "Some of them are, but most of the real bad ones aren't. I still don't think you should hang with the Terror, but that's not my decision to make."

"You didn't have to bring me today."

"True." She hesitates. "I hurt someone recently because I was too dead set on making them think the Terror are evil. Call this my penance."

"Do you still think they're evil?"

"As sure as I am that Satan's real, and in case you're wondering, he is. I still think you should run and never look back, but you're a big girl and can make your own choices."

I digest that and decide to switch the subject. "That's cool—that they look out for you."

Her smile falters. "My dad died. I'm not interested in anyone replacing him."

Wrong change of subject. "I'm sorry."

"Me, too. I have a feeling that isn't the question you were going to ask."

No, none of this is the conversation I planned on having. I rub my forehead and push forward. "How bad was it when that picture of you was posted on Bragger?"

Violet eases her foot off the gas and the car slows from her breakneck speed. I find the courage to look over at her and she mirrors the agony I felt when Kyle sat across from me in the library. "How bad is the picture they have of you?" she asks.

My throat tightens as the urge to share and the self-preservation to keep this secret quiet wages war within me. Violet focuses on the road again and her knuckles go white on the wheel. "Those assholes never know when to stop, do they? I mean, me? I walked into that mess, but you, what the fuck have you ever done wrong?"

"I went to Shamrock's. I drank and I ended up outside with Razor and someone took a picture. Razor was leaning into me, but we didn't kiss. We didn't do anything. We were talking, but the picture looks a million times worse and they were going to..." My chest constricts and my eyes burn.

"Label you a whore," she finishes for me. "They were going to post it and label you a whore."

Violet slams her hand against the steering wheel and pain slashes through me. She's lived through this torment. Even worse than me because people have gossiped about her for as long as I can remember, since she's a child of the Terror.

"I'm not going to lie. I knew you were being blackmailed. Not because Razor told me, but because Razor asked about the picture taken of me."

My eyes widen and she waves me off. "I put the pieces together. He didn't tell me, and because he's so damn set on playing rogue, I bet he hasn't said anything to anyone else. And, by the way, it's in direct violation of club rules for him to keep a secret like this, but that's neither here nor there. Tell me what they're blackmailing you for."

"I'm being blackmailed to write papers."

"Kyle Hewitt is a fucking moronic asshole," she spits out with enough venom that a chill courses through my blood.

"Was he the one that posted the picture of you?"

"No. Someone else. I was being blackmailed, too, but I didn't give in and look what happened to me. What sucks is, I have given in to keep more pictures from going up, but the damage was already done."

"What was it like?" I whisper, almost terrified of the truth. "When the picture went up?"

Violet's expression clouds over. "Awful. So awful I considered if life was worth living. So awful that some days I don't want to get out of bed. So awful that I have made myself a whore just to not go through it again."

It takes several heartbeats to ingest her honesty. She's

painting the horrible future that I've created in my mind. "Razor's trying to help. He'll fix this for both of us."

She yanks out a chain around her neck that had been hidden by her shirt, and she fingers a silver cross. The charm is about two inches long and it's thick, like it belongs to a man. "Computers?"

"Yes."

"He's smart. But I'm not sure he's smart enough. Before Razor pulls the trigger on whatever he has planned, make sure he's a hundred percent sure he's keeping you safe. Otherwise this group of guys will make it rain brimstone and fire." Pity fills Violet's eyes. "No offense, Breanna, but you're not the type to dance in the rain. Especially the type that burns."

Hysteria wells up within me. "What do I do, then? Because I'm starting to go crazy. Always wondering if he's going to put it up, the guilt of keeping a secret, and if I do give in, I'll be doing something wrong. I'm not sure how much longer I can keep going like this."

Violet plays with her necklace and drives. Waiting for her response is skull-crushing and each second that passes makes this entire situation nauseating.

"I was up for a scholarship," she finally says. "To someplace far away from here and I was told by a college recruiter that they were seriously considering me until they did a search for me on the internet. He told me their board of trustees couldn't in good faith give scholarship money to a candidate with a questionable reputation."

Hot moisture pools at the bottom of my eyes.

"No matter what happens, don't let Razor talk you into going to the club with this," she says.

"Why?"

"The Terror plays by their own rules when push comes to

shove and I don't want blood on my hands." It's not an answer, yet it is one at the same time.

"You said most of the stories were lies."

"I did, but I didn't mention which ones were true."

My bottom lip trembles and I suck in a breath to prevent tears from falling. Violet places her hand over mine and I link our fingers together. "What am I going to do?"

"One of us is going to get out of this town. When you make it, remember me when I come asking you for a job." Violet squeezes my hand. "In the meantime, I would plan on writing those papers."

RAZOR

BREANNA IS STRANGLING my hand so tightly she could rival a tourniquet. Gotta admit, the girl may be frightened, but she owns a bigger pair of balls than most men.

It's Friday and we're still standing near the row of parked bikes. We arrived at the clubhouse a few minutes ago. She took her time to gain her land legs and then bought more time by combing her fingers through her hair, then checking her cell to see if her cover story is holding. It all adds up to stalling.

I swipe my thumb over her frozen hand. It's been a cool day, but I'm betting it's nerves causing her to be cold. "You ready?"

She nods too quickly. "Do I look okay?"

"Yeah." She's fucking gorgeous. Jeans that hug her right and a blue top that sets off that black hair. What I really love is that she's wearing my leather jacket. "Stick with me at all times. If I get pulled away, you stay with Rebecca or with Oz or Chevy. You never leave our sight."

Breanna blows out a shaky breath. "I thought this was a big old family-friendly dinner."

"It's the same type of rules as if you went to Shamrock's. Stick with who you know."

Breanna's eyebrows rise and a ripple of uneasiness rushes through me when I remember she didn't stick with who she knew that night. She danced with a whole lot of guys who would have knocked the hell out of each other for the chance to be with her—the girl who had no fear.

"New rules—when you go to someplace unknown, you stick with who you know."

Breanna's face brightens as she watches my annoyance… fuck it, my jealousy.

I grab on to her belt loops and drag her into me as I sit on the seat of my bike. She's between my legs and she has this contagious smile that locks me into her. My hands settle on her hips and I imagine all the things I plan on doing with her tonight. After she meets the club, after we eat some dinner, I'm getting her back on my bike and we're riding to someplace private.

Breanna nervously glances around. "We aren't alone."

We're not. "No one's going to rat. What happens at the clubhouse stays here."

"Good to know." Breanna wiggles as if that nonverbal cue is enough to convince me to release her. "But there are a lot of people around."

The crystal ball grows clear. Breanna doesn't like an audience, but if she's going to hang around here, she's going to have to get used to a few things. My fingers stay on her hips and I attempt to distract her with a change in conversation. "My jacket looks good on you."

"Do you want it back?"

"No. I want every guy to know you belong with me."

"It doesn't have your name on it, so how do they know it's yours?"

"They'll know." Because it has a hole in the arm from when I got shot. Next time I go into Louisville, I'll buy a new one and let her keep this one. I'll tell her it's for protection on my bike, and it is, but it's also a nice calling card of get-the-fuck-away-from-my-girl. "Wear the jacket."

"Should I go feminist and say I belong to myself?" Breanna wraps her hands around my neck and her fingertips tease the ends of my hair. Fire invades my veins and my thoughts of where I want to kiss Breanna leave the realm of respectable territory.

"This isn't your world. It's mine. You're safer with that jacket on."

"Guess it's good that I like wearing it. It smells like you."

Damn, she always says the right thing. I pull her closer to me, tunnel my fingers in her hair and capture those sweet lips.

She's hesitant and I have no doubt it's because people are near. Breanna plays a little, then will slightly draw away, but I continue to coax. A nibble here, a slide of my tongue there. My hands sneak under the jacket so I can massage her back and skim my fingers along her spine. Each and every movement slowly thaws Breanna and makes her as hot as a flame. Her sighs and her caresses cause me to want to drop to my knees and beg for more.

A dog barks and Breanna jumps. She laughs as she eases back and that sound soothes some of my rough edges. Another bark, and when I glance down, a part of me discovers the excitement of being ten on Christmas morning. "Well, fuck me."

"What?" Breanna asks.

I stand and give her a quick kiss before letting her go. "It's my dog."

Breanna

HIS DOG. RAZOR has a dog. It feels strange that I never knew, but then again, our conversations lately have been so seriously set on my family or his family or schoolwork or on kissing that we've left out the small, fun things like dogs.

Razor's crouched near the ground scratching behind the ears of a pudgy basset hound with the largest dark eyes I've seen. "I didn't know you had a dog."

"I don't," he says, and then the dog leaps around Razor. The dog's tail wags, his tongue is hanging out and he continuously licks his master.

"Have you told him that?" I ask, but the big, bad biker has been reduced to cooing.

"What are you doing here, boy?" A rub behind the ears, a lick on the face in return. "Did you walk all the way from Florida?"

The dog chases his own tail three times before collapsing on the ground. He rolls over to show his belly and proves he really is a boy. I'm smiling as Razor rubs the dog's stomach with both hands, declaring him a "good boy."

Razor eventually peers over his shoulder at me and I'm knocked breathless with how happy he appears. "This is Lars."

At the mention of his name, Lars hops up on all fours, sniffs Razor's face and then plants another wet, sloppy kiss on him. Razor chuckles but moves Lars's snout away as he begins petting him again. "Lars, this is Breanna."

The dog's tongue rolls to the side again and he pants, surveying me as if he can understand Razor. "My mom gave me Lars the Christmas before she died." Some of the sadness that's always attached to Razor returns.

"So this is really your dog?" I kneel beside Razor and Lars pads over to me. I pet his head as Razor continues to run his hand over the length of the dog's back.

"When I was a kid, Cyrus's wife, Olivia, used to watch me when Mom and Dad had to work. She let me bring Lars with me to her house. When Mom died, I lived here for a while. Dad split after the funeral, and when he returned, he was a mess. When Dad got his shit together, he came and got me but left Lars. Dad wasn't sure he had enough in him to take care of a kid and a dog."

My heart honest-to-God breaks. Like someone reached into my chest, ripped it out and has cracked it in two. "What happened?"

"To the dog or me?" Razor forces a grin like what he admitted doesn't matter—that it's not absolutely soul-shattering.

"Both," I answer seriously, and he frowns, unhappy that I'm not offering him the easy route.

"We both know I'm fucked-up."

"That's not true—"

"Olivia kept Lars," he cuts me off. "I was here enough anyhow, so it's not like I didn't see him, but everyone eventually forgot he was mine and he became Olivia's. Then Olivia died this summer. When her granddaughter, Emily, returned to Florida, Eli had Emily take Lars with her."

I sort of crave to hit this Eli guy. "Why?"

Razor stops petting Lars and the dog whines as it peeks pathetically up at him. "Because Emily needed a reminder of this place more than anyone else did at the time."

Razor straightens and then takes my hand. "Which means if Lars is here, then so is Emily."

"Is that a bad thing?"

"The opposite. Let's go prove to you that some of the Terror are normal." And in the next breath, he says to Lars, "Let's go, boy."

There's this mixture of adrenaline and pure fear and I'm thirty seconds from throwing up. Razor is leading me through smaller groups of men in cuts and we're walking toward the enormous building on the other side of the property. The closer we get, the less normal the world becomes.

The building—this clubhouse—it's a huge two-story garage, or at least it once was. Both of the doors are raised and men pack the place. Razor guides me inside and I feel like Alice wandering into a demented Wonderland. There's a long bar along the left side and men rest against it with alcohol in their hands. A guy wearing a cut with a patch on the back of it that reads *Prospect* is behind the bar accepting orders.

Neon signs are everywhere and so are bras. Lots of bras. They are tacked up on the wall, lying across the shelves behind the bar, and I try not to think of Violet's mother.

The place smells of stale beer and my feet stick to the floor. A woman laughs too loudly and so do some of the men. My hair stands on the back of my neck as instinct screams to leave.

Razor stops short and I have to adjust quickly so I don't

collide with his shoulder. Two little blond-haired boys are chased by a girl of maybe five. All three are giggling as they weave fearlessly through the towering men. There's pure joy on their faces and I tilt my head as I recognize the little girl.

"She's a friend of Elsie's. She's played at our house and I've dropped Elsie off at her parents' house." My forehead furrows. "I mean, her parents are so—"

"Normal?" Razor asks. "Oddly enough, some of us are capable of that. Wearing a three-piece patch doesn't make you psychotic. It makes you a part of something bigger than yourself."

I scan the wall of bras again and none of the information I'm consuming makes logical sense and that causes my head to throb.

"Razor!" someone yells, and a deafening round of applause and cheers fills the room. From the corner comes an earsplitting whistle. Every person is solely focused on him.

A hand on my back and I jump. Razor's head snaps to check on me and to the left is Rebecca. She inclines her head to Razor and he nods his in response. It's like the two of them have their own specific language.

"Take her to Emily," Razor says.

"That was my plan all along," she answers.

Razor sends me an encouraging glance. He's leaving me and I need to be okay with it, but I'm so not. I sort of trust Rebecca, but in the end, I've spent only a handful of minutes in her company.

The clapping and shouting continues and Razor enters the crowd of men. They pat his back, hug him, purposely avoiding his injured side. There's something beautiful in the way they smile at him and I love how he practically glows in return.

Rebecca leans over to me. "This is his moment. It's huge that he shared it with you."

"Is this because he was shot?"

"Yes and no. They respect him for taking his job seriously, but this moment is because he saved one of his brothers."

A sense of awe overwhelms me and then I remember Razor as he stood with me outside the school, how he whisked me up in his arms outside the bar, and how he was willing to fight for someone he didn't even know because I asked. Warmth settles into my heart—saving people is what Razor does.

"I'm proud to be with him," I tell her as guilt tiptoes along my stomach lining. He's introducing me to his family and he's fine with keeping us a secret from mine. In fact, he's fine with keeping us a secret altogether, explaining that our relationship is no one else's business.

"You should be. But at the same time, life in the Terror isn't easy. Most people will draw dividing lines and will make you choose between us and them. I'll be honest, you're too young to make that choice."

Rebecca wears a cut, too, but this one is much different from Razor's. It's black like his and she has a nickname patch sewn on, but there are no other patches. The back simply states *Terror Gypsy* and a small patch at the bottom contains a name I've heard Razor use before—the name of another member.

She notices me studying her cut and she touches Razor's jacket. "Keep this on. It'll make tonight easier for you."

So I've already been informed. "Any other tips?"

"Don't come here without Razor. In fact, you aren't allowed in the clubhouse without Razor, and if you're under eighteen, you have to leave by eight. No exceptions."

I can live with that. "How old were you when you chose this life?"

"The same age as you, and most days I don't regret it."

My stomach bottoms out. "Most days?"

"Demons haunt the souls of some of these men. It's what drives them to belong to a part of society most can't understand. Razor's not exempt and loving someone like that can be hard."

Razor's demon is his mother. I haven't told Razor, but I'm still working on the second code. Maybe this is a demon I can help exorcise.

"Have you had enough of the clubhouse yet?" she asks.

I force my lips to move up like I'm fine even though I'm practically quaking.

Rebecca laughs. "Emily feels the same way. She's at a picnic table outside. Let me introduce the two of you."

RAZOR

I'M IN THE BACK of the clubhouse and I have a line of
guys willing to buy me a beer. Conversation is flowing fast.
Everyone has something to say and they're saying it at once.
I'm the one who's silent, so to them, it means I'm the one
who listens.

Pigpen slips in between a group of guys and waves two
fingers at the prospect behind the bar. The prospect slides
two longnecks to him and, with them in hand, Pigpen motions with his chin for me to follow. Brothers pat me on the
back, on my good side, as I tail him. Pigpen cuts into the
kitchen, holding the door open for me with his foot. When
I'm through, he hands me the other beer and the entire board
claps.

The door shuts behind me and the serving window is
closed. We aren't in the boardroom, so whatever is about
to happen isn't official, but serious enough that they prefer
privacy.

Pigpen sets his beer on the counter, then lifts himself to sit
on it. Eli leans his back on the wall next to him, and Dad's

beside Cyrus near the stainless-steel table in the middle of the room. They stare at me as if they're expecting something, and I'm at a loss.

"We're dying here," Eli says. "Spill."

Still doesn't help.

"You brought a girl," Eli says slowly as if I'm mentally impaired. "Is this Breanna?"

"Better be." Pigpen grins. "Otherwise she's going to be pissed when you roll over and whisper another girl's name in the morning."

My head lowers. I'll never live that down. "Yeah, that's Breanna."

"Miller?" Dad asks.

I nod, curious how he knew her last name.

"Her mom works in accounting at the hospital," he says.

It's not new knowledge, but it's something I never gave a second thought to. Curiosity creates a stab of physical pain. How is it we've been together and I never asked about her family?

"Breanna's mom and your mom worked closely together. Your mom considered Breanna's mom a good friend." There's a mournful smile on his face that slices me deep. "She said Breanna's mom was pregnant all the time. Then she'd come into work with a baby and your mom used to come home begging for us to have another once she got a whiff."

I want to ask why I was an only child, but then I think better. It's not like he'd answer.

"Does her family know about you?" Eli asks.

"No, neither does anyone else. I don't want her taking shit for being with me."

Eli and Cyrus share one of those glances that leads me to believe they read minds.

"They're a good family," Dad says. "She, and they, deserve better than for you to be sneaking around in the shadows."

"The bastards at school will crucify her if they know she's on the back of my bike."

"He didn't say school, pinhead," Pigpen interrupts. "He said her parents."

Acid churns in my stomach. "And what if they keep us apart?"

"Then you come to us," Dad says. "You come to me. For the millionth time, son, you need to trust us." He leaves out "trust me" because we're both aware of where I stand on that.

"I don't want to lose her."

"You won't. Trust us to help if it comes down to that."

"Just like you helped Mom?" I spit.

He and I glare each other down and the tension in the room is so thick that it's strangling me. For one night, Dad and I found a way to let our past go, and he was right, our problems sure as hell didn't waste their time plowing into us again.

"I heard your girl's smart," Pigpen pipes up to ease the building tension. "In fact, I've heard she's fucking Einstein, which brings up the question of how the hell she ended up with you."

I flip off Pigpen. He suggests something anatomically impossible, and as the familiar ribbing begins, we sober up when Cyrus says, "She's the other person in the independent study."

Silence as I understand what they must be assuming—that somehow our brains are the bond between us, but what they don't understand is that I don't hold a candle to Breanna.

"Yeah," I answer. "She is."

"See," Pigpen says. "The boy does have brains."

"Not like hers." Before they can argue, I jack my thumb

over my shoulder. "Breanna's freaked enough about being here, so I'm going to find her."

"She under eighteen?" Eli asks, and I nod. "Then she's out of here by eight. A few other chapters are riding in later tonight in your honor. Shit's going to get crazy."

I'll be expected to show later, and maybe I will after I get Breanna safely home, but right now, my focus is her. All on her. I nod again to let him know I heard and leave to find my girl.

Breanna

PAPER PLATES WITH the remnants of our dinner are stacked at the end of the picnic table, and there are enough red plastic cups on the table that I've lost track of which one is mine. I'm drinking water. Emily is drinking a diet soda. Oz and Chevy are drinking beer. They've had multiple cups and, when they first sat at the table, Razor had a beer, too.

He drank one and after that he's stuck to my water. It's intimate that we share the same cup and it's odd to watch people my age drink so freely with so many adults around. What's crazy—no one, not a single adult, cares.

"Tell me more!" Emily's grin grows. In a lawn chair, Emily sits on the lap of Oz—a guy who graduated from my high school last year and scared the crap out of me when he walked by, but he's hard to find intimidating as he watches Emily as if the sun rises and sets by her.

The other guy from our school—Chevy—shakes his head. "You're killing us, Breanna. Razor, ask your girl for some mercy."

We're all smiles: me, Razor, Chevy, Emily, Oz and this

other guy from school they call Stone. He's a couple of years younger than us and he's the kind of guy your soul hurts to look at because people at school torture him. My soul withers further as I realize that could be me.

Razor moves beside me to straddle the bench seat. He hooks an arm around my waist and glances down at my legs as a silent request for me to do what he's done. I also straddle the bench and end up with my back flush to him. I wait for everyone to whisper about us sitting so cozily, but like with the beer, no one cares.

"Breanna's lying." Oz runs his finger along Emily's knee and it's the type of touch that suggests they share very personal secrets. "I was a Boy Scout at school."

Ha. That's a lie. "So you're saying during my freshman year you didn't punch Adam Jones in the face, causing him to spew blood in my direction?"

"In my defense, it was your boy that started the fight." Oz mocks this innocent expression, but there's no way I'm buying it. "I was helping a brother out."

Razor makes a disgusted noise. "Guy I hit was already down. You were feeling left out."

I snap my body around. "I babysat other people's children for months to earn enough for that sweater and I never got the blood out of it. Anyhow, I don't remember you there."

"I was already in the office being suspended. First part of the fight happened in the parking lot. The guy I fought hit me hard, Breanna. So hard my hair moved and then I had to really hit him back. I'm the one who should be getting the sympathy points." He bats his baby blues at me and I shake my head at him because I'm melting.

"What were you guys fighting about?" Emily asks.

Oz, Chevy and Razor look at each other, then go quiet. I

drop my hand to cover Razor's fingers that are firm against my stomach. I know why they fought. The rumors at school were brutal and guilt consumes me for being the person who brought up the subject.

Adam Jones called the Terror worthless, and when Razor told him to keep his mouth shut, Adam told Razor he must be worthless, too, since his mother preferred death over being with him.

"What was your first impression of me?" Chevy asks, moving the conversation forward. I adore that about him and Oz. They read Razor well and form a protective bubble around him.

"First impression of you," I repeat. It's what started my stories. Oz asked point-blank what I thought of him and, through coaxing from Razor and Emily, I gave in. "Eighth grade stands out. That was when you gas-lighted our science teacher into believing he was crazy."

I look over at Emily. "Chevy stole things from him and then a few days later he'd put it back someplace different, and when our teacher found it, Chevy and Razor would tell him the item had been there the entire time."

Chevy chuckles. "Fucked-up bastard didn't have a chance when the rest of the class joined in. The asshole was starting to lose his mind at the end."

"You didn't?" Emily's eyes widen. "I thought you were the good one."

Oz and Razor bark out a laugh and Chevy flashes a sly one-sided smirk. "I am the good one, but then I hang out with these two. I'm telling you, I'm trying to save their souls, but they keep dragging me down."

"Seriously," Emily says. "That wasn't very nice."

Chevy shrugs and Oz wraps both his arms around Emily

in a hug. "The guy was sick in the head. He used to call girls to his desk, drop his pencil and then look up their skirts or down their shirts when they bent over to pick it up."

"Why didn't anyone do anything?" Emily asks. "Tell another teacher. The principal. Somebody."

"We tried." Razor's voice vibrates against the skin of my shoulder as he sweetly presses his lips to a sensitive spot on my neck and it's hard not to shiver from the pleasure. "No one listened."

"The board listened." Chevy rolls his plastic cup in his hand. "Cyrus and Oz's dad hounded the principal and the school board."

"Lot of good that did," answers Razor.

"The bastard's not teaching anymore, is he?" Chevy challenges.

"Not because the board tried the appropriate way first." Razor picks up my cup again and drinks while he keeps his eyes locked on Chevy. What makes me tremble is how Chevy grins like a satisfied asylum inmate. Chevy offers his fist, Razor bumps it and my stomach twists.

Everyone, including Razor, has said the same thing—the Terror try to abide by the law, but they play by their own rules. But then I recall how girls cried before and after class. How Addison used to throw up on Monday mornings because of what we had to endure in science, and then I think of those horrible moments that I had tucked away to the back recesses of my mind... "I'm glad you did it."

They had hopped on to another conversation and they pause and stare at me.

"What?" Razor asks.

I should say I didn't mean to speak. I should continue to carry the secret like I have since eighth grade, but for some reason, this group, this place, these fantastically raw people—maybe I don't have to hide anymore.

"He did it to Addison." The memory causes the fried chicken I ate earlier to war with the potato salad. "Mr. Mull did it to Addison a few times. He kept me after class because I was ahead of everyone else, so the school was giving me extra assignments, and she would stay because she didn't trust him alone with me. He would drop his pen and he wouldn't let us leave until she picked it up. It had to be her. It always had to be Addison. And she would never leave me behind, even when I begged her to, because she was scared what he would do if it was just the two of us alone."

I remember feeling ashamed and used and all I did was stay after class. Addison was the one who took the brunt of the abuse. "So...yeah, I'm glad you did it."

Razor's arm around me tightens and he mumbles a low curse. There's a wildness in both of the other boys' eyes that frightens me.

"You don't need to worry about anyone making you feel like shit again." Razor's threat is ominous and made with the promise of death.

"Amen," Chevy adds. "Anyone ever makes you the slightest bit uncomfortable, Breanna, you tell one of us. You're with Razor, which means you're family."

Family. My eyes flicker up with the word and there's a sincerity in Chevy's face that causes a small part of my heart to ache. He means what he says. Without knowing me... without really understanding me...he's already accepted me...he's suggesting I belong.

"It's true," Razor says in this soft voice that's almost a whisper. Our eyes meet and I wonder if he can spot my bewilderment. It can't be that easy. Nothing is that easy. I have a huge family. People who are supposed to love me regardless, and it's never this easy.

"Reign of Terror," Chevy says, and his statement rips Razor's attention away from me.

Razor tips his head to him and repeats, "Reign of Terror."

Oz turns his head toward the men crowding the bonfire and yells, "Reign of Terror."

A sense of awe and fear runs through me as a loud, deep chorus of "Reign of Terror" is shouted into the night. Not once, not twice, but three times, ending in a warrior cry that causes me to shrink into Razor.

Razor gently hugs me to him as if he can sense my unease, kisses my temple, then slips off the seat, leaving my back cold. He stands beside me and places his fingers under my chin. "I told you months ago—I got your back."

He did and I never understood how much he meant his promise. He swipes his thumb across my cheek and it leaves a burning trail along my skin. "You ready to head?"

I power on my phone and it reads seven forty. Twenty minutes until the proverbial Reign of Terror midnight for minors. "Sure."

He inclines his head to the clubhouse. "I gotta say some goodbyes."

It's implied he's telling me to stay. I grin an okay and he does that heart-stopping caress one more time before looking over at Oz and Chevy. They both nod at whatever he silently requested.

"Do you visit Snowflake often?" I ask Emily after Razor disappears into the swarm of bodies.

"Not as much as I'd like. Eli's all paranoid about the Ri—"

Oz interrupts her with a clearing of his throat and her cheeks redden. Something important was about to be revealed and my mind grabs the mystery. There's a heavy silence that follows and none of us can figure out what to say to make it any less awkward.

I choose the old standby for awkward. "Do you mind if I use the restroom?"

The thought of going back into the clubhouse causes my stomach to flip, but it's the only excuse I can think of to get me and Emily alone.

Emily shifts off Oz. "I'll take her to the cabin."

"Eli said no one but you and the board goes into the cabin." There's a bit of repentance in Oz's expression, but his words are firm enough that he obviously won't break this rule.

Emily stiffens like his statement was a blow. "I like her, and she shouldn't have to go into the clubhouse if she doesn't want."

"And you promised to follow the rules," Oz says as if he's implying something else.

Emily shrugs like she doesn't care and pivots away from him. "Fine. Then I'll show her where the bathroom is in the clubhouse and then you should go home or stay in the clubhouse or do whatever you want, since that rule means you can't come in the cabin, either. And according to *the rules*, I've been ordered back to the cabin after eight, so have fun without me."

Oz's head falls back as Emily snatches my hand and weaves us through the throngs of men.

"You don't mean that," Oz calls out, and I know he doesn't see Emily's smirk. Oh my God, she's a little devil playing him like a violin.

"Yes, I do," she yells back, then spins in his direction, smirk completely gone. "Have fun being by yourself tonight."

The men around us laugh and I blush when someone suggests something about Oz becoming good friends with his right hand. I expect Oz to be angry, but he chuckles as he and Chevy stand. Emily pulls on my hand again and sweeps me into the clubhouse. I don't understand any of these people or how they interact with each other.

Oz and Chevy track us. It's weird yet chivalrous and it's then I understand what Razor was asking them to do—to protect me.

We enter a hallway adjacent to the kitchen and there's a deep line for the woman's bathroom. Most of the women don't have cuts like Rebecca's and there's more skin than there is clothing.

"It must be getting seriously close to eight," Emily mumbles, then shouts, "Eli's daughter coming through."

"Emily!" Oz yells, and I wish I could own the flirtatious yet angry expression Emily throws Oz.

"What?"

"She can use the bathroom in the cabin."

Emily places a patronizing hand to her chest. "Why, thank you, Oz, what would we ever do without you?"

She lets go of me when Oz invades her space. Every part of them touches. "I have a few ideas of what we can do together."

Emily smiles wickedly up at him, winks, then grabs my hand again. It's a blur as we slink past bands of men and eventually we trot up the stairs to the log cabin. Once we're in and she checks to see that Oz and Chevy have chosen to stay on the front porch, she whispers, "You have questions, don't you?"

"Yes." It's total disorientation. The clubhouse was so… beyond normal and this…this is like a modern-day storybook cottage. I'm shocked. In a good way. The walls are made of massive tree trunks, but everything about it is straight out of one of my mother's home magazines. Nice but comfortable furniture, a television, bright lighting and pictures. A ton of framed pictures hang out on tables and bookcases.

"Breanna," Emily urges. "We don't have much time. What do you want to know?"

I jerk back to reality. Questions. Razor. "What is the RMC?"

"I had a feeling you were going to ask that," Emily says as a curse, then peers outside. At the foot of the stairs, two huge men with cuts that say *Prospect* stand as if they are sentries to a kingdom. "We can't have ears for this conversation."

Emily drags me down the hallway, we take a sharp left and she shuts the door to the bedroom. On the bed, Lars lifts his head and wags his tail.

Emily peeks out the window as if someone might be eavesdropping. "We have maybe five minutes, so let's get to the point. You can't tell anyone I'm telling you this, okay? Because the reason I'm doing it is that they stupidly tried to keep it from me and it backfired and you're dating Razor now, so you should know."

"Okay."

Emily tugs on the ends of her long hair. "The RMC is a rival motorcycle club in Louisville. The Terror and the Riot hate each other. In the past, it was bad, but they have a peace treaty now, but it seems to be on the edge of falling apart. I'm telling you this because if you see anyone from the Riot, you need to get out quick, especially if they know you're the girlfriend of one of the Terror."

The click in my head is so audible that I'm surprised Emily didn't hear it. I unlocked part of a threat and that threat was from the Riot Motorcycle Club.

"Eli and the club are freaking out. The Riot ran through on their bikes a couple of weeks ago and then Razor went after them on his own. If Cyrus hadn't caught up to him, there is no telling if Razor would have been hurt. Because of that Eli has been stonewalling me on visiting."

My mouth is completely dropped open. "Razor what?"

"Went after them," she repeats.

"Is that who shot Razor?" It's like I can't draw enough air into my body.

Emily goes completely still as if she's a statue. "Say that again?"

Secrets. Violet told me that this is a life of secrets. "Razor was shot. It's part of the reason why they're throwing this party."

Emily's eyes dart to the thoughts in her head. "I was told it was for me, but this makes more sense. But we're off track. Look, I like you. You're funny and nice and everyone in the club is seriously praying you two work because, to be honest, Razor's freaking suicidal."

I blink several times and Emily's expression falls. "I don't mean, like, he's tried it or he's vlogging his last words or anything. I mean he does these stupid things like that fight you talked about or chasing after the Riot or…"

Teetering on the ledge of a bridge over a rushing river. "I understand." I try to force myself out of the long tunnel of shock. "Then it's safe now? You're here in Kentucky, so the Riot is no longer a problem?"

"I don't know. I wasn't supposed to know about Razor going after the Riot, but I overheard Oz and Eli talking about it when they visited me in Florida. It drives me freaking insane, but this club is super secretive and that's not going to change. I mean, for God's sake, I consider Razor a friend and he was shot and no one told me."

"If it isn't safe, then why are you here?"

Emily gestures to the dresser and on it are two wooden boxes. "Those are Olivia's ashes. She was like a mom to Oz and Razor, but she was my biological grandmother. She left us instructions of what she wants us to do with her remains. One box is for me and Oz and the other is for Razor. Her letter to me and Oz said that we had to spread her ashes in Kentucky. Eli let me come because I told him we were being disrespectful to his mother if we pushed it out any further."

I walk over to the boxes and take an interest in the one that has an envelope with Razor's name resting on top of it. "What is Razor supposed to do with the ashes?"

"No one knows. Not even Razor. Olivia left him the by-laws of the club and said when he figured it out, he would know what to do with her ashes. What's even odder is that Oz and I received our letter after she passed, but she had specific instructions for when Razor was to get his. He received his a few weeks ago and it was related to some sort of event that no one will tell me about. Olivia was awesome, but she could be weird."

I note the wistful tone in her voice—the same one Razor has when he speaks of Olivia. She must have been someone truly amazing. Behind the box is a stack of papers stapled together and I tilt my head. "Are these the bylaws?"

"Yes, but we need to go. Razor will be looking for you and Oz will be pissed if he finds out I'm telling you this."

A screeching of a screen door, boots down a hallway, and Emily is pleading, but my focus is on the page. The first code's a cipher...a key to unlock something else...

Razor involved me with the code because a detective brought him a file on his mother. Olivia—a woman he admitted he loved and who loved him in return, a woman married to the president of this club—this Olivia left bylaws to be given to him after a specific event. An event where Razor was trying to discover what happened to his mother?

I snatch the bylaws off the dresser and Emily rushes toward me. "What are you doing? I know you're new, but you cannot read those. Seriously, they will freak out and—"

"I need a printer." I fish my cell out of my pocket. "I have a file and I need to print it."

Emily squints in confusion and there's no way she can understand. No one knows what this is about and I won't tell her, but even worse, this isn't only about Razor anymore. This is also about me. I've seen the code. It's there in my head, when I sleep, when I eat. A constant nagging.

The door to the room opens, Razor enters, and when he spots what's in my hands, he warily eyes Emily, then me. I show him my cell. "She needs to go, and I need a printer. Full page. Eight-by-ten. Nothing smaller. Nothing bigger. This has to be precise."

A shadow crosses his face as he notices the picture I had promised to delete off my phone. "Get out, Emily."

I don't cower at the pure anger radiating from Razor, but Emily is out the door in seconds. I maintain eye contact with Razor, and he steps closer, towering over me as if he could will me into compliance. He can glower, he can yell, but this is Razor and he could never hurt me because he is built to the core to protect.

"I can crack this code, but I need this printed out."

"This isn't a game. It's not a crossword puzzle or a seek-and-find. What's on your phone is a powder keg and I will not allow you to be a casualty of the explosion."

My heart aches at the pain in his eyes. He's lost so much, more than I could ever comprehend. "No one will know I cracked this unless you tell or I tell, and we're both capable of keeping secrets."

Razor's head falls back and he stares at the ceiling. A battle wages inside him between protecting me and gaining the answers he craves. "You don't understand how bad this is."

"I don't understand. None of it, but I understand me. You think I can stop hunting for a solution, but I can't. This code is in my brain and the wheels won't stop, not even for you."

I take his hand and squeeze it. "You know more about me than anyone else. I've told you more, told you secrets about my brain, and while you're the one that understands me better than anyone, you still don't truly understand. I'm not able to stop what happens in my mind. I'll go crazy if I don't solve this, so you can help me or you can fight me, but here's the thing—the reason we get along so well is because you're like me. Once something's in our brain, it doesn't stop."

Razor's shaking his head as he cups my face. There's a desperation in his voice I've never heard. "It's not the same. My mind is nothing like yours, and you're right, I don't fully understand, but I can't drag you any further into this. I can't lose you."

I lay my hands over his. "You won't. Because where my brain won't stop, you can't stop protecting the people you care for. I can crack this code, Razor, and I can do it knowing that whatever it is you're scared of, you will never let it touch me. I trust you."

Razor searches my eyes for an answer to a question he has yet to pose. "Stay here. I mean it, Breanna. You don't move a foot." He yanks the bylaws from my hands and he's out the door.

RAZOR

EMILY'S SITTING IN Cyrus's recliner, and her eyes are puffy. She wipes at a tear, but damn if her chin isn't lifted in that pissed-off way of hers. Not sure what happened, but it could be on the same radiation fallout level as what's going on with me and Breanna.

Oz is a wall in front of the screen door with his arms crossed over his chest, glaring at Emily in the same angry way she's glaring at him. "Emily told Breanna about the Riot."

Fuck me, this night keeps getting better. "Why?"

"Because she needed to know," Emily spits out. "The same way I deserved to know."

Emily's not from our world. She's Eli's daughter, but she was raised far away from here and then was dragged into the middle of our worst nightmare earlier this summer.

There's a reason why we keep our business to ourselves and Emily has a lot to learn about being a club girl. It isn't lost on me how much Breanna will have to accept if she sticks with me and what I'm about to do will make it tougher for her to understand why I keep secrets.

"Do you remember what happened when Violet told you things she shouldn't?" Oz says.

"Are you talking about the things that would have been easier to tell me from the beginning? Yes, I do remember. If Breanna's life is going to be in jeopardy, it should be up to her whether she wants to be in the line of fire."

Oz morphs into twelve shades of red and I'm out the door. Emily's right. Oz knows it, but Emily promised Oz and Eli that if she visited, she'd play by their rules, not her own. Oz and Emily are a blowtorch and gasoline together and odds are they'll be in the horizontal position within the next fifteen minutes.

I head to my motorcycle, slip Breanna's folder out of my saddlebag and fly back into the house. Emily and Oz aren't kissing on the couch, but they are in the kitchen and they aren't screaming. Instead, he's hugging her, comforting her, and by the way her shoulders shake, she's crying. The two of them shared a seriously fucked-up summer. Turns out I'm not the only one still capable of crushing fireflies.

Breanna's watching the party unfold from the window seat. I close the door behind me and it doesn't cause her to jump or tear her gaze away from the window. It's like the world that seemed hurried before spiraled into slow motion.

"There's a lot of drunk people out there." Her voice is lifeless.

There are. "Lot of drunk people at Shamrock's, too."

"Are the girls you had sex with out there?"

Why doesn't she just put a nail gun to my head and continually shoot one sharp piece of metal into my skull after another? That'd be less painful. "Probably. They love parties."

She doesn't respond and my boots sound too heavy on the floor as I walk toward her.

"When I'm eighteen, will you take me to these parties?" she asks.

I sit beside her and lean my back against the wall. Outside a guy from the Lanesville chapter is enjoying a lap dance near the bonfire. If Breanna's hung up on that, she ought to love the debauchery going on within the clubhouse. "If you want."

"What if I don't want to go?"

"Then you don't."

"But you'll still go, won't you?"

"Already told you, if you're with me, then I'm yours. You either trust me or you don't. But it's my goal to remain in the club."

I extend the bylaws and the folder I stole from her. Doing this could buy me a ticket out of the club, it's putting Breanna in danger, but... "I trust you."

Her face crumples as her shoulders roll forward. "This is so different from my life."

"But it doesn't make it wrong. The party is what you make of it. Stuff goes on that may not be your thing, but it doesn't mean you won't have a great time hanging with Emily or Rebecca. Don't let your fears create walls or define you."

Breanna accepts the folder and I'm not sure I like the way she studies me. "Have you tried living up to that advice?"

A punch straight to my heart, and the fucked-up thing? I don't know why her words hurt. "This place doesn't scare me."

"I'm not sure about that. I think your demons haunt you wherever you go."

My mother's ghost haunts me like a second layer of skin. I strive for numb within the chaos of my emotions, but the emotions win every time. Breanna's right, it doesn't matter where I'm at—home, the clubhouse, Olivia's, even my bike—

my mother's death claws at me like an evil spirit bound to rip through my skin so it can gain possession.

"You really do trust me," Breanna says in a quiet voice.

"Yeah."

Breanna opens the folder and I lose her the moment she spots the crossword code. Her eyes narrow and dart and her expression completely smooths out. She lays the bylaws next to the code and her eyes dance between the two pages. Her fingers flitter in the air as if she's writing on a chalkboard. If I didn't know better, I'd guess she's in a trance.

It's because of those demons she mentioned that I'm permitting her to have a crack at the code again. If she has a chance of finding my answers, then I have a shot at doing what the club is desperate for me to do—to let go of Mom and finally trust them.

"It's a cipher," she says to herself. "A cipher. So how does the key go into the lock?"

Her fingers skim over the bylaws and she flinches, reminiscent of the day she solved the puzzle in class. My muscles tighten and nausea spins through my gut. What if this has nothing to do with Mom? What if this is old or new bullshit between the Terror and the Riot and I'm dragging Breanna into a world that will make her a target?

The need to protect her bulldozes through my veins. I can't lose her. Losing Breanna is not an option. My hand flicks out to seize the paper. "I change my mind—"

She's faster than me and is on her feet and across the room. Breanna grabs a pencil and stabs holes into the code—taking out the letters and numbers that are supposed to contain the answers. It's like her mind has fractured.

"What are you doing?" I demand.

She ignores me, tearing at the letters and numbers in such

methodical movements that I'm not sure she's aware of anything beyond her thoughts.

"Breanna!" I shout, but she rips out the last number and then slides the paper she mutilated over the bylaws. My world stills, but Breanna tears another piece of paper from the folder and begins to write.

A slow pulse forms in my brain. Letters poke out through the bylaws and the first word is a name. All the years of twisting comes to a head—it's my mother's name. It's Layla.

The first code, the one that caused me to forbid Breanna to continue, said to consider this our warning shot.

"Razor," Breanna says as if she's attempting to talk me off a ledge. "Look at me."

I can't. I can focus only on my mother's name. In the detective's file, that code was the first and the one containing my mother's name was the second. The first code a warning—the second one…

"Razor," she says again. "You don't know for sure what it means."

Yeah, I really fucking do know. Anger reverberates between my muscles and bones. The Riot killed my mother and everyone in this club fucking knew. Everyone but me.

I round for the door, feeling like a freight train. My fists ball at my sides. The answers are coming, even if it means beating the hell out of someone.

Breanna's voice calls behind me, but it's like she's on the opposite end of a long tunnel. She sure as shit is shouting, but there's a vibration in my brain driving me now. The storm within me has been building for years and I'm seconds away from destructive landfall.

Oz bolts from the kitchen, clutching my biceps, shouting, but I don't hear any words. Just a loud buzz, just my brain cracking in half. He's pulling on my arm, but I'm a bull going for the target. My hand slams into the screen door and I'm on the front porch.

Chevy had been laughing, but his face falls. He plants his feet and tosses out his arms in an attempt to slow me down. Another yank back and it's Oz still pulling on my arm. The buzzing in my brain gets louder, Oz and Chevy are in my space, but they can't halt my momentum.

The guys from the board are at a smaller bonfire near the tree line. They're laughing. Talking shit. Enjoying the fact that they've tried to play with my life. Yelling. Loud shouts. It's near me, but the chaos controlling me makes it incoherent.

Each man glances up and, like Chevy, they stare at me like I've lost my mind. I have. I've gone fucking crazy. Pigpen's on the move. His hands are a stop sign and Eli's hustling fast to the left, his mouth spewing something, but I'm tracking my father.

He tosses down his beer and has the nerve to act like he's concerned.

"You can't hit a brother! You can't hit a brother!" It's Oz and Chevy. They're tackling me. Reminding me of a club rule. Fuck the club because the club has fucked me over.

I'm fighting them like I'm the Colts' offense, but when I gain no ground, I look my father straight in the eye. "The Riot killed her. The Riot fucking murdered my mother!"

It's silence. A stillness that causes a cold chill to slither down my spine. The buzzing is gone and my two best friends are no longer battling me, but curling their fingers into my arms as if to hold all three of us up.

"All those years." A wave of hurt crashes into me. "I blamed myself. I carried her death like a cross, and this club, this *family*, let me slowly die because I wasn't worthy of the *truth*."

"Who told you?" Anger replaces my father's shock. "Did you visit the detective?"

Oz and Chevy release me as they also regard me like I'm capable of that type of betrayal. "That's what you think of me, isn't it? Disloyal?"

"How else?" Dad shouts.

"Enough!" Cyrus expects compliance. "This isn't the time or the place."

"There's never a time or a place!" I yell. "We're doing this now!"

Cyrus steps in front of me and he's not the man I've claimed as a surrogate grandfather but the badass biker I've seen take men down in a brawl. "Either you take your girl home or I have someone do it for you. Seventeen and here this time of night is nonnegotiable."

His eyes sway to beyond my shoulder and my stomach knots. Breanna. Fuck me, I forgot about Breanna. On the front porch steps, Emily has an arm around Breanna's shoulders and the two prospects assigned to Emily's protection have created a barrier at the bottom of the steps. I abandoned her, just like I promised I wouldn't.

I swing my glare back at my father. "There was a code in the detective's file. Two of them. I took pictures."

There's a muttered curse behind me as they solve the puzzle of how I figured it out.

"I never talked to the detective again. Doing it would have made life easier, but I'm loyal." I shove the words like a knife into his heart. "Nice to know what everyone thinks of me."

As I walk for my girl, Eli captures my arm and exerts enough force that I stop because I'm too fucking exhausted to throw a punch. "What?"

"There are moving parts to this problem. Shit you can't

begin to comprehend. You get her home, then you come back here. You're still a part of this club and that is a fucking order."

Am I still a part of this club? Was this cut mine to begin with? Was it nothing more than a pity offering from men who don't respect me?

Eli releases me, and as I continue toward Breanna, I remember what she's said about her family, about how happiness in numbers is an illusion. Maybe she's right. Maybe no matter how much faith we try to put into the idea of family, in the end, we're fucked.

True words!

RAZOR

I FLY INTO the open space near the clubhouse going double what I normally do. Kerosene's running in my veins and I'm thirty seconds away from someone striking a match.

Breanna appeared lost when I dropped her off. She hugged me, I hugged her and it was difficult to let her go and return to this nest of liars. My fists are aching to punch someone for this entire damn day. Everything's a fucking mess and I don't know how to stem the bleeding from the multiple hits I've taken.

The party that was supposed to be for me is out of control, just like I am on the inside. I stalk through the crowd and a couple guys call my name, wondering where I've been, and one girl has the nerve to slip in front of me like I'll skid to a halt because she's wearing next to nothing. But I'm on the warpath, stopping for no one.

I'm up the stairs and don't bother knocking as I enter the boardroom. There had been conversation, but it goes silent when the door shuts behind me. All of them are here, all of them seated at the long wooden table, and they all look at me. Each and every member of the board including Cyrus, Eli, Pigpen and my father.

Pigpen hooks his foot around the metal folding chair Eli sat in weeks before and it scrapes against the tiles. The floor beneath me pulses with the beat of the turned-up bass from the music downstairs. My steps fall in time with the rhythm. I take the seat, and this time it's not Eli sitting across from me, but my father.

We're eye to eye. His green ones peer into Mom's blue ones. There're a million questions in my head. A heart full of anger, rage that belongs to a man, but there are times when I'm before my father that a part of me feels like I'm ten.

A cramping in my gut.

Ten.

Years have passed. My body has aged. Knowledge has been gained, but a piece of my soul has remained frozen.

The board's right—I've never moved past Mom.

"Did you love her?" I ask.

Dad jolts as if the question shocks him.

"You fought," I continue. "A lot. So tell me if you fucking loved her."

Dad rests his arms on the table and leans toward me. "I loved her more than I loved anything else in my life. You're my son, and you've gone through hell, but ever question my love for her again and I'll lay you out."

I nod and on the outside I'm still as stone, but that ten-year-old boy on the inside collapses in tears. Lots of tears. Tears that I have never fucking shed.

"I was on the phone with her while they chased her," he says. "I listened to her as she was begging for me to help. I listened as she understood we weren't going to get there fast enough and I listened as she told me that she loved me and you more than she loved her own life. Did I love her? Yeah, I loved her and I had to listen helplessly as the woman I loved died."

I drop my head into my hands and wetness burns my eyes. She loved me. My mother loved me.

"Your mother drew the Riot away," says Cyrus in a quiet voice that's too sorrowful for the loud noises seeping in from below. "When she came out of work, she found the code stuck under her windshield and she knew the Riot was near. She didn't know what it meant, but she knew it was bad. She called your father, he told her to get to the clubhouse, but she refused to go there."

"Why?" My voice comes out cracked.

There's silence in the room, and when I glance up, most everyone is focused on the table, but Dad's watching me. "Things were building up to bad with the Riot. It's why your mom and I fought. Same shit that had gone down with the Riot years before was happening again and she was scared for me."

Because years ago, Dad almost died in the fight for Emily's safety. Dim memories of hushed hospital rooms and the man I believed invincible in a bed. Mom in tears by his side, Olivia whispering to me that he was strong and me clinging to Cyrus's hand like if I let go I would tumble down a dark hole.

"Olivia was watching you and your mother refused to draw them anywhere near you, which meant she wouldn't come anywhere near the clubhouse."

It's too much. Too fucking much and I breathe in but the air doesn't reach my lungs. "Did she know about the code?"

"Yes and no," Dad answers. "She saw a different piece of code once in my belongings. Your mom was quick. Realized by my reaction when I saw it in her hands it was related to the Riot, but didn't know much else. This was that messed-up period after Eli was released from prison. The Riot was pissed he got out on parole and they wanted to renege on the deal made to keep peace between our clubs. They demanded we hand over Eli. We told them to go fuck themselves. So we began negotiating. Communicating through the code and short meetings."

"Why code?" I ask.

"Law enforcement has always been after them," Eli explains. "Made them paranoid. They didn't like putting anything in writing. Face-to-face meetings were risky for both sides—too many pissed-off people with guns. We first used the code when they found out Meg was pregnant with Emily. She knew all their different ways of translating the code. When the stakes between our clubs were being raised and they felt that law enforcement was on the edge of cracking the code we were using, they stole a copy of our bylaws, sent the code to Meg, and she knew how to decipher it. That's how we've always communicated with them. The code worked. Kept our people safe while we tried to keep the Riot calm."

"Eventually," Dad adds, picking up the thread, "when it was clear we weren't handing Eli over to them, they sent the list."

Cyrus slides a piece of paper in front of me and I recognize my father's handwriting. Dad must have been the one to translate the Riot's message. The name at the top is my mother's. The next Olivia's, and it goes down the line of the wives of club members. Anger ripples through me. "They were willing to go after women?"

Eli's seat creaks when he adjusts. His legs are out straight, his arms crossed over his chest, and it's one of the rare times he won't make eye contact. "When holy hell broke out over Emily and her mom before I went to prison, the Riot went after club members. After I lost custody of Emily when I went to prison, they decided to make it personal."

My hand slams on the table. "Why the fuck didn't you take the warning shot seriously? I saw the message. Breanna broke it. They warned you this was coming."

He lifts his dark eyes and the regret swimming in them smacks me in the stomach. "Both codes came together and we got it five minutes before your mother called. We didn't even have it completely deciphered before your mother was being tailed out of the parking lot."

"Why did they leave the code with Mom? She wasn't Terror."

The room falls silent and all eyes are on Dad. Finally, he speaks. "They wanted me to find it. Guess they figured she'd call, figured I would find it in her car if they abducted her, or if they did mean for her to go over the bridge, I guess they thought I'd find it in the aftermath. The Riot wanted me to know that I couldn't save the woman I loved from them. They wanted to show that they were in control, that they held the power."

"Razor," Eli says, "I would have handed myself over on a damned platter for your mother, but I was never given the chance. Your mother was the warning shot."

My body sways as if I've been sucked into an undertow. My mother never had a chance. She never had a fucking chance and she drove away from help to save me. My lips turn down and it's hard as hell to ignore the raw ache in my throat. "Was she forced off or did she go over to save herself?"

Dad and Eli shrug their shoulders to show that they're both haunted by the unknown.

"She died on impact," Eli says. "Your dad stayed at the clubhouse talking with her while the rest of us tore off to try to catch up. She told your dad that they were coming up beside her. Our best guess is that they tried to cut her off at the bridge to force her out of the car and that's when she went over. Maybe she lost control of the car. Maybe she saw that as her best chance at life. I'm sorry, but we don't know."

Fear. My mother's last emotion was fear. My fingers tunnel in my hair and I pull, hoping the physical pain can somehow wipe this internal agony away. "Why not tell me? Why lie to me about how she died?"

"You were ten," Dad says like he's experiencing the same pain. "When I walked in Olivia's house with your mother's blood on my hands, I went down the hallway and found you on that bed with your friends and with your arm slung over that dog. You looked peaceful. I couldn't wake you and look you in the eye and tell you that I fucking failed you. That your mother died because some asshole club ran her off the road and I failed to protect her."

I thrust back the seat so that I'm no longer at the table and settle my elbows on my legs. My foot begins to bounce on the floor as the sadness and anger within me builds to the brink of explosion. "But I'm not ten anymore. I haven't been ten for a long time."

"No, son, you haven't, but there were eight other names on that list and we had to make sure no one would suffer the same fate as your mother. We did what needed to be done and we secured everyone's safety. Olivia, Rebecca—the two women you loved the most after your mother would have been next."

It's not an answer and this insanity that has always crawled along my skin demands the truth. "I spent eight years of my life thinking she left me on purpose. Eight years of thinking I wasn't enough."

"We didn't know that's what you thought. We—"

"Bullshit," I shout. "That's fucking bullshit, and you know it. Why didn't you tell me?"

Dad collapses back in his seat. "Because I promised not to."

"Because the board told you not to?" I demand.

A muscle in his jaw jerks and his eyes pierce me. "Because the last words your mother said to me were to make sure you never joined the club, and if I couldn't promise her that, that I never tell you what happened, because she knew me."

He pounds his hand to his chest. "She knew how broken I was on the inside. She knew how fucking crazy I'd become after her death, and she didn't want those demons inside you. She knew what I would do if she died, and she sure as hell didn't want you to grow up and become the dead man I am. She begged me before she went off that bridge to make sure this war did not become generational. You and I both know that if I told you, that if you grew up knowing that the Riot was responsible for your mother's death, this entire club would be at war. She knew that when you became old enough, you would be leading the charge."

"It's too late." All the anger, all the pain pours out. "I'm already dead. There's nothing inside me. The first time someone told me she chose death over life, I died and it's too damned late for me now."

"That's not true." Dad's expression turns into a plea. "Maybe it was, but I've been watching you. Over the past few weeks it's like seeing you reborn. The boy who loved his mother. The boy who laughed when his mother laughed, I've seen him."

I'm shaking my head. "It's not me. It's being around Breanna. She loves me, but I'm still dying." Every second of every day, I'm still withering.

"This girl may love you, but you had to alter something inside you for the changes we're seeing. Someone's love can only hold together broken pieces for so long. The glue, that's you—and I've been witnessing you piece yourself back together."

It sure as hell doesn't feel like I'm on the mend. "You're wrong."

"I'm not, because I've loved you and so have half the people in this club and we've never been enough. She might love you, but you're happy because you're loving her back."

"I've loved you back."

"You haven't," he says with finality. "Not fully. You can't fully love someone unless you trust them and you have never trusted any of us."

He leaves it unsaid that I somehow found a way to trust Breanna, but not them. It's like I'm on a forsaken merry-go-round. The ride starts. The ride stops. We never go anywhere but in circles. I slump forward, too heavy to hold myself up. Too heavy to continue to shoulder all the shit that constantly tears me apart. "She's never lied to me."

"You're the same as me. We keep our promises. I made a promise to your mother and I love her enough to keep it."

"Even if it hurt me?"

Dad contemplates the question. "Maybe I agreed with her. Maybe I decided I wanted you to grow up in peace. Maybe I couldn't stomach watching you fall into a pit of vipers. Maybe I'm the complete bastard you think me to be."

Everything that's been said whirls in my brain and the insanity I've fought for so long pulses as it longs to be released. "Did whoever send Mom over that bridge—did he pay for his sins?"

The atmosphere practically crackles with pissed-off energy. I'm staring Dad down. He's doing the same to me. I over-pronounce my words so there's no mistaking my thoughts on his efforts to prevent a generational war. "Was there justice for my mother's death?"

Dad angles forward on the table and his low voice rumbles along the wood to me. "Know that trust I was talking about?"

I nod.

"You will show it to me and to this club before you ever get that answer. Now the question is on you, son. Can you trust your brothers to have taken care of this, or are you going to do what you've done time and time again and take matters into your own hands, even if it means blowing this club to hell in the process?"

Breanna

THROUGH THE PROPPED-OPEN back door to the Barrel of Fun, the cool autumn breeze rushes through the trees and a waterfall of vibrant leaves falls to the ground. My eyes and lungs burn from the harsh cleaning products infecting the air. The ice cream shop officially closed last night and today I'm making extra cash by preparing it for the winter.

My boss hacks as the bleach in the bucket sloshes over the sides. I prop my mop on the wall and jack my thumb toward the back door. He nods. We both quit talking an hour ago. Either to prevent ourselves from inhaling more poison than we should or because we both lost the ability to speak.

I seriously need to find a new job.

I step outside and the intake of clean oxygen is like a pillow for my lungs. The stray pieces of hair that had escaped the bun stick to my sweaty face and I peel my sweatshirt off my skin in an attempt to cool down. As much as today's manual labor has been constant, it hasn't been enough to ease my concern for Razor. I'm not sure anything will ever erase the memory of how he looked so absolutely broken.

My boss coughs again and I head for the thick trees. In the distance, a car honks and a semitruck rumbles past on the road out front. My cell never vibrated in my pocket, but I pull it out anyway, hoping for a message from Razor. But like last night, there's nothing.

> Me: I've been thinking of you. I'm here if you need to talk or not talk. Either way, I

Razor and I have never said certain words aloud. We've definitely expressed our emotions physically and in the calm silences in between those precious kisses and touches. We've also referenced how we feel about each other, but we've never fully admitted it.

I bite my bottom lip. In my daydreams as a child, I imagined a guy saying it first, but I care so much about Razor that he needs this—especially since his world has been torn apart.

> Me: Either way, I love you.

The edges of my mouth lift when I see the words on the screen. I do love him and it's not as scary to confess as I thought. In fact, it feels natural.

> Razor: I cut out on my bike last night to clear my head. I'm in Tennessee, but I'm heading back now. Straight to you. I want to hear those words out of your mouth.

The smile on my face grows. He's coming home to me.
Another vibration. Razor: I love you too.
Butterflies. A million gorgeous butterflies. My fingers are

flying across the screen and not keeping up with the gazillion thoughts in my head and then my phone is gone.

Gone.

Ripped from my fingers, and when my head snaps up, a hand goes to my throat and my back slams into a tree. The air rushes from my body as two soulless eyes bore into mine. It's Kyle and he's gone insane.

Panic floods my system. No air in, no sound out, nothing. Dizzying thoughts overwhelm me as the pressure on my throat nears painful. He's killing me. Kyle is killing me.

My fingers scramble for my neck, claw at the stranglehold. My feet kick and, with a flick of his arm, pain shoots into my spine as he rams me against the tree again. A flash of black as consciousness is on the verge of being lost and I fight to keep my eyes open.

"Did you and Razor honestly think you could play me?"

White dots mar my vision and my lungs hurt. I crane my neck, desperate for air, and only a pathetic squeak erupts from my mouth as he pushes on my body again.

Kyle leans forward and his breath is hot on my ear. I flinch at the way his mouth moves against my skin. "We found how your boy was hacking us, and for that you are going to pay."

The pressure on my neck releases, a gasp of air from my body, and I drop to the ground. Coughing, choking, my hands landing where he was crushing my bones.

Kyle paces in front of me. A short loop and his eyes are on me. "The day you asked to work with me instead of against me. You used me. You helped him get into my phone."

Tears well up in my eyes and I throw my head back to yell, but no sound escapes.

"He has four of us, but not all of us, and you tell that asshole that the one he can't find, he won't. He's the one that figured out we were hacked. He's the one that noticed we were connecting to a dummy server. I don't know what the hell Razor was planning on doing, but I'm back in control of this game. I want my damned papers, Breanna. I want the first one on Friday and I expect perfection."

He crouches in front of me. "And in case you're wondering how far I'm willing to take this, I left a present for your parents at your home. Manila envelope. Your mom's and dad's names on the front. I dropped it off, rang the doorbell, then watched from across the street as your mom answered and picked it up. In case you're wondering, inside was the photo. Fucking push me again and that photo will be up on Bragger before you can say my name."

Kyle stands, throws my phone at my feet, then a piece of paper drifts from his hands. It's the picture of me and Razor and it's spelling my demise.

I've been banished to my room, but I'm not sure what the consequences will be if I leave. They've already told me I'm forbidden to set foot outside the house, forbidden to talk to anyone on the phone, forbidden to do anything more than breathe.

When I walked in from work, my parents confiscated my cell. My father then grew angry red when what they thought was my password didn't work and I refused to give them the real one. Razor's codes are on my phone. So is the picture of me and him together at Shamrock's and the ones of me drinking. They've seen the picture of me and Razor, but somehow for them to find it on me would be worse.

Funny how I was terrified of them seeing that photo and being disappointed in me. Now I'm scared they'll see that photo and judge Razor. I'm holding out hope my parents will calm down and grant him a chance.

It's one in the morning and my parents are fighting. So loud I can decipher most of what they say from my bedroom. Mom's blaming Dad for being busy at work, Dad's blaming Mom for ignoring me when I went to her for advice and Elsie's crying in her room.

Neither of them seem to hear her or care.

Part of me had been praying Razor would show under the streetlamp on his motorcycle, beckoning me to climb down so we could run away. It hasn't happened and it won't.

My door creaks when I open it, and across the hallway, Clara, Joshua and Liam are gathered on Joshua's bed. They stop their intense whispers and study me as if I'm a stranger. In the end, I guess I am. It's never been a secret that I'm the outsider.

"Mom told you to stay in your room." Clara's home on break and I wish she would get a life like my two oldest siblings and never return. "Did you hear what I said?"

Clara reminds me of a dog nipping at another's heels to force them back in line. She's always been snapping at me and I've always turned tail and fled, but I'm not her submissive puppy anymore.

"Elsie's crying," I say.

Her sobs grow louder and so does Mom's voice. "...do you expect of me? I can't handle all of this on my own! My job is important, too..."

"Do you think acting perfect is going to make them like you again?" Clara smirks as if her words were sharp enough to draw blood.

"You won, Clara. They hate me. Everyone in this family

hates me. If you don't mind, I'm going to let you continue your gloating party while I take care of Elsie."

She rolls her eyes and she calls out, "You're getting what you deserve."

"You never know when to stop, do you?" Joshua reprimands, and I'm not sure if he was talking to me or Clara and I don't care.

Elsie's My Little Pony bedsheets are twisted around her legs, and her nightshirt, which is actually Liam's old T-shirt, dangles off her shoulder. The night-light plugged in on the wall near her bed casts a faint glow over my youngest sibling. Her face is red, her eyes swollen. Tear tracks mark her face.

She lifts her arms in the air, and when I'm within jumping distance, she launches herself at me and buries her head in the crook of my neck. Hot wet drops land on my skin and I close my eyes as I hug the little girl I wanted desperately to evade months ago.

I sit on her bed and she keeps herself curled around me, but the sounds of despair have ceased. Across the room, Zac watches me from the bottom bunk, Paul from the top. Both of them peek out from under their covers like owls terrified to wander from the safety of their nest.

"Is it true?" Paul asks. "Are you dating someone from the Reign of Terror?"

Elsie throws her fears into the mix. "Are Mommy and Daddy going to be mad at you forever?"

"Are they going to make you leave?" asks Zac.

Elsie's dark eyes fill up again and her lower lip trembles. "I don't want you to go."

More questions pour from them about Razor and my parents and leaving and then the light flicks on. Liam and Joshua stride in and Clara hangs back to cock a hip against the door frame. From downstairs, Dad yells something about how Mom never has enough time for him and Mom shouts back asking why she should spend time with someone who doesn't acknowledge her existence or worth.

I smooth back Elsie's hair from her hot, sweaty face and consider laying my palms over her ears until the argument is over. Joshua picks up a pillow and swats Zac with it until he allows him room to sit and Liam rests his back against the frame of the bunks.

"You should be at work," I say to Liam.

He hooks his thumbs into his jeans. "Getting a text telling me that there's a picture of my little sister making out with a guy from the Terror at a bar changed my plans."

"We didn't do anything that night." The making-out portion had come much later. "And Thomas is more than a member of the Reign of Terror." Using Razor's real name feels like a better strategy than his road name.

Joshua's eyes narrow into slits. "They're killers."

"You don't know that. You don't know anything about them other than what people say."

"Is it true?" Liam barks, and I rub my hand along Elsie's back when she shudders. "Did you tell Mom and Dad you're in love with this bastard?"

Anger tightens my muscles. "His name is Thomas, and yes, I am in love with him. He's in love with me, and if you'd give him a shot, you'd find out what a great guy he is."

Liam throws out his arms. "He carries a gun!"

"So what if he does? He's a million times better than half of the people at school!"

He bangs the back of his head against the bunks so hard that the frame shakes. "Jesus, Bre, you're too smart to be brainwashed. You're too smart for any of this, but evidently you're having a brain lapse and it's time for you to get your head out of your ass!"

"What is that supposed to mean?"

"You gotta break up with him." Joshua squishes Zac's pillow in his hands. "One—he's dangerous. Two—the people he's around are lethal."

"I'm not going to break up with him." I press my lips to Elsie's forehead when she sniffs like she's going to start crying again. "I'll introduce him to Mom and Dad. They'll see how great he is and how smart he is and—"

"Mom and Dad are sending you away." Liam cuts me off and the breath is knocked out of my body.

"What?"

"The private school. The one you were accepted to. I'm here because they called me over to see if I would move home so I can pick up the slack that will be left when you leave."

It's what I wanted. Months ago. My mouth gapes, and like when Kyle had tried to squeeze the life out of me earlier, no sound leaks out. If Liam had told me this in August, I possibly would have leaped into his arms and cried like a newborn, but now I'm encased in cold numbness.

The bunk squeaks when Paul hops out of the top and scurries to Elsie's bed. He tucks a pillow to his chest and doesn't look at anyone. A few seconds later, Zac bolts over the invisible line that has always separated me from everyone else.

Zac encircles his arms around my waist as Elsie tightens her hold on my neck. I'm leaving them. I glance around the room. Joshua has his head down and Liam's staring at the ceiling as if we told him of an impending death.

"What did you tell them?" I whisper.

"I told them I'd do it. I'll do anything to keep you safe."

My mouth feels like a desert and it's difficult to breathe. "What if I don't want to go?"

Liam meets my eyes. "It doesn't matter what you want. The decision's already been made. You're leaving this week."

RAZOR

WE NEED TO TALK about Kyle as soon as you get back. That was the last text Breanna sent before I hauled ass to Snowflake.

Sitting on my motorcycle in the student parking lot, I can hear the time bomb ticking in my brain. There was no other contact from her. No other text, no voice mail. Kyle did something to shake Breanna and each second of silence from her is causing my mood to become deadly.

A growl of motorcycles and two bikes from a pack of Reign of Terror driving past the school break off and turn in to the parking lot. Only one wears a three-piece patch and, from his bike, I can tell it's Oz. Chevy rides beside him. They fly into the empty spot beside me and I do little more than glance at them as they dismount. Where the hell is Breanna?

"Where have you been?" says Chevy. "No one's heard shit from you since Friday."

No, they haven't, but I can't deal with the club. Breanna's best friend, Addison, slips out of the passenger side of a car and her gaze hits mine. The wires that are crossed inside me cause the ticking to speed up. Everything is wrong.

"Razor!" Oz steps in front of me. "What's going on?"

I push past Oz and he easily gives as I stalk toward Addison. She waits for me and the lone sign that she's nervous is how she adjusts the backpack she carries on one shoulder.

"Addison!" her other friend chides as she looks at me as if I'm the devil bent on stealing their souls. "Let's go."

"Go on without me. Thomas and I need to talk." Addison rips her glare from me to behind me, and because we have always backed each other up, I have no doubt Chevy and Oz are coming up on my six.

Her friend leaves and I don't waste time. "Where is she?"

"Home. Reagan and I pulled in to pick her up this morning and her older brother Liam came out and told us she's not going to school."

An edge of worry shakes my frame. "Is she sick?"

"He said she's not going to school anymore. Breanna's parents are sending her away." The perfect cheerleader leans into me like she's the Riot willing to go to war. "I'm assuming they found out about you, and if you're the reason why I'm losing my best friend, I'm going to make sure you pay."

She wants a piece of me, she can have it, but not now, not until I know how deep this hole goes. "Have you talked with her?"

Addison grimaces like I struck her, but she's quick to recover. "I was allowed to hug her goodbye. Thirty seconds. I've been her best friend for years and because of you I got thirty seconds and you know what she told me to tell you? That the warning shot was sent. Not sure what that means, but I hope it means you'll rot in hell."

My entire body straightens as pissed-off energy rolls off me in waves. "Did she say anything? About Kyle? About a picture?"

Addison's head ticks back. "No, but what do you mean Kyle and a picture? Is Breanna in trouble? Is—"

No time. The seconds are counting down in rapid succession. The explosion's imminent and Kyle will be part of the damage. I'm through the crowd, scanning faces, and there's footsteps behind me, and unlike on Friday, they aren't trying to stop me, but they're moving with me as if we're a synchronized machine.

The son of a bitch is by his car, chatting with a freshman girl who believes he's God.

"Get her away," I growl, and Chevy maneuvers past me, catching the arm of the freshman and navigating her away with a smile and a daisy popping out of thin air. She's confused and amused, and she's officially out of the impact zone.

Like the moron he is, Kyle's dumbfounded as he regards Chevy's show and he doesn't see my fist until it makes contact with his face. A smack of flesh against flesh and Kyle falls sideways into the hood of his car.

Before he can recover, I grab him by the lapels of his football jacket and drag him to his feet. "You're a fucking dead man."

His eyes widen with fear, but his lips twitch like he's attempting to laugh. "Only sent the picture to her parents, but if she doesn't write that paper, it's going live." He puts his hands over my wrists. "I'm in control of this game now. We found the back door you placed on our phones and we won't be falling for your shit anymore. Because you care for her, you won't do a thing to me. If you do, I'll make sure everyone knows that she's your whore."

I go cold on the inside and the world tilts. He's dead. The guy in front of me is inhaling air, but he's as good as dead.

My fingers curl tighter, but there're hands on my shoulders.

The power of horses pulling me away and Chevy's in my face. "Not now. We'll take care of this, but not now."

Kyle is ripped from my grasp and the world is in fast-forward as the pieces on the board shift to his side. I promised Breanna I could save her from this. I promised I would protect her. Like everything else in life, it's completely fucked-up.

The asshole works his jaw. "I'm going to the office to get your ass kicked out over this. Have fun working on your GED, asshole."

My gut cramps and I circle to find Oz and Chevy acting as if they're ready to catch me when I fall.

"What's going down, brother?" Oz asks.

The world grows hazy on the edges, but my bike becomes clearer as I walk toward it. I mount it and Oz is in front of me with his arms stretched out wide. "What's going on?"

"Find me Pigpen," I say. "He's the only one that can help me."

Oz yanks out his phone and Chevy pats Oz's arm as the two of them head for their bikes. My motorcycle grumbles beneath me and I tear out of the parking lot as if I'm being chased by the flames of hell.

Breanna

MOM WENT TO WORK and so did Dad. Elsie, Zac, Paul and Joshua are off to school. Clara and Liam have been tasked with babysitting me, but like they did when I was younger, they suck at it and I'm sitting on the front porch.

I used to love autumn. The sound of the wind chimes tingling as the northern wind gently pushes through to the south. The way the leaves float to the ground and the constant chirping of crickets.

In essence, fall is the signal of everything dying, but I love how the world seems more vivid then. But today, I don't enjoy the subtle warmth of the air or the radiance of the leaves. I feel only empty and alone.

I overheard Mom and Dad this morning and Dad mumbled something about how he never thought I'd be a Terror whore. I lower my head as my heart hurts. He believes I'm a whore.

The front door opens and Clara yells, "She's out here sulking." Then to me, savoring her power trip, "We didn't give you permission to leave the house."

They didn't. "Why do you hate me?"

I expect myriad answers and excuses, but it's the silence that surprises me enough to glance over my shoulder.

"I don't hate you," she says quietly.

"Yes, you do."

Clara nibbles on her top lip, then closes the front door as she struts out. "I hate how everything comes easy for you, so sue me for enjoying something being hard for you for once."

I laugh and then laugh harder when I realize how crazy I sound. "You're mistaken on the easy."

She snorts and leans on the porch railing. "You have no idea what hard is. Do you know what it has been like to be your older sister? Everyone's like *Look how smart Breanna is, Why can't you be more like her?* and then there's my favorite pitied comment of *Poor Clara, everything will always be a struggle for the poor dear because she's stupid.*"

I flinch. "You're not stupid. You're as smart as I am. In fact, you're smarter—"

"Save it," she spits. "Mom and Dad have been giving me the pep talk for years. You know what the world looks like to me? Chaos. My mind tries to merge letters together, it starts to do math problems from two years ago. I can't focus. Not like you. I'll never be you."

For years, this is the same conversation we've had. That somehow I'm responsible for her misery and I'm sick and tired of the guilt. "I'd switch brains with you if I could."

She chokes on a laugh. "Sure you would."

My throat runs dry and I swallow, but it doesn't help. "I don't sleep."

"What?"

"I don't sleep. In fact, I don't remember sleeping. I mean, I do and it's enough to get by on, but it's hard to fall asleep, and when I wake up, I can't go back because my mind starts working on things, but I didn't want you and Nora to know, so I would lie in bed for hours counting the plastered dots on the ceiling. There are four hundred and thirty-eight over my bed."

Clara sleeps. It's one thing she has been able to do. Her forehead wrinkles, but she quickly recovers from her shock. "So there's one drawback for you."

There is and there're so many others. "I'm like you…more than you know. When I'm not working on something, it's like a painful itch I can't reach. Sometimes my head hurts when I can't find the logic in the every day. There's a throb in the front of my head and it shifts to my temples and then I'll feel like I need to vomit because I don't understand how it doesn't make sense. And if none of that was annoying enough, I would freaking rip off my arms if, for thirty seconds, I could fit in with someone, somewhere." Like I have with Razor.

I briefly close my eyes as all of the taunts from my past pound me like a wave. "At school. At work. At home. With you. All I've ever wanted was to be a part of this stinking family, but all you have ever done is made me out to be the freak show and maybe I am. Maybe I am the weird girl who no one will ever like, but at least my family should love me. At least somewhere in the deep recesses of your soul you should like me."

A knot forms that cuts off my breathing. My eyes water and I try to blink the tears away, but more appear in the corners.

"Bre…" Clara starts but then stops.

"Home is supposed to be safe. Home is supposed to be the one place you can go and know that the horrible things people say to you won't be said to you there. It should be that place that forms a protective shield and it's okay to be quirky and messed up and…and…accepted."

Yes, I stood up in seventh grade and I explained how I made an operating telegraph. I smiled as I explained my experiment. I stumbled over my words as I attempted to chase the thoughts in my mind, and I even experienced a slight high when I saw several classmates' faces light up when they saw it truly worked.

My heart sinks when I recall the first insult and then nausea strikes me in the stomach when I recall the laughter. But if it's the truth that is to be told, it's when I walked into the house to find Clara crying alone in the kitchen over her ACT score that my life changed.

"You'll score higher than me. You could take it now and score higher than me. I know the answers. Everyone knows that I know the answers, but I can't focus. I lose my focus. I can remember all these things and it makes you smart and me stupid. Everyone is always better. Everyone knows that you're better. And I'm tired. I'm so tired of never measuring up."

It wasn't her words that shredded me, it was Clara hovering over the kitchen sink. It was her wrist poised over the basin. It was the knife that was being held at her wrist.

I loved her. Even though she blamed me. She was my older sister and I loved her.

Clara had looked over at me with wide eyes and she pleaded. Pleaded so much that it appeared her legs were about to give. *"Can you try to not be you? Can you just try to be less?"* She choked on the sobs and red-hot tears began to flow over my face as they ran over hers. *"Maybe then I can keep up. Maybe if you pretend to be less, it won't be so bad."*

And then she threatened to go through with killing herself if I told anyone what I saw and her burden became my burden. Her pain was my pain.

My head falls into my hands and the same tears I cried that

day threaten to spill over now. "I tried, Clara. I tried to be less. I tried to be quiet and to be someone else and I'm sorry it wasn't enough for you, but I can't do this anymore. I did what you asked. I never told anyone what you were going to do. I never told anyone how I spent months terrified I'd come home and find you dead and I never told anyone that the reason I stopped being me was that you asked, but I can't do this anymore because I'm dying. I can't continue to kill myself in order to save you."

When I lift my head, Clara's completely pale and she holds on to her elbows like she's about to break. She gently rocks back and forth. "I didn't know that still haunted you."

Every second of every day. "There are some things I wish I could forget, but, like you, I'm cursed."

A rumble of a motorcycle and I stand. Razor pulls in front of my house, and when his gaze meets mine, I know the answer to his silent question.

Clara steps toward me. "No, Bre."

Unfortunately for her... "This isn't your decision to make."

RAZOR

BREANNA GLANCES AROUND my house. It's the first time I've brought a girl home. This moment's huge, and I'd share how much this means to me, but we don't have time for my emotions. We have problems.

"You have a nice home." By her slight grin, I can tell she means it.

"It's small." But pride leaks out. I could never be ashamed of the place Mom loved.

"Bigger isn't better." It's a reference to her family, and I hate the sadness in her eyes.

I snag her hand and draw her forward. "Want to see my room?"

Breanna blushes as she threads her fingers with mine. I flip on the light, and Breanna takes in the narrow room with the Reign of Terror banner, the dresser and the mirror hanging over it. She touches the pictures taped on the wall. Most of them are of me, Chevy, Oz and Violet in various stages of life. There's two of me and Dad and at the top is one of me and Mom.

"She didn't commit suicide," she says.

It's a mixture of relief and anger. "No." I'm grateful that Breanna doesn't press for more, because she already knows more than she should.

"The code helped?" she asks.

"Yeah." A sickening sensation crawls along my insides. "It helped." And I haven't helped her. "This stuff with Kyle—we're going to figure it out."

Breanna's pursing her lips like she's about to disagree when the sound of a motorcycle gains our attention. She twists her fingers in her hair and her eyes shoot to the closet as if she's searching for a hiding place. "Am I allowed to be here? Holy crap, you're cutting school. Your dad is going to freak. I did not mean to get you in trouble."

I slip into her personal space, circle an arm around her waist and kiss the next string of worries from her lips. It startles her, and when I lick my tongue across her lips, she sucks in a breath and molds completely into me. Her sweet scent overwhelms me, and when she eases her soft curves into my body, I become very aware of the bed less than a foot from us.

A knock on the front door and I begrudgingly release her. "I'm not in trouble, you're fine in my house and stay here. I need to talk to Pigpen alone."

"How do you know it's him?"

Because I asked to see him and I don't ask anyone for anything. "I just do."

Breanna lowers herself to my bed, and I pause. Damn, she looks good there and leaving is the last thing I want to do, but in order to help her, I need Pigpen. He knocks again and I cross the room, open the door and step out onto the porch.

Pigpen leans against the railing and nails me with his stare. "This is the second time you've gone AWOL on the club.

Let me tell you, that shit got old the first time. Next time I fucking text you to see if you're alive, you text back."

Hell, I'm so caught up in Breanna's problems I forgot about Friday night. After the board laid it out for me in regards to Mom's death, I split as I needed time to digest.

"Do you hear me?" he demands.

"Loud and clear."

"Good. So what's this 911 Oz sent out on your behalf?"

"I'm against the ropes on a problem." Quick and to the point. Hopefully less painful.

"Knock and the door shall open…"

…ask and you shall receive. How many times has he said this to me? Breanna might consider this a betrayal, but it's one person, not the whole club. "Breanna's being blackmailed by some guys at school with a picture they took of me and her. I thought I could nail them and erase the picture by using the backdoor program, but they found it."

"Thought I taught you to move fast when you work with hacks like that."

He did. "I couldn't figure out one of the guys. I was waiting for them to slip his name in an email. If I moved before I had the last of the group, I would have tipped my hand."

Pigpen crosses his arms over his chest, clearly pissed that I'm not following his set rules for hacking. "You should have come to me when you hit that snag."

"I fucked up."

"You did, but now you're playing straight. What was your endgame?"

"Figure out who was involved. Go through their phones and computers, then wipe the picture clean in one swipe."

"It's a hell of a risk to take that they haven't stored the picture someplace else. I taught you to never underestimate."

Until they found my hack, I was convinced they were minor-league players. I crack my neck as I do something I hate—repeat myself. "I fucked up and Breanna's suffering for it. If you can't figure it out, I'm asking for help." And doing so is like offering a pound of my flesh.

"Give me what you know and we'll get it taken care of."

"I promised Breanna this would stay out of the club. I'm asking this as a personal favor."

Pigpen shoves off the railing and studies me like I got caught knocking over a liquor store. "I told you, no more personal favors. You have a problem, then you lean on your brothers. That's the point of the whole fucking club."

"I promised her—"

"You made a promise to us first," he cuts me off. "Here's the thing, I know the past couple of months have been tough. Fuck, I'm not going to even pretend what the past couple of years have been like, but you have a family willing to take the same type of bullet that you did for us. You expect us to trust you, but it's a shitty position to be in when we're the one giving all the blind faith. It's a two-way street with us. You either start trusting us or you need to give up your patch, because without trust, those colors on you don't mean shit."

"That how it is?" I ask.

"Yeah," he says like it's simple addition. "That's how it is."

We glare at each other as it crawls under my skin that he won't look away.

"And another thing...you say you love her, then you better figure out quick if you can trust us, because if you want to get her out of this mess, you're going to need the club. Just so you know, brother, you think it's impossible to trust us with you, it'll probably kill you to trust us with what you love the most."

A muscle in my jaw twitches. "If you help her, I want in."

Pigpen shakes his head. "We offered that help the night you brought her to the club. We saw you weren't budging. This is it, kid. End of the road. The stakes are high everywhere and it's time for you to go all in or to fucking fold. Which one is it going to be?"

Breanna

I'VE BEEN DRAWN to Razor—like a possessed moth to an inferno. So many reasons explain why: his beauty, his understanding, the way he protects, but it's not until my chat with Clara that I understood what attracted me to him emotionally… at least initially. He understood what it was like to feel as if you had possibly driven someone to take their own life.

The guilt.

The self-hate.

The feeling that your existence is absolutely worthless.

I saw it in his face the night outside of Shamrock's and I hurt for him because I still hurt for me. Clara pulled the knife away from her skin. She sank to the floor, tears streaming down her cheeks, telling me that she would do it if I ever told anyone what I saw.

I never betrayed her secret. Instead, I've let it eat me from the inside out.

A rush of air escapes my lips. His mother didn't commit suicide. I'm utterly relieved for him and still devastated for me. Year after year, Razor grew up tortured by the gossip of everyone in town, grew up believing that his mother chose to take her own life rather than to be with him. The entire time, the people who think they know everything knew nothing, but the emotional damage has already been done. The same damage that's already been done to me.

I stare at his mother's picture. She was beautiful. Blond hair. Sky-blue eyes. She has a fantastic smile. Mom says she was smart and full of life and Rebecca said that being a club girl isn't for everyone. Is it for me?

My eyes dip to a picture of Razor, Chevy and Oz crouched near a motorcycle. They're flipping off the camera and they grin as if they were laughing like children.

"I like it when you smile." Razor strides into the room and I jump. I hadn't realized I had been smiling, but I got lost in the pictures. As weird as his world is to me, I do strangely find myself gravitating toward it. As if I do belong.

An undertow of sadness yanks me down. I finally find a place I belong and I'm being ripped away. I'll have to tell him and doing so is going to break my heart.

I gesture to the picture. "This reminds me of the night of orientation. You were working on your motorcycle then, too."

Razor gathers me so that his front warms my back. He props his chin on my shoulder and his breath tickles the sensitive spot behind my ear. A wave of pleasure races through me.

"So you were checking me out that night." The smugness radiating from him is so sickening that I mock elbow him and he fake flinches as if I hurt him. I drank Razor in that evening, and I lean back into him now, reveling in the fact that, at least in this moment, he's mine.

"We need to talk." Razor loses his lightness, and I'm not ready for us to confront reality—the logic of our situation.

"We do." I pivot in his arms so we're face-to-face. "But

you made a promise to me about you healing and then us being alone, and I know how you are about your promises."

Razor goes completely still, and as he blinks back to life, he tunnels his fingers into my hair. "Breanna, those are words I fantasize about hearing you say, but we have time."

I shift my weight because we don't have time.

His fingers ease farther into my hair until he cups my head. "I know Kyle sent the picture to your parents. Addison told me they're sending you away. I know you're scared this is—"

"The end," I finish for him. "I need us to make memories."

Razor's eyes shut like my words cause him pain and it's not what I want. He lowers his forehead to mine. "We're going to figure this out."

We won't, and a lump in the back of my throat confirms this. "Their decision is made. There's nothing I can do or say to make any of this go away."

"No, Breanna." His voice cracks and it causes a flash of agony in my chest. "Let's take a few steps back, talk this out, solve the puzzle—"

I kiss him. My mouth on his. Without fear. Without thought. All of my emotions, my love, my trust wrapped up in this embrace. Our lips move in time. Too fast, almost desperate.

There's an ache within me—a curling of warmth in my stomach. It's like an indescribable, beautiful need, a desire even, and it's calling for Razor to touch me, to ravish me, to bring me to this glorious high only he has brought me to before.

His fingers gently pull on my hair, creating pleasing tingles that zap to my toes, and my hands find his chest. Through the fabric of his shirt, I explore his muscles, but this isn't enough.

I crave the warmth of his skin, and for there to be absolutely nothing between us.

As I reach the hem of his shirt, my wrist bumps his cut and my eyes snap open. I draw in a breath and Razor is looking down at me with the deepest blue eyes.

"You can take it off," he says, and the thought of doing so terrifies me and causes a spark of joy. He doesn't allow anyone to handle his cut, and when someone does touch it, they're careful to avoid his patches.

I reach under the leather, up to his strong shoulders, and keeping my hands safely inside the cut, I slowly edge it off his arms. It's like a countdown. The moment this is off, everything will become discarded. My shirt and his. His jeans and possibly mine. We'll be tangled and touching and everything I need this moment to be.

I lick my bottom lip and heat rushes through me as Razor's eyes track the movement. That provocative feral glint appears in his eyes again. It's like we're becoming victims of pure, unadulterated instinct.

My fingertips graze along his arms, over his biceps, along the inside of his wrist, and with each second that passes, my heart rate increases. Faster and faster and faster.

His cut skims over his hands, and when he grips it, my heart stutters with the switch in pace. Razor takes over. Easing his cut off, he folds it, then reverently places it on his dresser.

Razor circles an arm around me, and a smile bursts from me when he lifts me off the floor and carries me to his bed. He's gentle as he lays me down. My head settles into the huge pillow and my body is cradled by the blanket beneath me.

Razor yanks his shirt over his head to reveal all his beauty and he kneels. One knee against my outer thigh. The other tucked between my legs. His fingers pace the inner seam of my jeans—the area above my knee. A heightened sense of awareness causes my cells to awaken.

He leans down, situates his hands on either side of me, but hovers his body wickedly away from mine. "I'm in love with you. This isn't a memory, but a promise, do you hear me?"

I hear him and his words cause a pain in my chest. One of my hands slides along his spine and another touches his cheek. His jaw is smooth and his blond hair falls so that it almost covers his eyes. I'm in love with him and I'll take whatever I can get from Razor—his love, his memory, a promise. "I love you, too."

He drops his head and kisses my neck. It's a long kiss, an enduring one. It causes goose bumps along my arms and my blood to hum. His hands are magic, creating a tingling sensation wherever they roam. Down my arms, along my sides, up again as he tugs at my shirt.

His lips meet mine and we're both leaning up, my hands over my head. We briefly separate as the material is eased off my body and tossed to the floor. My back arches as he begins this slow, seductive trail of kisses.

Soon, there's no material between our chests and he touches and kisses and nips and his hands move lower. My body and Razor's rock in the same rhythm that's being synchronized by our pulses. I suck in an audible breath that partly describes the intense pleasure.

Razor moans and the sound drives me close to the brink of insanity.

His body glides against mine as he drags himself toward me for more kisses. These are on fire and intense and it's like we can't satisfy this building hunger.

The world spins, several times, and I'm touching and he's touching and we're kissing and there's whispers. Lots of whispers of love and of God and there's this warmth. Oh, this warmth. It's hot and it's consuming and it's spreading and then my muscles tense and an explosion.

Colors and sounds and a rush and then I'm gasping for air.

Lots of air. Razor's breathing hard beside me, cradling my head, kissing my lips, my cheeks, and whispering that this was right, and he utters those magical words again. "I love you."

RAZOR

CLOSE TO NAKED and tangled with me in my bed, Breanna's head is on my chest and she tells me everything. From Kyle, to her parents, to her siblings' reaction and the bad news I had hoped was wrong—that Breanna is being sent to private school—that she's being sent away from me. I'm not Chevy and I don't have any more tricks up my sleeve. Her parents are packing her up and Kyle still holds all the cards.

As she talks, I stare at the ceiling, graze my fingers up and down her bare back and search for a solution, but I keep circling back to the same place—with a solution she won't easily accept.

Breanna falls silent, and I give her a few seconds in case she remembers something else or I can create some brilliant plan. Neither happens.

"Can I tell you something?" she asks.

I fist her long raven hair and kiss her forehead. "Anything."

Breanna lightly brushes her fingernails over my chest and her apprehension is palpable.

"Tell me," I say.

"The night I met you, going to that private school was my dream. I would have given anything for my parents to say yes."

I swallow the fear nagging at me. "And now?"

She lifts her head and the pain in her eyes is her answer. "I don't want to go, not like this. Not because of this. Not because I'm in love with you and they won't give you a chance."

I trace her cheekbone and weigh her words. There's a part of her that wants to go, and why wouldn't she? This is a place that can challenge that perfect brain of hers, a place where she'll meet other people like her, a place where, as she said, she'll fit in and meet her tribe.

Just like how I have a tribe—my club. A group of men who understand there are days I want to talk and days I don't. A group of men who I have proudly taken a bullet for and who would take the same bullet for me again and again. A group of men who are begging me to love and trust them the way they crave to love and trust me. A group that I've hurt because I can't get past my own demons.

"I fucked up with Kyle and I'm sorry it's costing you."

She offers a sad smile that breaks my heart. "You tried, and that means everything to me. It's okay. I'll write the papers. At least being a hundred miles away will keep Kyle from tormenting me on a daily basis."

But he'll still torture her, possibly worse because he'll hate the loss of control that comes with not being able to confront her in person. Fuck that. Trying isn't good enough. "There's a way to fix it with Kyle. The path I should have taken and I was too stupid and prideful to do it."

And she's now paying for my moronic choices.

"What do you mean?" Breanna leans forward on her bent arm and drags a sheet up to cover her breasts. Her modesty reminds me how different we are.

I stare straight into her hazel eyes, which are widening. Twenty dollars she already knows. She's Einstein and those pieces are already put together in her head.

"It's the only way," I say.

She's shaking her head. "You promised me the club would stay out of this."

"They can do what I can't. They can make this problem go away."

"How?" Her voice grows in volume. "How are they going to make it go away? Are they going to hurt him? Are they going to make him disappear like Mia Ziggler?"

"Is that where we're at? Back to believing rumors spread by a bunch of assholes?"

Breanna slams her mouth shut and looks down, but anger causes her body to tense. "I've told you, I trust you. Just because I trust you doesn't mean I trust your club—"

"I am the club." I cut her off and point at the tattoos of fire on my arms. "I have never not been the club."

"That's not true. You've been doubting them since we met. That's the whole reason why we continued to talk. You needed proof about your mother because you didn't trust them. I don't claim to understand everything that happened the other night, but I saw the look on your face, I heard you yelling at them. I know they lied to you and I know you aren't okay with it."

"That's between me and them." I scoot to the edge of the bed, grabbing my jeans. "I'm talking about you and me. I'm talking about keeping you safe."

She laughs and it's a bit hysterical as she grabs for her clothes. "You didn't trust them to take care of your mother and yet you expect me to trust them with my problems? With my life?"

I flinch as if her words were a switchblade. "I'm asking you to trust me and I've already explained I am the club. I will not allow Kyle to continue to blackmail you."

Breanna works under the sheet to get her bra back on and I use that time to shrug on my jeans. I'm so fucking pissed that when I shove my foot through, I rip the already frayed cuff. She slides out of the bed and she's also brewing with enough ticked-off energy that it's not long before, like me, her shirt and jeans are on, too. The silence is sharp enough that it could cut us. I roll my neck and try to fight the feeling she's slipping away.

"In case you're wondering." A snap from her laces as she double knots. "None of this is your decision. It's mine. I asked for your help, you tried and it didn't work, so now I'm choosing to write his papers."

"Is that what you want? Because it won't stop there. It will never stop. Shit like this, Breanna, it's not about the endgame of the fucking papers, it's about control."

"You don't think I know that? You don't think I know this is about control? I'm the one under his thumb. I'm the puppet being played. I'm the one whose future is being decided by some guy who has to act dominant to make himself feel better."

I stretch out my arms, desperate for her to understand. "Then let me help. Let me do what needs to be done."

"Why? So *you* can be in control?"

"Are you comparing me to that bastard?"

"Yes. No. You and Kyle are two different people. Not just on the outside, but the inside, as well. You would never treat a girl like he's treating me, but you guys do have one thing in common and that is control. You want to fix things, you want to protect people, you want to take the bullet, and I'm telling you, it's not your choice to take the bullet on this."

"When Kyle's around, do you know what I see? Fear. And fuck me for not wanting the girl I love to be scared. Fear—that's not you. You are one of the few people I know who is truly fearless."

"You've made that girl up in your head! She doesn't exist. At least she doesn't exist in me, because all I am is scared. I've been scared for years! Scared someone will make fun of me. Scared someone will make me the butt of their jokes. Scared I'll stick out too much. Scared that if I do too much or say too much or do too well, that I'm going to hurt the people around me, and I can't take that burden, not anymore."

She claws at her shirt as if she's suffocating. "I don't want to hurt people and I'm scared, but what terrifies me the most is that I will never be as free to be myself as I am with you. I'm terrified I'm going to be in this box forever and I have to be. I have to stay just as I am."

Breanna's chest rises and sinks too fast and my instincts flare. There's more happening than Kyle. "What's going on?"

"Nothing." It falls out of her mouth as an automatic response and I'm not buying it.

"You're talking like I'm an outsider. You act like I'm not involved with this."

Breanna knots her hair at the base of her neck. "I am not your club! There is no in or out. This is my problem, not yours and it sure as hell isn't the club's problem, either. I'll handle this my way because my way won't end up with someone possibly being hurt."

"So you're going to do what you do at school? You're going to hide?" A wave of anger and hurt ripples through me and it's building into a tsunami.

Her eyes narrow into slits. "What happened to me being fearless?"

"I don't know. Maybe I have it wrong, because the girl I love wouldn't be asking me to butt out, but would keep me involved."

"This isn't about you! This is about me and I'm trying desperately to keep my world from falling apart. That picture can destroy what little I have left."

"Are you ashamed of me?" I spit out. "Was I a piece to a puzzle for you and now that the puzzle isn't working I'm being discarded?"

Shock and hurt cloud her face. "Why would you say that? I just did things with you that I have never done with anyone else. I have loved you like I have loved no one else. I'm standing here in your house, defying my family, hurting them because I love you!"

Pissed at myself, my entire body becomes a steamroller and I throw my fist into the wall. Breanna jumps and I press my hands over my face and scrub the skin as if that could erase the past few minutes.

I don't know what the fuck I'm saying anymore. She's leaving. After she walks out that door, I don't know when I'll see her again, if I'll see her again, and she's leaving with more problems than she had to begin with.

I'm hurt, she's hurt and we're only hurting each other more. As always, I'm cursed. She came searching for a memory and I'm sure as hell giving her one. Just the nightmare version everyone else in town also shares of me.

I take a deep breath and search for a semicoherent thought. "Breanna, I'm sorr—"

"Take me home." She wraps her arms around herself and I curse when I spot the tears lining the bottom rim of her eyes.

"We can't leave it like this between us."

"I'm not ashamed of you." Her voice cracks and that tears me up.

"I know." And those words that other people are good at saying, I find myself lost trying to form.

"Tell me you aren't going to the club about the picture and Kyle."

I wish I could lie to her, but I can't. I fucking can't. "I don't know."

"If you go to them, then we're over."

If I don't go to them, she'll forever live in that box she's terrified of being chained in for the rest of her life. I love Breanna. Love her more than I thought I was capable of loving a person. She brought me peace, light and happiness and I should give her something in return.

I step into her, and because Breanna is brave at her core, she doesn't step back.

"Don't do it," she whispers as I run my fingers through her hair. "Don't make my life more complicated than it already is. I can't trust them. I can't do what you're asking."

I hear her words, but I'm too busy making my own memories to respond. Breanna's hair is soft, and when my fingers glide through, it's like touching silk. I caress her face next and enjoy the smoothness of her cheek against my knuckles.

Her lips are perfect. Dark pink to light red. Curved just so that when she smiles it has this seductive tease. I'll go to bed night after night thinking of her lips. Kissing them. The feel of them on my skin. I curl her into me. Our time is almost completely gone. Not nearly enough left for me to love her properly—enough for memories.

"Razor," she says as a plea. "Please tell me you aren't choosing to end this."

I lower my head so that our foreheads are touching. "I'm choosing to love you."

"What does that mean?"

I kiss her. Slowly. Softly. As if she's glass on the verge of breaking, because that's what I am. I'm shattering on the inside. Her lips move with mine with as much deliberateness. Her taste is so sweet, her smell so enticing, this moment is fucking shredding my heart.

"What will they do to Kyle? He's wrong, Razor. He's more than wrong, he's sick in the head even, but I can't live with the idea of someone being hurt over me."

The front door to the house opens and the voices of multiple people talking at once cause Breanna to ease back, but I keep my arms locked around her. We stare at each other. She's still begging for an answer I don't possess. Screw it, I know the answer, but it's not the one she craves to hear. But for her happiness, for her safety—I'd do anything.

"I love you," I tell her. "I don't have fancy shit inside me or other pretty words to say, but know that, no matter what, I love you."

She opens her mouth, to possibly say it back, but someone knocks on my door. "Come in."

"Aren't you supposed to be at—" *School* dies on Dad's lips as I glance over my shoulder at him. His gaze lands on Breanna, then jumps to me. "Pigpen didn't tell me you had company."

"He didn't know. Did I hear Rebecca?"

"Yeah."

I rest my arm over Breanna's shoulders and edge her forward for the living room. I kiss her temple and briefly close my eyes with the embrace. This could be the last time I touch her. "I need her to take Breanna home."

Breanna

RAZOR'S GOING TO tell his club. The way he kissed me, the way he told me he loved me, the return of the frozen blue eyes as he watched me riding away in the passenger side of Rebecca's car—it was all there, the answer I didn't want to hear. The answer that is tearing us apart.

Rebecca's car idles at the end of the driveway and she waits like I'm walking the last few feet of my life. Maybe I am. Maybe when I enter the kitchen, my family will literally kill me, but when I round the corner, Mom's and Dad's cars are still missing.

I slip in the back door to buy myself as much time as I can without Clara and Liam and drop into a chair at the kitchen table. Weeks ago, I stood at the sink washing dishes—being the good little girl most everyone has predicted me to be. The smart girl, the best friend, the one who follows every command, the sister keeping a secret.

A secret.

I now have so many secrets that I'm buried alive—still in

the box, still chained inside, and I'm losing air. Razor's words come hurtling back at me... *Are you ashamed of me?*

What causes bile to slosh around in my stomach was the internal hesitation. How come I never told my parents? Why didn't I proudly hold his hand at school? Why wasn't the love from this fantastic man enough for me to rise above the thoughts and fears of everyone else?

Because I'm a coward... I'm afraid...

Around the room, everything is the same. Dirty dishes piled up. A half-eaten apple turning brown on the counter. A stack of mismatched shoes in the corner near the door. The same scene, another day, but I left this house one person last August and I'm sitting here someone new, someone changed, and it's time not to be afraid anymore.

Across the kitchen on the island is my phone, because in truth, my parents assume me to be the good little dog. They're convinced I'll obey.

Just like Clara expects me to forever keep her secret.

Just like Kyle expects me to write his papers.

But there is one person who expected the unexpected from me and the only time I noticed disappointment on his face was when I cowered like a sheep. And I had to take a moment to figure out I'm not ashamed of him. It's him who should be ashamed of me.

I've put Razor in an unfair position. He introduced me to his world. Welcomed me with open arms. Made me feel like I belonged and I've asked him to keep a secret when doing so is killing him. And I told him that we would be over... I did the same exact thing to him that Clara did to me and that's not okay. No part of it is okay.

I cross the kitchen, and when I pick up my cell, it feels epically heavy. My heart picks up pace and dizziness causes me to lean against the counter. I can do this. I can end this nightmare and Razor won't have to choose between me and keeping my secret.

With a swipe of my finger, my phone powers on. I never knew that being fearless could be so terrifying.

RAZOR

I WISH I HAD Breanna's mind. If I did, maybe I could sort through the possible solutions faster. Find the way to protect her without risking that picture going live on the internet. Find a way to convince her parents to let her stay. But I don't have her mind. I have mine and I can't think of an answer that will work.

The board is here. All but Pigpen inside the house. He's sitting on the railing on the opposite end of the porch from me, staring. Just staring.

It's an eerie sensation that my mother's cramped house is filled with so many men and there's hardly a sound. It's like everyone has their guns loaded, are lying in a ditch, watching a hill, and they're waiting for someone to yell "charge."

Messed-up part? They're waiting on me.

I'm in the same place as when Rebecca left with Breanna— my left shoulder leaning against the corner post on the front porch. I'm putting off the inevitable. As though if I remain in the same spot I was in the last time I saw her, I won't cause myself pain.

"There's a Bible story." Pigpen breaks the silence. "About this guy named Jacob and how he wrestled with God. Have you heard it before?"

I blink a no.

"The two of them went at it all night," he says. "Think about it—you're Jacob and he's God and you're evenly matched enough that you fight for hours. Jacob had to believe he was kicking ass. Thinking he was big and bad enough to do it on his own, but do you know what happened?"

It's a biblical story, so nothing good. "A plague? Pillars of salt? Brimstone and fire?"

"God touched him." Pigpen points one finger in the air. "And with that one touch, he dislocates Jacob's hip. One touch and it was over."

God smashed him like a bug. I crushed fireflies. Mom's dead. Breanna's floundering. And Pigpen wants to spin a story about how shit happens. "Working on a seminary degree?"

A smile stretches across his face. "Naw, but we had a chaplain over in Afghanistan. Cool son of a bitch. And he'd do this. Out of nowhere tell a story that would put it in perspective."

"Got a point?"

The grin slips off his face. I hate it when he goes dead serious. It usually means bad shit is about to go down. "God could have flattened Jacob, but he didn't. God knew that Jacob was stubborn, was prideful, so he let the poor bastard wear himself out before God does what he does—prove to Jacob he's nothing compared to God."

"Still waiting on that point."

He shrugs. "I was thinking you look like I expected Jacob would have after he realized he was fighting something bigger than he was, and I wonder, like Jacob, how long it's going to take you to figure it out that you don't have to be fighting alone."

Sometimes, I hate this guy. Especially when he makes sense. "I'm in love with her."

"Figured," he says. "Is she making you choose between us and her?"

"She's making me choose between keeping her safe or keeping her."

"That fucking sucks."

It does. Sucks enough I don't need to respond.

Wind blows across the field and the cold air causes the hair on my arms to stand on end. Breanna still has my jacket. I'm glad she does. Maybe she'll take it with her. Maybe it will help her remember me.

"How's that wrestling match with God going?" Pigpen asks. "From here you look mighty tired."

I'm fucking exhausted. "Breanna doesn't want me to go to the club with her problem, and when I tried talking her into it, she drew the line."

"Where you at on this line?" he asks.

I shove my hands into my jeans pockets and toe a piece of faded wood splintering off the deck floor. "If I cross it, I lose her. I might be losing her anyhow, because her parents are sending her away, but she'll walk if I go to the club for help."

"Hate to say this, but the way you sent her away, you already made the decision."

That's what is killing my soul. I know the choice has been made and so does Breanna. The agony of letting her go strikes deep. "I love her. Enough that I'll do anything to keep her safe."

The graying wood of the porch creaks under Pigpen's weight as he crosses it to join me. "Sounds like the decision your mom made when she drove away from the clubhouse—sacrificing herself to protect you."

My heart stalls out, but Pigpen's not done torturing me yet. "Also sounds like the decision the board and your dad made by keeping how she died a secret from you. And before you say shit, you and I both know how ugly that demon is inside you when it comes to her. I know it when I see it because that warped monster lives inside me. If you grew up knowing the truth, you would have gone into Louisville guns blazing by the time you were sixteen, starting a war that this club can't win, costing lives we couldn't save."

My head swims like I was involved in a head-on collision. "So he let her die and moved on? He just accepted it? The Riot wins because the Terror was weak?"

"The Terror is strong because we don't act like the Riot." Pigpen spits like he's a viper showing his fangs full of venom. "My old man—he's Riot."

"What?"

"I grew up in their clubhouse. I understand you because I am you. I also learned to crawl on the sticky floors of where guys made their oaths. But here's the difference, I grew up watching people make stupid mistakes in the name of revenge."

"You grew up Riot?"

Pigpen flicks my questions away with a shake of his head. "Another conversation for another day. Point is I'm Terror because the Riot don't play straight."

Anger rumbles through me like a thunderhead about to hit land. "They killed my mother. Are you telling me that's worth letting go? That justice shouldn't be served?"

"I've killed people before, Razor, and that shit…it changes everything and it doesn't just change you. It's an avalanche to everyone around. What your father did, lying to you about how she died, it may not have been the definition of right, but he did it because he loves you...because he wanted to keep you and the people he cared about safe.

"What your father did—it wasn't weak, and he sure as hell didn't accept it, but that's his story to tell, not mine. Here's the thing, kid. You are the product of your parents, a product of this club, and you've been denying us for months, and the man I'm standing next to now, the one wrestling with God—you're beginning to understand what it means to make a sacrifice for the one you love. Question is, can you forgive us for loving you the same way you love her."

There's a shifting of wood and Pigpen and I both snap our heads to catch my father near the screen door. How long he was there and what he heard, I don't know. But I think of how he sat with me after I took the bullet, the night I came home and he stood proud next to me, the way he looks at me now like a broken man waiting for his son to return home.

Right and wrong begin to get muddled. Black and white merge into shades of gray. My father loved me enough to do something so huge in regards to my mother that the Terror respects him and it brought a fragile peace to two warring clubs. He also did what he could to maintain that peace throughout the years—including lie to me...because he loved me.

I gesture with my chin and he's hesitant as he strides toward us. Like he's ready for me to pull back and swing instead of joining him in conversation. "What do you need?"

The muscles in my neck tense as I throw everything I have with Breanna away, but I'm giving her up to make sure she's safe because, sometimes, that's what love requires.

Just like my mom did. Just like Dad did, too. And maybe someday, Breanna will understand, like I'm starting to now. "Kyle Hewitt and four other guys from school are blackmailing

Breanna with a picture of me and her, and if we don't stop them, they're going to torture her and then eventually try to ruin her life. I tried to stop them, but I couldn't. This..." Is killing my pride. "It's too big for me and I need your help."

Dad takes a relieved breath, a lot like the moment I opened my eyes after the bullet. He even rubs his hands over his face like I was raised from the dead. Pigpen claps my arm and smiles at me like he did the night I was patched in. "Welcome back, brother. Now let's get to work."

Breanna

I'M SITTING ON the front porch again, my head between my knees. Nausea and dizziness are often caused by the lack of proper blood to the brain. Doing this places the brain at the same level as the heart so the blood doesn't have to fight gravity to reach the brain. That's the theory. Personally, it also keeps me from having to bend over too far if I do vomit.

I'm cold and clammy and hot at the same time, yet I'm free.

I lift my head and the autumn breeze feels good against my skin.

Free. I'm officially outside the box. I'm free.

Free is terrifying and open and it's similar to being a bit lost—but it still feels...free.

My cells vibrates and pings over and over again. Reagan has called twice. Addison three times. My cell sings again with her ringtone. The count is now up to four.

Elsie wanders from the house and plops down beside me. Her black hair is in a ponytail and half of the strands are falling out. She's in her school clothes and there are Band-Aids over her scraped knees. I put those bandages there last night. I wonder who will do it when I'm gone.

"You look sick," she says.

"It's been a rough afternoon. How was your day?"

"Rough." Elsie straightens, then her eyes wash over me. In a few seconds, she leans forward and rests her combined hands on her legs. A complete mirror image of me.

"What made it rough?" Typically this conversation would happen in the kitchen with me pouring a glass of milk while she and Zac swipe cookies off the plate I have waiting for them.

"Lauren," she says as if a word could be a scowl.

Lauren. I sigh for her. We all have a Lauren who's the bane of our existence. While I had two older sisters and two older brothers, Elsie is the product of being a girl with three boys ahead of her. She's a proud tomboy and Lauren isn't.

"You shouldn't let what other people say bother you." My advice feels hollow.

Elsie flashes me a brief smile. "At least I have you."

My heart sinks. How many times have I told her that and all this time I had planned on leaving. "You do, but you also have Zac, Paul and Joshua. And you heard Liam last night, he might be moving back in to help."

"Not the same. Clara and Liam are fighting because you went someplace you weren't supposed to go again."

I could lie to Elsie, but she's smart enough to know the difference. Where I'm built for facts, her little brain reads people very well. "Mom and Dad tell me I should be like you. That I should listen. You aren't listening anymore and now they're sending you away. If I don't listen, will they send me away?"

I shake my head. "I wanted to go away. It took me not listening for them to listen to me. Sometimes people don't listen until bad things happen. They realize then they should have listened instead of talked. Sometimes people are too busy hearing what they want to hear, seeing what they want to see, and they don't care what's real, only what they think is real."

Elsie shifts away from me. "You want to leave home? But you have another year before you have to leave. Why would you want to do that?"

Another piece of her hair falls and I beckon my youngest sister to sit on the step between my legs. She does and I begin the task of undoing the knot of hair I had put up this morning. "I wanted to fit in someplace, and I thought if I left, I would."

"You fit in here."

I brush her hair out with my fingers and then smooth it back up. "I didn't think I did."

"Sounds like you were the one not listening."

The rubber band snaps her hair in place, but it's the snap inside me that hurts. "What?"

Elsie glances at me from over her shoulder. "Like when I don't fit in with the other girls, you tell me I have you, which means you have me. And if I have Zac and Paul and Joshua and Liam, then that means you do, too. It sounds to me like you aren't listening."

My body goes numb as my mind begins to disseminate the information. Is it possible... No, I mean Clara has always treated me like... But there are eleven people in my family and she's one. And Liam—he's willing to give up his dreams of independence because he's concerned for me.

"If you're sad because you're in trouble," Elsie says, "then don't be. I get in trouble all the time, and sometimes after I cry, those are the times Mommy hugs me the hardest and you look like you need a hard hug."

And she does it. Elsie hugs me hard, throwing her entire being, soul and all, into loving me. I hug her back and try to fight the lump hardening in my throat.

"It's like you said when Daddy forgot to pick me up at ballet. Sometimes these bad things happen to prove you're strong enough to be a Miller."

My eyes shut with the wetness forming there. I did tell Elsie that. She was sad. I was sad for her and I made being forgotten in the pickup rotation a badge of honor, and it's not until this moment that I realize how right she is. This family is messed up, but it's still my family.

Just like the club is Razor's family. Razor loves me so much that he's willing to go to any length to protect me...even involving his family.

A sense of urgency rushes through me. I need to find Razor. I need to talk with him and tell him I understand his drive to inform the club, his family, but there has to be a way that we can stay together without anyone getting hurt.

"I love you, Elsie." I kiss her temple, and when she eases back, I touch the end of her nose. "And I'm glad Mom and Dad didn't stop at eight."

She grins widely to show two adult teeth and a bunch of crooked baby teeth. "Me, too."

"Let's go get some cookies." I offer my hand, she accepts, and the two of us walk in. Elsie continues to chatter as we pass the living room, and when she settles into the seat at the kitchen, eats her cookie and drinks her milk.

Razor loves me and he's going to freak when he sees the post. When Elsie hops down from her seat and races off to play with Zac, I stare at Liam's car keys on the island.

I'm already in trouble. Not sure I can go much deeper. Especially when my parents discover the post and how I ran off with Razor earlier today. One more outing won't matter.

Before I lose my courage, I snatch Liam's keys and text Razor: Meet me at the bridge. We need to talk.

RAZOR

WAITING.

It's never been my strong suit and, until Breanna, neither had trusting.

Right now, I'm doing both.

Waiting and trusting.

I'd rather get shot and take a spill on my bike with no jacket and have my skin scraped off by the blacktop than wait for the board to decide how they're going to handle Breanna. Unfortunately, my single option is to sit here in the beat-up chair near the pool tables.

Oz sinks the eight ball in the corner pocket, then tosses the stick onto the table. It rolls until it hits the other side of the green felt. He obviously isn't into this waiting shit, either. "You should have come to me."

I tip the chair until the back of my seat smacks the wall behind me so I can rap my head against it. I came clean over an hour ago and I'm already sick of hearing how everyone has faced a demon similar to mine. Truth is—what I hate is how they're right.

Oz eyes me like he's pissed. "I handed my cut to Eli thinking I couldn't make it in this club."

My seat falls forward with a crack. "You serious?"

"Dead." He doesn't once blink as he holds my gaze. My best friend isn't lying.

Chevy barrels through the door to the clubhouse. "Try answering your damn phone!"

Great. Another guy to lay into me. "Board took my cell." To look at the pictures I took of the detective's files. To research how deep this detective is digging to threaten either us or the Riot. They're also studying the info I gathered on the guys blackmailing Breanna. "They're in Church now."

Church is how the club refers to their private board meetings.

"We got problems."

I stand, hands out in a stop sign. "I told the board and we're working on it."

Chevy yanks his phone out of his pocket, slides his finger across it and tosses it at me. "It's Breanna. She's dropped a mother of a bomb."

On the screen is Breanna's account, but confusion muddles my thoughts. It's the picture of me and her. "Did the son of a bitch hack her account?"

"She posted it and she named Kyle. Whether she realized it or not, Breanna started a war. And here's the thing, we were at practice when he found out. Kid looked crazy and he tore off."

Ice water seeps into my veins. "Why didn't you stop him?"

"I tried," Chevy says. "But coach physically held me back. As soon as he left, so did I and came straight here. If I was Kyle and my world was falling apart, I'd go after the source of the pain, brother, and we need to get to Breanna before he does."

I could race out of here now. Return to controlling this

problem. It's what I've done for years. What instinct screams at me to do, but I can't continue to rely only on myself. This doing it on my own…it's what makes me weaker. The club is what makes me stronger.

I turn to Oz as I dial Breanna's number. "Interrupt Church. If Kyle's on the warpath, I need a wall of cuts surrounding her."

Chevy pulls out his keys as Oz runs up the stairs. He pats me on the back as we head for our bikes. "Never thought I'd say this, but let's go win you the girl."

Win me the girl. It's what I want, but for now, I'll settle for her being safe.

Breanna answers after two rings. "Hello?"

I almost swear with relief at the sound of her sweet voice. "It's me. Tell me where you are. I'm coming to get you."

"The bridge. I'm driving to the bridge because I want to talk to you."

Breanna Miller @breanna212 · 2 hrs

I'm Breanna Miller. The smart girl. The quiet girl. The one who belongs to a large family. I'm Breanna Miller. Number 5 in the line of 9. The girl who everybody knows and nobody sees. I'm Breanna Miller. A girl who went to Shamrock's and ended up falling in love with Thomas Turner—Razor of the Reign of Terror. The boy who everybody sees and nobody knows. I've been with him for months. I'm in love with him and I don't care who knows.

I'm Breanna Miller. I don't know what I want to do with my life. I don't know yet who I want to be. I'm Breanna Miller and I'm not sure what my future might hold.

I'm Breanna Miller and Kyle Hewitt took this picture of me and Razor after Razor saved me from a potentially dangerous situation. Kyle took pictures of me when I was vulnerable. He took this one when Razor was being a perfect gentleman. He took it in a moment where it looked like more happened than what really did.

And even if something did happen, that is between me and Razor and not between me, Razor and the rest of the world. Private lives should remain private. Period.

Kyle has been blackmailing me to write his papers. His first one is due on Monday. I won't be writing it. In fact, because of this picture, I possibly won't be in school anymore, nor will I be in Snowflake, and any dreams I've had for my life might be ruined.

I'm Breanna Miller and you'll think of me whatever you want. Some of you might call me a freak. Some of you might call me a slut. Call me whatever you want, but I'm Breanna Miller and I know who I am and it officially doesn't matter what any of you think.

Share, like, comment. It doesn't matter. At midnight tonight, I'll be deleting this account.

Breanna

LIAM'S ENGINE WHINES when it hits forty-five, so I've kept the speedometer to under forty. He's going to be furious when he discovers I "borrowed" his car without his permission, but there's too much at stake.

The muscles in my neck tighten as I turn onto the access road that leads to the bridge and my skin vibrates with nervous anticipation. This dread is like a sixth sense screaming at me that the world is collapsing. That's because it is. It's been a bad day, a bad night, just a bad…life.

But then I think of Razor's hands touching my bare back, the way his lips feathered kisses along my neck. It's not all bad. Some of it has been very, very good.

Razor. It's like my soul breathed his name.

Razor is the only thing that's been right in my life.

A rumble of an engine from behind me and my eyes flicker to the rearview mirror. The late-afternoon sun glints off the windshield and nausea strikes my stomach hard and fast. Cherry-red muscle car. It's Kyle.

He lays on the horn and uneasiness tiptoes through my

bloodstream. This area is isolated. No traffic, no houses, no farms. Just very, very alone.

Kyle blares his horn again and my palms sweat. Fading fall grass borders both sides of the narrow road. There's nowhere to go. No sanctuary in sight.

He revs his engine and his horn sounds off again as he swerves. Kyle pushes alongside of me, the left side of his car angling up as he races along the grass. My heart beats hard and a million thoughts collide in my mind. *Stop. Don't stop. Grab my phone. Call for help. Go faster. Hit the brakes. Be better. Be smarter.*

A flash of red. Metal crunches against metal and the steering wheel jerks. My body jars with the impact and I fight the losing battle to keep the car on the road. The frame shudders as I press the brake, but the car hurtles toward the tree. I'm going faster, why am I going faster? The brake, the brake, the brake.

I lift my foot off the gas, rip the wheel to the side, slam on the brake and miss the tree by inches. My body whiplashes to the side. Pain against my skull. And the entire world possesses a dreamlike haze.

The door to the car creaks. A combination of the warm sun and the cold autumn breeze drifts across my skin.

"Come on!" It's Kyle's voice, but his face is nothing but a blur.

The seat belt is unbuckled, my body is moving because of a pull on my arm and it's odd how my legs work. There's a humming in my ears and I close my eyes to gain my bearings.

When I open them, it's too bright, and as I strain to make sense of my surroundings, the blue sky appears. The tugging on my arm grows stronger. My feet instinctually pick up the pace.

Kyle's mouth is opening and closing. Words I can't hear fall from his lips. There's just the loud buzz and my moving feet. I blink. One time. Another. Recognition in the form of a memory causes me to trip over my feet.

"This is where Razor brought me." My own voice sounds muted. Far away. As if I'm talking through a thick glass.

The hold on my arm tightens and it's painful enough that a sharp "Ow" leaves my throat. That one declaration causes the fog in my head to sweep away in time for Kyle to step on the bridge looming before us.

My breath catches in my throat. Kyle.

Kyle has me and he's yelling and he's furious. His face red, his eyes wide, he's spitting as he continues to scream at me and this isn't Razor's bridge. This is the other bridge. This is the one that the trains use. I snap my arm back and it slips in his clammy hand. "No!"

I spin on my toes and spot motorcycles. Four of them, then two more. They park in the grass next to the abandoned car. Racing off their bikes, yelling at us to stop. One of them has blond hair and he's faster than the others, running as if he's watching his life coming to an end.

"Razor!"

An arm around my waist and I'm being dragged. Onto the train tracks, onto the bridge, and below us the rapids swirl. The roar of the water replaces the buzzing in my head. White foam waves lash up, then get sucked into the undertow.

I have to get off this bridge. I need to get to safety. I prepare to kick, raise my elbow to strike a blow, then Kyle circles us and I can't breathe.

We're on the edge and he's leaning me over. My feet scoot back and smack his and I recoil, but the more I struggle, the more he uses his body weight.

"Stay back," Kyle shouts. "Stay the fuck back!"

Not quite a hundred feet—the drop is easily that huge. Into the rocky ravine. Into shallow rapids. At forty-eight feet, the chance of surviving a fall is fifty percent. At eighty-four feet, ten percent. I wish I had never read that article. Wish I could remain ignorant.

"Why did you do it? Why did you write that post? Why did you ruin my life? I'm going to lose everything. Everything."

"You did this. You're the one that took the photo."

"But I never would have released it." We shake as he yells and I press back, into him, away from the edge. "It was just a threat. To scare you. I never would have released it."

"You released the one of Violet."

"That was them. Not me!" He shoves us closer to the edge again. "That wasn't me!"

"Calm down," comes a voice, and it's not Razor's. I rip my focus away from the water and there's a man with blond hair and a cut like Razor's slowly approaching the bridge. His hands are up—a sign of submission. "Just calm down."

"I said stay back!" Kyle's voice vibrates against my back.

My pulse pounds in my ears. "Please, stay back!"

"Breanna," Razor calls. "It's going to be okay. I promise."

A promise. Razor's next to the other man and I don't see the terror inside me reflected on him. Razor is calm, too calm, and he subtly nods at me. "I promise," he repeats.

I swallow to ease my dry throat and nod back. Razor never makes a promise he doesn't intend to keep. It's then that I realize that my fingers have a death grip on Kyle's arms. The one wrapped near my throat, the other snaked around my waist.

"Were you stalking her?" the guy next to Razor asks. Pigpen. I bet this is the Pigpen Razor has talked about.

"No!" Kyle shakes his head, bumping mine. "I drove by

her house to see her and I saw her taking off. I followed her. That's it."

"Now you're holding her over a bridge. How do you see this playing out, kid?"

"Get on your bikes and leave." Kyle's voice trembles and so does his body. "That's what's going to happen. I'll let her go then and then I'll leave. I'm not the bad guy in this. I didn't take or put up the picture of Violet. I'm not the one!"

"Promise you won't hurt him," I say.

Razor tilts his head to show he's consumed with the thought of hurting Kyle, but he remains silent as Pigpen says, "Hurting you was never an option on the table. We don't operate like that. Hurting kids isn't how we work."

"I'm not a kid!"

"A man wouldn't be holding a girl on a bridge like he's about to toss her over. I swear on my patch, killing you is not in the Terror's plans."

I blink as I hear the promise and Razor raises his head for me to not tip their hand. They don't have plans to kill Kyle, but anything else, like maybe jail time, is up for negotiation.

"How can I believe you?"

"You can't," says Pigpen. "But I'm not seeing your other options."

"I'm not bad," Kyle whispers into my ear. "I'm sorry, Bre. I promise I'm not bad."

The desperation in his voice, the way he's hugging me instead of holding me, causes me to loosen my grip. For months, Kyle has been this shadow of a monster haunting my life and he's been the epitome of evil, but listening to his brokenness— he doesn't sound much different from Zac or Paul or Elsie. He doesn't sound much different from a scared child.

The big, strong football player who everyone knows is

frightened. Frightened enough to blackmail me, frightened enough to do something that causes him to feel guilty, frightened enough to take on the Terror, frightened enough to drag both of us onto a railway bridge.

"I'm scared," I say to him.

"I'm sorry," he says again.

"You and I, we've made bad choices. It doesn't make us good, but I'm not sure it makes us bad."

"What have you done?"

"I didn't love my family enough to let them love me back."

A disgusted sound slips from his lips and a new rush of fear overtakes me, but I press forward. "I hurt people. People that I said I loved. They hurt me, too, but I'm not sure I tried to give them another chance. It's like tearing off my arm because I didn't want to feel the pain of a paper cut on my finger."

Kyle doesn't move. He doesn't speak, either, and a wave of dizziness disorients me when a strong gust sweeps over the bridge, causing us to ease a centimeter toward the edge.

"Easy now," says Pigpen in a smooth tone.

"I said—" Kyle starts, but I shush him.

"Listen to me, not them. We've both made mistakes, and the point is, what makes us bad is when we don't know when to stop. When we keep covering for the things we've done wrong and never stop. If you say you aren't bad, then prove it. Walk us off this bridge, let me go home and I'll tell my family that they've been wrong, but I've also been wrong."

"But you don't understand." There's a break in his voice. "What has happened…what you did…what I did…everything is ruined."

If I lie, and he doesn't believe me, he's crazy enough to toss us both over. "You said you wanted me to write the papers because you need out of this town, and I never thought of it until now, but that must mean you feel like you're dying here. Maybe this is our moment. Maybe everything is gone, but maybe this is what we both need. Maybe both of us need to stop playing the parts assigned to us by this awful town and find the courage to be somebody new. Somebody different."

"The Terror are going to kill me. They think I put up the picture of Violet. Razor's going to kill me for hurting you."

"They won't hurt you."

"You don't know—"

"Promise you won't hurt him," I call out. "Swear to me as Razor's girl that you won't hurt him."

"Doesn't work like that," Pigpen says real slowly, and my blood pressure plummets. It's a boys' club. Violet had said that. A boys' club that's going to get me killed—

"On my life," Razor calls out. "He'll walk out of here."

Pigpen assesses Razor with a half-sarcastic grin. "Now, that's how we work. Razor calls this clean, so I'll drive Kyle home to Mom and Dad myself."

Kyle's arms give, and when I inch to slip out of them, he grabs on to my wrist. My heart shoots to my throat, but then he slides his hand into mine. Nausea knots my stomach. I don't want to hold his hand, but I do want off this bridge.

With every step, I'm terrified he'll change his mind. We're farther onto the bridge than I thought. Too far for my liking, but at least we're walking on the tracks in the middle.

Pigpen's telling everyone to fall back and Razor's staring at me as if his gaze is what is protecting me. Kyle pauses and anticipation builds. Not the good kind like the morning of your birthday. The bad kind. The type that suggests that death is taking note of exactly how your last moments should be.

"Let's go," I encourage him.

"I'm sorry. I mean it." He releases me and a sickening

sensation twines its fingers around me like a January wind. "Make sure you tell my mom that I said it and that I meant it."

No. I know that hopelessness. I've seen it before. On Clara. The day she held a knife at her wrist. No one should look that way. Not ever. Kyle steps toward the bridge and I'm the one clutching his hand. "Don't do this. Not now. We'll figure it out. I swear we'll figure it out."

The metal beneath my feet vibrates and mind-numbing fear freezes my heart. "Kyle, it's the train."

A whistle in the distance and there are multiple shouts. Men yelling my name. Telling me to get off the tracks. "Go, Bre." His eyes are hard and his jaw determined. "Go now."

Kyle attempts to shake off my hold, and when I won't let go, he shoves me. I stumble and the words rip so loudly from my throat that it scratches the vocal cords. "He's going to jump. He's going to jump or stay on the track! I can't let him!"

Another whistle and it's so loud that the hair on my arms rises. He's going to die, and if we don't run, we're both going to die. "Don't do this! Please don't do this!"

The entire bridge shakes and Kyle quakes as he studies the churning water. "Tell my mom I loved her. Just tell her that I loved her."

"Move, move, move!" Pounding of footsteps and an arm around my waist. "Let's move!"

Tears flood my eyes, but the roaring of an engine causes my feet to scramble, me to move in the same direction as I'm being dragged. Pulling me forward, running with me, it's blond hair, a black cut.

The green of the trees blur as we race for our lives, as we race to beat a train.

My lungs hurt, my legs burn, I trip in the rush forward and the strong arm lifts me and then we're rolling. The scent of fall grass, then the air's knocked out of me as we land and we continue to roll. Dirt and rocks embed into my skin.

I reach out, clawing into the ground. We finally skid to a halt and there's only the deafening grumble of the train flying past. I whip my head to confirm Razor's safe and then I scurry back, my arms and legs colliding against each other. It's blond hair and blue eyes, but that's not Razor.

"Where's Razor?" I shout, but the train drowns me out. Pigpen's on his feet and a wave of nausea crashes into me. Dizzy with dread, I yell Razor's name, but there's no reply.

Lots of black cuts. Lots of men wide-eyed and scanning the area. I'm frantic, desperate for a sign of him, desperate to see everything at once.

"Where is he?" Pigpen demands, and my mind rejects someone's answer of "He went over. He was dragging that kid and it was close. He shoved the kid and they both went over."

There's a pain in my heart. So massive, so intense that I bend over. "Razor!"

My shout is swallowed by steel grinding against steel and the rhythmic clank, yet I try again. "Thomas!"

I can't lose him. I can't. The last car passes, the rumbling fades and a crow caws in the distance. I'm stumbling through the field, next to the track, and the men march toward the ravine.

"Thomas, answer me!"

"I told you, it's Razor, but I like that name off your lips, too."

My heart pulses hard as I drop to the ground and peer over the edge. A few feet down, sitting on a rock ledge, Razor raises his beautiful face in my direction. Dirt stains his cheek and there's a rip in his jeans with a small amount of blood, but he's alive. The mix between a sob and a laugh escapes from my mouth. "So I can call you Thomas now?"

"Considering the past few minutes, you can call me anything as long as I can hug you again."

"Deal." Movement near Razor and it's an odd sensation of relief when I spot Kyle propping his back against the rock wall.

Razor catches my eyes and rocks his head for me to stay silent. "Get us help."

Razor saved Kyle's life—from suicide, from a train. "He's over here! Razor's over here!"

"Why'd you do it?" I overhear Kyle ask. "Why'd you save me?"

"Because somebody loves you," Razor answers, and my heart twists for all of us—me, him and Kyle. "Because somebody out there fucking loves you and doesn't deserve the type of hurt you jumping would have caused. Killing yourself doesn't solve your problems. It just hands them to somebody else."

"Razor—" Kyle starts.

"Shut up," Razor cuts him off. "Just shut the fuck up."

Pigpen rushes to my side. "Is he okay?"

Oddly enough? "Yes. In fact, he's amazing."

RAZOR

ELI'S EDGY AND that causes my skin to crawl along my muscles. We're in Louisville and in Riot territory. It's not the first time he's been here since the Riot tried to hollow out his chest with a few bullets, but it's the first time we've been here specifically to meet with someone from the Riot. The peace between our clubs continues to be unsteady. Today is an information-gathering session, and according to my father, judgment day.

Not sure what that means, but I was asked to ride along.

We're at a public park. A few women jog on a concrete path in pairs or in threes. Kids squeal and laugh from the towering playground that's on the far side from where we left our bikes. I'm sitting on top of a picnic table staring at my cell.

Me: You there?

Breanna doesn't respond.
Because I'm a glutton for punishment: I miss you.
And love her. It's been a month since I've seen her, since

I've held her, since I've had any contact with her. This text, it's in vain, and watching my cell like she's going to respond hurts as bad as having a bullet rip through my arm and my skin scraped off by the road.

Naw, that's wrong. It hurts worse.

A month ago, when everything went down with Kyle, her parents deactivated this number, but it doesn't stop me from calling. Doesn't stop me from searching for a connection with her. Doesn't stop me from hoping.

I run a frustrated hand through my hair. Hope. Never had it before, but Breanna taught me anything's possible. That a gorgeous, intelligent girl like her could love a guy like me.

The picnic table shakes as Pigpen climbs it from behind, then plants himself next to me. "We should change your road name to F-U-F. Fucked-Up and Forlorn."

I flip him off and pocket my phone.

"It's going to get better," he says. My father chooses a seat on a bench about fifty yards away. "You've done good trusting us and I promise it's going to get better."

I haven't seen Breanna since the night of the bridge. Dad, Eli and I brought Breanna home bruised, scratched up and dirt-stained and we were met on her front lawn by her pissed-off father. When the instinct was to toss Breanna on the back of my bike and take off for good, Dad and Eli asked me to trust them. To trust the club. To leave and trust them to fix everything with Breanna's parents.

Killed me to do it, but I left. One month later, she's gone and I still think about her. I still love her. I'm still trusting the club.

"Rebecca had lunch with her mom again," Pigpen says, and I pop my neck to the side. Rebecca's a nurse. Breanna's mom works in accounting at the hospital. They're bound to share a lunch hour. But there's more to it than that. Rebecca and Breanna's mom never talked before the day of the train bridge, but Rebecca has been trying to bridge the gap between the club and the Millers by using lunch.

My cell vibrates once, then again. I don't bother checking the messages. They're nondelivery notices from Breanna's disconnected cell. Each one tears off pieces of my heart. "Found the fifth guy yet?"

Pigpen frowns. "He's been slippery, but I've got him. I'll be fucking up his world real soon."

Pigpen produced hard evidence against Kyle and his three other buddies who had been using that Bragger site to blackmail girls from school. All of them were suspended. All of them blackballed from whatever team or after-school activity they were on. Because the justice system is messed up, no one's sure on criminal charges yet, but Kyle told the truth—Breanna had been his sole target.

Because of that, she's refusing to press charges against Kyle as long as he meets with a counselor every week until he does graduate. The asshole's doing it, too, and I know for sure because I follow him there and then make sure he leaves an hour later. Breanna will get her last Snowflake wish.

Pigpen pats my shoulder. "Heads up because we're live. Your dad gave the sign."

Dad's flashing two fingers. Download before we left was that someone involved with the Riot was defecting and is willing to pass us info that could protect our club. Dad, being the sergeant at arms, volunteered to be in the line of fire to meet with this person to see if he's legit.

I scan the area and Pigpen stiffens. "Son of a bitch."

I'm off the table. That's my father. He and I might not have figured out our crap yet, but he's still my dad. Pigpen jumps off as well but snatches my arm, gripping me like he means to cause pain.

"That's my younger brother." Pigpen reacts like a viper coiled and ready to strike.

Shock ripples through me like a drop of rain in a puddle. Pigpen and I have been tight for years and it twists my gut how little I know about him. First the fact his father rode, possibly still rides with the Riot, and now that his brother does, too.

Pigpen starts to turn and I shove at his chest. "Stay back."

"Fucking cute, but that's my brother."

"And that's my father. We agreed to a plan. Trust the club, remember?"

Pigpen practically snarls at me, but he retakes his seat on top of the picnic table. "I liked you better rogue."

"No, you didn't." My attention flickers between Pigpen and Dad. The guy about my age walks up to the bench and Dad scoots over. Pigpen's brother sits.

"Stupid kid," Pigpen mutters. "Didn't check his six before he sat down. I like you better true to the club, but in this moment, it sucks."

Convinced Pigpen isn't going to rush his blood brother, I settle back beside him. "Guessing you didn't know he was the defector?" Which suggests Pigpen's brother didn't reach out to him, but to another member of the Terror.

"I also liked you better mute," he mumbles.

Even though Pigpen's stinging, I can't help the slight tilt of my lips. "No, you don't."

"No, I don't," he repeats. "Our club won't take him if he patched in to the Riot."

I may be expressing myself more, but there are times when a man talks that he needs people to be silent. This is one of those times. After a few minutes of watching Pigpen's brother talk and watching my father listen, I attempt to be the man Breanna brought out in me. "Maybe he hasn't patched in yet. Maybe he's seeking asylum with us before he gets that far."

Pigpen works his jaw like my attempt at hope is fruitless, but he says, "Maybe."

His brother offers my dad his hand and, after two beats of glaring him down, Dad accepts. The tension leaves my body when Pigpen's brother strides across the street. At least that didn't collapse into an ambush and then an all-out dogfight.

Dad switches his attention to us, and when he locks eyes with me, he jerks his head for me to join him. With one are-you-going-to-live glance at Pigpen, he rolls his eyes, and I sit with Dad on the bench.

He says nothing as the two of us check out the passing traffic. Two red lights and a near collision of a minivan with a pickup later, Dad speaks. "Three o'clock might interest you."

The detective who snowballed this entire saga with the club observes us from his car to our right. He notices me staring. "What's he doing here?"

"I called him," Dad says.

Wasn't expecting to hear that. "Why?"

Dad rubs his hands together as he leans forward. "When your mom died…" He sucks in a breath like it hurts for him to talk. "I left town."

This part, I remember. Nothing like burying your mother, then spending night after night looking out a window wondering if your father was going to be next.

"I came here, to Louisville. Eli and Oz's dad were with me. At times Cyrus rode along. I was determined to find who ran your mom off the road…to hunt down who was responsible."

Nerves cause me to shift. I thought I wanted this answer, but there's an unsettling in my soul. After pushing and pulling Kyle off that bridge, the thought of being the man pursuing justice by taking a life tastes sour in my mouth. "And?"

"And I found him. Sat outside his house. Waited to make him pay, and when the moment presented itself, I couldn't do it. I couldn't put a bullet in his head."

I close my eyes. Half relieved. Half feeling like I'm losing Mom again.

"He had a son," Dad continues. "Your age, and when I saw that kid running out to greet that damn bastard...I couldn't do it. So I improvised."

My eyebrows rise and Dad bitterly chuckles. "More like I bluffed. I didn't have hard proof of what they had done, but I told the Riot I did. The deal was made that the Riot would back off us and I would make sure that the evidence I said I had would disappear."

Growing up, I'm not sure I could have accepted that, but now I can.

"What's this have to do with the guy you talked to?" In case Dad had no idea it was Pigpen's brother, because that's info he should drop, not me. "With the detective?"

Dad circles the wedding ring that he still wears on his left hand. "Thought about how you felt about us lying to you. In fact, the entire board has. What do you think about nailing the bastard that killed your mom? Finding the evidence that can put him away?"

I collapse back against the bench. "What about the peace between our clubs?"

"It's something we'll have to consider, but for the first time since she died, the possibility of hard-core evidence exists."

The pieces click in place. Pigpen's brother might be volunteering to rat. "I don't know."

"Neither do I, but it's worth at least thinking about."

We both regard the traffic again and it's like doors I thought were closed open, but I'm not sure if they should be walked through. "Do I have time to think about this?"

"You have some."

I nod and Dad twirls his wedding band again. "I'm in love with Jill."

He is. I've had dinner with them twice. Dad looks at her like he used to with Mom. Jill makes him laugh, makes him think. Challenges him, I guess. A lot like Breanna challenged me. It's acid and a Band-Aid at the same time. "Are you going to marry her?"

"I'd like to."

I wish I could talk to Breanna. "Then you should." And I meet his eyes to let him know the words rolling off my lips are sincere.

Dad somewhat smiles, but he strokes his goatee to hide it. "I know it's been hard, but you've done good with giving the Millers space."

It's what they requested when they agreed to meet with Dad and Eli a few days after the train incident. Breanna had told them everything and I guess they met with the club so they could confirm her story.

Dad and Eli explained how the club intended to find evidence on the guys blackmailing Breanna. Turns out that's what the board agreed and voted on after I had come to them for help.

The club has kept the Millers updated on what they've discovered and Breanna and I have been allowed no contact. Last image I have of her is with dirt on her face and pain in her eyes as she walked into her house the day Kyle lost his mind. Last words she said to me were "I love you," and I told her, "It'll be okay."

"I promise the club will work this out," Dad says.

I nod because there isn't much else I can do. Dad, Eli and Pigpen set me straight after their first meeting with the Millers. Rushing over and disobeying her parents would make things worse on Breanna and she's had enough of bad. I wanted her to have good.

"Ready to go?"

I stand and so does Dad. He pats my back as we head for our bikes. We have one more stop for the security business before we return home.

Breanna

THIS GIRL IS smarter than me. Way smarter. Where I remember random facts, she remembers everything. For instance...

"You wore those socks two days ago." Her name is Denver and she bites on her pinkie nail. She's always nibbling on her nails, and it's odd how in the four weeks we've been roommates, it's stopped bothering me. "There's a small hole under the blue stripe."

She sits cross-legged on her perfectly made bed. Denver continuously calls attention to these types of things. At first it annoyed the crap out of me, and it was easy to understand why every roommate she had jumped ship, but then I noticed how she sat by herself in the dining hall and how most girls whispered as she walked by, and the annoyance dissolved.

Somehow I had been making friends, because my level of freak-of-nature brain activity was the same as most everyone else here, but Denver had become the outcast. She didn't know how to talk to people, because she was either too intelligent or too awkward. Either way, I wasn't interested in being like the people who tortured me in Snowflake. Instead, I decided to be her friend.

Denver's eyes flicker to my socks again and I note her white ones that are perfectly folded over. I pull a pair of pink socks with crazy red stripes out of my dresser and toss them to her. "You can have these if you want. I have two pairs of that type."

"We have to follow the dress code or we'll be in trouble."

"In class. Outside of class and school events we don't have to wear the uniform."

We're both wearing a plaid skirt that hits our knees and a white button-down shirt. My side of the room is filled with posters of puppies I bought at the campus store. I also went old-school like Razor and taped pictures of my family by my bed. I also have a few of him I was smart enough to print out before everything fell apart.

A sharp ache causes me to close my eyes. It's been over a month since we last talked. Since he last held me in his arms and told me he loved me. I tell people I have a boyfriend, but I'm not sure if that's the case anymore. How long can I expect a guy to wait when we haven't had contact for so long?

I reopen my eyes and Denver's weighing the socks in her hands like I offered her a loaded gun. "It's just socks."

"My mom won't approve," she whispers like she's afraid her mother might hear her in California.

"Well, that may be true, but she's not here, is she?" A wicked smile spreads across my lips and it widens when I spot the spark of an evil smile start to form in response.

Denver is definitely sealed shut inside her box, and if Razor taught me anything, it's that boxes are meant to be broken down and thrown away.

A knock on the door and my happiness fades. Nervous

adrenaline seeps slowly into my veins and Denver grabs her purse and slips on her shoes. My parents are here. They visit every weekend and meet with my school counselors so they can review my phone records to confirm I'm contacting only them and Addison.

They freaked over my post on Bragger and then freaked more after I told them what happened with Kyle. Mom and Dad promised I would never see Razor again. They didn't care that he protected me from Kyle. They saw Kyle and Razor as the same problem instead of one guy being the issue and the other being the solution. I informed them I'd be eighteen soon and their opinion didn't matter much to me after that.

Mom cried. Dad yelled. I remained defiant. A few days later they told me they would give Razor a chance if I showed I could be trusted again. It's an argument that caused all of us to bleed.

I did break their trust, but there's not a part of me that regrets it. Those few months with Razor were the best of my life.

But my relationship with my parents isn't the only one that needed repair. Addison wasn't too happy I was keeping secrets from her, either. A couple of times I thought about asking her to play go-between for me and Razor, but then I figured that wasn't fair. Addison and I just need to be friends and I need to deal with the consequences of a whole lot of decisions.

Denver opens the door and my mother says, "Hi," as my roommate bolts. I sigh. Denver has a long road ahead of her with socialization skills.

My room fills with my family. Elsie attaches herself to my side. Zac and Paul act like they're going to mess with Denver's stuff and I continually threaten their lives. Dad tells me how he won the client and saved the factory. I congratulate him, then Dad, Liam and Joshua ask about school, drilling me on my classes, and my mother stays unusually silent near my desk.

She studies the pictures of me and Razor and once she touches his leather jacket, which hangs on my desk chair. "Will you guys give us a few minutes?"

It was one of those moments where everyone was talking at once and then no noise. After several beats of awkward silence, Dad offers to buy ice cream and everyone but Mom vacates.

Mom stays quiet long after the door to the room shuts and I consider taking a page from Denver's book and bite my nails. Mom and I...we don't know how to talk anymore. I mean, we do talk, but it's nothing more than her asking about school and me filling her in. There's no ease to our conversations. It's like we're strangers now.

"You're still in love with him?" Mom meets my gaze. "You're still in love with Thomas Turner?"

"Yes," I say simply. "And if you're wondering, I've done what you've asked. I haven't had contact with him."

"I know. Truth is, I don't know, but everything we check on says you haven't, and deep in my heart, after everything that has happened, I still trust you."

That statement felt more like a sharp knife to my stomach than a compliment, and I try not to wince with the impact.

"I don't approve." Her utter expression of disgust reinforces this. "Neither does your father, but we're realizing that if we don't figure something out with this issue, you're going to end up like Mia Ziggler on the back of a Terror bike and we will never see you again."

I scowl. Mia Ziggler is becoming a thorn in my side. If I'm ever granted a free pass to ask any question about club business and receive the answer, I'm so inquiring about her.

"So this is how it's going to be," she says. "We have reached an agreement with the board of the Terror. Your father and I will allow supervised visits between you and Thomas as long as his club promises that they'll continue to make sure Thomas follows our rules."

I'm bouncing. I'm on my bed and I'm bouncing. "I get to see him?"

Mom holds up her hand. "With rules, Bre. Lots and lots of rules."

"I don't care. I'll take the rules." Because as I'd pointed out to my parents already, I'll be eighteen and will be graduating in the spring and then nothing can keep us apart. But to be honest, I'd love to be with Razor and still have my family.

Mom leaves the safety of her side of the room and sits on the bed next to me. "I'm aware of the role or lack of a role that your father and I played in this and we've apologized for that."

She has and so has Dad, multiple times. Possibly as many times as I've said I'm sorry for seeing Razor behind their back and for keeping the blackmailing a secret, but somehow even though the words have been said, we can't find a way to move forward.

"I can't make this a rule, Bre, even though I would love to demand it." Mom picks up a lock of my hair, and instead of trying to force it to curl, she smooths it out. "I wish you would talk to me again or maybe…"

Mom's lower lip trembles and then she shakes her head as if to get hair out of her face. "Or start talking to me. I thought I knew you. I thought I knew your hopes and your dreams and what you wanted out of life and it's killing me to realize I might not ever have known you at all."

Mom lowers her hand and I link my fingers with hers as the sadness and hurt from over the years climb out of the box I had shoved them into. "You know me."

The pain registering in her eyes says differently and it hurts to know there's nothing I can do about that, but there is something I can do about going forward.

I suck in a deep breath and dive into uncharted waters. "In seventh grade, I walked in on Clara trying to commit suicide, and she told me if I told you, she'd do it, and if I kept silent, she'd never try it again, so I didn't say anything. I didn't say anything and I realize now that was wrong and it eats me alive to think the reason she is how she is now is because I didn't speak up then."

Mom places a hand over her heart, and when I draw back, thinking I've made a mistake, she engulfs me in a hug. It's warm and it's solid and it's all I've wanted since I walked in that door in seventh grade. Hot tears gather in the corners of my eyes, and as my body starts to quake, Mom rubs my back and whispers, "It's okay, baby, it's going to be okay."

RAZOR

WE PARK AT what appears to pass as a convention center in this small town between Louisville and Lexington. I scan the area, trying to figure out which client would want to meet us here and come up empty. Never claimed that rich guys made sense.

A prospect is with us and he stands by his bike as Dad, Eli and Pigpen take off their cuts and lay them on the back. Pigpen flashes that I've-been-judged-mentally-insane-by-a-court smile at the prospect. "This better be here when I get back."

The prospect turns green and Dad pats the guy's arm for him to suck it up. Eli jerks his head to the building. "You're in on this, Razor."

I slip off my cut and lay it with the others. Sometimes, like school, this happens. There are places that refuse people wearing club colors and then there are times that, out of respect, we take them off. It's rare, but as I said, it happens.

We enter the building and receive plenty of terrified glances. Lots of people here. Families mostly, and people my age. Most of them dressed like they're at a fancy business meeting. My stride slows when I realize how many people are in uniform…a private school uniform.

Pigpen grins at me when he opens a door but then puts a finger to his lips. "We're running late and they just said they'll kick anyone out who makes a sound."

The world moves in slow motion when we walk into the back of a darkened auditorium. On the lit-up stage are two tables full of people and in the middle is one person explaining rules of how the academic competition will play out.

My heart stops and I'm frozen in place. At the end of the table is long raven hair and the most beautiful face in the world. It's Breanna and I almost drop to my knees when a burn hits my throat and eyes.

"You okay, brother?" Pigpen asks.

"It's Breanna." My voice is rougher than it should be.

Pigpen cups the back of my head. "You showed faith in us and we came through. Her parents have laid down some serious rules, but if you follow them, that girl is yours as long as she still wants you."

I nod and join Pigpen in a seat in the last row and sit back and watch something I wasn't sure I'd ever see—Breanna on stage, showing the entire world how her mind works.

Breanna

I CAN'T STOP touching Razor.

Not that we can really touch—not in the way he touches me in my dreams, but at least we're touching and he's here and he's looking at me and we're still together.

On a blanket at a park across the street from my private school, Razor and I hold hands. He's been catching me up on what's been happening at school, with Violet, Oz, Chevy and Emily. Nothing he says is too detailed. He speaks in generalities as my older brothers are also sitting on the blanket staring at Razor like they would happily toss him into a meat grinder.

But I don't care… I'm touching Razor.

My parents are at the picnic table full of fixings from KFC. Chicken, mac 'n cheese, mashed potatoes. Name it from the menu, it's there. All courtesy of the Reign of Terror. Across from them are Razor's dad, his girlfriend and Rebecca. Eli and Pigpen are playing kickball with my younger siblings.

Razor squeezes my hand, then clears his throat. "Mr. Miller?"

Talk about epically weird. Razor from the Reign of Terror

just properly addressed my father and I try to stymie the silly grin on my face.

The picnic table falls silent and my father answers, "Yes?"

"Can I take Breanna on a walk? I've been watching the joggers and there's a loop that runs along this place."

I hold my breath with each second of awkwardness that follows. It's extremely obvious they'd like to scream no, but instead Dad says, "We'll be keeping an eye on you."

Yes! Razor stands and I waste no time accepting his hand to help me up. I glance back at my parents and I wonder if the smile on my face is insulting. The thought causes some of the joy of this moment to falter, but then Mom offers me a soft encouraging lift of her lips.

"Thank you," I say, and Mom nods a "You're welcome."

We're quiet as we walk on the path and there are a million thoughts in my mind. All the things I've been dying to tell him, all the things I'm dying to know from him, and then this nagging fear that maybe he doesn't fully feel the same way I do, that maybe this road is going to be too difficult for us to navigate, that... "Forty percent of long-distance relationships break up and seventy percent of long-distance relationships fail when there's a change in plans."

Razor's lips tug up and he rubs his thumb over my hand. "Then we'll have to make sure we have a plan in place in case plans change."

I giggle and Razor chuckles.

"I read up on it," I say. "In case my parents did let me see you again."

"Are you happy here?" He doesn't look at me when he asks and I wonder what he wishes my answer would be, but then I chastise myself for thinking such things. Razor craves the truth.

"Yes. It's, oddly enough, still high school and there are still high school problems, but the classes are phenomenal. It's like mind crack without killing the brain cells."

"Good." By the way his blue eyes soften, he means it. "Good."

"Did you ever doubt this moment would happen?" I ask. "Being together again?"

"Did you?" He turns the question around to me.

It somehow feels like a betrayal to admit I had no idea if we would stay together.

"I was scared I'd never see you again," he admits. "That once you got here, you'd change your mind about me."

"Never. Just never, but, yeah, I was like you. I wasn't sure if it would happen or if you would have second thoughts."

A quick squeeze of my fingers. "Never."

We near the spot where the path is engulfed by the neighboring forest and my heart quickens. No one can see us here. No one will know what is done or how we do it and—

Razor moves, lightning-fast, and my breath rushes out of my body. One arm encircles my waist, the other caresses my face, and in a moment that feels like an eternity, he lowers his head and brushes his lips to mine.

Everything inside me explodes. Our mouths move, tongues dance, hands explore and we soon remember the precious and delicious parts of each other. Heat builds, but it's the emotion that causes me to go weak.

The way Razor's palms frame my face, the gentle way his hands run through my hair and the reverent way his fingers skim along my back. It's as if he's kissing me like I'm a dream, as if he doesn't believe I'm real.

A buzz of Razor's cell and we break away. He's breathing

hard and so am I. A glance at the message. "Pigpen says your brothers think we're taking too long."

I laugh because we totally are and there's no way to hide what we've been doing. Razor's hair is tousled and his lips are swollen. He grins as he slides a finger along my neck, where there are no doubts that my skin has flushed.

"No one said we couldn't kiss," I say.

"True. That was not one of the rules."

His laughter fades as he tucks my hair behind my ear, then pulls me into the shelter of his body. I lay my head on his shoulder and let one of my hands rest on his solid chest.

"I've missed you." Razor nuzzles my hair, then kisses the top of my head.

"I've missed you, too." I hug him tight and breathe in his scent of autumn air and leather. The smell of freedom. "We're going to make this work, right?"

"Yes," he says. "That's a promise."

RAZOR

THE FIELD FEELS lonely without Breanna, and because of that, I had promised myself I wouldn't come unless she could join me, but I'm on a mission for someone I loved before Breanna. I have a promise to keep to Olivia.

I take off my leather gloves and stick them in my jacket and my warm breath billows out into the cold air. The trees have lost their leaves, the grass is now brown, but the memories of Breanna's laughter, the feel of her body pressed against mine make this place as colorful as it was this fall.

My cell vibrates and I pull it out as I pause near the abandoned bridge. It's Breanna: Am I late? My meeting ran over and then I couldn't get a signal until I stepped outside.

Even a hundred miles away, at times, it's like she's beside me. Me: Just in time.

Breanna: I wish I could have met her.

Having Breanna on the other end of my cell steals away some of the ache. Me too.

Olivia would have loved her. Me: Give me a few and then I'll video call.

Breanna: Sounds good. I love you.

I walk onto the abandoned railway bridge and peer at the bridge upstream. I haven't been here since the day Kyle forced Breanna onto the tracks. Haven't had the guts or the desire to. This field belonged to me and her, and the bridge Kyle dragged Breanna on and then the bridge a little farther down has affected my life in ways I'm not sure anyone can understand.

Bridges are meant to connect. They're meant to defy drops and distances, but occasionally we lose our way...we fall off, we drive off, we consider jumping.

Mom's bridge—I lost my way. The bridge I'm standing on—I had spiritually jumped. The bridge where I tackled Kyle—I saved myself.

The colder air carries the sound of the tractor trailers crossing over the busy state road a few miles ahead and off in the distance a train whistle blows. Six months ago, I was mourning the loss of Olivia and my mother, I never knew I'd know love and I was estranged from my club and father, if not in body, then in spirit.

Now I'll be the best man in my father's upcoming wedding, I'm being mentored for a future board position in the club and the girl I love includes me when she talks about her future.

I open the box in my hands and pull out the bag containing Olivia's ashes.

Yeah, there are certain lies in life we convince ourselves we have to believe and those are the ones that lead us to self-destruction. But as we grow, as we mature, we learn how to search for the truth. We learn that our lives are not determined by fate, but by our own free will.

Olivia said I'd know what to do with her ashes when I found peace and she was right. I open the bag and let the wind carry her remains off the bridge and into the valley below. "I've finally learned how to let go, Olivia. I've finally learned how to let you and Mom go."

When the bag is empty, when the burning in my eyes and in my throat no longer feels like it's going to consume me, I sit and let my legs hang over the edge. A few swipes of my phone, a beeping, and the most beautiful girl in the world pops onto the screen.

"Did you do it?" she asks, and concern mars her hazel eyes. "Did you release her ashes?"

I nod. "Thanks for being here with me."

"Anytime. Do you want to talk about her?"

I've done that—told Breanna stories about Olivia, but the past isn't where I desire to be. I belong to the present and even maybe my future. "Are you still interested in those northeastern colleges?"

Breanna gathers her hair away from her face while she nods. "I'll be home this summer."

She's worried about distance, but I'm not. "I talked to the board. We think it's time the Terror and the security company expand, and those places you mentioned—New York, Massachusetts—sound like areas that need someone like me to plant a new chapter."

She shrieks with joy. "Please tell me you aren't kidding."

"Never." Breanna may never understand how much I love her. "I would never joke about something like this with you."

Breanna blinks like she's on the verge of tears, and hating that I can't hold her, I press forward with conversation. "Help me narrow down the field of where the Terror are headed. I have a lot of work to do and only a few months to do it."

She wipes her eyes, sucks in a breath and begins telling me everything she knows about the places where our future together might begin.

★ ★ ★ ★ ★

ACKNOWLEDGMENTS

TO GOD: ECCLESIASTES 4:12 (NIV): Though one may be overpowered, two can defend themselves. A cord of three strands is not quickly broken.

For Dave: You are the love of my life and my best friend. Each day with you is a gift.

Thank you to...

Kevan Lyon and Margo Lipschultz. Your continued faith in me means more than you could imagine.

Colette Ballard, Angela Annalaro-Murphy, Kristen Simmons, Kelly Creagh, Bethany Griffin, Kurt Hampe and Bill Wolfe. You are my tribe and I would be lost without you.

Again, to my parents, my sister, my Mount Washington family and the entire McGarry "Madness" clan... I love you, always.

Read on for an exclusive sneak preview
of the next THUNDER ROAD *novel*
from Katie McGarry and Harlequin TEEN...

Violet

DAD'S CROSS DANGLES over the engine of his Chevelle while my other necklaces stay tucked in my shirt. I'll admit, I don't have a clue what I'm looking for and using the flashlight app from my cell has done nothing to help. Maybe if I stare at the inner workings of the car long enough a magic fairy will pop out and tell me to smack this, turn that, jump in a circle three times naked and then the engine will wondrously rev to life.

I'd perform the act if that would make Dad's car run again. Who am I kidding? I'd do it if it would make anything in my life work again.

Behind me, Brandon paces and the rocks crunch under his footsteps. We're two miles from home and off to the side of a quiet country road. Thank God there's a full moon as my brother can be terrified of dark places. Dad used to tell Brandon that a full moon is nature's night-light. I'm banking on Brandon remembering that tidbit of fatherly wisdom, because unless steam rising from my engine means my car is about to evolve into some next generation of superpower vehicle, we're stuck.

"We should call the club," Brandon says. "They'd come. They'd help fix your car."

With strings made out of spiderwebs. The Reign of Terror would suck us in and then suck us dry. It's how they work. You don't get something for nothing with them. "If you remember, Eli and Pigpen tore off from the football game because they have business to take care of, meaning we wouldn't be high on the priority list. Besides, Mom's on her way."

She's put out, but she's on her way. Mom will take her time to prove how annoyed she is with my "careless behavior" of driving at night without the protection of a man. That's how Mom thinks. Girls, to her, are the weaker and fairer sex waiting for a man to save them, and Mom is constantly annoyed that I don't play up my femininity.

Yeah, that's bullshit.

I straighten and the bracelets on my wrist clank together. If I was alone, I'd head home on foot, but Brandon walking along the woods in the dark could cause problems I'm not giddy about dealing with. At least he feels somewhat safe next to the car.

"Are you hungry?" I ask. "I didn't eat all my popcorn at the game and you can have what's left. I should warn you, most of it is burnt."

"The club would send somebody if you called," he mutters. "If you called Chevy, he'd come. At least he'd come for me."

Knife straight to where I'm weak and I lose the ability to breathe. Yeah, Chevy would come, but what girl wants to play damsel in distress and then be saved by her ex-boyfriend? "I can't call Chevy."

It wouldn't be fair to Chevy and it wouldn't be fair to me.

The love I had for him was consuming and powerful and raw, and the attraction? I briefly close my eyes as memories of Chevy's hands on my body and his lips on mine cause warmth to curl in my bloodstream… Even when we fought, we never had problems with attraction.

My breakup with Chevy hasn't hurt only me, but my brother, and I'm not sure if he'll ever forgive me. I'm not sure if a lot of people will forgive me, but none of that matters. I've got a plan and none of it involves staying in town past graduation.

A motorcycle rumbles in the distance and it's weird how a flutter still enters my bloodstream at the sound. When I was younger, I used to sit at the window in the living room and wait for that beautiful growl. The moment I heard Dad's motorcycle, I used to run through the house telling my mom and my brother that Daddy was on his way.

I'd bust out the front door just in time for him to swing his leg off his bike and then he'd catch me and toss me up into the air. A squeal would always rip through my throat followed up by giggles as he would tickle me in his big, crushing hug.

Those days are long gone.

The motorcycle engine grows louder and I lift my head, looking up at the road that leads to town, and a single headlight breaks over the hill. Most sane people would be terrified at the idea of being alone on the side of the road at night with an approaching motorcycle, but I'm just annoyed with a mixture of slightly relieved.

If someone from the Terror wants to stumble upon me and help make Dad's car move, I'll suck up the animosity long enough to get my brother home. But at the same time, accepting their help will only make them want to go dictator over everything else in my family's life.

As much as I need help, anything from the Terror comes at a price. My father paid with his life.

I step back from the open hood and watch as the motorcycle slows to a stop behind my car and then blow out a rush of air. Why does my life have to continually suck? I would have taken Eli or Pigpen over this. But I didn't get Thing 1 or Thing 2. I got my ex because that's the way my life works.

Chevy slips off his bike and grimly assesses the car. He's been under the hood of this Chevelle more than once. Chevy and my dad were close. It also hurt him when Dad died.

"Mom's on her way," I say. "You're fine to move along as she'll be here soon."

But nothing I said matters as my brother rushes past me so quickly that his arm smacks mine and he doesn't look back to confirm I'm still standing. Brandon offers Chevy a hero's welcome.

My brother is all words, most of them tripping and running into the other, as he attempts to express his excitement and undying love and loyalty. "We were at your game and Pigpen bought me a hot dog and Eli bought my ticket and I didn't see your first touchdown but I saw your second and you just plowed right through that line and I'm so glad to see you."

Because Chevy is patient, more patient than most grown men, he stands in front of my brother with his thumbs hitched in his front pockets and that sexy slouch of his like he's prepared to stand there and listen to every single word Brandon could ever say or think to say.

As long as I've known him, he's always kept his hair trimmed, but today strands of his dark brown hair slightly cover his forehead and it's incredibly endearing. The type that's teasing and begs to be swept away.

A wave of very unwanted jealousy rages through me. I

used to be the one who could touch. Last I heard, I'd been thoroughly replaced with the revolving door of girls who have lined up to spend the evening with the school's star running back and waterfall of muscle.

Brandon's still gushing, Chevy's still listening, but then his eyes stray in my direction. As if our relationship had never been interrupted, he looks at me. Eyes straight to mine and I can't breathe. Returning his gaze is a lot like coming home after a long night and falling into bed.

I fell into way too many things with Chevy. The suck part about falling is that eventual crash landing. I tear my eyes away and force air into my aching lungs.

Thank God, Brandon's still going. "Dad's car broke down and Violet wouldn't call you, but I said we should call you. I told her that you'd come—at least you'd come for me. I told her to call the club, but she wouldn't."

Twice in one night my brother decides to go traitor. See if I take him to a football game again.

"Did Violet bring you to the game?" Chevy interrupts.

Brandon's forehead wrinkles. "What?"

"Did Violet bring you to the game?"

"Well...yeah."

"Then you should be grateful she did. Not all sisters are like that."

My bracelets clink together when I shift, uncomfortable that anyone is taking up for me, even if it is Chevy. Since Dad died, Chevy joined the ranks of people thinking I'm the devil because I'm trying to break free of the Terror.

"Your car's broke." Chevy glances in my direction again, and there's a softness in his eyes that I hate and love. It's the same unguarded look as when we whispered our most intimate thoughts into each other's ears.

I hold his eyes this time for as long as he can handle. "Thanks for the update, Captain Obvious."

Chevy mocks tipping a hat that isn't on his head. "My pleasure."

The right side of my mouth tips up. Damn him for being so charming, because it makes me miss him more and I'm not sure how much more missing him I can take.

Headlights shine in the distance, and my shoulders relax. This has been an awful day and I'm ready to pull the covers over my head and stay in bed for days, maybe weeks.

I step out onto the road and, using the flashlight cell, wave to signal Mom. This isn't the first time Dad's car has broken down, and unfortunately, it won't be the last. Mom has passed us up before. Though I'm not convinced those times were a mistake as much as Mom attempting to teach me another lesson about how unsafe I am in the world.

Footsteps against the rocks and Chevy walks up beside me. The car weaves in and out of the center lane, and my arm hesitates in the air as a sense of unease tiptoes through me.

Chevy places his hand on my arm and forces it down. "That's not your mom's car."

It's not. Mom would never drive like that and those aren't the headlights to a minivan. Those belong to something with some muscle. A scary sixth sense creeps along my skin.

Growling engines and three single beams appear. Motorcycles. My stomach lurches as I stumble back and Chevy steps forward, knife out, his arms stretched wide ready to fight.

I swallow as my hands begin to shake. The Terror never come from this direction unless they were coming to see me and none of them have a muscle car they would be following. There's only one group it can be. "Brandon, get back into the car."

"What's wrong?" he asks.

My internal warning system is blaring like a foghorn, and instead of slowing down, the car picks up speed. I grab Brandon's arm and I shove him toward the passenger side. "Get back into the car, lie down on the floorboard in the backseat and don't pop your head up until I say so. Now!"

Brandon moves with me and slides in when I open his door. I shut it the second his foot clears the frame.

"Get in there with him, Violet," Chevy demands. "In the backseat, on the floorboard."

"They've already seen me," I hiss. "Odds are they didn't see Brandon. We have to protect him."

Chevy glances over his shoulder at me and someone else's death is written on his face. "Then in the front seat. Doors locked and call the club."

"Chevy," I begin, about to ask him to join me, and he cuts me off.

"They're looking for someone and I'll be it. I'm first wave of keeping them off Stone. You're second. Call the club. Get me backup."

Absolute fear seizes my body. I can't leave Chevy to stand on his own. I care for him too much for that.

"Get in, Violet," he repeats.

But as the headlights draw closer, I remain glued to the ground.

PLAYLIST FOR
WALK THE EDGE

Theme:
"American Kids" by Kenny Chesney
"Small Town Saturday Night" by Hal Ketchum
"Am I Wrong" by Nico & Vinz
"Refugee" by Tom Petty
"It's Time" by Imagine Dragons

Razor:
"I Hold On" by Dierks Bentley
"Demons" by Imagine Dragons
"Blank Space" by I Prevail

Breanna:
"Everything Has Changed" by Taylor Swift
"What Makes You Beautiful" by One Direction
"Reflection" by Christina Aguilera

Songs for Specific Scenes:
Razor and Breanna at the Bridge:
"Rewind" by Rascal Flatts and "Night Train" by Jason Aldean

Razor and his relationship with his father:
"Wrecking Ball" by Miley Cyrus

Razor and his relationship with his mother:
"Ghost" by Ella Henderson

Razor and Breanna see each other at the bar:
"T-R-O-U-B-L-E" by Travis Tritt